A few people to thank....
reading and found a few
otherwise.

Many friends who encouraged me to keep writing after they read parts of the novel that I sent them.

This book is dedicated to all people who believe as I do that things will get worse before they get better but in the end they do get better.

Copyright © 2012 by John Tod
All rights reserved.

This book or any parts of it may not be copied or distributed in any form without express consent of the author except for small parts which may be quoted in a review.

Reach me at: **FURRYFACE47@YAHOO.CA**

ISBN-13: 978-1478315650
ISBN-10: 1478315652

This book is a look at one possible terrifying future. The world economy is coming apart at the seams. Criminal elements have taken over many of the inner cities and in some cases, whole countries. One man, Malcolm Beacham, has a bold plan to save humankind. A habitable planet has been detected orbiting Alpha Centuri and he has a bold plan to build a generation ship to travel there and start a human colony. But would it work and could it be completed in time? It would be a race against time on a global scale.

I have studied economics on a global scale and some global economic details in the early parts of the book were coming true before the time line in the book so I had to change the time line to compensate. So what I had forecast IS coming true faster than I had predicted.

Hope: A Space Novel

Prologue

23,246 B.C. Somewhere in Africa

A hunter-gatherer party was returning to their tribe in the near darkness. Today was not a successful hunt. He hoped the other hunting parties of his tribe were more successful or they would not have much to eat again until tomorrow. The stars had just begun to come out with Venus shining brightly near the horizon. What were these lights in the sky, he and other members of his tribe wondered? They must be a gift from the Gods providing light when the sun went down.

The moon was also up in the sky and it was full. He stopped and gazed at it in wonder. Why was only some of the moon was visible most of the time but on nights like tonight it was fully lit, a beautiful ball of light in the sky. It must be a sign that tomorrows hunt would be a successful one. He hoped that was what it meant. He could make out what looked like a face on the moon. Was it the face of a God?

Human kind had reached the point in evolution when they had the capacity of thought and reason. There were many questions but few answers. No one knew where everything, including themselves, had come from or where they would go when they died. It was believed that every living thing had a life source within it. What happened to that life source when life ended? It had to go somewhere. He and elders of the tribe had begun to ask questions of themselves about such things. There must be a God or perhaps several Gods with their own powers that had created everything at the beginning of all. Where else would it have come from? He did not know it at the time but he and his tribe were becoming founders of a religion to explain the unexplainable. They must talk to these Gods and ask questions. Whenever they did they never received answers but things would happen when certain conditions were right. Maybe when they did things that made the Gods happy with human kind the Gods rewarded them with a successful hunt or protected the tribe from their enemies or attacks from wild animals. He himself had begun to wear a bone that he had carved around his neck hung by a strip of animal hide. He believed that it protected him in some way and never left the tribe without it.

When he found the tribe, other hunting parties had been successful. He could hear the whoops and hollers as he got closer to the camp. He smiled. Tonight he, his mate and their child and the rest of the tribe would eat. He thought no more of the moon and stars that night but on many other nights he and the elders would talk much of them and what they meant and about the Gods and where everything had come from and went. Why had the hunt been successful for others and not for him? Had they done something that pleased the Gods while he had not? He would have to talk with the others and compare what he had done different. He fingered the carved bone about his neck as he walked toward the camp. He could see the bright fire and the dancing of joy of members of the tribe. He saw his mate and his child. He hungered for food but he had other hungers too. They would be satisfied this night as well. Perhaps the Gods would give him another son. That would be good. Another hunter for the tribe. If he had two sons that would elevate his position in the tribe as the maker of hunters. Perhaps one day he or one of his sons would be chief.

Much talk had been done about their nomadic ways. It was being discussed heatedly around the fire to stay where they were and build better shelters. Some had even suggested planting the vegetables they needed rather than harvesting them further and further from the camp. The ways of the animals had been tracked and remembered. They were close to a favorite animal pathway from the plains and water holes to the safety of the brush. They only had to sit and wait and kill what was needed. He was one of the people who believed in settling but the final decision when all talk was done rested with the chief. His word was tribal law. But what of the Gods? What did they want them to do? He asked the Gods many times and as always never received an answer but he had a warm feeling inside when he thought about establishing a permanent camp rather then wandering. Maybe that was a sign from the Gods that his thinking was right? He would think more on this and discuss with other members of the tribe and his mate.

He saw his mates silhouette against the light of the fire. He would satisfy his other hunger later that night when his belly was full and she lay beside him.

A Brief History of Space Flight Evolution

1945 - After the Invasion of Germany

Wernher von Braun

World War II in Europe was drawing to a close. The Allies including the Soviets were deep in German territory and it was only a matter of days when German surrender was imminent. Wernher von Braun and his brother Magnus were in hiding along with most of the V-1 and V-2 rocket design team. They talked a lot about who to surrender to. It was rumored the Nazi's were about to assassinate everyone that could be of use to the Allies including Wernher and his rocket engineering team. Magnus was selected to go to the Americans because he could speak some English and tell them Wernher and the rest of his team would like to surrender to the Americans because as Wernher said, "The team was afraid of the Russians and the the British couldn't afford us." It took a while because the Americans did not know who Magnus was or whether they could believe him and his claims. No Allied scientists or advisers were available at the scene but he was finally able to convince U.S. troops that Wernher von Braun and his closest associates, now living at an inn behind German lines, wanted to surrender to the Americans. Magnus von Braun did this by convincing U.S. troops that America was the best nation to continue the research started by his brother, Wernher von Braun, with the ultimate goal of interplanetary travel. He also asserted that Wernher von Braun's life was in immediate danger due to a German directive to kill key personnel prior to surrender.

Wernher and some of his rocket team were taken to the U.S.

as part of the then secret Operation Paperclip. In 1955, ten years after entering the country, von Braun became a naturalized U.S. citizen. Wernher von Braun and his team of rocket scientists would be indispensable in the U.S. space program which reached its height (according to many people's opinion) in the moon landing on the 20 July 1969.

1947 - Chuck Yeager – Breaking the Sound Barrier

The Americans tested several models of jet aircraft to try and break the sound barrier which was considered impossible by many engineers. All the aircraft used up to this point had disintegrated in mid-air just as they approached the sound barrier. A new series of aircraft called the "X" series for "eXperimental" were on the drawing boards. The first of these jet aircraft was the X-1. An experimental test glide was done as the plane was dropped from high altitude and dead stick landed by Chuck Yeager. A powered flight was planned for October 14th, 1947, Chuck was to be the pilot. Chuck and his wife were horseback riding two days before the flight and Chuck was thrown from his horse and suffered two broken ribs. A veterinarian taped up his ribs because if a doctor had done it the base may have found out and not let him fly the X-1 to attempt to break the sound barrier.

His movement was restricted with the broken ribs so a friend fashioned a "tool", a 10 inch length of broomstick to enable Chuck to close the canopy of the jet for the flight. A B-29 bomber was used to lift the plane to an altitude of 20,000 feet where the bomber was put into a steep dive to achieve an air speed of 250 mph needed by the X-1 to fly and then after a short countdown the X-1 was dropped. With full rocket power, Chuck used his controls to maintain smooth flight as he accelerated and passed the sound barrier. He later, wrote,

"We were flying supersonic! And it was as smooth as a baby's bottom. Grandma could be sitting up here drinking lemonade. I sat there feeling kind of numb, but elated." The tachometer in the plane was pinned at the mach 1.0 point, as far as it could go because most engineers believed the sound barrier of mach 1.0 could not be broken. Alone in the sky, he celebrated by rolling his plane to make the landscape spin, as he glided down to his landing. This was one of the most significant flights in the history of aviation.

1952 - Early Rocket Development

Up to 1952, 64 German designed V-2 rockets were launched at White Sands. Instruments, not explosives, packed the missiles' nose cones. A V-2 variant saw the missile become the first stage of a two stage rocket named Bumper. The top half was a WAC Corporal rocket. The need for more room to fire the rockets quickly became evident and, in 1949, the Joint Long Range Proving Ground was established at remote, deserted Cape Canaveral, Florida. On July 24, 1950, a two stage Bumper rocket became the first of hundreds to be launched from "The Cape." The transfer of launch operations to the Cape coincided with the transfer of the Army's missile program from White Sands to a post just outside a north Alabama cotton town called Huntsville. Von Braun and his team arrived in April 1950. It was to remain his home for the next 20 years, a period in which the towns population increased ten fold.

1956 – The Redstone Rocket

The Wernher von Braun team worked to develop what was essentially a super-V-2 rocket, named for the U.S. Army arsenal where it was being designed, Redstone. In 1956, the

Army Ballistic Missile Agency was established at Redstone Arsenal under von Braun's leadership to develop the Jupiter intermediate range ballistic missile.

1957 – The Soviet Sputnik

The Soviets amazed the world and shocked America by launching Sputnik, the first artificial satellite to orbit the earth, on the 4th of October 1957. Its orbital speed was 18,000 miles per hour and remained in orbit for 3 months until its orbit destabilized and it burned up in the atmosphere.

1958 – United States Explorer 1

A version of the Redstone rocket, known as the Jupiter C, was used on January 31, 1958, to launch into orbit, America's first satellite, Explorer I. Three years later, Mercury Redstones launched Alan Shepard and Virgil "Gus" Grissom on suborbital space flights, paving the way for John Glenn's first orbital flight.

In 1958, NASA (National Aeronautics and Space Administration) was established, and, two years later, von Braun, his team, and the entire Army Ballistic Missile Agency were transferred to NASA to become the nucleus of the Agency's space program.

1960 – The First Living Space Passengers

The Soviet Union launched a spacecraft into orbit with two dogs on board, Belka and Strelka. They were the first live passengers to be sent into space and be returned successfully. The Soviet capsules were designed to be landed by parachute on dry land. The U.S. capsules were designed to be landed by parachute on water.

12 April 1961 – The First Human in Space

The Soviet Union launched the first human into space, Yuri Gagarin, on the 12 April 1961.

25 May 1961
President Kennedy's "Man on the Moon" Speech

John F. Kennedy, then President of the United States gave a special address to Congress where he gave his historical speech:

"First, I believe that this nation should commit itself to achieving the goal, before this decade is out, of landing a man on the Moon and returning him safely to the Earth. No single space project in this period will be more impressive to mankind, or more important for the long-range exploration of space; and none will be so difficult or expensive to accomplish."

He continued, "We choose to go to the Moon in this decade and do the other things, not because they are easy, but because they are hard, because that goal will serve to organize and measure the best of our energies and skills, because that challenge is one that we are willing to accept, one we are unwilling to postpone, and one which we intend to win, and the others, too. Many years ago the great British explorer George Mallory, who was to die on Mount Everest, was asked why did he want to climb it. He said, 'Because it is there.' Well, space is there, and we're going to climb it, and the Moon and the planets are there, and new hopes for knowledge and peace are there. And, therefore, as we set sail we ask God's blessing on the most hazardous and dangerous and greatest adventure on which man has ever embarked."

20th of February 1962 - John Glenn

John Glenn became the first American to orbit the earth on 20th of February 1962. His space capsule was known as Friendship 7 which orbited the earth 3 times. There was a bit of a scare as ground controllers thought the heat shield was loose and might break during reentry. Ground Control told Glenn to leave on the retro rocket bracket as "an entry of that kind posed no problems." It was thought that leaving the retro rocket bracket on would help hold the heat shield in place during reentry if indeed it was loose. Glenn made a successful splash down and was treated to a heroes welcome.

Three decades later, after serving 24 years in the Senate, Glenn lifted off for a second space flight on 29th of October 1998, on Space Shuttle Discovery, in order to study the effects of space flight on the elderly. At age 77, Glenn became the oldest person ever to go into space. Glenn's participation in the nine-day mission was criticized by some in the space community as a junket for a politician. Others noted that Glenn's flight offered valuable research on weightlessness and other aspects of space flight on the same person at two points in life thirty-six years apart — by far the longest interval between space flights by the same person — providing information on the effects of spaceflight and weightlessness on the elderly, with an ideal control.

1962 – The Cuban Missile Crisis

The Cuban Missile Crisis was the closest the world has ever come to nuclear war, before or since. The United States armed forces were at their highest state of readiness ever and Soviet field commanders in Cuba were prepared to use battlefield nuclear weapons to defend the island if it was invaded. Luckily, thanks to the bravery of two men, American President John F. Kennedy and the Soviet Premier, Nikita Khrushchev, war was averted.

In 1962, the Soviet Union was desperately behind the United States in the arms race. Soviet missiles were only powerful enough to be launched against Europe but U.S. missiles were capable of striking the entire Soviet Union from the continental United States.

In late April 1962, Soviet Premier Nikita Khrushchev conceived the idea of placing intermediate range missiles in Cuba. A deployment in Cuba would double the Soviet strategic arsenal and provide a real deterrent to a potential preemptive U.S. attack against the Soviet Union.

Meanwhile, Fidel Castro was looking for a way to defend his island nation from an attack by the U.S. Ever since the failed Bay of Pigs invasion in 1961, Castro felt a second attack was inevitable. Consequently, he approved of Khrushchev's plan to place missiles on the island. In the summer of 1962 the Soviet Union worked quickly and secretly to build its missile installations in Cuba.

For the United States, the crisis began on October 15th, 1962 when reconnaissance photographs revealed Soviet missiles under construction in Cuba. Early the next day, President John Kennedy was informed of the missile installations. Kennedy immediately organized the EX-COMM, a group of his twelve most important advisers to handle the crisis. After seven days of guarded and intense debate within the upper echelons of government, Kennedy concluded to impose a naval quarantine around Cuba. He wished to prevent the arrival of more Soviet offensive weapons on the island. On October 22nd, Kennedy announced the discovery of the missile installations to the public and his decision to quarantine the island. He also proclaimed that any nuclear missile launched from Cuba would be regarded as an attack on the United States by the Soviet Union and demanded the Soviets remove all of their offensive weapons from Cuba.

During the public phase of the Crisis, tensions began to build on both sides. Kennedy eventually ordered low-level reconnaissance missions once every two hours. On the 25th Kennedy pulled the quarantine line back and raised military readiness to DEFCON 2. Then on the 26th EX-COMM heard from Khrushchev in an impassioned letter. He proposed removing Soviet missiles and personnel if the U.S. would guarantee not to invade Cuba. October 27th was the worst day of the crisis. A U.S. U-2 spy plane was shot down over Cuba and EX-COMM received a second letter from Khrushchev demanding the removal of U.S. missiles in Turkey in exchange for removing Soviet missiles in Cuba. Attorney General Robert Kennedy suggested ignoring the second letter and contacted Soviet Ambassador Anatoly Dobrynin to tell him of the U.S. agreement with the first.

Tensions finally began to ease on October 28th when Khrushchev announced that he would dismantle the installations and return the missiles to the Soviet Union, expressing his trust that the United States would not invade Cuba. Further negotiations were held to implement the October 28th agreement, including a United States demand that Soviet light bombers be removed from Cuba, and specifying the exact form and conditions of the United States assurances not to invade Cuba.

22 November 1963
President John F. Kennedy Assassinated

President John F. Kennedy was assassinated on November 22nd, 1963 in Dallas Texas. Lee Harvey Oswald was charged with the crime but he was shot and killed two days later by Jack Ruby before he made it to trial. The Warren Commission concluded that Oswald acted alone. Many people believe even to this day that other people were involved in the assassination and there was a cover up of the facts. John F. Kennedy never lived to see his dream come true of a manned lunar landing by America.

1961 to 1975 - The Apollo Years

The Apollo spacecraft program ran from 1961 until 1975. The first Apollo capsule Apollo 1 caught fire on the launch pad killing all three astronauts on board. After a delay of twenty months and many upgrades and mechanical changes such as an outward opening hatch, the manned Apollo program resumed. The Apollo program was designed specifically to journey to the moon and back using a spacecraft composed of two parts, a Command/Service Module or CSM and a Lunar Module or LM. The original name for the LM was Lunar Excursion Module or LEM, a pronounceable acronym.

A new rocket had to be designed for the moon project. Several designs were proposed and the final choice was the Saturn V designed and developed under the direction of Wernher von Braun and Arthur Rudolph at the Marshall Space Flight Center in Huntsville, Alabama. The Saturn V's huge size and payload capacity dwarfed all other previous rockets which had successfully flown at that time. With the Apollo spacecraft on top it stood 363 feet tall and without fins it was 33 feet in diameter. Fully fueled it had a total mass of 6.5 million pounds (3,000 metric tons) and a payload capacity of 260,000 pounds to propel an object into low earth orbit.

(Authors note – It would have made more sense to use two smaller existing rockets and launch the CSM and the LM into space separately and then assemble them once in space. The design was for the LM to be extracted from the payload rocket that launched both vehicles into space and then assemble them into one spacecraft anyway).

The first stage was fueled with RP-1, a highly refined form of kerosene, and liquid oxygen. When the Saturn V's first stage ignited it rattled windows and shook loose ceiling tiles in the broadcast booth located four miles from the launch pad. The first stage rocket had a dry weight of 288,000 pounds and fully fueled weighed 5,000,000 pounds. The first stage used five F-1 engines, the center engine was fixed and the four outer engines were computer hydraulically controlled or "gimbaled" to allow fine control of the rockets direction and ascent. The first stage fired for 168 seconds and developed 7,500,000 pounds of thrust, ignition occurring about 7 seconds before liftoff to generate enough power to lift the massive rocket assembly off the ground. The first stage took the rocket up to an altitude of about 42 miles, downrange about 58 miles, and moving about 5,352 mph.

The Saturn V was a three stage rocket, the second stage was used to propel the spacecraft most of the rest of the way into low earth orbit. The third stage was used to insert the spacecraft into a stable low earth orbit and then shut down and was designed to be re-ignited to hurl the spacecraft out of the earths gravitational field and send it on its way to the moon. Once the spacecraft arrived at the moon it would circle behind the moon and then at a predetermined time, fired again, to slow the spacecraft down so that a stable moon orbit could be achieved.

A first test flight was eventually made to the moon, circling behind it and then returning to earth. A subsequent mission by Apollo 8 put the lunar module assembly in orbit around the moon at Christmas in 1968. One of the most famous photographs of all time was taken during this mission. It showed the entire earth suspended in the blackness of space showing how tiny and vulnerable earth was compared to the cosmos. It also showed people that earth was a planet, the home of ALL humankind and that we should ALL work together to make it humanities home rather than fighting amongst ourselves. In early 1969 Apollo 10 did a dress rehearsal for the real thing by coming within 50,000 miles of the lunar surface but did not attempt a landing.

1966 - Present - Soviet and Russian Soyuz Spacecraft

Soyuz is a series of Soviet and now Russian spacecraft designed for the Soviet space program by the Korolyov Design Bureau. The spacecraft was also referred to as a Cosmic Chelnok or simply chelnok which literally means "spaceship" in Russian. The Soyuz succeeded the Voskhod spacecraft and was originally built as part of the Soviet Manned Lunar program. The Soyuz spacecraft is launched by the Soyuz rocket, the most frequently used and the most reliable launch vehicle in the world, even to this day. Soyuz spacecraft were used to carry cosmonauts to and from the

Salyut and later, the Mir Soviet space stations, and are now used for transport of personnel to and from the International Space Station. The International Space Station maintains docked Soyuz spacecraft at all times to be used as escape craft in the event of an emergency.

20th July 1969 - The Moon Landing

Neil Armstrong, Edwin (Buzz) Aldrin, and Michael Collins were chosen for the Apollo 11 mission to attempt the first ever manned landing on the moon. The Command/Service Module was nicknamed *Columbia* and the Lunar Module was named *Eagle*. Communication with the spacecraft and Houston was made possible by several stations around the world picking up conversations between the spacecraft and earth and relaying them to Houston so no matter where Houston was located on the revolving earth they always had a clear channel to the Command Module and the Lunar Module.

The verbal exchange between the spacecraft and Houston Mission Control was weighted with cryptic exchanges of scientific data, but still it rang with the stupendous drama of the greatest achievement in the history of space exploration up to that time. For these were the voices of Apollo 11, voices carried over nearly a quarter of a million miles to tell of mankind's first steps on the moon.

Neil Armstrong was the pilot for the LM. He watched as the LM separated from the Service Module and began its fall towards the moon's surface. The trip down was all under computer control and was directing the LM to the chosen landing spot. The computer beeped and displayed a code. He radioed this information back to Houston and was told it was a warning the computer's memory was getting full and to ignore it. The computer would have been considered quite primitive by today's standards. One of today's ordinary desktop computers has much more computing power and memory than this computer being used to land on the moon.

Neil looked out on the moon's surface and thought, "Oh, oh....we can't land there.", as he saw the chosen landing spot was strewn with boulders the size of houses. He immediately took the computer off line and switched to manual control. He knew he had only less than a minute to find a suitable landing site.

"I got to find somewhere to land this bitch or we're all screwed.", he thought.

The only way to save himself and Buzz was to separate the LM and use the ascent stage to return to orbit and all this effort would be wasted. As he flew over the boulder strewn chosen landing area he saw a better landing site a short distance away.

"Its gonna be close.", he thought as he gauged the distance and looked at the fuel pressure still left.

"Hang in there, baby.", he thought to himself.

He used the controls to settle the LM on the moon's surface.

"Whew, that was close.", he said and grinned at Buzz. He looked at the fuel pressure gauge and figured he had less than 20 seconds of fuel remaining.

The world listened as Neil Armstrong, Edwin (Buzz) Aldrin,

and Michael Collins spoke to each other and to CapCom (the Capsule Communicator) in Houston. Eagle (the Lunar Module) had separated from Columbia (the Command/Service Module) and had touched down on the dust of that desolate, windless world on July 20th 1969, at 4:17 and 43 seconds PM EDT, 102 hours, 45 minutes, and 43 seconds after launch. At the moment of touch down the following conversation was recorded between Armstrong and the Houston Control Center:

ARMSTRONG: *Houston, Tranquility Base here. The Eagle has landed.*

CAPCOM: (Astronaut Charles M. Duke): *Roger, Tranquility, we copy you on the ground. You got a bunch of guys about to turn blue. We're breathing again. Thanks a lot.*

COLLINS: (in Columbia): *Fantastic!*

ARMSTRONG: *Houston, that may have seemed like a very long final phase. The auto targeting was taking us right into a ... crater, with a large number of big boulders and rocks ... and it required ... flying manually over the rock field to find a reasonably good area.*

Six and a half hours later after checking everything over to make sure the ascent stage was okay for the eventual lift off, the crew of Tranquility Base as the LM was now called and Houston Control decided it was time to open the hatch and descend the ladder to the Lunar surface. The following historic conversation was recorded along with Neil Armstrong's famous sentence as he was the first person to step onto the moon:

ARMSTRONG: *The hatch is coming open.*

ALDRIN: *Neil, you're lined up nicely. Toward me a little bit. O.K., down.*

ARMSTRONG: *How am I doing?*

ALDRIN: *You're doing fine.*

ARMSTRONG: *O.K., Houston, I'm on the porch.*

CAPCOM (now Astronaut Bruce McCandless): *Man, we're getting a picture on the TV.*

ALDRIN: *Oh, you got a good picture, huh?*

CAPCOM: *There's a great deal of contrast in it, and currently it's upside down on our monitor, but we can make out a fair amount of detail. ... O.K., Neil, we can see you coming down the ladder now.*

ARMSTRONG: *I'm at the foot of the ladder. The LM footpads are only depressed in the surface about one or two inches, although the surface appears to be very, very fine grained, as you get close to it. It's almost like a powder. Now and then it's very fine. I'm going to step off the LM now.*

Then Neil Armstrong said one of the most famous sentences of all time when he said:

ARMSRONG: **That's one small step for man** [pause] **one giant leap for mankind.**

Some people were upset about Armstrong's use of the

wording "one small step for man", mostly coming from feminists groups who objected to that phrase and said it should have reflected an achievement for all "humankind". A news release from Houston later explained the words he used were "one small step for 'a' man", the word 'a' having got lost due to a communications glitch.

Neil and Buzz stayed on the Lunar surface picking up rocks and loading up the Lunar Lander, performing various experiments and setting up some scientific equipment that was to be left on the moon. An American flag was raised and some wire had to be used to display the flag as there is no atmosphere on the moon, no wind, to extend the flag. On the Lunar Lander ladder was a plaque bearing two drawings of the earth of the west and east hemispheres along with an inscription that read:

"Here Men From The Planet Earth First Set foot Upon the Moon, July 1969 A.D. We Came in Peace For All Mankind."

It was signed by the astronauts and President Nixon who was President of the United States at the time.

After the astronauts planted a U.S. flag on the lunar surface, they spoke with President Richard Nixon through a telephone-radio transmission which Nixon called "the most historic phone call ever made from the White House." Nixon originally had a long speech prepared to read during the phone call, but Frank Borman, who was at the White House as the NASA liaison during Apollo 11, convinced Nixon to keep his words brief, out of respect of the lunar landing being Kennedy's legacy.

The astronauts then collected rock samples using scoops and

tongs on extension handles. Many of the surface activities took longer than expected, so they had to stop documenting sample collection halfway through the allotted 34 min. Neil and Buzz went back into the LM to get some sleep and after about seven hours they were awakened by Mission Control in Houston. Two and a half hours later they lifted off in Eagle's ascent stage carrying 21.5 kilograms (about 43 pounds) of lunar samples to rejoin Columbia in lunar orbit. The blast from the ascent stage blew over the flag which was only 25 feet away from the descent stage. Future moon missions would place the flag 100 feet away so the flag would not be blown over. To link up with Columbia, Eagle had to "chase" Columbia in lunar orbit until they were able to link up. After rendezvous with *Columbia*, *Eagle's* ascent stage was jettisoned into lunar orbit where it was expected to eventually lose altitude and crash land on the lunar surface.

On the 24th of July 1969 the astronauts returned home and were immediately placed in quarantine for three weeks. It was considered remote that any contamination was brought back from the moon but no chances were being taken. It was discovered that no contaminates were brought back from the moon and after the Apollo 14 moon mission the crew quarantine phase of the mission was skipped.

1970 - Apollo 13 – a successful failure

The Apollo 13 mission was the third manned mission to the moon on 11 April 1970. Two days into the flight an oxygen tank in the Command/Service Module ruptured severely crippling the spacecraft. Enroute to the Moon, approximately 200,000 miles (320,000 km) from Earth, Mission Control asked the crew to turn on the hydrogen and oxygen tank stirring fans, which were designed to de-stratisfy the cryogenic contents and increase the accuracy of their quantity readings. Approximately 93 seconds later the astronauts heard a loud "bang", accompanied by fluctuations in electrical power and firing of the attitude control thrusters which tossed the spacecraft all over the place until control was achieved. The crew initially thought that a meteoroid might have struck the craft.

Jack Swigert, the Command Pilot spoke to Houston and said, "Hey, we've got a problem here!" Somewhere along the way that line has been changed to "Houston, we have a problem", and is still used in common language to this day to describe a problem when something has gone wrong. The crew was forced to shut down the Command Module completely and to use the LM as a "lifeboat". This had been suggested during an earlier training simulation but had not been considered a likely scenario. Without the LM, the accident would certainly have been fatal to the crew.

The damage to the Service Module made safe return from a lunar landing impossible, so Lead Flight Director Gene Kranz immediately aborted the mission. The quickest way home was a Direct Abort trajectory, which required using the Service Module engine to achieve a large change in velocity to essentially reverse the direction of the craft back to earth. Though this would get the men home quickest with the least drain on consumables, it was highly impractical for the following reasons:

- It was practical only in an earlier stage of the mission, before the craft entered the Moon's gravitational sphere of influence.
- There was no practical way to get electrical power to fire the engine.

- It was feared the engine might have been damaged in the explosion, preventing it from being fired safely.

For these reasons, Kranz and Flight Director Chris Kraft chose the circumlunar "free return" option, using the Moon's gravity to return the ship to Earth, with an acceleration burn shortly after pericynthion (closest approach to the Moon) to help speed the return. Considerable ingenuity under extreme pressure was required from the crew, flight controllers and support personnel for the safe return. The developing drama was shown on live television. Because electrical power was severely limited, no more live TV broadcasts from the spacecraft were made; TV commentators used models and animated footage as illustrations. Low power levels made even voice communications difficult.

Several problems had to be solved on the way back. The LM had been designed to provide enough oxygen for two men for 2 days, not 3 men for 5 days. Also the Command Module had been completely powered down to conserve electrical battery power. A power up sequence had to be found to power up the Command Module in space with limited battery power. For starters, the Command Module had never been designed to be completely powered up in space never mind with limited battery power. Solutions to both problems were found to save the lives of the three astronauts.

As Apollo 13 neared Earth, the crew jettisoned the Service Module so pictures could be taken for later analysis. It was then the crew were surprised to see the Sector 4 panel had been blown off. The Command Module *Odyssey* began its lone re-entry through the atmosphere. A normal earth re-entry was accompanied by four minutes of communications blackout caused by ionization of the air around the Command Module. This was normal for all space-to-earth re-entries. The possibility of heat shield damage had been feared from the explosion, heightening the tension of the blackout period which took 33 seconds longer than normal. The entire United States and most of the rest of the world held their collective breath. However, *Odyssey* regained radio contact and splashed down safely in the Pacific, southeast of American Samoa and only four miles from the recovery ship, the USS *Iwo Jima*.

The Apollo 13 mission has been called "a successful failure", because the astronauts were brought home safely notwithstanding the failure of the mission. The crew and the Apollo 13 Mission Operations Team were awarded the Presidential Medal of Freedom for their actions during the mission. And so ended the most famous space rescue ever, before or since.

1971 – 1982 – Russian Salyut Space Stations

The Salyut program was the first space station program undertaken by the Soviet Union, which consisted of a series of nine single-module space stations launched over a period of eleven years from 1971 to 1982. Intended as a project to carry out long-term research into the problems of living in space and a variety of astronomical, biological and Earth resources experiments, the program allowed space station technology to evolve from the engineering development stage to long-term research outposts in space. Ultimately, experience gained from the Salyut stations went on to pave the way for multi-modular space stations such as Mir and the International Space Station, with each of those stations possessing a Salyut-derived core module at its heart.

The program consisted of a series of six scientific research stations and three military reconnaissance stations, the latter being launched as part of the highly secretive Almaz program. Salyut broke several spaceflight records, including several mission duration records, the first ever orbital handover of a space station from one crew to another, and various spacewalk records. By the time the program concluded, in 1991, it had seen space station technology evolve from basic, single-docking port stations to complex, multi-port orbital outposts with impressive scientific capabilities, whose technological legacy continues to the present day.

1973 to 1979 - Skylab

Skylab was the United States' first space station, and the second space station visited by a human crew. It was also the only space station NASA launched alone. The 100-ton space station was in Earth's orbit from 1973 to 1979 and it was visited by crews three times in 1973 and 1974.

1975 - Apollo and Soyuz Test Project

The Apollo-Soyuz Test Project entailed the docking of an American Apollo spacecraft with a then-Soviet Soyuz spacecraft. While the Soyuz was given a mission designation number (Soyuz 19) as part of the ongoing Soyuz program, it was referred to simply as "Soyuz" through the duration of the joint mission. The Apollo mission was officially not numbered, though some sources refer to it as "Apollo 18".

Though the mission included both joint and separate scientific experiments, its primary purpose was symbolic. The mission was a symbol of detente the two superpowers were pursuing at the time, and it ended the tension of the Space Race.

1986 to 2001 - Mir Space Station

Mir (Russian for "peace" or "world") was a Soviet and later Russian space station, operational in low Earth orbit from 1986 to 2001. With a greater mass than that of any previous space station, Mir was the first of the third generation type of space station, constructed from 1986 to 1996 with a modular design, and was the largest artificial satellite orbiting the Earth, a record now surpassed by the International Space Station, until its deorbit on 21st of March 2001.

1981 to 2011 - United States Space Shuttle

The Space Shuttle, part of the Space Transportation System (STS), was an American spacecraft operated by the National Aeronautics and Space Administration (NASA) for orbital human spaceflight missions. Millions of people in North America and around the world watched on live TV the launch of the first Space Shuttle and its successful landing. The Shuttle system was scheduled to be retired from service in 2011 after 134 launches and 30 years in service. Major missions included launching numerous satellites and interplanetary probes, conducting space science experiments, construction and servicing of the International Space Station and launch and placement of the Hubble Space Telescope.

Each Shuttle is equipped with a crane-like arm called the "Canadarm" that is used for lifting objects out of the shuttle payload bay and for retrieving objects in orbit. The arm was designed and built in Canada as Canada's contribution to the Shuttle program.

At launch, the Space Shuttle consists of a dark orange colored external tank (ET); two white, slender Solid Rocket Boosters (SRBs); and the STS Orbiter Vehicle (OV), the Shuttle spacecraft itself, which contained the crew and payload. The Shuttle "stack" launched vertically like a conventional rocket from the mobile launch platform on the "crawler" that was used since the Apollo missions after leaving the massive assembly building. It lifted off under the power of its two SRBs and the three main Shuttle engines (SSMEs), the latter fueled by liquid hydrogen and liquid oxygen from the external tank. The Space Shuttle launch used a two stage ascent. The solid rocket boosters were used only for the first stage, while the main engines on the shuttle burned for both stages. About two minutes after liftoff, staging occurs: the SRBs were released, and shortly began falling by parachute into the ocean to be retrieved by ship for reuse. The shuttle orbiter and external tank continued to ascend under power from the three main Shuttle engines and the Shuttle's inertia. Upon reaching orbit, the main engines were shut down, and the external tank was jettisoned downward and falls to burn up in the atmosphere. However, it was possible for the external tank to be kept in orbit and used for various applications. At this point, the orbital maneuvering system (OMS) engines may be used to adjust or circularize the achieved orbit.

The orbiter carried astronauts and payload such as satellites or space station parts into low earth orbit. Usually, five to seven crew members rode in the orbiter. Two crew members, the Commander and Pilot, were sufficient for a minimal flight, as in the first four test flights. A typical payload capacity is about 22,700 kilograms (50,000 lb), but could be raised depending on the choice of launch configuration. The orbiter carried the payload in a large cargo bay with doors that open along the length of its top, a feature which makes the Space Shuttle unique amongst spacecraft at that time. This feature made possible the deployment of large items such as the Hubble Space Telescope, and also to capture and return large payloads such as failed satellites in low orbit back to Earth for repair and eventual redeployment.

When the orbiter's space mission was complete it fired its OMS thrusters to slow down and drop out of orbit. It then made a "dead stick" or unpowered landing to a long runway as a space glider. The aerodynamic shape was a compromise between the demands of radically different speeds and air pressures during reentry, hypersonic flight and subsonic atmospheric flight. With more than 2.5 million parts, the Space Shuttle has been called the most complex machine yet created by humanity.

1986 – The Space Shuttle Challenger Disaster

It was January 28th, 1986 in the morning and Christa McAuliffe looked up at the clear blue Florida sky at the Kennedy Space Center.

"What a beautiful day for a launch.", she thought.

She was a teacher by profession and had been selected from over 11,000 applicants to go on this flight. She was going to do two teaching sessions from orbit to thousands of classrooms in the United States. The launch of the Space Shuttle Challenger had been delayed several times over the last few days but she was sure today's launch would be perfect. She just had that feeling. She looked up at the shuttle stack as it stood on the pad ready for launch. Even though she had seen it many times it always impressed her that such a huge machine could be shot into space. She took the elevator up to the orbiter with the rest of the crew and got strapped into her launch couch. All the crew had duties to perform and she was no exception. She was in constant communication with Mission Control and her Controller. It had been cold the last few days and she had heard rumors about the effect the cold could have had on the rubber O-rings that separate the different sections of the Solid Rocket Boosters (SRB's) used to assist the launch of the orbiter. All the crew had been assured that nothing was going to go wrong.

The launch was planned for 10:38 AM local time and as that time approached she started to get butterflies in her stomach, partly from anticipation of this amazing journey she was about to start and part from the fact this was her first real launch. She had taken all the standard training in the simulators but nothing was like the real thing. At 6.6 seconds before launch the shuttles main engines were started. The fuel for the engines was stored in the huge pressurized external tank which the shuttle orbiter and the two SRB's were connected. At 0 count the two SRB's were ignited.

She was told about what to expect at launch when the main engines start and the SRB's ignite. The noise would be deafening and the whole orbiter shakes from the power of the huge engines and the firing of the SRB's. She was not to be disappointed. The shuttle stack slowly rose off the pad and she heard the Shuttle Commander, the Pilot and Mission Control talking through the loop in the headphones in her helmet.

Shuttle Commander: "*There they go guys!*" (Shuttle main engines started)

Mission Control: "*All right!*"

Shuttle Commander: "*Three at a hundred.*" (meaning all three Shuttle engines were firing at 100%)

Shuttle Pilot: "*Here we go!*"

Public Affairs Officer: "*Liftoff of the 25th space shuttle mission, and it has cleared the tower.*"

At 57 seconds into the flight:

Shuttle Commander: "*Throttling up*"

Shuttle Pilot: "*Throttle up*"

Shuttle Pilot: "*Feel that mother go!*" "*Wooochoooo!*"

Shuttle Pilot: "*Thirty-five thousand going through one point five.*"(35,000 feet at speed of Mac 1.5)

At 68 seconds into the flight:

Capsule Communicator (CAPCOM): "*Challenger, go at throttle up.*"

Shuttle Commander: "*Roger, go at throttle up.*"

At 73 seconds into the flight:

Shuttle Pilot: "*Uh-oh...*"

Christa heard a tremendous explosion and the orbiter was violently thrown to one side. She followed her training and punched the panel to release the breathing mask to supply her with oxygen. The orbiter was tearing itself apart around her. The G-forces were off the scale as the orbiter was blasted free of the external fuel tank. This was the last thing she felt as she slipped into unconsciousness. Death came quickly from lack of oxygen and the extreme G-forces. The external fuel tank carrying liquid oxygen and hydrogen fuel for the Shuttle main engines had exploded.

After the remains of the orbiter were recovered off the ocean floor it was discovered that three air packs had been manually deployed indicating that at least three of the crew were alive after the explosion but the air packs were never used so it is assumed these crew members died within seconds after deploying the air packs. The explosion tore apart the orbiter so there was no chance of the crew surviving at the speed (Mach 1.92) and the height (48,000 feet) they were traveling.

The break up was found ultimately due to the failure of an O-ring on its right solid fuel rocket booster (SRB). The O-rings are used to seal the joints between the multiple segments of the SRBs. The failure was due to a variety of factors, including unusually low temperatures prior to liftoff. Many fingers were pointed after the catastrophic failure as it was later discovered that several engineers had expressed concern over the low temperatures and the possibility of moisture freezing in the joints making them open up and thus creating the possibility of a failure. The failure allowed a plume of flame to leak out of the SRB and impinge on both the external fuel tank (ET) and the SRB aft attachment strut. This flame could be clearly seen in videos of the launch shown after the disaster. The Shuttle Challenger spacecraft, traveling at about Mach 1.92, was forced into an attitude that caused it to endure extreme aerodynamic loads, with the resulting stresses causing it to break apart so there was no hope of an emergency landing after the explosion. The Shuttle fleet was grounded for a year and half due to the investigation of the accident.

1990 - Hubble Space Telescope

The Hubble Space Telescope (HST) is a NASA space telescope that was carried into orbit by a space shuttle in 1990. Although not the first space telescope, Hubble is one of the largest and most versatile, and is well known as both a vital research tool and a public relations boon for astronomy. The HST is named after the famous astronomer Edwin Hubble.

Hubble's orbit outside the distortion of Earth's atmosphere allows it to take extremely sharp images with almost no background light. Hubble's Ultra Deep Field image, for instance, is the most detailed visible-light image ever made of the universe's most distant objects. Many Hubble observations have led to breakthroughs in astrophysics, such as accurately determining the rate of expansion of the universe.

Hubble is the only space-based telescope ever designed to be serviced in space by astronauts. Four servicing missions were performed from 1993–2002, but the fifth was canceled on safety grounds following the Space Shuttle *Columbia* disaster. However, after spirited public discussion, NASA administrator Mike Griffin approved one final servicing mission, completed in 2009. The telescope is now expected to function until at least 2014, when its 'successor', the James Webb Space Telescope (JWST), is due to be launched.

1995 - Mir and Shuttle Docking

The March 14th launch of Soyuz TM-21 carried expedition EO-18 to Mir. The crew consisted of Cosmonauts Vladimir Dezhurov and Gennady Strekalov and NASA astronaut

Norman Thagard, who became the first American to fly into space aboard the Soyuz spacecraft. The expedition's crew returned to Earth aboard Space Shuttle Atlantis following the first Shuttle–Mir docking mission. The Mir Docking Module, positioned in Atlantis's payload bay, ready to be docked to Kristall. The primary objectives, launched on June 27th, called for the Space Shuttle Atlantis to rendezvous and perform the first docking between an American Space Shuttle and the Mir station. On June 29th, 1995 Atlantis successfully docked with Mir, becoming the first US spacecraft to dock with a Russian spacecraft since the Apollo-Soyuz Test Project in 1975.

2003 - Space Shuttle Columbia Disaster

The Space Shuttle Columbia disaster occurred on the 1st of February 2003, when Columbia disintegrated over Texas spreading debris stretching from Trophy Club to Tyler and into parts of Louisiana during reentry into the Earth's atmosphere, resulting in the death of all seven crew members, shortly before it was scheduled to conclude its 28th mission. The loss of Columbia was a result of damage sustained during launch when a piece of foam insulation the size of a small briefcase broke off the Space Shuttle external tank (the main propellant tank) under the aerodynamic forces of launch. The debris struck the leading edge of the left wing, damaging the Shuttle's thermal protection system (TPS), part of the "heat shield" which protects it from heat generated with the atmosphere during reentry. The majority of Shuttle launches recorded such foam strikes and thermal tile scarring. During reentry, the damaged area allowed the hot gases produced during reentry to penetrate and destroy the internal wing structure, rapidly causing the in-flight breakup of the vehicle. A massive ground search in parts of

Texas, Louisiana and Arkansas recovered crew remains and many vehicle fragments.

Space Shuttle flight operations were delayed for two years by the disaster, similar to the Challenger disaster. Construction of the International Space Station was put on hold, and for months the station relied entirely on the Russian Federal Space Agency for resupply until Shuttle flights resumed for crew rotation.

1998 – Present - International Space Station

The International Space Station (ISS) is an orbiting laboratory and construction site that synthesizes the scientific expertise of 16 nations to maintain a permanent human outpost in space. The average stay aboard the ISS is six months. Astronauts must exercise for two hours each day to counteract the detrimental effects of low gravity on the body's skeleton and circulatory system.

The International Space Station station has been under construction since November of 1998. In that year the first piece of its structure, the Zarya Control Module, was launched into orbit using a Russian Proton rocket. In 2008, the two billion dollar science lab Columbus was added to the station, increasing the structure to eight rooms. Canadarm2 is another important feature of the space station. This Canadian built apparatus is a large, remote-controlled space arm that functions as a crane and can be utilized for a wide variety of tasks. The International Space Station was completed by the end of the 2000 decade. When construction was finished, six crew members could live and work in a space larger than a typical five bedroom house.

American Spacecraft Development - 2000 Decade

The X33 and X34 programs will develop reusable vehicles, which significantly decrease the cost to orbit. The X33 will be a manned vehicle lifting about the same payload capacity as the Space Shuttle. The X34 will be a small, reusable unmanned launch vehicle capable of launching 905 kilograms to space and reduce the launch cost relative to current vehicles by two thirds.

The first step towards building fully reusable vehicles has already occurred. A project called the Delta Clipper is currently being tested. The Delta Clipper is a vertical takeoff and soft landing vehicle. It has demonstrated the ability to hover and maneuver over Earth using the same hardware over and over again. The program uses mostly existing technology and minimizes the operating cost. Reliable, inexpensive rockets are the key to enabling humans to truly expand into space. Civilian space companies have also been encouraged to come up with space vehicles of their own. Some companies now offer space flights to near space for the passengers to experience weightlessness and to easily see the curvature of the earth.

On the 25th of May 2012 a privately developed space craft the SpaceX Dragon successfully docked with the International Space Station. A new era of spaceflight had begun as private companies were beginning to take over the job of ferrying supplies back and forth to the ISS.

SpaceX was created in 2002 by Elon Musk, the same entrepreneur who created PayPal and Tesla motors, an electric car company.

Hope - A Space Novel - Chapter One

Stephen Hawking
"The Greatest Theoretical Physicist Since Einstein"

"Mankind must abandon earth or face extinction."
- Stephen Hawking

Stephen Hawking is a British Theoretical Physicist whose career has spanned over 40 years. In 1962 he showed the first signs of "Amyotrophic lateral sclerosis" (ALS, known colloquially in the United States as Lou Gehrig's disease). Once at University College, Hawking specialized in physics. His interests during this time were in thermodynamics, relativity, and quantum mechanics. After receiving his B.A. degree at Oxford in 1962, he stayed to study astronomy. He decided to leave when he found that studying sunspots, which was all the observatory was equipped for, did not appeal to him and that he was more interested in theory than in observation. He left Oxford for Trinity Hall, Cambridge, where he engaged in the study of theoretical astronomy and cosmology.

His physics tutor, Robert Berman, later said in The New York Times Magazine:

"It was only necessary for him to know that something could be done, and he could do it without looking to see how other people did it. He didn't have very many books, and he didn't take notes. Of course, his mind was completely different from all of his contemporaries."

Hawking was passing, but his unimpressive study habits

resulted in a final examination score on the borderline between first and second class honors, making an "oral examination" necessary. Berman said of the oral examination:

"And of course the examiners then were intelligent enough to realize they were talking to someone far more clever than most of themselves."

Hawking was elected as one of the youngest Fellows of the Royal Society in 1974, was made a Commander of the Order of the British Empire in 1982, and became a Companion of Honor in 1989. Hawking is a member of the Board of Sponsors of the Bulletin of the Atomic Scientists. Hawking's achievements were made despite the increasing paralysis caused by the ALS. By 1974, he was unable to feed himself or get out of bed without assistance. His speech became slurred so that he could be understood only by people who knew him well. In 1985, he caught pneumonia and had to have a tracheotomy, which made him unable to speak at all. A Cambridge scientist built a device that enables Hawking to write onto a computer and with small movements of his body, then have a voice synthesizer speak what he has typed. The DECtalk DTC01 voice synthesizer he uses, which has an American English accent, is no longer being produced. Asked why he had still kept it after so many years, Hawking mentioned that he has not heard a voice he likes better and that he identifies with it. As of mid 2009, he was said to be using NeoSpeech's VoiceText speech synthesizer.

"Mankind's only chance of long-term survival lies in colonizing space, as humans drain Earth of resources and face a terrifying array of new threats.", warned Stephen Hawking.

"The human race shouldn't have all its eggs in one basket, or on one planet. Our only chance of long-term survival is not to remain inward looking on planet Earth, but to spread out into space.", he added.

He warned that the human race was likely to face an increased number of events that threaten its very existence, as the Cuban missile crisis did in 1962.

"We are entering an increasingly dangerous period of our history.", said Hawking.

"Our population and our use of the finite resources of planet Earth are growing exponentially, along with our technical ability to change the environment for good or ill. If we want to survive beyond the next century, our future is in space.", added the scientist. "That is why I'm in favor of manned, or should I say 'personned', space flight."

His comments came after he warned in a recent television series that mankind should avoid contact with alien civilizations at all costs, as the consequences could be devastating. He said aliens would likely be roaming marauders who have depleted their own planets resources, be probably far superior to us and will want to plunder our planet for its remaining natural resources. This scenario was the basis for the popular movie "Independence Day" in 1996.

2009 – 2012
Decline of the United States and the World Economy

The banking institutes on Wall Street who provide loans to other banks in the United States were in serious trouble. Many of the smaller banks had loaned money for houses and other big ticket items to people who could barely afford it. When the world economic decline and the decline in the United States economy hit, many banks were forced to repossess houses because buyers could no longer afford them as businesses started laying off large numbers of employees in an attempt to survive. This left the Wall Street banks in serious trouble with a debt load of 700 billion dollars.

President George Bush was trying to pass a bill to bail out the banks and avoid a 1929 type crash where the economy literally collapsed like a house of cards. The Presidential election interrupted this process and the new President, Barack Obama, submitted the same bill to Congress for approval which was finally passed. It was hoped that it would shore up the economy and save the U.S. banking system. The economy kept sliding downwards putting millions out of work. President Obama increased the amount of time that Unemployment Insurance benefits could be collected to help those out of work and as he put it, "To put money in the hands of those people who will spend it" in the hope this would be one step to help restore the economy as people spent the money to keep businesses alive.

Actually the seeds of this decline had started decades before as American corporations started shutting down manufacturing plants in the U.S. and moving manufacturing "off shore" to other countries like Taiwan, Malaysia, Mexico and later to China to get products made with cheaper labor. It meant that consumers could buy almost anything a lot cheaper than if it was made "on shore" using unionized labor, labor costs that were far higher than could be had in the "off shore" manufacturing companies. This meant far fewer jobs for Americans as plants closed. More items were being imported than exported resulting in a trade imbalance. The U.S. had to borrow more and more money until the national debt was in the trillions of dollars. The American economy had moved from manufacturing jobs to jobs in the service, retail, fast food outlets, research fields and different levels of government. The average American family income was becoming less all the time because salary increases were not keeping up with the cost of living while prices for essentials kept rising. This meant less money to spend keeping the economy robust, and slow but sure over the years the economy steadily declined.

Most Americans still believed in the American dream of home ownership, a new car in the driveway and state-of-the-art electronics like a big screen high definition flat screen HDTV in the family room or living room. Unfortunately most Americans went seriously into debt to realize these dreams so when a job was lost by someone in the household it put many families in serious trouble.

The wars that had started in the early 2000's in Afghanistan and Iraq were taking a heavy toll on government expenses and human life. Billions per year were being spent on wars that were supposed to have been short in and out campaigns. Year after year these wars dragged on further draining the American economy. The American people were getting more and more disgruntled with the way things were going until the U.S. government finally decided on a pull out date and hand over military control and policing to these countries.

Up until the early 1940's most women stayed home to run the household and look after the children. When WWII broke out many men from the factories joined the armed forces so women were recruited to take their place. After the war many women stayed in the workforce as by this time many saw the advantage of having two incomes in the family and the extra income to afford a better life. No one today except for the really well paid can afford not to have two incomes in the family. It took two salaries to maintain the American dream or even just to live comfortably. In the 1950's just after the Second World War the U.S. economy was booming as most products were made in the U.S. as manufacturing plants switched from making war supplies to making consumer goods. The unemployment rate was extremely low and jobs were plentiful.

The United States tried to help Germany and Japan rejuvenate their recovery and allowed lower priced items produced in those countries to be imported into the United States in order to give them a market to sell their products. The economy was growing by leaps and bounds as more and more families started moving to the suburbs and buying houses which meant more highways had to be built connecting the suburbs to the cities which meant still more employment. Shopping malls started to appear in the suburbs to service this movement. A lot of these collections of houses and shopping malls quickly became small towns. Stores in or near the cities began to be affected by the loss of business as more people in the suburbs began shopping closer to home. Manufacturing plants and research companies began moving to the suburbs as well to be closer to their labor pool and cheaper taxes which left the cities occupied by low income service industry workers and their families living in cheap rentals in older decaying buildings. Over time, many inner cities in large metropolitan areas began to decay and were full of abandoned houses, factories and so became denizens of crime, homeless shelters and drug houses.

Japan began manufacturing American products cheaper and better as time went on and their economy started to flourish. Japanese auto companies began manufacturing vehicles and importing them into the United States and Canada competing with the American auto makers. Soon Japanese auto plants began appearing in the United States and Canada as Japanese auto companies started to manufacture automobiles within their North American market. The inner cities began to decline over the years as some old manufacturing and warehouse properties were simply abandoned and left to decay. By the 1960's some American companies tried to compete and started to have products manufactured in other countries using cheaper labor. Salaries were high in the U.S. so companies started to close manufacturing plants as manufacturing was sent out of the country to be produced by much cheaper labor "off shore" and then brought back into the country for sale.

A brief upswing to the economy was made possible by the Apollo project to put a man on the moon at the end of the 1960's and again with development of the microchip in the mid 1970's. Companies in California appeared overnight and started hiring tons of people to produce these chips. Microprocessors began to appear which made possible small computer designs and was the start of Apple Computer Corporation in the late 1970's which is still in business today and doing very well with its line of "i" products, today mostly produced offshore. Apple introduced the first generally accepted personal and business computer and many companies started writing programs and games for it.

IBM introduced the IBM personal computer in 1981 and business owners jumped on it because of IBM's "big blue" name and mainframe computer history even though these first computers did not have a hard disk and sold at $6,000.

Computers have become more and more popular until the present where almost every home has at least one computer and a lot of homes have home networks to share files and photos with networked printers and other devices. Today, the price for computers has dropped making the ownership of a personal computer available by almost everyone. The manufacture of most computer components is done in other countries such as Taiwan and China to name just two.

In the 1990's the Internet was made available to the general public and many "dot COM" companies were created making their creators instant millionaires overnight. Many of these web sites went bust in the famous "dot COM" bubble burst but several managed to survive to this day like Yahoo!, Google and eBay and are worth billions to their owners and investors.

By the 1980's and '90's the first serious signs of a faltering U.S. economy started to show. By the 2000 decade more and more families went from home ownership to renting and having to move back to the cities and take service jobs that were becoming more numerous than manufacturing jobs were in previous decades as many could no longer afford the American dream. Even Telemarketing and Tech Support lines were being run in foreign countries like India to take advantage of the cheaper labor rates. Personal bankruptcies rose sharply in America as more families could no longer service their debt loads. Banks, loan companies and credit card companies started to feel the resulting pinch as more and more people went bankrupt. The resulting personal defaults were trickling back to the banks on Wall Street who loaned the money to the smaller banks that loaned the money to their banking customers. Private banks in the United States began to fail leaving investors and account owners left with pennies on the dollar as these banks went bankrupt themselves. Over a period of a couple of decades the result was a 700 billion dollar loss to the Wall Street banks.

The best job to have was one in the federal, state or municipal governments, in research and development companies or in solid investment institutions where senior members received huge salaries and bonuses even though these institutions themselves were in serious financial trouble. Finding good work of any kind was getting harder to find. Jokes were made such as, Question: "What does a university graduate say?" Answer: "Do you want fries with that?"

2010 – 2015
The American and European Economies

Riots broke out in several European countries as governments cut back pay for government workers to reduce government debt while inflation in these countries kept climbing. The wars in Iraq and Afghanistan took a terrible tole on the U.S. economy and military personnel. Public sentiment for these wars declined rapidly and riots and marches broke out all over the U.S. to put an end to these conflicts and bring the military home for civil defense and quit spending money "over there" and put it to use reviving the economy. By 2011 most military personnel were pulled out of Iraq leaving the Iraqi military force to try and keep order in the country. Some U.S. soldiers were left as advisers. Al-Qaeda began making a comeback despite the efforts of the Iraqi forces trying to maintain control. Many Iraqi soldiers deserted to Al-Qaeda. It was the same in Afghanistan where the Taliban quickly took control of most of the country as Allied forces started evacuating the country and Afghanistan forces could no longer keep control.

Pakistan was accused of offering a safe haven for the Taliban and even allowing Taliban training sites in that country. In 2011 Osama bin Laden was finally killed. He was considered the head of Al-Qaeda and the mastermind behind the destruction of the Twin Towers in New York City on the 11th of September 2001. Many thought Pakistan knew that bin Laden was living in that country and the American public sentiment for Pakistan dropped sharply as a result.

The America government had not learned their lesson from the Vietnam conflict in the late 1960's and early 1970's where they had to withdraw from Vietnam under public pressure after spending billions of dollars and paying the high price of loss of life, both civilian and military. North Vietnam quickly took control of South Vietnam after the Americans left. The South Vietnam armed forces could do little to stop them.

The jobless rate in the U.S kept climbing no matter how many stimulus packages were introduced to spur the economy. People started to group together sharing houses in the hope they could all afford to live without having to resort to living in the cities or in a shelter or in subsidized housing that had waiting lists years long. Many jobs were done "under the table" which meant state and federal taxes were not being paid which worsened the situation. The number of people with taxable income was growing less and less. By 2011 there were 14 million people unemployed in the United States and the country was in debt to the sum of over 14 trillion dollars. Money to pay welfare recipients was getting harder to find as less tax revenue was being brought in. The United States began printing money that it could no longer back up and the U.S. dollar began to slip on the international money markets. Bills were continually being put through Congress to raise the U.S. Debt ceiling allowing them to borrow more. Standard and Poor's lowered the U.S. Credit rating from AAA to AA+ which briefly upset the stock market and a crash was likely as panicked stock owners tried to sell, sell, sell. There were outcries for calm which finally settled the stock market down briefly but gold prices skyrocketed as investors put their money into the precious metal seeing it as the most stable item on the market.

As the decade carried on, money began to be worth less and most people started to use the barter system to get done what needed to be done. People started to trade skill for skill rather than work for money if work could be found at all. Many desperate people died in gun fire exchanges with law officials as they barricaded themselves in their homes rather than be evicted with no where to go. Women resorted to prostitution to raise money for essentials for the family to live. Men started joining gangs for protection and would often be given the job of battling rival groups. It was either do that or lose their homes and end up on the street with their families. Theft and the street drug trade was high. Pawn shop businesses and prostitution rings, mostly owned by criminal elements, were flourishing.

By 2015 chaos was slowly taking over the inner cities as people fought to survive. The government tried to use the military to keep order and martial law was imposed in all of the larger cities. If someone was caught outside curfew or stealing they would be arrested or shot on the spot if caught in the act and resisted arrest if armed. Many small businesses were robbed on a routine basis. Store owners were often armed and some even hired armed men as guards. They would be given food in return for providing protection to the store and its owner. Money was used less as anarchy took over much of the inner cities.

Rural America was not immune from problems. Rural people who could live off the land or barter and trade with their neighbors were better off than people in the city. City people would often try and beg or steal food or trade labor for food. Some farms turned into armed camps as people moved into these areas to help protect the camps being formed and be rewarded with shelter and food. Large commune style enterprises began to appear as more people were accepted from the cities and other farms started to join the communes or risk being taken over by force. Armed barricades were built for protection to keep out outsiders as perimeters began to be established. The military rarely intervened as they had their hands full in the more populated cities. Food was being imported from the commune farms at high prices into the cities to be quickly distributed to the half starving populations.

The Process of Detection of Habitable Planets

As early as the 16th century the Italian philosopher Giordano Bruno, an early supporter of the Copernican theory that the Earth and the other planets orbit the Sun, put forward the view that stars similar to the Sun are likely accompanied by their own planets.

Carl Sagan, famous scientist and astronomer predicted as far back as the 1970's that other planets would be found around other stars similar to our own that could sustain life. There may be other civilizations similar to our own living on these planets, he said. His conclusion was reached by saying there are billions of stars in our galaxy alone and around those stars are probably planets in orbit and some of the planets may reside in "the right zone" similar to earth. Planets that are just the right distance from its star to have the proper temperature range to sustain life as we know it or where life has already started and possibly evolved. Even if less than 1/10 of 1% of the stars having planets meeting this criteria there would still be thousands of other planets like ours. Carl Sagan was also one of the founding members of SETI – The Search for Extra-Terrestrial Intelligence, an organization with several hundred thousand participating members who believe there are other civilizations out in space who are comparable with our own and that we can detect their radio transmissions with radio-telescopes. Hundreds of thousands of personal and business computers around the world are sent small amounts of data received from radio-telescopes for analyzing looking for intelligence in the signals. Nothing conclusive has yet to be found although there are some promising leads.

Extrasolar Planets or "Exoplanets" as they are sometimes called have been detected as early as 1988 when a stars wobble was detected and a theory proposed the wobble could be caused by a large orbiting planet. As of 2010, 490 such planets had been detected by more and more sensitive equipment being designed and used all the time. It has been observed that stars with planets are fairly common but detecting an earth-like planet in the right zone from its star to be capable of originating or supporting life are very hard to detect. Detecting a large planet the size of Jupiter or larger was fairly easy but detecting a far smaller planet like our own is almost impossible because a planet our size has very little affect on its star's wobble and is almost impossible to detect by telescope, even space based ones, the process used to detect the larger planets. Space-based telescopes such as the Hubble and the Webb telescopes have the ability to view far clearer and closer than ever before. Shadows of larger planets hundreds or thousands of light years away from earth had been noted back-lit by their stars.

By 2015 newer and more sensitive equipment had been designed to detect smaller earth-like planets orbiting in the "sweet zone", the correct distance from their star, to sustain life as we know it. Some of these planets were far closer to us than previously believed. An important discovery in 2017 was made when it was discovered that a probable earth-like planet was observed orbiting our nearest neighbor Alpha Centauri-A. This set the scientific world abuzz with excitement.

2019
Steady World and American Economic Decline

The jobless rate in the U.S. had now reached almost 30%. Inner city crime was extremely high with flourishing drug, prostitution and gambling rings controlling much of the areas. At night it was particularly dangerous. Murder rates were extremely high and the police or military rarely investigated. Many patrols refused to go into some areas at night for fear of their lives. Arrests were high and the prisons were jammed beyond capacity by criminals serving their sentences or waiting for trial dates. Temporary prisons were hurriedly built to try and ease the situation. Some American politicians even suggested building prisons in the Canadian far north as not many prisoners would try and escape because there would be no where to go if they were able to break out. Life in prison was controlled by gangs and factions. The only way to survive was to join a gang or risk being killed. As prison life worsened and more prisoner unrest began, many prison take overs were attempted by the prisoners with significant loss of life on both sides, between prisoners trying to escape or make deals, and peace officers, prison guards and the military that were trying to take back control. Many states re-introduced the death penalty for serious crimes like first degree murder in the hope these sentences would reduce serious crime but no difference was made. It was better to die fighting for your life outside of prison than risk being arrested and sent to prison.

2021
Malcolm Beacham

Malcolm Beacham was head of Microsoft Corporation and like its founder, William Gates, Malcolm had amassed a private fortune. He was only in his mid-forty's but looked younger. He was shaved, of medium height with a slim build. He was seen as a quiet man but had amassed his fortune with shrewd investing and stock options from Microsoft. He also was known to live simply and people that had been to his residence reported that it looked spartan with only the essential in furnishings and few pictures. The people under him respected him as a fair individual who was open to new ideas and recommendations. As CEO he could have led Microsoft with an iron hand but that was not his style. He had learned early in life that if you treated people with dignity and respect they would respond in turn.

He looked at the world wide situation and recalled Stephen Hawking's suggestion decades before to colonize space because if mankind kept going the way it was earth and civilization would be destroyed. He firmly believed this would likely happen and believed if humankind were to survive he had to convince the rest of the people like him that his Plan was the best answer to save humanity. The Plan he had in mind would need an incredible amount of money, many billions, more than he could provide. The Bill & Melinda Gates Foundation, established in 2000 had already promised several billion to the Plan. He made some discrete calls to other people who he knew that had amassed private fortunes, had influence in many corporations and made arrangements to have them all meet with him at a secret location in northern Canada, a remote but popular resort, to discuss the Plan. The area had an airport nearby but not large enough to accommodate the landing of large private jets.

These people had to fly in to airports further south and then hire smaller planes to make the rest of the trip. The people he invited were the heads of or heavy investors in companies like Wal-Mart, Shell Corporation, Exxon Mobile, British Petroleum, Toyota, Chevron, General Electric, ING Group, Bank of America, AT&T, General Motors, Hewlett Packard, J.P Morgan and Chase, Samsung Electronics, IBM, Nissan Motor, Sony, Panasonic and many others. He did not tell them about the Plan, he just told them where the meeting would be held, date and time and told them it was of the utmost importance to attend to save the planet in the the most forceful manner he could. He worded the message carefully and sent it out. Most replied but wanted more details. He said he would provide the details when everyone was there and it would be worth their while to attend. The meeting was scheduled for the weekend of April 6th. All he could do now was wait and see who would attend. It was a big gamble on his part because so much could go wrong. He prepared a short speech and presentation for the meeting. He knew there would be a huge discussion later with many detractors.

He knew that all these men and women were not going to be coming alone. No one who was worth what these people were worth traveled anywhere these days without a security team armed to the teeth. The location he chose had lots of room. He booked the entire site and had arranged for protection of the site perimeter in case news leaked out. If that happened there would be a huge riot equaling those of the G20 summit meetings. People would be very suspicious and would do their level best to breech security and shoot every last one of them. He gave his security team open orders to turn away intruders and if necessary to shoot to kill.

Malcolm's Plan

Malcolm went to the remote location first to oversee the entire operation and that everything that he had planned with his security chief was implemented. Most of it was in order except for a few details that needed to be addressed. Dixon from Shell Corporation was the first to arrive. Dixon did not look wealthy. He was dressed casually in slacks and a sweater. He looked to be in his early '50's, was tall and lean. He smiled easily which made his face topped with reddish hair very friendly. But Malcolm knew that Dixon did not get rich without making some shrewd and profitable investments. Malcolm shook hands with the man and thanked him sincerely for making the trip. Dixon had brought several security people with him as Malcolm had expected he would. Dixon of course wanted details of what this was all about but Malcolm told him he wanted the entire group to be present before telling anyone anything about the Plan. He explained that if he told some people ahead of time it may be seen that he was showing favoritism and that some may leave immediately before the presentation had even been shown and the Plan discussed. Dixon was annoyed but seemed to understand the concept.

The Plan would be presented to everyone at the same time. Personal security people would not be allowed in for the presentation. Everyone would be screened for "bugs" so no news would leak out to security personnel or any other people. Only the important people invited would know about the Plan and sworn to secrecy whether or not they agreed to it.

The rest of his guests started arriving and were shown to their rooms. The rooms were arranged so there was enough room around each guest to house their personal body guards that he knew each one would bring. The last guest arrived later in the afternoon. A reception was held in the main dining room later that evening and everyone mingled and talked and the main discussion of course was what the heck was The Plan all about and why were they all here. A few had approached Malcolm and had asked him directly about the Plan but he gave them the same answer he had given Dixon.

Security was tight in and around the complex. It was remote enough that protesters further south would likely not be a bother because by the time they heard about it the conference would be over and everyone would be gone. Hopefully, thought Malcolm, that is the way it would work out. Security personnel were strategically placed. Some were in plain view on roadways leading to the resort but the majority were hidden from view and could act on a moments notice in the event of any problems. There was a small town nearby where a lot of the population lived that worked at the resort. The cover story was that an important person had booked the resort for the weekend to host a gathering of his friends and associates and wanted everything to be as secretive as possible. This type of arrangement had been made before on other occasions so the staff and owners of the resort bought the cover story.

The next morning at 9AM everyone was to meet in the resorts large conference room. Some of the people were upset that none of their security people were to be allowed to accompany them in the conference room but Malcolm did his best to assure them of their safety. Their personal security teams were allowed to be in the vicinity of the conference room but not close enough to hear what was going on inside. His own security people had met with the security teams of his invited guests and had showed them the security precautions that were being taken to assure the safety of their bosses. Most were satisfied but a few were still concerned but in the end went along with the arrangements. There really was no other choice.

At the appointed time after breakfast in the main dining room everyone was escorted to the conference room attended by some of their own body guards and some of Malcolm's own security team. There were tables and security scanning equipment set up a discrete distance from the conference room where all guests were scanned for "bugs" of any kind. Some were discovered and the equipment was removed to the chagrin of the guests who were caught out. They were all escorted into the conference room. No security men were in the conference room, not even any of Malcolm's team. He wanted only the principal people to know the contents of the Plan.

"Thank you all for coming to this conference.", Malcolm said soon after all his guests had seated themselves at the conference table.

"All of you are wondering of course why you are here. That will be revealed now.", he said.

He gazed around the room and made eye contact with all of his guests. All of them had his complete attention.

Malcolm continued, "We all know the world situation is not good. The world economy is breaking down and a lot of countries are in serious trouble. Even the United States is not untouched by it, in fact it is one of the worst affected countries. Chaos and anarchy is spreading over much of the world. Most people are fighting just to stay alive and safe. Gangster elements are running the inner cities and in some cases entire countries where law and order have broken down completely. We are in a very serious predicament and there is a threat of world wide nuclear war. Every leader has their finger on the button and all it will take would be one country to launch an attack and it would be World War III which I am sure you all realize would be the end of humankind as we know it on this planet. All nuclear nations are in constant contact with one another which is a good thing but how long will that last? I am afraid that humankind has reached the brink of their existence. What can we as rich and powerful people as we are to do and try to stop it? We can't. Even with all our money and resources we are powerless to stop the events taking place."

Malcolm paused for effect and looked around the room. It seemed as though everyone was hanging on to his every word. So far, so good.

Dixon from Shell Corporation was the first to speak up. "What are you trying to suggest we can do? Is that why we are all here? Do you have a plan to restore the world economy?"

Someone else started speaking. "I'm not giving up any money to bail out some country in the hope of restoring order. With all the corruption that is going on, the money would simply disappear and we would never see it again."

Other men and women started to speak and soon it was almost out of control as everyone tried to speak at once, getting louder to be heard. Malcolm picked up his gavel and hammered it on the lectern to get everyone's attention and restore order.

Eventually everyone settled down and waited for Malcolm to continue. "I am not asking anyone to give up their personal fortunes in this manner. You are right. If we simply gave money to these countries in an attempt to shore up their failing economies I am also sure the money would simply disappear.

What I have in mind is much larger in scale. I have a slide presentation prepared as a visual aid to describe what I am about to suggest. Some of you may be shocked at the idea but please give it some thought. We can spend whatever time we need discussing the Plan as I have code named it to try and answer all questions and to persuade everyone that it is the right thing to do so that humankind can still exist and continue." All eyes were on him now as they realized the contents of the Plan would now be revealed to them. "All I ask is that everyone please not interrupt until the end of the presentation. You will all want to make comments I am sure but please restrain yourselves. All questions will be answered in the discussion to follow. I hope the discussion phase will be professional in nature. Let the person speaking continue without interruption. I will give answers to all questions and then the next speaker will be allowed to say their piece. Lets start the presentation."

Malcolm turned on the overhead projector that was mounted in the ceiling and the large screen at the front of the conference room lit up with the words '**The Plan....A Proposal to Save Humanity**'

Malcolm began reading from his prepared notes, "Everyone here knows the serious condition the world is in right now. Civilization is quickly breaking down. Most countries have imposed martial law and are arresting or killing any transgressors. People are panicking and suicide rates are the highest we have every seen. We have entire families being wiped out with mass murder/suicides. The Mafia and other gangs have control of most of the inner cities and are spreading across the countries they reside. Soon it will be gang warfare on a global scale. Its only a matter of time when these gangs get control of military installations and gain control to the nuclear arsenals that are in many of these countries. The nuclear countries had everyone at a stalemate because they knew that if any one country pushed the button then retaliation would be swift and would guarantee the annihilation of both or all countries that decided to respond. Civilization as we know it would cease to exist. The planet would literally be bombed back to the stone age. It would take years, perhaps generations to rebuild everything back to where it was, if ever."

Malcolm paused again to give his guests time to digest what he had just told them. It seemed they all knew that what he had said was true. It was only a matter of time.

Malcolm continued. "What I propose is this."

He clicked the next slide into view that showed a huge ship in space. It was hard to tell if it was a space station or a ship. It had a bullet shaped body with a huge space wheel surrounding it at the waist. The room started to buzz again as his guests started side conversation and comments with the others around them.

"Quiet please!", Malcolm banged his gavel once more on the lectern. "Please hear the rest of the presentation."

Malcolm gazed around the room until everyone stopped talking and a few of the guests were seen trying to calm down others in the room.

"Let the man speak, lets hear him out!", someone shouted.

"That's right. Please hear me out. That's all I ask for now.", Malcolm said. "What I propose is the building of a large spacecraft capable of journeying to another star system in the hopes of finding a habitable planet where the descendents of the crew of the spacecraft could start humanity anew."

He clicked the next slide into view. It showed a binary star system with some planets surrounding both stars.

Malcolm continued, "The nearest star to us is Gliesse 581-d known to most of us as Alpha Centauri-A. It is only 4.37 light years from us. Unfortunately with our current technology it would take us over 200 hundred years to make the trip. We know of no method to travel at or near the speed of light. The closer you approach the speed of light the more energy is required to go faster. To make light speed would take all the energy in the known universe to accomplish. This is all based on Einsteins theory of relativity that he developed decades ago and has been proven time and again as scientists all over the world have tried in vane to meet or break the speed of light barrier. That simple formula $E=MC^2$ has remained immoveable after all these years. The fastest speed we can achieve with present technology is two percent of light speed with our newest engines."

What I propose is the construction of a generation ship to make the journey. A generation ship would start out the voyage with a crew of men and women of many technical and scientific disciplines. They would procreate and raise children who then would be educated in the field of their parents to carry on the journey. There would be no marriages as we know of them now. If people wanted to bond together that is fine but inter-procreation with other members of the crew would be necessary to ensure the gene pool remained as varied as possible. The original members of the crew would grow old and be euthanized when it was generally accepted the persons usefulness was at an end. This would be done so as not to be a drain on resources by keeping older members of the crew alive when dementia, Alzheimer's, cancer or any other condition that would impede that persons contribution to the voyage. This would be done humanely by lethal injection at a ceremony of whatever type the person has indicated in their Will. The bodies would be recycled as would everything else aboard ship to use as food. I do not mean cannibalism. The food producing equipment would take all waste products, break it down and re-manufacture edible food for the crew. There would also be hydroponic farms on board as well raising quick growing high protein plants to use as basic food. Food supplements would be available to supply necessary elements to maintain good health. No animals would be aboard. Frozen embryos of various animals species would be kept in a cryogenic state until the destination is reached.

All evidence points to their being an earth-like planet orbiting Alpha Centauri-A. Once the planet is found some of the crew would land using the landing craft of Russian design. These landing craft would be carried outside the ship attached under the central section of the main hull. This would allow for maximum room inside the ship. There would be several of these landing craft to ensure all necessary items and personnel are able to be transported to the planet surface. The first wave landing crew would set up portable shelters in preparation for the rest of the crew and supplies to be ferried down. Once down the first concern is to ensure shelters are adequate and seed stock planted to start growing crops and to set up portable labs where the frozen embryos could be thawed and allowed to mature in artificial uterus's until the gestation period is finished. The resulting baby animals would have to be hand fed at this point because there would be no parent animals to look after them. The animals would be allowed to grow and procreate creating the needed herds to support the population. Once this process is well on its way, more and more of the crew would be transported down to join the rest of the colony."

The crew would have to be fairly small, maybe about 30

members maximum. All pregnancies would be carefully screened and if any defects were detected the pregnancy would be terminated. If any severe abnormalities were detected after birth, the babies would of course have to be euthanized as well as they could not be allowed to grow up because they would not be contributing members of the crew. This all sounds barbaric but necessary to ensure the quality of the crew remains at the highest standards possible. Charts would be kept to ensure the widest possible hereditary in the gene pool. Another idea would be the storage of frozen samples of eggs and sperm of unrelated individuals to be used for In Vitro Fertilization to further ensure the widest gene pool possible. Many generations would be required to be born, live and die on board the ship until it has reached its destination. I estimate the cost of this enterprise to be in the neighborhood of 100 billion dollars, more or less."

The room was silent as people were in shock at the idea. The expense and the moral methods proposed to terminate life when that life was no longer useful was shocking to many. There were a lot of ethical questions.

The first member to put up his hand was of course Dixon who asked, "So you propose for us to give you several billions of dollars apiece for this enterprise?" "Yes.", answered Malcolm.

Pandemonium broke out in the room with comments of:

"impossible"
"who does he think he is"
"how can he think he can pull this off"
"how long would this project take"
"this is no investment, there is no return"

Malcolm allowed the room to blow off a little steam and then started banging his gavel again for silence. Some guests tried to leave only to find the doors securely locked. Some people shouted that Malcolm had imprisoned them here. Eventually the room settled down.

Malcolm continued, "We can now begin the discussion phase of the presentation. Would you like to start Dixon?"

Dixon asked, "How long would it take to build such a ship and how would you get construction materials into orbit?"

"I am glad you asked that.", said Malcolm. "We cannot use one of the established launch centers for if word got out there would be riots from people to stop the project or people who would want to try and hitch a ride or take over the whole project. What I propose is building our own launch facility somewhere in northern Canada in a remote area. I have already been in contact with some high level Canadian government people and they seem to be on side with this idea. The cover story is we are building a space station, nothing more.

The facility would have to be heavily guarded because eventually word will leak out about the 'space station' and the money being spent for it when there are plenty of problems on earth to be fixed. We could design our own launch vehicles or perhaps use vehicles supplied by the European Space Agency or other countries. There are also private companies who have developed low cost disposable low orbit space vehicles that deserve to be considered. We could of course build our own launch vehicles copying existing designs but that would take more time. What we need are available inexpensive launch vehicles, a lot of them will be required, to get all materials needed into low earth orbit. Assembly crews would live aboard the old International Space Station that is still in orbit. I have discretely checked with NASA and they tell me the ISS was mothballed years ago but could be started up again and be useable in a few weeks time. They have told me they are willing to help with the restart of the ISS. When our ship can be inhabited then assembly crews would live there and work on it. I estimate that if we start as soon as possible we can start building the ship within the year. That will give us time to build and equip a launch facility and begin transporting earth assembled modules into orbit. Some modules would be too large to transport up to orbit whole and would have to be assembled or welded in space. The actual assembly of the ship would take about three years if we start now and hope the earth survives that long to allow its completion."

Someone asked, "Word is going to get out about the true intention of the 'space station' when we start sending up engine components. Space stations are designed to orbit the earth or stay in a fixed orbit. They have attitude rockets to maintain orbit but that is all."

Malcolm responded, "Yes that is true. That is why the engine components will be shipped up along with everything else a piece here and a piece there so it would not draw attention. But you are right, sooner or later word is going to leak out, hopefully near the end of the assembly project, that our 'space station' has an engine and is capable of leaving earth orbit. We hope to be able to protect the ship and the launch facility until the final moment when the ship leaves orbit."

Someone else asked, "Where do you intend to get the people that are required in space to assemble something this large.

What about the ground crew, where are those people going to come from?"

Malcolm replied, "I have been financing a company that is almost finished designing the ship as we speak. We have sent out discrete invitations to anyone with space experience or at least ground based training to work with us. Invitations have also been sent out as well to people that have worked or are working in launch control positions in the U.S. We will build a community at the launch site. No one will be allowed to leave that community until the project is complete for obvious security reasons. Everything they need will be in the community; stores, schools, churches, factories, housing of course, movie theaters and other activity centers such as gymnasiums and anything else we think people will need."

Everyone was silent for a few moments and were looking around the room trying to read other peoples thoughts.

Malcolm said, "We all know the earth is on the brink of disaster if present conditions continue and if we as a species are going to survive we will have to complete this project as quickly as possible. The project will run 24 hours a day, 7 days a week in three shifts on the ground and in space.

Unmanned robotic rockets will be sent up continuously from at least two, maybe three launch pads around the clock to keep the supplies needed flowing to build the ship in space. All supplies will be either flown in or sent in by sea to the launch base which will be on the shores of James Bay in northern Ontario Canada. With the global warming affect the Northwest Passage is now open all year around so shipping by sea will not be a problem. Crews in space will need to be rotated every so often so they don't suffer the long term effects of living and working in zero gravity. This won't be a problem on board the ship as it has a space wheel incorporated into its design which will produce an artificial gravity, about half what is experienced on earth. All the living quarters and work areas will be located in the space wheel around the waist of the ship. All of the propulsion systems, hydroponics, storage and so on will be located in the hull of the ship where zero gravity will not be a problem. The sooner we start this project the sooner it will be complete and the sooner the ship can leave orbit to begin its long trip. The crew on the ship can communicate with earth but as the ship travels further away from earth the communications will take longer as it will take radio signals longer to get to earth as the ship travels further away and just as long for a reply to be sent.

When the ship arrives at its destination in 200 years or so for instance, it will take over 4 years for the message to reach earth.....if there is an earth as we know it to receive the message. Our earth-bound descendants could all be living in caves or not exist at all. I'll need everyone's answer on this project as soon as possible. Time is of the essence as I have stressed. I would love to get a confirmation from everyone right here in this room but some of you may need to think about it but don't take too long. The more people that are ready to transfer money to this project the less per person we will need. Earth may survive but personally I have my doubts and as for myself I would rest easier knowing that the human species has at least been given a chance to start over somewhere else. I have created a bank account in the Cayman Islands to accept the funds you wish to donate to this project. I can give you the account number before you leave if you wish to think about it or want to ask me more questions about the project."

Malcolm looked around the room. He saw people talking quietly with each other in hushed tones about what they had just heard.

Malcolm spoke, "If any of you wish to break into groups to discuss this, feel free to do so."

Someone asked, "What if we want to leave right now?"

Malcolm said, "I would really prefer you all to stay until this is finished and we have done all we can do here then the doors will be unlocked and everyone can leave at once. But please remember that you all signed confidentiality documents which stated what you heard here was to be kept to yourselves. There is not a lot I or anyone else can do if you decide to break that agreement but I am counting on everyone to honor the agreement. Please feel free to partake in the refreshments that you see on the tables around the room and take a break. I know I need one." He smiled.

After about fifteen minutes everyone slowly returned to their seats and the talking gradually died down. Malcolm decided it was a good time to carry on and take a vote as to the people who were willing to join the project right now and those that wanted a little more time to decide.

Malcolm asked, "Everyone has had a chance to think about what you have heard and most of you have talked it over with others. Who is ready right now to join this project?"

He looked around the room. One person, a large shareholder who made her fortune with HP slowly raised her hand. Someone else raised their hand, then another and another. As soon as others saw that others were ready to commit to the project they too raised their hands. Soon almost all had indicated their willingness to put money into the project. All was calm here in the conference room and at the resort but everyone knew that in the world outside chaos reigned and something had to be done and done quickly in the event humanity killed off civilization as they knew it or obliterated themselves and the planet as a whole. It was better than Malcolm had expected. There were a few holdouts but hopefully they would join later. The more money the project had to work with the faster it could be completed and speed was of the essence.

Hope - A Space Novel - Chapter Two

Early 2022
Building the Launch Facility

Malcolm had already chosen the site on the shores of James Bay to begin building the launch facility and the town to support it near the existing town of Moosonee. The first bit of business was to build the town for everyone working at the launch facility to live and a dock for the freighters that would be shipping in material to build the town, the launch rockets, the equipment for launch control and parts for the spacecraft and all the supplies. The list seemed endless. The first order of business was to upgrade the existing airport at Moosonee to accommodate large jet transport aircraft. The existing runway was far too small and only could accommodate propeller driven aircraft. Jets needed a much longer runway to land and to take off and have equipment at the airport to support them.

Crews and material would be transported by tracked vehicles from Moosonee to the launch site center where the town was to be built. A road would be built later so that materials could be transported more easily to the town site. Tents were erected for the workers to live in temporarily until the first barracks were erected. The workers would work in three shifts around the clock. Electricity was supplied at first by portable generators, other workers would start building the diesel generator building that would produce the electricity required by the town and the launch facility. Day by day the town quickly took shape after the airport had been upgraded and some building supplies flown in. Other workers with equipment flown in started improving the dock facilities to enable ocean going freighters to unload at Moosonee. Within a month the dock was ready. It wasn't pretty but it was functional and that is what counted. The first ship came in ready to be unloaded. The bars in the town of Moosonee were doing a booming business. There was often line ups at the doors because the crowd inside exceeded the safe capacity of the building fire regulations. Malcolm realized that he had forgot to add some bars to his town plans. He made a note to have some built. He had forgot because he had not drunk in years. But hard working "hard hat" workers needed a place to have a few drinks and let off a little steam after their shifts.

Once the town and launch perimeters had been established, Malcolm ordered a fence erected around the entire facility. The fence was 15 feet high and topped with spools of razor wire. There was a mine field installed just outside the fence to deter outsiders from attempting to gain access. Signs were erected at regular intervals alerting intruders to the mine field. The fence served two purposes, to keep people out and to keep people in. The entire project had to be as secretive as possible.

Malcolm had hired a site boss that seemed to fit the bill. Murphy was about six feet four inches tall and weighed in around 250 pounds or so, all solid muscle it looked like. His hair was a little long but not overly so. He needed a shave. Murph had all black hair, no gray in it yet, and a rugged looking face of someone who had worked outside in all kinds of weather. Malcolm had read the big man's resume and he had a lot of experience with large projects. His resume said that Murphy was 37 years old. He had taken a few courses here and there on construction management and time management but it looked like most of his training had been done "OJT" (on the job). He looked like the kind of guy who rarely started fights but would always finish them. He needed a no-nonsense type like Murphy who insisted Malcolm call him "Murph" as everyone else did. His resume was well written and laid out. Malcolm asked if this was his work or did he have it prepared.

Murph assured him the resume was his work. "I'm as at home with a computer as I am with a hammer." He laughed. "I use the computer on every job to lay out a time line for each phase of the project and estimate where we should be at any stage."

Malcolm was doing the same thing. It would be interesting to see how each project time line looked when compared. Murph looked and talked with intelligence belying his rough exterior.

Malcolm showed him the plans for the town site, the launch facilities and the launch control building. "Of course the main thing to get finished first is the town site so the workers and their families will have somewhere to stay other than tents, then the launch control and then the launch pads themselves.", Malcolm said to Murph.

Malcolm told Murph that he was the site boss in charge and told the big man if he encountered any problems with any of the workers to let him know.

"Don't worry Sir.", Murph said, "There won't be any problems." Murph didn't smile.

He looked directly into Malcolm's eyes as he said it. Malcolm was sure there would be no problems, not with

Murph around.

"Put whoever you think is best in charge of each shift and be sure that each shift is given achievable targets.", Malcolm said. "Plan a schedule what you want achieved each day and give each shift boss what you want completed by the end of their shift the next day. Be sure to overlap each shift by at least a half hour so that each shift boss has a chance to bring the next boss up to speed on what has been completed and what still needs to be done. If you have to switch people around on the shifts due to personality or skill necessities, just go ahead and do it."

"Sure thing boss.", Murph said to Malcolm. "Call me Malcolm, everyone else does.", Malcolm smiled and extended his hand.

Murph grabbed Malcolm's hand and squeezed. He could feel the firm grip in the big man's handshake.

"Sure thing Malcolm.", Murph grinned back at him.

"If you ever have any suggestions as to how to speed things up or make things more efficient just go ahead and do it but keep me informed.", Malcolm said.

Murph said, "Sure thing Malcolm.", and just grinned back.

The first freighter carried more building supplies, transport vehicles and two large diesel generators that would be housed in the generator building. One generator would be the main one and would be running most of the time, the other generator would be used in emergencies as a backup or when the main generator had to be shut down for maintenance.

Within two weeks after the generator building was erected and the generators had been installed, power lines started to be run into the rapidly expanding town site. The freighter also carried two unassembled launch towers which were transported to the launch site. Another freighter was waiting off shore to come in to dock. The dock facilities could handle only one freighter at a time. The first freighter was unloaded and had left the dock as the second freighter was coming in. Malcolm had chosen a privately designed and built American rocket to be used to ferry materials to the spacecraft.

As soon as the designer found out his rocket had been selected for the program and the number of rockets required he realized that his small factory was completely unable to supply the demand and so talked Malcolm into shipping all rocket building material to the launch site and building the rockets there. This suited Malcolm just fine. It was one less thing the rest of the world would have to watch for clues to what was going on at the northern Canada launch site. It would also speed up the supply chain of the rocket manufacturing.

Some of the plants supplying parts for the rockets had been shutdown due to lack of orders. These plants were quickly reopened and started producing the necessary parts for the rockets around the clock. This supplied much needed jobs in the various areas and manpower was plentiful. These particular rockets were going to be the unmanned robotic rockets that would launch into space the bulk of the parts necessary for the spacecraft. Rockets from Russia would be used to ferry space workers to and from the International Space Station to begin work on the spacecraft assembly and to ferry up larger parts. The Russians had designed a successor to the long used Soyuz spacecraft that was as reliable and bigger to launch larger payloads. The Russians had been told the same cover story, the construction of a new privately funded space station.

Other nations particularly China began to notice the new activity in space as the International Space Station (ISS) was put back into service. The launches to the ISS had taken place in Russia to ferry crews up to the space station. It took a couple of weeks and another unplanned for launch when it was discovered that a number of pieces of equipment had to be replaced. Russia launched an unmanned robotic rocket to the ISS with the needed parts. Russia was another country that was surviving, for the most part, the world wide economic melt down. Russia and Canada had largely been spared the brunt of the economic problems, Canada because of its carefully controlled banking system, exports and nation wide medical coverage and social services and Russia because of its material wealth, sound manufacturing base and strong government and was one of the few nations left with a functional space launch facility.

China had their own space station and was steadily adding to it the same way as the ISS had been assembled. It was able to house six person crews with the objective to house a dozen in a couple of years. Research was already being carried out in the Chinese space station. China had been largely unaffected by the global economic melt down mostly due to the fact that China was still the nation of choice for off shore manufacturing. China had their own spacecraft which was considered to be on par with the old Russian Soyuz rocket which was in service for several decades becoming well known as the oldest but most reliable rocket in the world. The Chinese had designed their rocket after the old Soyuz rockets from stolen Russian plans and updated them. News reached NASA the Chinese had noticed the reactivation of the ISS.

The news soon reached Malcolm and he wondered what the Chinese would think as the spacecraft was being assembled. The cover story was a privately funded space station was being built as America and the rest of the countries that had been involved in building the ISS (with the exception of Russia and Canada) could no longer afford to build an updated version of a space station because the countries were near bankrupt and economic collapse. Chinese spies had learned of the secret town being built in the Canadian north and the huge shipments of parts and supplies being sent in. They wondered why wasn't the existing American launch facilities being used. Why build another launch facility from scratch in such an inhospitable area? Malcolm had his spin doctors start a rumor cover story the reason for the new location was because of the civilian unrest in America. If the existing American launch facilities were used the people may not believe the rocket launches were privately funded and riot to protest against the government asking why money was being wasted on space launches when the American economy was in such bad shape. News eventually reached Malcolm the Chinese government had mostly bought the story. That was good news as it would give the team a little more breathing room to build the spacecraft if the Chinese also thought it was a privately funded space station.

The two launch towers were nearing completion. There were only parts to build two launch towers but Malcolm had wanted three to be built but was told that a manufacturing problem had stalled the construction of the third tower. It would have to be completed later. Soon the parts for the launch vehicles began to arrive. The American designer had brought his team to the town and so additional housing had to be built to house them and a manufacturing facility built to assemble the rockets. Shifts worked around the clock to build these extra facilities. Malcolm consulted his computer to see where they were on the project time line to completion of the spacecraft and realized the project was falling behind. There was little he could do about it. Everyone was working three shifts around the clock to complete their various projects. Soon, he hoped that launches would begin to ferry parts into space for the new spacecraft and he hoped the Chinese or other governments would not find out the true nature of the spacecraft project until it was too late.

"Especially the Chinese.", thought Malcolm.

On another front people were being chosen and trained who would be the first passengers on the spacecraft. They were carefully screened using the NASA facilities at Houston and only accepted after a battery of tests were passed. People chosen had to be 100% healthy both physically and mentally. They were also selected for the skills that would be needed during the flight and when they reached their final destination. Questions were carefully asked about a long term space flight. Anyone who did not pass these last questions and it was felt they would not be right for the project were quietly rejected without telling them the true nature of the project. The only knowledge they left with was that a new privately funded space station was being assembled in space as a launching point for spacecraft to go to Mars and some of Jupiter's moons to look for past or present signs of life. Those that passed all tests and were finally told of the true nature of the project and if they accepted it were passed onto the first phase of the training. Those that were told the true nature of the project and did not want to accept entry into the project were sent off to a camp especially prepared for these people. They could not be trusted to keep the true nature of the project secret. Malcolm was afraid that someone would break the code of silence and the Chinese or other nations may try to sabotage the project. They would be released after the launch of the spacecraft.

The camp location was a closely guarded secret guarded by people who were being paid very well to stay there and promised a big bonus once the project was finished and the spacecraft was on its way. The guards were also told they would be hunted down and killed by another group of perimeter guards that were hired to watch the camp guards, a double guard system. The people chosen for all these positions were carefully screened. They had to be single with no outside ties of any kind. Malcolm knew that lack of sex for the term of the project would be hard on both layers of guards so prostitutes were sent in to service the men. The prostitutes were carefully picked out from various cities, blind folded and sent to the guard buildings in and around the camps. Afterwards they were again blind folded and sent back from wherever they had come. They too were well paid for their services. The services of the prostitutes were often bought from gangs or the Mafia who controlled the crime in virtually all American cities. The crime bosses were told the prostitutes were for a private party at an undisclosed location which wasn't far from the truth.

The First Launches

To get the rockets from the assembly factory to the launch towers, special hydraulic controlled vehicles were used where the rockets were assembled on and then driven the short distance to the launch towers. The rockets were raised from their horizontal positions on the trucks to a vertical position at the launch towers using a hydraulic system built on the trucks. Solid rocket boosters were bolted on to the first stage assembly of the rocket. The cargo modules were loaded on the ground and then hoisted into position atop the rocket by crane where they were then bolted in place. The cargo carriers were quite large, almost the same capacity as the old shuttle payload bays. The same was done with the external fuel tanks. They were lifted from trucks then attached to the rocket assembly and all lines were attached. It would take the combined power of the solid boosters and the first stage of the rocket to lift the heavy cargo carriers off the ground. Cable assemblies between the launch platform and the rocket were connected to allow Launch Control to monitor and check the condition of the rocket prior to liftoff. Assembly was done at the launch pad for the quickest and easiest way possible for speed and efficiency.

The first rocket was ready for launch. It was checked and rechecked prior to launch. Everything seemed to be working fine. Malcolm could not afford any disasters such as a launch pad explosion or an explosion during flight. The robotics had to function perfectly as well. His team of engineers that had picked the rocket as the best and cheapest one to use had assured Malcolm of the reliability of the rocket. It had been designed to be similar to the old space shuttle rocket used decades before but far simpler in design. It was, after all, a civilian designed rocket. The rocket had three stages and used an external tank like the old shuttle rocket to hold fuel and liquid oxygen just like the old shuttle. It used solid rocket boosters on the external tank for assist while launching the rocket. Instead of a shuttle, the rocket was topped with a large cargo container, streamlined to enable the rocket assembly be able to achieve the almost 18,000 miles per hour needed to achieve orbit. The external tank was used to provide fuel for the first and second stages and then ejected and allowed to fall and disintegrate back to earth. The third stage was internally fueled and used for the final insertion into orbit and for maneuvering along with the OMS system as the rocket neared the construction site in space.

The go ahead for the count down was given and the people in the launch facility watched their monitors and were to report any abnormalities to the Flight Director. The count down proceeded with no stops for anything then came the final fifteen seconds. The outside speakers were turned on for the benefit of the workers watching the launch from a discrete distance. There were block houses near the launch site for people to go to protect them in case of a disaster. Malcolm hoped they would never be necessary. It was dead quiet as everyone held their breath including Malcolm that everything would go as planned. At three seconds before launch the first stage rocket engine fired up followed three seconds later by the solid rocket boosters. Flame and smoke belched from the launch pad. The rocket wasn't moving! Malcolm broke out in a cold sweat then the rocket began its slow ascent and passed the top of the tower gaining speed quickly as it went.

Malcolm had a pair of binoculars for the event. The first stage and the solid rocket boosters were still firing and at less than 30 seconds the rocket was barely visible to the naked eye. Malcolm went outside the block house and put the binoculars up to his eyes and followed the rockets path as it sped up towards its destiny in space. The solid rocket boosters were ejected as the first stage kept firing. The solid rocket boosters were designed to be ejected and sent back to earth using parachutes to be retrieved and reused similar to what had been done with the old Space Shuttle. There was a plume of smoke as the first stage was ejected and the second stage ignited . The rocket was getting hard to see even with the binoculars. The rocket was tilted over in preparation for its orbital insertion. Malcolm picked up the phone and called the launch facility and spoke directly to the Flight Director asking him how everything was going so far.

The Flight Director assured Malcolm the rocket was performing exactly as expected. There were no concerns from anyone sitting in front of their monitors checking the rockets telemetry. One of the Flight Controllers was communicating with one of the astronauts at the ISS. He was asking the astronaut to keep an eye out for the supply rocket by radar and by sight. After several minutes the Flight Controller was informed the rocket was in visual range and was slowing down. Its retro rockets had turned the rocket 180 degrees as it neared its destination. Its third stage fired briefly prior to docking with the ISS to slow the rocket down slightly. Maneuvering jets docked the cargo carrier to the ISS. Astronauts left the ISS to start unloading the cargo carrier. The first mission from the new launch facility was a success. Malcolm started to breath again. He had forgot to take in a breath during the last couple of minutes of flight.

There was already another rocket on the second launch platform ready to go but the astronauts on the ISS had to unload the first rocket and detach it from the ISS. A gentle push sent the rocket away from the station. Steering jets maneuvered the third stage and the equipment storage capsule attached to the correct position and fired briefly to send the rocket into earths atmosphere where it would burn up. When all this was complete the second rocket count down proceeded as Flight Controllers checked their monitors for any malfunctions. There were none detected. The second rocket lifted off like the first one and was propelled down range and up to its eventual orbit and docking with the ISS. When enough parts were ferried up the crew of construction astronauts aboard the ISS began to assemble the spacecraft. The body of the spacecraft would be completed first and then the parts to assemble the space wheel would be ferried up and assembled. Most parts were simply too big in size for the rockets to send up in one piece so they were sent up in several pieces and if necessary were to be welded together in space. When welding the pieces they were put in the sunlight to warm it up because welding something at -250C in any sun shielded area would warp the piece and it would have to be discarded. This same process was repeated many times over the next several weeks. The astronauts took pictures and relayed them back to Launch Control to show Malcolm how the spacecraft assembly was coming along and to keep a historical record. The spacecraft was going to be the first and probably last of its kind.

Someone asked Malcolm what the ship would be named. The question stunned him at first because he had spent so much time handling all the logistics the thought had never crossed his mind. He always thought of it just as "the ship" without a thought to its name.

"Hope", he said. "Hope", he repeated and walked away.

The ship could be humanities last chance to survive as a species. Yes, he thought. 'Hope' would be the perfect name. Simple but applicable as it was hopeful the ship would complete its mission with no serious problems and the descendants on board would be able to restart the human species on the newly discovered planet. The third rocket launch pad arrived on the next freighter and was set up with all haste. Malcolm was happy at this turn of events. He was starting to think they would have to make do with only two launch pads.

The Chinese

Chang, the Chinese Premier wondered about the news he was receiving about the new space station being assembled in orbit near the old International Space Station (ISS). He thought to himself why go to all the trouble and expense of building a whole new space station when the ISS was still perfectly useable. The information that he had been given was the new space station was to have a space wheel incorporated into its design to provide an artificial gravity for extended stays in space. Then why not just build a space wheel? Why bother to build a bullet shaped hull in the middle? He was informed that it was to be used for storage of items not affected by zero gravity and to allow for a launch point for spacecraft to go to Mars and perhaps sometime in the future to go to some of Jupiter's moons where life was thought to exist.

The entire project was being funded with private corporate money and funds from wealthy people in the world in the hope it would help fix the crumbling economies. He smiled to himself when he thought how well China was doing compared to the rest of the world. Most of the countries got to the state they were in because for decades they had been sending all their manufacturing to China and other countries where labor was cheap and then sent the product back to their own countries for resale. But who was left to buy them if most of the manufacturing facilities in these countries had been shut down? The only jobs left in these countries were in various levels of government, research, sales, distribution and service areas. Without a manufacturing base the economies of these countries were bound to fail.

Building a new space station would of course provide much needed jobs in the short term but what happened after that? It was just a band-aid fix for the present with no thought of the future. He knew of many of the people that had funneled money into the project and they would not have done it if they had little chance of making a profit. It just didn't add up. Sure, the stocks in the companies that were involved in the project would go up in the short term and with a little bit of careful stock trading some of the money could be recovered by investors, but not it all and certainly no profit. It just didn't seem to make sense to him. He knew Capitalists very well and if a profit could not be made they rarely ventured into it unless there was some other motive. Was there some other underlying motivation? His spies could find no other explanations.

He would have his espionage people keep a close eye on what was happening and try to get more information. With the decline of the economy in most of the rest of the world, information was fairly easy to come by. People would be willing to sell information for a price and often cheaply. But the people on the project were not forthcoming with much information. Careful questioning had brought out little in the way of additional facts. Even NASA which was riddled with spies had found out little except for a request for assistance in restarting the International Space Station and training of the first crew for the space station when it was completed.

He had also learned through his spy network that a number of prostitutes were being hired and sent off to undisclosed locations and returned without knowing where it was they had been taken. He must take advantage of every opportunity to learn more facts. Perhaps he would get some female spies in America to join the prostitute rings in the hope of being selected to go to these locations and try and gather more information. He knew of the American liking for Asian and Chinese women. He had spies in the launch facility town that had sprung up in northern Ontario in Canada. These spies worked under cover as laborers and had reported nothing out of the ordinary except for the frantic pace of operations which went on 24 hours a day. Why such rush? What was the need to build the new station as quickly as possible? He sent a request to the Ministry of State Security (MSS) to send in some female spies already in America to try and gain access to the prostitute rings in the hope they would get a chance to be selected to go to these unknown locations and find more information.

Camp Alice

Camp Alice had been constructed in a very desolate area of Montana near Fort Peck Lake. The population was very low. One could drive for hours without seeing another vehicle. It had been selected for this very reason. Camp Alice was not large, it housed maybe a couple of dozen people with support staff like the mess hall and the barracks where the "guests" stayed. There was a small movie theater, a gymnasium and a common area with a range of activities. There was always at least two guards in the common area at all times. They never stopped any activities or conversations, they were always just 'there'. There was no communications possible in or out of the Camp. The entire camp was enclosed with high fences topped with coils of razor wire if anyone was dumb or brave enough to try and escape. They had been told that guards routinely patrolled the area outside the camp to keep the curious away and ensuring the quick capture of anyone attempting an escape, assuming they got past the Camp guards and the perimeter fencing. Once in a while the gate to the Camp would open and a vehicle or two would enter carrying supplies. Guards were evident every where, not a lot of them but enough that no one dared to try escape or revolt.

The "guests" had been told they were there for their own protection. All of them had applied for or been selected for space missions. They had all gone through a battery of mental and physical tests. They had been told the missions would be long duration space voyages to Mars and in the future, to some of the Jovian planets. All of them had accepted these missions. Then they had been told the truth. A ship was being built in orbit that would travel to Alpha Centauri to a planet that had been detected that could support human life. They were told the voyage would take over 200 years and the rest of their life would be spent on board ship. Their descendants would be born on board then their responsibility would be to train them in their parents skill set. These descendants would have offspring of their own, train them and live out their lives and die naturally or be euthanized if it was thought they would be a drain on ship resources and they were no longer useful members of the crew. This process would be repeated several times until the ship reached its destination. Camp Alice had been built to house the people who refused to go on the trip once they had been told the real reason for the project and about the ship being built in orbit. They had all been assured they would be released once the ship had departed. They could have all been quietly executed but instead had been brought to this Camp wherever it was. No one knew where they were. Most thought they were lucky to still be alive. They could have all been killed and their deaths quietly hushed up. Their families and friends could all have been told they had been killed in a training exercise or some other accident. Perhaps they had been already been told that and everyone thought they were dead. In actual fact they had been told they were in training for a mission and could not be contacted but assurances were made to keep their family and friends updated on their condition and money was sent to them as requested by the crew. It was hush money and seemed to be working.

The Launch Facility – One Year Later

The rocket factory was assembling rockets as fast as they could. Speed was of the essence but so was safety. There was a book of checklists that went along with every rocket being assembled. Every check was completed, no exceptions. As soon as the rocket cleared final inspection it was transported to the launch area where cargo for the spacecraft was loaded and the rocket set up in its firing position. Each rocket had to pass a battery of tests by Launch Control with the Flight Director having the final say to launch. He relied on the Flight Controllers to report all information to him. There was a switch at each Flight Controllers station and if an abnormality was seen, they would flick the switch which would alert the Flight Director of a possible problem that could delay the launch. A rocket was ready for launch on the new tower and the countdown had begun. At the final 15 seconds the countdown was sent out to the launch area speakers so everyone would be aware of an impending launch.

At the end of the countdown the solid rocket boosters and the first stage ignited and as usual the rocket slowly rose off the launch pad, cleared the tower and quickly gained speed as it sped to its destination in space.

It had become so commonplace to see a launch that quite a few workers never even bothered to look anymore. This launch was special as it contained the first modules for the space wheel along with a few engine parts. The body of the spacecraft was nearing completion. The space wheel was to be built separate from the body of the spacecraft and then joined to it later when it was almost complete. The final job would be to attach it to the spacecraft body. By that time all airlocks would be operational and the crew could start moving into the space wheel to complete the work necessary inside. There was a lot of equipment needed to be ferried up to go inside the space wheel and the spacecraft body. It was decided to build most of the space wheel and then move the equipment up and install it later. When all that was done the final assembly would be completed and the space wheel would be tested to ensure that it would spin as it was designed to do to provide about half earths gravity.

Decades ago after much testing in space it was discovered that half the gravity experienced on earth was sufficient to keep everyone aboard healthy, reduce bone and muscle loss and avoid circulation problems. The space wheel would easily provide this amount of gravity and could be sped up if necessary to simulate near the same gravity as experienced on earth.

In Space

The astronauts were working putting together the body of the spacecraft and had already started on the space wheel. Hardly any of them knew that it was a spacecraft except for two of them whose job it was to assemble the orbit breakaway engine. The parts that had been ferried up from earth had to be moved from the rocket to the spacecraft. Moving something heavy in space with no gravity was easy. Just a gentle push would get anything moving. The hard part was getting it stopped. Even though there was no gravity there was the mass of the object to keep in mind. Once a part had been pushed gently in the right direction it had to be stopped at some time otherwise it would just keep going. The astronauts had parts movement down pat. Once the parts were removed from the rocket cargo space they were positioned in the direction they wanted it to go and gently pushed towards the spacecraft and the astronauts would just hang on for the ride. When they were approaching the spacecraft they used the suit rockets which were just spurts of compressed gas to slow down and the astronauts at the spacecraft would help as well.

The trip from the ISS to the assembly area of the spacecraft took several minutes. You couldn't go too fast otherwise you would have a hell of a time trying to stop the piece from keeping on going so just a gentle push was all that was needed to get the piece moving in the right direction. In the vacuum of space with no gravity nothing could be done fast. Everything was done in slow motion. The spacecraft was coming along nicely. The body of the craft was almost complete. Sometimes an odd piece would be in with the rest of the cargo and it was sent over to the spacecraft with everything else. These were parts for the engines. Only two of the astronauts knew what they were and went ahead and installed them. The rest of the team asked no questions. They just assumed it was some specialized equipment. They were right of course but they did not know it was engine components they were handling.

Ling Wong

Ling Wong was her real name but she had assumed the name of Cathy Lee. She was a third generation Chinese woman. Ling was attractive by anyone's standards. She was 25 years old and medium height for someone of Chinese descent. She had a very curvaceous body and knew how to dress to get attention. She was also very pretty with a typical Chinese face. She spoke fluent English with only a hint of an accent making her all that more attractive to the men who wanted her. She was also a member of China's notorious spy network, the Ministry of State Security (MSS). She had been born in America where she had been recruited and trained by a senior MSS operative. She was paid very well for her services. Jobs were very scarce if there were any at all and this position beat the alternative of living on the street. She had been persuaded to join the MSS with promises of rising through the ranks and becoming a senior operative herself one day.

What she did not know was that she could be eliminated at any time if it was thought she would betray a mission or her mentor. She had a capsule surgically hidden in her cheek, that she was told to bite hard and ingest the contents of it if she was ever found to be a Chinese spy. The Americans were good at interrogation techniques but not near as thorough as their Chinese counterparts. The MSS had a very good record at getting the truth out of anyone who they knew had information to tell them. A lot of these methods were not very pleasant. Once she had been recruited and her training had begun with her mentor she had been told that if she betrayed anyone in the MSS that she and her family would be brutally murdered. She knew the consequences but was serious about making the MSS proud of her.

She was sent on some routine spying missions to see how she performed. Unknown to her she was secretly and carefully monitored. She performed her duties well and she gained the trust of her handlers. The only person she knew and had contact with was her mentor, a Chinese woman called Li. If she was ever captured and interrogated all she could tell her capturers was the name "Li". Even if she was subjected to torture, which the Chinese were doubtful would happen as the Americans had little stomach for this, all she would be able to tell them was that she took her orders from someone called Li. What she did not know could not be forced out of her even with drugs or hypnosis. She was also told that she could never have a boyfriend or get married. That didn't bother her because she didn't want any relationships and never wanted children. If she wanted sex, she would take on a one night stand and then disappear.

Her latest operation was to infiltrate a prostitute ring in the hopes of being selected to go to the secret camp that was known to exist as part of the space station project. The MSS knew of the camps existence but did not know what its purpose was or its location. She underwent an operation under local anesthetic to have a tiny GPS unit inserted in her left buttock near her anus to hide any scarring so she could be tracked. It was thought the people being selected for prostitution duty at the camp would not be screened for such devices as most of the women that were in prostitution were there willingly in desperation because there were no other jobs they could find. She was sent to New York where a number of prostitutes were known to have been selected to go to the camp.

She was given the name of the gang leader who she was to see to join his stable of prostitutes. Once she got to New

York she checked into a seedy hotel and changed into her "working clothes", those of a prostitute. She took a look at herself in the mirror. Her blouse was red and unbuttoned to expose the top of her breasts. The black skirt was very short with a revealing slit up one side exposing a good portion of her well shaped thigh. She wore a pair of light violet lace panties that could be easily seen through the slit in the skirt or if she sat in a chair and crossed her legs. She finished off her outfit with a pair of silver high heels which made her calf muscles nice and tight. She checked out of her hotel room and walked out on the street carrying her suitcase. A man she passed shouted out to her, "Hey baby, how much?" She didn't respond. She had an appointment to keep.

Ling or "Cathy", as she was known, found the address she had been given and entered the building. There was a smiling receptionist behind a desk who asked how she could help. Ling told her she had an appointment with a Mr. Jacobs. The receptionist checked her calendar on the computer and confirmed the appointment.

"Please have a seat over there and I'll tell Mr. Jacobs you are here.", said the receptionist.

Ling took a seat and waited. After about five minutes a small man entered the reception area and looked at Ling. He indicated that she follow him. Ling got up and straightened her skirt and followed Mr. Jacobs where they went into an office with a couch, a desk, a chair for Mr. Jacobs and a couple of chairs for visitors.

"So.......you're the girl who was referred to us?", he said.

"Yes.", said Ling. "Stand up please.", said Mr. Jacobs. Ling stood up. "Take off all your clothes please.", said Mr Jacobs. Ling hesitated for a moment and then started to undress. She was told in advance about this phase of the "interview." She carefully placed her clothing on one of the chairs and stood facing Mr. Jacobs attempting to cover herself a bit pretending to be shy. She thought if she looked a bit shy she would be more convincing. In actual fact Ling was not at all shy of taking her clothes off. It was part of the mission and the mission was everything.

Mr. Jacobs looked her up and down and smiled. "He looked like a little rat smelling a piece of cheese.", thought Ling to herself. Mr Jacobs got out his chair and came around to her side of the desk.

"Put your arms at your sides.", he said.

Ling did so. Mr. Jacobs started to rub his hands over Lings body paying special attention to her breasts and her buttocks. Ling winced a bit as his hands moved over her body. This was no act. She was actually repulsed by this little weasel of a man touching her but this is something she had to get used to in her new role.

"Get on your knees.", said Mr. Jacobs.

Ling did as she was instructed. Mr. Jacobs unzipped his fly and fished his penis out of his pants and put it in front of Lings face. She hadn't expected this.

"You know what to do with this.", he said leering at Ling on her knees in front of him.

She slowly took his penis in her hand and put it in her

mouth. When Mr. Jacobs was finished with her he took a Kleenex from his desk and wiped himself off and threw it in the garbage can. Ling felt sick. She had done this sort of thing before but to do it to this weasel of a man....it just turned her stomach but duty was duty.

"Okay, you'll do.", said Mr. Jacobs. "Go back out and see the receptionist and she will tell you where to go."

Ling dressed and went out to the receptionist who almost looked sorry for Ling because she knew what had gone on in Mr. Jacobs office. The receptionist wrote an address on a piece of paper and handed it to Ling.

"Go to this address and ask for a man called Ken. He will tell you what is expected from you."

Ling took the paper and looked at it. "Where is this?", Ling asked.

The receptionist gave her directions. The address was a couple of blocks down and one over from where they were. Ling walked the few blocks to the address that was on the paper the receptionist had given her. She walked into the building. It looked like a run down hotel inside. There was a clerk behind the front desk.

"Can I help you?", asked the man.

"I was told to see Ken.", Ling said.

"That's me.", he said.

Ken took her into a small room at the back of the front desk and asked Ling if she had ever done this type of thing before, meaning prostitution.

"No.", Ling replied. "But my family.....we need the money."

She had been told to act the part of a shy naive girl who had never prostituted herself before. Ling was acting the part beautifully. Ken never suspected otherwise.

"Okay, here is how it works.", said Ken. "You work when we tell you. You will get a room assigned to you. When we call you, you will come downstairs and go into that room over there." He motioned toward a room off to the side of the front foyer. "We get customers coming in all hours of the day but mostly at night. If a customer picks you, you are to take him to your room and do whatever he wants you to do. We charge by the half hour. We'll let you know how much the customer has paid for. Keep a watch on the time. Don't give any extra time to anyone. If the customer tips you, you can keep the tip but don't expect a lot of tips but if you make your customer real happy he may tip you. We pay you half of what the customer pays us. If you get customers you get paid. If you don't get customers then you don't get paid. Its that simple. Its to your advantage to make your customers as satisfied and as happy as possible because if they like you they will ask for you again and may refer you to some of their friends."

"Oh yeah!", said Ken. "One more thing. Always have the customer wear a condom. No exceptions even if the customer says he will tip you extra if he can screw you without a condom. We run a clean place here and we want it to stay that way. Our customers expect that from us. We have become well known for our disease control procedure.

Besides, its for your protection too. Once in a while, it doesn't happen very often, but we do get the occasional dyke in here looking for some girly action. That doesn't bother you I hope?"

Ling asked what a dyke was. She knew but was playing the part of a shy girl who didn't know a lot. Ken explained to her that a dyke was another word for a girl that only likes other girls. Ling pretended to look shy and said she understood. Ling hoped that would not happen as she had never had the desire to have sex with another woman. Ken gave her a key to her room and told her to go up and have a rest. It was Friday afternoon and Friday nights were usually busy. Ken also explained she would get time off once in a while if business was slow but admitted there wasn't much to do or see in this part of town. He also explained there was a kitchen and if she felt hungry she could go and ask for something to eat but don't expect a banquet and don't eat a lot. "We don't want any fat whores.", he said.

Ling went up to her room, unlocked the door and entered. The room was fairly neat and tidy. The sheets had been changed and there were extra sheets in the closet. There was a small older TV set. She guessed that she was supposed to change the bed herself when it needed changing. She needed a shower especially after that weasel, Mr. Jacobs. She could still taste him. She had a long hot shower and dried herself off. She wondered if she had time to have a snooze before getting dressed. Ling normally slept naked. She decided to lay on the bed and rest for a moment. Suddenly she was snapped awake by the phone ringing. It was Ken.

"Come on down.", said Ken. "We got a customer here that wants to see the new girl."

Ling dressed quickly and then went into the room indicated by Ken and noticed most of the girls she had yet to meet looked bored and their eyes looked empty.

She sat down and one of the men, a well dressed black man with a gold chain looked Ling over and said, "So....you are the new one?"

"Yes.", replied Ling.

"You'll do fine woman. Come with me.", he said.

She followed him out of the room to the front desk. "I'll take this little Chinese one for a spin.", he said. He handed Ken a handful of bills.

"One hour.", Ken told Ling.

Ling took him up to her room. When they got there he started to undress so she started to undress as well.

"No, no!", he said. "I'll undress you."

Ling stood there while he finished undressing and then came over to Ling. She noticed that he was already partly erect. He started unbuttoning her blouse and slipped it off. He slowly removed the rest of her clothing.

"You look fine!", he said.

He took her by the hand and led her to the bed. She told him about the condom rule. She looked at him again and saw that he was fully erect. He was big! She selected a condom that she hoped would fit him and handed it to him. He opened the package, took out the condom and rolled it on himself. She laid down on the bed and he laid down beside her. He took a little of the lubricant that was on the bed side table and rubbed it on the condom. He fingered her vagina a little and found it was moist enough so he positioned himself on top of her and slowly inserted his penis into her.

"He is big!", Ling thought, she might actually enjoy this.

She remembered what Ken had told her that she might get a nice tip if her customer enjoyed himself and she wanted to get well known so she might get picked to go to the camp. She started to move against him and moan. She rubbed his sides with her hands. He plunged into her again and again as she continued to moan and move against him. She was only partly acting. She was enjoying herself with this large black man. He had to stop several times and wait until he had cooled down. He started thrusting into her again and then he went really fast and hard and grunted as he came. She felt his penis swell inside her and pulse as he came. When he was finally done he rolled off her.

He asked her if she minded if he smoked. She said she didn't mind. He offered her one but she shook her head no. They talked for a few minutes and then he asked her if she would help him "get it up" again. She wrapped her small hand around his penis and pumped gently until he was erect again. He rolled off the condom and he replaced it himself with a new one.

"I want to take you from behind.", he said.

She stood up and then knelt at the foot of the bed and bent from the waist over the bed and rested her upper body on the bed. He positioned himself behind her and gently eased himself into her. He grabbed her by the hips and started thrusting hard into her. She responded by moving back toward him.

"Damn!! You're good!!", he gasped between breaths.

He slowed down a little and stopped once in a while to stop himself from coming too soon. He did this several times until he grabbed her hips hard and started thrusting harder into her. She gasped from the pleasure of it as he came into her once more. He stayed in her for several moments enjoying the afterglow and then pulled back. He removed the condom. She went to give him a tissue to clean himself off but he asked her to lick him clean. She did this for him with no reservations. This man was a lot different than that weasel this afternoon. She was sweating from all the energy of having sex with this man. He got dressed and opened his wallet and gave her a $100 bill.

"You earned this.", he said. Ling thanked him and smiled.

He left the room and Ling went to have a shower and wait to be called again.

The Launch Vehicle Assembly Factories

The launch rockets were made up of many different parts manufactured in several different factories in the U.S. Once they were produced they were all sent to a central warehouse in Baltimore to be stored and shipped to the northern Canada launch site. All the workers were aware where the parts were going but didn't care. All they cared about was getting paid for the work they were doing. Once the parts were in the warehouse they were either transported to the harbor for loading on freighters or were sent to the Baltimore-Washington International Thurgood Marshall Airport for transport by air to the Moosonee Airport. There were a couple of Chinese workers at one of the plants who were asking questions of some of the other workers that would be embedded in normal conversation. Most of the questions were about what the rockets were being used for and what they were transporting into space. None of the other workers knew or cared about such things. All they cared about was getting paid for what they were doing. One day the two Chinese workers failed to show up for work and were never seen again. No one knew they were Chinese spies and had left because there was no more information to be had at this plant. It was the same situation at other plants where there would be one or two Chinese workers that stayed for a while, asked a lot of questions and then left. No one seemed to notice.

There were a couple of Chinese workers working at the warehouse where everything manufactured for the launch vehicles were being stored prior to shipping. When no one was watching they would be checking various crates and boxes looking for something. One of the workers noticed this and just thought they were curious and paid no mind to it. He never bothered to report it to any of his superiors. Both of these Chinese men were members of the Chinese spy agency, the Ministry for State Security. One of the spies, Chen, who had assumed the English name of Brian came across a crate that looked interesting. It had come from a different manufacturer, Electro HydroDynamics in Houston, than most of the other crates and boxes. He made a note of the company name. He must come back later and see if he could open the crate to look at its contents.

Later that night, he and his accomplice sneaked into the warehouse passed the guards and went over to the crate. They found some tools and being as quiet as possible, opened the crate. The contents were well packed in styrofoam and plastic wrapping. They opened the plastic wrapping and took pictures using a miniature spy camera. They tried their best to replace the plastic wrap and sealed the crate back up. They were able to sneak out past the guards and make good their escape. No one had noticed them.

Once back in their quarters, Chen turned on his computer and attached the camera to the computer using a USB connection cable and downloaded the images he had taken with the little spy camera. The images looked good. He wrote a short message that contained the manufacturers name and attached the images he had taken. He encrypted the message and sent it to an email address in China that gave no indication that it was eventually going to the MSS. The message was encrypted so even if it was intercepted it would be difficult to decode. It was written in Chinese to start with and then encrypted with a MSS developed algorithm.

MSS Headquarters

The message was received by an operative working at MSS headquarters. She looked at the manufacturer name and looked it up in her database of American manufacturers. The company, Electro HydroDynamics, was located in Houston Texas. The company was mainly a research facility but had another company produce a limited number of engines designed by the company. She took a look at the photos. She recognized they were pictures of a component for a spacecraft engine. What part exactly could not be determined but the spies in the American warehouse had said this crate was one of very few that were seen from that manufacturer. Most crates were from a handful of other manufacturers and were the bulk of all the crates in the warehouse. She sent a reply message to the two spies to travel to Texas and try to check out the company this crate had come from. She gave them the address of the company. She was betting it was for a part for a spacecraft engine and not for one of the launch vehicle rockets otherwise there would have been a lot more crates from this manufacturer. Chen received the encrypted message and decoded it and informed his partner. They started packing their belongings to leave for Texas in the morning.

Engine Design

The engine that Malcolm's design team had selected was a hydrogen fueled engine powered by hydrogen atoms floating freely in deep space. The engine was a low thrust type which suited the spacecraft design perfectly. A high thrust engine would put too much stress on the space wheel during acceleration. A gentle but continuous thrust was what was required. The engine design was quite old and had been tested before with limited success. The engines of years passed had used hydrogen carried on board. This engine used hydrogen atoms freely available in deep space. A static field generated in front of the ship would scoop the hydrogen atoms into the engine.

The design was based on the Bussard Ramjet engine system proposed years ago in 1960 by the physicist Robert W. Bussard. The general idea was to collect free floating hydrogen atoms then compress them using magnetic fields into a smaller and smaller orifice and heated with lasers until nuclear fusion occurred. The resulting energy was ejected backward propelling the spacecraft forward. The only drawback was the spacecraft would have to be traveling quite fast before the engine would collect enough hydrogen to "ignite". Standard rocket engines would be used to eject the spacecraft out of earths orbit into inter-planetary space and then use the planets themselves to slingshot the spacecraft faster and faster until the hydrogen ramjet engine could ignite. The nice thing about the engine design is that it had no moving parts. There would have to be a small on-board nuclear reactor to provide electrical power for the ship interior, the static scoop, the magnetic field magnets to compress the collected hydrogen and the lasers to heat the hydrogen to a plasma to create fusion.

At The Launch Facility

A few specially labeled crates began arriving. They contained the engine parts for the spacecraft main engine. The parts were sent up along with other assemblies so as not to attract too much attention. The spacecraft actually had two propulsion systems. One was a standard refined kerosene and oxygen fueled engine. It could not be tested until launch so it was hoped there were no assembly glitches, but the two rocket engineers doing the assembly were the best in the business. Some prelaunch testing could be done but the moment of truth would be at the actual launch time. The other engine was to be used in deep space once the spacecraft had achieved enough speed for it to work. Malcolm had been told the general design details of the engine but did not understand its design thoroughly, only that he was assured it would work. He had been told the engine was extremely reliable because it had no moving parts. That was good, one less thing that could go wrong.

A small nuclear reactor was required to generate the electricity for the engines electromagnets, lasers and for the ship's internal power needs. The small reactor was being sent into orbit by a Russian rocket as the launch vehicles being used here did not have the required thrust for such a heavy payload. The reactor would be installed at the rear of the craft and outside the spacecraft. This way minimal shielding would be required around the reactor. He received news the standard rocket engines were almost completely assembled. The rocket design was kept as simple as possible. Little thought had been given to its power output. As long as it was powerful enough to send the spacecraft out of orbit and give it sufficient speed to reach Mars. This method had been used with great success in the earlier days of space research to get more speed out of research space vehicles when investigating the outer planets. The spacecraft would hopefully be traveling much faster, and use Jupiter as the next sling shot and then on to the outer planets and use some of them as slingshots to provide even more speed. It was hoped by this time the main engine could be ignited then or while inside the Oort Cloud, the ring of debris left over from the creation of the solar system, where a large mass of hydrogen gas was thought to exist and the real journey could begin.

Ling Wong

Ling had worked as a prostitute for two weeks now but it had seemed a lot longer than that. Some of her customers had been downright crude and disgusting but she had put up with it. One of her customers had asked her for anal sex but she refused. The customer had used the room's telephone to call the front desk and talk to Ken to complain. The customer had handed the phone to her and she had talked to Ken again refusing to accept anal sex. Ken tried to threaten her by telling her she might have to leave if she refused but she steadfastly refused. It was lucky for her that many of her customers had told Ken how good she was and would be coming back and sending their friends. Ken finally told her she didn't have to do the act. She handed the phone back to the customer and Ken told him that service was not available from this girl. He slammed the phone down and demanded she perform oral sex on him. This she did as it was better than disgusting anal sex and he was, after all, wearing a condom.

The next day she was called downstairs by Ken. She was expecting to see a customer or two in the waiting room to choose one of the girls. Instead there were two well dressed men in suits and sun glasses. All the girls were in the room. The two men looked at all the girls and then talked quietly between themselves and then told Ken they would take six of the girls and pointed out which ones they wanted. Ling was one of the girls chosen. She wondered if it was for the camp. She hoped so. She wanted this mission to end. All the girls were escorted outside to a waiting van and they were driven to the airport.

They were led to the rear of the plane where all the windows were painted black so they could not see out. There was a curtain separating this area from the rest of the plane. The plane was given the go ahead by the tower to take off. They taxied to the runway and sat there for a few minutes and then the planes jet engines roared and the plane lurched forward as it quickly gained speed and took off.

One of the men came to the rear of the plane and explained

the rules to the girls. "You're being taken to a location where your job is to screw the men there. Before the plane lands you will be blindfolded and put into a truck for the rest of the journey. One of us will be there with you. If any of you attempt to take your blindfold off you will be punished or maybe shot, it depends on my mood. If any of you have to use the washroom, it is right behind you. We will bring you some drinks and sandwiches during the flight. Are there any questions?"

He looked at all the girls. None of them asked any questions. About an hour later one of the men came back with a tray of sandwiches and some bottled drinks. He put them down and left without a word. A few hours later the plane started to slow down and a clunk was heard as the landing gear was deployed. The plane landed on a rough runway and the girls were tossed about a bit. The plane came to a stop and one of the men came back with blindfolds for the girls.

"Put these on!", he said.

All the girls did as instructed. He went from girl to girl to be assured the blindfolds were on correctly. They were told to hold hands and follow each other in single file off the plane. They were led to a waiting truck and were helped to climb in the back. They were told the trip would take a little over an hour and he reminded them one of them would be in the back of the truck with them to be sure none of the girls tried to take off their blindfolds. The truck bounced and lurched down the rough road. Sometimes the truck had to slow down as they went through a heavily wooded area where branches of trees brushed against the side of the truck. After a little over an hour, it seemed a lot longer, the truck screeched to a halt. They were told they could remove their blindfolds. The light was hard on the eyes after being blindfolded for so long. They climbed out of the back of the truck and saw a group of men waiting for them. They all wore guard uniforms.

"Yes!!", thought Ling, "This must be the secret camp." She hoped her GPS device was working so MSS could tell where she was. As she suspected none of the girls were inspected for any devices they might have on or in them. The girls were told to line up. The guards were handed a box that contained numbered pieces of cardboard. They all drew one piece.

"Okay", asked one of the men that had brought them, "Who has number one!"

A man shouted, "I do", and walked forward. He was told he had first choice. Of course he picked Ling.

The guard looked like he was in his late twenties, quite handsome and in good shape. That pleased Ling because some of the guards were older and rough looking but she felt this guard would treat her right and she might actually enjoy it. The numbers were all called and the guards all had selected their girls.

"You have an hour with your girl and then we take them to the next set of guards!", he yelled. "You all know the drill."

Ling's man took her by the hand and led her away towards a small cabin.

"What's your name?", the guard asked.

"Cathy.", answered Ling.

Cathy was her chosen American name that she used. They entered the cabin. It was small. There was a bed, a dresser, a shower and a small counter hot plate and a small refrigerator. A generator hummed in the distance. The guard closed the door and started to remove his clothes. Ling did the same. In moments they were both naked. The guard was quite muscular and handsome. She glanced at his penis. It was quite thick and he was already almost erect. Ling had been given a stock of condoms. She selected one that was large and handed it to him.

"Do I have to use this?", he asked. "Sorry, its the rules.", Ling told him.

He looked sour but ripped opened the condom package, removed the condom and rolled it over his penis. He took Ling to the bed and she laid down on it. Instead of getting on top of her as she had expected he put his head between her legs and opened them. He smiled as he looked at her vagina. He started to perform cunnilingus on her. He was good at it and she began to enjoy it and moved her hips forward to the touch of his tongue. He was hitting all the right places. She came a couple of times because none of her customers before ever cared if she was satisfied or not. Finally he finished and moved his body on top of hers and inserted his nice fat penis into her. It felt good to Ling. He kissed her and she tasted herself from his mouth. He started rocking back and forth ramming his penis into her and she responded by moving against him and moaning. She was enjoying this so much she almost forgot she had a job to do.

She gasped as she asked him, "What do you do here?" He

didn't respond right away and finally answered that he guarded the camp. "Who is in the camp you are guarding?", she asked.

"I don't know, there is a rumor they are scientists or something.", he told her.

That was good information. "I should not have told you any of that.", he said. "Forget what I told you."

Ling said okay and that it was none of her concern anyway, to put his mind at ease. He stopped thrusting into her and stopped for a moment to rest and not to come too soon. They kissed gently for a while and then he started thrusting into her once more. After a few minutes he started moaning loudly and then thrust into her hard and came. She could feel his penis pulsing inside of her as he came. She thought he would never stop. He stopped finally and rested on top of her until his afterglow was diminished and then pulled out of her and rolled off.

"Wow, you're good!", he said.

Ling thanked him and told him she had enjoyed it too. She had but she said this to make him feel better and maybe loosen his tongue some more. She asked him how long he had been here and how long he would have to stay. He told her he had been here for over a year and was told he would be here for at least another two years. He told her it was boring but he was being very well paid and would be a rich man when this was all over. Ling asked again about the prisoners in the camp.

"You told me the prisoners are all scientists. Where did they come from?", Ling asked.

He told her he wasn't sure but there was a rumor they came from Houston. As Ling was questioning him she was gently rubbing his penis to put him in a relaxed mood to loosen his tongue. It had worked. She noticed his penis was once more fully erect. He told her he wanted to "make love" to her again. She asked him to replace his condom which he did and then positioned himself on top of her again and this time his love making was slower and more relaxed. She laid back and moved against him enjoying it as well.

"Don't tell anyone what I told you.", he asked. "I could lose my job or worse." Ling assured him she wouldn't. She would only tell Li her senior operative.

After he had come again they both got dressed and he hugged her.

"You're the best girl they ever sent here. All the other girls just lie there and don't do anything. Its almost like screwing a mannequin.", he said.

Ling laughed. She had seen the other girls and they all had slack faces and dead eyes and never smiled. She didn't doubt his words one bit. She was selected by some of the other guards but did not question them. She already had all the information she needed. She just performed her duty. Some of the guards wanted her to perform oral sex on them before they screwed her which she did. She was glad most of them didn't want to come in her mouth. She didn't like that much but it was surprising that some semen tasted better than others when she had performed oral sex without a condom. She didn't know why or cared. After a couple of days and several men her job was finished. Her blindfold was put back on and she was escorted back onto the truck for the long trip back. As soon as she got back she would leave the whore house and report back to Li with the information that she had gained. She hoped the GPS in her buttock had worked and that one of the Chinese satellites in orbit had been able to track it for the camps location.

In Space

The spacecraft construction was coming along nicely. The body of the craft was complete, at least on the outside. There was a tunnel inside the body of the craft. No one knew what is was for. Some equipment was installed inside it. The tunnel had been lined with ceramic tile. Some equipment was installed at the mouth of the tunnel. The tunnel went all the way to the back of the craft where there was an exit port. Just below this were the nozzles of what looked like a spacecraft engine.

"What would a space station need with an engine like that?", some of the astronaut workers wondered.

They had been told to do their jobs and not ask any questions or discuss what they saw there. None of them did. They were being very well paid for their work and their silence. Work was proceeding on the space wheel. It was huge! It was going to take a lot of time and many supply flights to assemble this thing. All this activity was not going unnoticed. The crew of the Chinese space station were observing the construction as well and the Chinese on the ground with powerful telescopes.

Ling Wong

Ling left the whore house after telling Ken she was just going for a walk. He told her to be careful in this part of town. When she didn't come back he would probably think that she had been abducted to work in another whore house or maybe raped and killed. That often happened but mostly at night. This was in the afternoon. Ling quickly made her way to the airport by taxi. She had lots of money from tips. She didn't care about the money that Ken said he was holding for her. She took the next flight back to her home town and reported to Li who seemed pleased with her mission. She told Ling to take some time off and spend it with her family or friends. She would be contacted again when she was needed. She decided that she would go and visit her family. A couple of nights after she arrived, a group of men burst in the door and methodically shot everyone with silenced pistols including Ling. Her usefulness to the MSS was finished.

Space - Progressing Construction

The body of the spacecraft was almost finished and a good start on the space wheel was being made. Regular shipments of material were being sent into space from the launch facility. "Things are going well", thought Malcolm. "almost too well." He had remembered that old slogan 'if things are going well you have obviously overlooked something'. Malcolm thought through the project and everything that he could think of had been resolved or a solution was in the works. Murph had done as promised. The big man reported to Malcolm on a regular basis as he promised and kept Malcolm informed of progress and any changes he had made. Malcolm had told him if changes to shift or processes had to be made then go ahead and make them, just make sure that he was told somewhere along the way. Murph said he had to break up a fight at one of the town's two bars the other night.

"I had 'em out numbered.", laughed Murph, "There was only four of them."

Malcolm chuckled as well. He knew he made a good choice when he selected Murph as head foreman of the whole project. Murph was smart and tough enough to keep the men in line. The men respected him and did what Murph asked them to do. He kept in constant contact with each shift supervisor to see if things were running on time and being done properly. The rocket assembly plant had started to run behind on production and the designer/owner of the rockets being used had asked Murph if he could spare a few of his guys. Construction had slowed down a lot and Murph had men to spare so he selected men off each shift who were good workers and were conscientious. The head of rocket assembly said the new men were working out good. They had to be trained of course which slowed production down in the short term but had picked up substantially once the men had been trained and joined as productive workers in the rocket assembly line. All of them were happy with the change as this was something new for them and got them away from general construction and maintenance of the town.

The rockets were performing well. It surprised Malcolm they had all performed so well. He was told the rocket engines were very simple in design but when he saw the inside of one for the first time he was amazed at all the pumps, tubing and wiring that made up the engines. If these were simple in design he would not want to see a complex one! It was basically the same type of engine installed in the spacecraft to get it out of orbit. Malcolm was not concerned with a few percentage in efficiency. He wanted something simple that as little as possible could go wrong. It would be needed to get the ship out of orbit and used again in over 200 years time to slow the ship down when it reached its destination. Malcolm hoped that in 200 years time it would still work. The amount of fuel needed had been calculated and a some extra added just in case. The fuel would be stored in tanks in the body of the craft. The tanks had been designed to be as leak proof as possible. He was told that some leakage was to be expected over that length of time since it was under pressure so that's when he was told to add extra to the calculations.

Some parts of the space wheel were quite heavy and the Russian launch facilities were used on a regular basis to send these parts up. The Russians were happy to cooperate. They needed the cash as much as any one else. The Russians had even offered some help to assemble the 'space station' but their offer was gently turned down as the fewer people that knew the true intent of the spacecraft, the better. As soon as the Russians saw the 'space station' close up they would know right away that it wasn't just a station but a ship. Malcolm was worried about the Chinese. They had always been outspoken about America trying to lay claim to bodies in space.

International Space Agreements

The Outer Space Treaty of 1967 known formally as the "Treaty on Principles Governing the Activities of States in the Exploration and Use of Outer Space, including the Moon and Other Celestial Bodies" had been written and signed by most of the nations on earth, including China, agreeing to its contents. It prohibited any one country laying claim to any celestial body including the Moon. It also prohibited sending nuclear weapons into space. Any bases established on the Moon had to be research only in nature, not military or fortified. It is similar to the treaty governing Antarctica. No one country was allowed to claim ownership (a few had tried) but any country was allowed to establish research bases. The Outer Space Treaty of 1967 was based on this concept. China had signed the Outer Space Treaty although they were a late comer in the space community.

Malcolm thought they might try and launch a similar mission and claim another star system as their own and not honor their agreement. Maybe even Alpha Centauri where his ship was going was a long range plan of the Chinese. If they reached there first he had no doubt the Chinese would lay claim to the planet that was thought to be in the right zone for human habitation. That could not be allowed to happen. The colonization of other planets in nearby star systems would use Alpha Centauri in many years in the future as a base of operations as basic industries were established and other industries were off sprung from this as had been done on earth over the centuries.

Launch Control

One of the routine material space flights had just taken off when a malfunction was detected by Launch Control. The rocket was veering off course. Launch Control's attempt at changing the rockets course was proving futile. The rocket had passed all assembly and preflight tests and was considered passed to launch but something had gone wrong in its guidance system. After several attempts to regain control had failed and it was possible the rocket could crash land it was decided to abort the mission and destroy the rocket. Several confirmations were need for this drastic decision and all controllers agreed to the decision as they had no further ideas on how to regain control. The Launch Director opened the destruct button cover with a special key. He looked at all Launch Controllers and then pushed the button. The destruct order was designed so the cargo module at the top of the rocket was detached and allowed to fall away before rocket destruction. The cargo module was to parachute to ground in the hope the cargo could be rescued and used again on another rocket. The cargo module was ejected successfully and fell away from the rocket. A few seconds later the rocket exploded into a fiery fireball instantly obliterating it. A large Sikorsky helicopter was immediately dispatched to rescue the cargo module which had a locator beacon to assist in finding it.

An investigation was immediately started to find the cause. All assembly checklists were gone over and launch control records reviewed looking for a clue as what might have happened. It was thought that a new worker in the rocket assembly plant had missed a step or not connected something properly. Production was stopped as everyone was reviewed as what their job was and making sure it was done properly. This stopped rocket production for a few days. Produced rockets were opened up and rechecked. Nothing wrong was found. A new launch was scheduled and went without a hitch. What went wrong with that particular failed rocket would forever remain a mystery.

The Chinese

The two Chinese spies that were ordered to go Electro HydroDynamics in Texas to find out what they could, found the facility heavily fenced and guarded and probably had motion detectors on the grounds that would alert the guard headquarters that someone unauthorized was on the grounds. They went to a local library to look for a weak point to gain access. Night would be their best time to gain access. Chen looked at the sewer system as one way to get in. He found what he was looking for after about an hours search. There was a sewer access cover located about a half mile away from the facility. One of the passages led right onto the grounds at the back of the facility. That would be their way in. He hoped the sewer cover had not been welded shut as a security precaution.

Chen and his partner left the library and went to a hardware store to buy a crowbar needed to pry open the sewer cover. They also bought a couple of flashlights as it would be pitch black in the sewer. They quickly located the sewer they were entering and pried open the cover and slipped in and dragged the cover over into place. The sewer pipe was quite large, big enough they could walk through with their heads bent slightly to make their way through. A half mile in total darkness. But they had two flashlights which they had tested. If one failed they had the other as a backup. After about 20 minutes they reached their destination. Chen pried open the sewer cover carefully. It had not been welded. He peered out carefully to see what was around them. They were in the back of the facility which was dimly lit. Chen moved the sewer cover open all the way and eased himself out followed by his partner.

They immediately went to the nearest wall and looked carefully for any cameras or motion detectors. There didn't seem to be any. Chen notice a door not far from where they were. They went to the door and tried it. It was locked. It was a steel door inset into a steel frame. Chen inserted the end of the crowbar into the door frame near the lock and pried. Nothing happened. He pried harder and it seemed to move a little. He motioned his partner to give a hand and the two of them pried with all their might and the door frame bent just enough for the door to be opened. Chen gently opened the door. No alarm sounded. So far so good. They both slipped in and closed the door behind them.

They appeared to be in a basement location. The floors were painted cement There were other doors here and there down the hallway. They need to find where the planning and research labs and where the records were kept. They found a set of stairs going up and quietly went up. Once on the next floor it was much better. Lighting was better and the floors were tiled. All the doors were marked with different department names on them. They found one door marked "Records" and decided it was a good place to start. Chen tried the door and it was locked. This door was easy to break into. It was a wood door in a metal frame. A little prying gained them access. They went in and closed the door behind them.

They started looking through the vast amount of records and finally Chen's partner made a 'Sssss' sound and motioned Chen to come over. He had found the plans for the hydrogen engine to be used in the spacecraft.

"So, it wasn't a space station after all.", thought Chen.

They quickly took pictures with their tiny spy cameras and then put the plans away. They opened the door carefully and looked out. No one seemed to be around. They made their way down the hall quietly but quickly to the door leading to the stairwell to go down.

"Hey!! What are you two doing here!!", bellowed a guard from behind them.

Chen pretended to be an engineer working overtime. The guard looked them over.

"Where are your badges?", he asked.

Chen pretended to fumble in his jacket looking for the pass when he swung the crowbar catching the guard on the side of the head. Chen whacked the guard a couple more times and then Chen and his partner quickly went down the stairwell and found the door they had forced open and went out. The sewer cover was still open so they dropped down and then Chen's partner slid the cover closed. They half ran, half walked down the sewer pipe until they came to the cover they had entered. Chen listened, everything seemed quiet. He slid the cover open carefully and looked out. No one seemed to be around. They both climbed out and headed back to their rental car and jumped in and quietly but quickly drove away.

They went back to their rented room and retrieved the pictures from the cameras. The pics looked good and clear. Chen created a message in Chinese to an address that looked innocent. He encrypted the message and sent it. Soon the MSS received the message and decrypted it. They looked at the pictures of the blue prints. It was obvious it was an engine but of an advanced design. The pictures would be given to some engineers to go over and see if they could figure them out.

A day or so later the report came back from the engineers. The blue prints were indeed plans for building a new unknown type of engine. They guessed it was based on the Bussard Ram Jet first thought of in the 1960's. But it was only theoretical at that time. It was considered too costly to attempt to build a prototype and the project was shelved. Obviously someone has thought otherwise and revived the project. But who? The blue prints gave no indication of the company or organization but a name was scribbled in the corner of one of the blue prints. Malcolm Beacham. Who was this man? A quick search revealed that he was a heavy investor in Microsoft and made a fortune.

The Chinese spies at the launch facility in northern Canada had identified Malcolm Beacham as the head of the space station project. This was the link they had been looking for. If this engine was being built for the space station then it wasn't a space station at all but a spacecraft. What was its purpose? Where was it going? Why wasn't the project more publicized? Why all the security and secrecy? Something was going on that this Malcolm Beacham didn't want everyone to know. Did the Americans know the real reason for this project? Chinese spies at NASA reported that a group of about 30 people were undergoing training for a space mission. The cover story was these people would be working on the space station in preparation for deep space voyages to Mars and Jupiter. But why use such an advanced engine as this for interplanetary travel? According to available information, a spacecraft would have to be going damn fast for this engine to work as designed, perhaps as fast as a percentage of light speed.

All the facts seemed to indicate a much further journey than just a voyage to another planet in our solar system. But what about a planet in another solar system? This had the MSS very troubled indeed. The Premier needed to know this information as quickly as possible so that action could be taken.

Premier Chang was informed by a report from the MSS. He read the whole report and read certain parts of it again. The Americans were up to something. He knew that. He didn't trust the American government at all. Their companies were sending lots of work to China but that didn't mean he had to trust their government. Corporate America and the American government were two separate things as far as Chang was concerned. He picked up the phone and called his Chief of Defense and asked if they were capable of sending a destructive missile into low earth orbit. The answer was yes. Chang could not allow the spacecraft to leave orbit. He would have his embassy people in America make some discrete inquiries to find out if the American government was aware of the real reason for the 'space station.' He got his answer in a few days. According to his ambassador in Washington the American government was aware of the privately funded space station but that was all. They had no knowledge that it was a spacecraft possibly capable of extrasolar travel to another star system. This inquiry had raised a few eyebrows in Washington and government agents had notified the Secretary of Defense, Charles Debin, of this news. He thought he better make the President aware of the situation and made an appointment to see her as soon as possible.

The Oval Office – The White House

Charlotte Henderson was the United States President. She had spent years in politics and had been voted in by the American people as America's second female President. She was well known in global affairs as a no-nonsense leader. At 53 she was young for a President but well experienced in politics and tough as nails. When she said she was going to do something it was done. She was not one to threaten but promise. She had her hands full with the deteriorating situation with the economy. Her plan was to put a stop to all the violence and chaos and then try and reverse the economy but it was going to be a long hard struggle. All aid to foreign countries had been cut. All U.S. military forces serving in other countries had been recalled to deal with the chaos at home. All federal elections had been canceled due to the country-wide martial law. Elections would resume after order was restored.

"I hope sooner than later", she thought.

The stress on her and her staff was enormous. She checked her calendar and saw an appointment had been made by her Secretary of Defense to see her as soon as possible. What now? He was scheduled to visit her in the Oval Office in an hour. She asked her aide to get her a coffee. Two cream, no sugar. She spent the hour reading the report on her desk about the privately funded space station that was being built in orbit as that was the subject of Charles' visit. It must be very important if he wanted to see her personally. At the appointed time her receptionist buzzed her and informed her that Charles had arrived. She told her receptionist to show him in. Charles walked into the Oval Office. He used to be a high ranking general in the U.S. forces and had seen service on many fronts. Charlotte thought he was a good choice for the position of Secretary of Defense. Charles was in his 60's but still walked straight up with a purposeful stride. His bright eyes showed attention and intelligence. His hair was graying but his face had that craggy look of an experienced soldier.

"Do you want coffee?", Charlotte asked. Charles shook his head no but asked for a glass of water instead.

She buzzed one of her aides to bring in a glass and a pitcher of cool water.

"What brings you here in such a rush?", asked Charlotte.

"Its about the space station being built in orbit.", said Charles. "There is every indication its not a space station at all but a spacecraft."

Charlotte's eye brows shot up. "Oh really?", she said. "And what makes you think that?"

Charles replied, "Our Chinese friends have been investigating and our operatives have discovered their findings. It appears the space station is equipped with an extrasolar engine."

Charlotte was not an engineer and had to ask what that was. Charles explained to her that it was a theoretical engine capable of driving a spacecraft to a small percentage of light speed. If it worked. It had never been tested.

"Our Chinese friends think we, the U.S. government, are aware of it and are backing the project."

Charlotte thought about that for a few seconds and replied, "But we don't have the resources to build anything of that magnitude, the Chinese must know that."

Charles replied, "Yes, they are aware of that but they think we are aware of the project and are helping out with it with the aid of NASA. Apparently some of NASA's training facilities are being used for the training of the crew for a space mission in this new space station. We have learned this is being done but the members of the training team insist its just to train the crew members of the space station on how to use space suits, get used to lift offs, that sort of thing that is always done for anyone going into space to visit the International Space Station for instance. Most of these crew members are from the scientific community and some of them are experts in in-vitro fertilization for instance while others are experts in crop growth for instance."

Charlotte sat back in her chair and thought about this for a moment and then asked Charles what he suggested.

"I suggest we contact this Malcolm Beacham who is apparently the head honcho of this project and tell him what we have found out and ask him point blank what the spacecraft is all about and that we know it is a spacecraft and not a space station."

Charlotte said that was an excellent idea and asked where Malcolm was at the moment. Charles informed the President he was overseeing the project from the launch facility in northern Canada.

"Okay, get a message to him telling him he is wanted in Washington. I want to talk to him directly. I want you in attendance along with the following people."

She quickly scribbled a list on a piece of paper and handed it to Charles.
"Tell me when this Malcolm Beacham will be here and I will make the necessary arrangements."

That signaled the end of the meeting. "What Charlotte wants Charlotte gets.", thought Charles.

Charlotte buzzed her personal secretary and asked him to contact a list of people to be in Washington and to be ready at a moments notice to attend a meeting in the Oval Office. They were to be given further instructions as soon as it was available.

At the launch Facility

A messenger from Launch Control came up to Malcolm.

"Here is a message for you.", said the messenger.

The message was sealed in an envelope. Malcolm opened it and read the contents.

"It looks like our little secret is out.", thought Malcolm.

The message was a "request" from the President of the United States to attend a meeting regarding the space station. A request from the President of the United States was not really a request, it was more of a command. He knew the meeting was because the secret was out, they had found out the real reason for the "space station" construction more than likely. Malcolm knew it was only a matter of time this would happen but had hoped it would not have happened so soon. The message contained a phone number to call to confirm his attendance at the meeting and be given instructions for his transportation to Washington. Some agents were coming to Moosonee and would meet him there to accompany him to Washington. He was being allowed to bring some of his own security people for the trip if he wished. Yes, he certainly would be getting some of his security people to protect him on the journey. He trusted the U.S. government to protect him but these days it was better to have more rather than not enough security.

He went to Launch Control and went to use the special phone in an out of the way area that was the only phone to use to call the outside world. Only the Launch Director and Malcolm had keys to access the phone kept in a secure lock up. He called the number in the message. A female voice answered the call.

"Is this Malcolm Beacham?", asked the woman on the other end of the phone.

"It is.", answered Malcolm.

"Can you give me the code phrase in the message, please?", she asked.

Malcolm looked at the message and quoted the phrase contained in the message. The woman confirmed the code phrase and explained to Malcolm the time he was to be at the Moosonee airport for his trip to Washington. It was only two days away. He better make some arrangements quickly to have someone else oversee the whole project while he was away. Murph was the only man other than himself who knew the project timelines as well as Malcolm. Murph did not know it was a spacecraft that was being built. Malcolm tracked down Murph and told him he had to leave the project for a few days on "business" and asked the big man to look after things while he was away. Malcolm asked Murph to accompany him to his office where he showed Murph the computer program he used for the project timeline to use as a guide where the project should be day by day while he was gone. Murph asked how long he would be gone. Malcolm answered that he wasn't sure, which was the truth. He didn't know what he was walking into.

A couple of days later he went to the gate where a security team was on guard 24 hours a day making sure no one who was not authorized got into the launch site and that no one left. He showed his ID to the guards and he was of course let through with his security team. He met one of the transport vehicles that brought materials and supplies to the town and showed his ID to the driver and asked for a van to be sent to pick him up and to be taken to the airport along with his personal security team. The driver said okay and left. After about a half an hour a van pulled up. Malcolm and the security team climbed in and took their seats.

"Take us to the airport please.", Malcolm asked the driver.

The driver looked nervous to have Malcolm, the head of the whole project, to be in his vehicle. The man asked no questions but instead drove directly to the airport. When they arrived an unmarked jet was waiting on the runway surrounded by a security team. Plain clothes military men thought Malcolm.

A man approached his team and asked for Malcolm

Beacham. "I am.", said Malcolm.

"Please follow me.", said the man and turned and walked away. Malcolm and his team followed. They were stopped at the guard perimeter at the plane and were electronically frisked for any devices. None were found. Malcolm had six security men with him.

"You're allowed to bring four personal security people with you. No more.", said the man.

Malcolm knew it would be useless to argue so he picked four of his men to accompany him and gave instructions for the other two to return to the launch site. He and his four security men were ushered onto the jet. The interior was somewhat different than a normal jet. He noticed a small conference room in the back of the plane. The rest of the plane that he could see were seats for everyone to sit with plenty of room. He was told where to sit and was allowed to have his security team to sit nearby. The jet sat there for several minutes while the pilot talked to the tower getting departure instructions. The engines spun up, the the jet started moving toward the runway and sat there for another minute or two and then the engines roared to life. The plane hurtled down the runway and was quickly airborne.

Not much was said on the flight to Washington. He and his team were asked if they would like refreshments. Malcolm said he would and glanced at his security team to see if anyone of them wanted anything. The steward rattled off a list of what was available and everyone said what they wanted. A few minutes later the steward and a helper brought a couple of trays and everyone helped themselves. The process was repeated with the rest of the planes team. The flight took several hours but everyone had a personal screen in front of them that they could view movies or television channels if they wished.

Washington – A Meeting With The President

The plane finally reached Washington and touched down at Ronald Reagan Washington National Airport, the closest airport to Washington DC. Malcolm and his team were escorted to a large armored vehicle that would hold all the members of both teams. They were driven straight to the White House. Once there they were escorted inside and told to wait in a room and someone would be there to get them soon. Malcolm and his team took their seats along with some of the plain clothes military guards that had accompanied them on the flight. It wasn't long before a well dressed young woman came into the room and asked Malcolm to follow her. Malcolm stood up along with his team.

"I'm sorry but only you are allowed beyond this point. One of his security men started to complain but Malcolm assured the man that he would be okay. He was, after all, in the White House, the most securely guarded building in the United States.

The young woman lead him to another room a short walk away and asked him to take a seat and wait to be called.

"Summoned is more like it.", thought Malcolm.

It wasn't long before a phone rang at a desk where a well dressed young man sat.

"Please follow me.", said the man who was the Presidents

personal secretary.

He led Malcolm to a door and opened it and motioned Malcolm to enter. Malcolm walked in and the room was partly filled with men and women, some in military uniform and behind a mahogany desk sat the President of the United States, Charlotte Henderson herself. Malcolm knew what she looked like but had never met the woman.

"I am going to meet her now whether he liked it or not.", thought Malcolm.

"Thank you for accepting our invitation Mister Beacham.", said the President. Malcolm just nodded. "I suspect you know why we asked you here?", asked the President.

"I have a good idea.", said Malcolm.

The President was not known to pussy foot around, she cut to the chase right away.

"We would like to know more details about the 'space station' your team is building. We have received information that it is in fact a spacecraft. I would like to know what its purpose will be.", asked the President.

Malcolm knew it was no use to try and bluff his way out of this one. Malcolm scratched his cheek and wondered where to begin. The President asked if he would like a refreshment before beginning. The President buzzed for an aide and asked what Malcolm would like.

"Just water.", replied Malcolm.

The aide disappeared and returned in moments with a tray with a glass and a pitcher of water. She placed it on a stand and poured a glass, handed it to Malcolm then turned and left the room, closing the door behind her.
Once she had left the President continued. "Please tell us what the purpose of the spacecraft will be."

Malcolm began at the beginning telling the President and the assembled guests everything. That he felt the planet and/or civilization as we know it now was headed for disaster and the spacecraft was a generation ship. He quickly explained what a generation ship was and that it was intended to travel to the Alpha Centauri star system to find the planet which had been detected that could support human life. The trip was to take a couple of hundred years plus and the descendants of the original crew would be tasked with creating a settlement there and starting a human civilization. He explained the original crew would teach their descendants their knowledge which would be passed down to their descendants and so on until arrival at the remote star system. After reaching their destination the crew would land on the planet using landing craft carried outside the ship. Some of the landing craft would be used to transport material down to begin life anew on the new world.

It took Malcolm about 20 minutes to tell the assembly and the President the whole story. After he was finished the President looked around the room and asked if anyone had questions. There were quite a few. Malcolm answered everyone truthfully.

"Will the United States help protect the spacecraft from possible attack until it is under way?", asked Malcolm.

The President nodded toward Charles her Secretary of Defense. "What threat do you you perceive?", asked Charles.

"Where did your information about the spacecraft come from?", asked Malcolm.

Charles confirmed the information came through channels that Chinese spies found out enough evidence that it was spacecraft and not a space station. Malcolm suspected as much.

"Are you prepared to help us protect the spacecraft until it has left orbit?", asked Malcolm.

The President was the one to answer. "After what we have heard, I agree with you. We are at a crossroads for human survival. Personally, I like the idea of your program. I see it as a backup plan in case we don't survive as a civilization or a planet. I am hoping it will not come to that. You are asking what we can do to help. I agree the Chinese are your biggest threat. They see your project as Americans getting the jump on them in the direction of the spread of humanity in the universe.

If your project succeeds I can see a whole new civilization on that planet that equals our own in several hundred years. It will take that long to build primary industries and then trickle down from that to the point we are at now with our technology. The Chinese see that as a threat to them as they are not any where near the stage you are at. We estimate it will take at least 50 years before they would be able to launch their own generation ship to reach Alpha Centauri. If that happens I firmly believe the Chinese will be prepared to attack the planet inhabitants and take it over by force if necessary."

That was a thought that had never even crossed Malcolm's mind. The Chinese could fill their ship with a crew of military people and weapons whose mission would be not to start a colony of their own but to take over and rule the inhabitants already there. Why had he not considered this possibility?

"So protecting us against harm until launch is only the beginning?", Malcolm asked.

"Yes.", confirmed the President. "If humanity survives and the Chinese continue on their present path in space advancement we can see this happening."

This was very disturbing to Malcolm. "Don't the Chinese know about the Outer Space Treaty? If they decide to build their own generation ship and reach Alpha Centauri in the distant future they would be welcome to join the colony there or start their own colony. I am sure the colony there would be more than willing to assist them.", said Malcolm.

"Do you really trust the Chinese to follow that course of action?", asked the President.

Malcolm did not know what to think. "I think the Chinese should be formally made aware of the project and if they do decide to build their own generation ship they will be welcomed as friends to join us in developing the planet and its technology.", said Malcolm.

"We could do that and maybe, just maybe, the Chinese will go along with that but since the project was hidden from them...damn!! Hidden from everyone, even us, they think we are in on the project and see it as a covert American project to settle another star system. You've put us in a very difficult position.", said the President.

She had brought up a scenario that Malcolm had not considered in his wildest dreams. Malcolm had a very hard decision to make. Let the ship leave on the voyage and hope for the best or leave the ship in orbit to see what will happen on the planet below and perhaps in the worst case scenario the ships crew could resettle earth if there was a WWIII and once the threat of radiation was gone, land on the planet and start civilization again using the ships crew of specialists? Or launch the ship if there was a WWIII and head to Alpha Centauri as planned.

"No!", he thought. Once a plan was made the best thing to do was to carry it through. He was sure if the ship remained in orbit and there was a WWIII the Chinese would shoot down the ship to ensure that no other humans especially Americans would not survive to start another civilization.

He took about ten minutes to explain all these thoughts to the President. What Malcolm had said was true, the Chinese would shoot down the ship if there was a WWIII. All it would take would be one small nuclear tipped missile to do the job. There was nothing America or anyone else could do to prevent it except to wipe China off the map. But China too had nuclear technology. That was well known. It was also well known they had a well developed space program and had missiles that could easily reach America. If WWIII started both countries would be annihilate each other and who would Russia side with? It was known that even though Russia had strong ties with America they also still had ties with China. Or they could sit and not choose sides and become the nation on earth that would be left as the sole nuclear power.

Then there was all the other nuclear powers such as India, Pakistan, France, North Korea was suspected to have nuclear weapons but their launch capability was unknown, the United Kingdom was rumored to have some and Iran was highly suspect of having nuclear weapons and mobile launch vehicles in hiding. The first thing Iran would would do would be to wipe Israel off the map. It was a mess that Malcolm had not considered. What he had thought as the threat was an attack by China with America retaliating but how to protect the spacecraft if WWIII happened? China was sure to launch a last ditch attack at the spacecraft. What course of action to take had to be carefully weighed. Maybe a preemptive attack at China was the answer but then other nuclear countries may retaliate against America. And if a preemptive strike was made against China it was a good bet that a nuclear missile would be sent toward the spacecraft in a last desperate attempt to sabotage the project.

Several people in the room were talking amongst themselves as to what to do. Malcolm meanwhile was thinking. He had a sudden idea. Complete the spacecraft and then wait for quite a while and then unexpectedly launch the spacecraft and get out of there fast!! If China tried to shoot down the spacecraft hopefully China would be caught off guard and be unable to shoot down the spacecraft once it had left earths orbit. The launch could be done while China was on the other side of planet and out of view to Chinese land based telescopes and missiles. The only problem was the Chinese spy satellites and the Chinese space station keeping their eye on the spacecraft. If the spacecraft were launched when China was on the other side of the globe they might have a chance. The spacecraft could be stocked with armaments in case China decided to send their own generation ship in the future and attempt to take over the colony. That seemed to be the only solution.

He voiced that plan to the President and she pondered that for a moment. It made sense. It might be the only solution. Another way to protect the spacecraft was with space based armaments to protect the spacecraft from attack while in orbit.

They would have a several year jump on the Chinese and be ready for them if China launched their own generation ship. If earth survived and China decided to launch their own generation ship in the future, the colony could be alerted but it would take 4.37 years for the message to reach the colonists, if there was an earth left to send the message. There was much discussion following. They had been in the Oval Office for several hours and would be there for several more hours she was sure. The President buzzed for her personal secretary. He entered the room and everyone stopped talking.

"I want food for everyone in this room along with refreshments.", she told her secretary. The secretary promised to take care of it right away.

The President asked if there were anyone in the room with special dietary requirements. No one mentioned any. The secretary quickly left to take care of the order.

"We should have some food and refreshments very soon." she said.

Some people expressed a need to go to visit the washroom

and others wanted to stretch their legs. She buzzed for the security people who arrived in moments.

"Escort the people who wish to use the washroom facilities please.", she asked the security people. Several people stood up and headed for the door quickly followed by security people.

When everyone had returned and sat down, the meeting resumed. There was a knock at the door.

"Come in!", said the President. Several people walked in carrying trays of food and drinks and placed them on the sideboard, turned and walked out of the room.

"Lets take a few minutes to get something to eat and drink, I don't know about anyone else but I am starving.", said the President.

She got up to go to the sideboard and then everyone else followed. After several minutes everyone had a plate on their laps and a drink of something in their hand. Malcolm felt a lot better now that things were in the open and the American government was agreeing to assist in whatever way possible.

Charlotte spoke, "What can we do Charles to put some defenses in space to protect the spacecraft until its launch?"

Charles replied, "We could place space based guns in orbit to shoot down any Chinese missiles directed at the spacecraft. These could be remotely controlled from the ground. We could also threaten the Chinese with war if they attempted to destroy the ship. This would be done after all diplomacy had failed. We could also, using Malcolm's launch facility, put satellites in orbit near the spacecraft that could be directed from the ground that could intercept a missile attack and blow up at or near the missile destroying it."

Charlotte responded, "How much time would that take to set up?"

Charles replied, "We would need about two months at the minimum to set it all up and get the hardware into space using Malcolm's launch site."

The President replied, "That's too much time. We need a solution faster than that."

A man raised his hand and spoke. He was Grimes, the head of the CIA. "I have an idea. We could send three Special Ops men to the spacecraft armed with laser cannons to destroy any enemy missiles coming toward the spacecraft."

The President asked, "How long would that take?" Grimes replied, "Give me 48 hours and I can have the men and equipment ready. We can launch the men and the weapons from the launch site in Canada."

Malcolm replied, "We are not set up for manned launches at the site. The site is only there to launch robot ships to ferry parts and materials to the spacecraft for assembly."

Grimes asked, "How big are the cargo containers that you launch?"

Malcolm said, "They are fairly large. We can send up quite a lot of material and equipment at one time."

Grimes asked, "Would there be enough room for three men in astronaut suits and some laser cannons?"

Malcolm replied, "I think so but again I repeat we are not equipped to send up people into orbit."

Grimes replied, "Don't worry about that. These men don't require anything too sophisticated. They have been trained to make do with what is available."

Malcolm said, "So you propose to send three men and laser cannons into orbit to protect the spacecraft?"

Grimes replied, "That is correct, until we have the time to come up with something better." Grimes looked at Charles for approval and then the President.

Charlotte asked everyone, "Does anyone else have any other ideas?" Everyone looked around.

Charles spoke, "I think it best to contact the Chinese formally and let them know what they mostly know already and hope we can head off a possible disaster. Maybe once they know all the facts, that it is not an American project for one, and they understand it is a peaceful mission for all mankind they may be less of a threat."

Charlotte spoke, "Okay, try that route and see what happens, keep me informed. Mr Grimes? You have the go ahead with your plan. Malcolm, we will send our three Special Ops people to your site. Give them all possible cooperation and assistance. Let them do their job."

Everyone that was addressed gave their assurances they

understood their roles and their responsibilities and everything would be taken care of.

The President said, "Unless anyone else wishes to propose anything else we can wrap this meeting up and get on with it." She looked around the room making eye contact with each and everyone. No one spoke. "Okay, that's it. Everyone has a job to do. Keep my office updated as to your progress. Charles, I want you to go ahead with your space based lasers or satellite plan, whatever you think is the quickest and the best solution just in case this situation drags on longer than anticipated."

Charles replied, "Yes Madam President."

Everyone stood up and shook hands all around. The President went to the door to personally see everyone out. When Malcolm was ready to leave she stopped him.

"Thank you so much for coming here on such short notice. I really believe in what you are trying to accomplish and wish you and your team the greatest success but I really wished that you had contacted us sooner."

Malcolm replied, "Thank you Madam President but I thought the best course of action was to be as discrete as possible. I knew the Chinese would find out sooner or later but I didn't anticipate the points you brought up. I really appreciate your help and support."

The President replied, "Good luck Malcolm and if there is anything else we can do or anything you think that you need, just contact us. You know how to make contact with us. The same way you were asked before."

Malcolm nodded and said, "I feel much better now that everything is in the open and that we have the assistance and backing of the American government."

The trip back was uneventful and soon they were back in Moosonee. He arranged transport back to the launch site. He had a lot of time to think about things on the trip back. There was no further need for Camp Alice, that would be shut down and everyone released with apologies. The guards would be paid off and the Camp destroyed. He decided to keep security tight at the launch site. It had worked so far and he saw no need to change that. It would not be a good thing if the launch site security access was removed because foreign agents, particularly the Chinese, could come in and destroy the launch center with explosives. He would not touch the tight security at the launch site. It had worked so far so why bother changing that? He pondered putting in a badge access program for the site to allow people to leave and come back at free will but decided against it. It would be just another way for agents to get into the site. Leave well enough alone he thought.

At the Launch Site

Things progressed normally at the site. Everything was at or near schedule both on the ground and in space. He sent word out to ask Murph to come to his office. A short time later the big man entered.

"Sit down please.", he motioned to Murph. He sat and the chair squeaked with his weight as he settled in.

"I just want to bring you up to date on my 'business trip'. I think it will make things a lot clearer as to what is going on and the crisis we are facing.", Malcolm said.

Murph looked concerned. Malcolm told Murph everything, that the 'space station' was not a station at all but a ship and what its purpose was going to be. He told Murph about the threat from the Chinese and the fear they may try and sabotage the project in space or maybe here on the ground now that they knew what the project was all about.

"I want to give you a new responsibility. I am taking you off temporarily as site boss and giving you a new role to perform. I would like you to beef up site security as tight as possible. If you need technical assistance just ask and I can have the appropriate people here quickly to assist. Will you help me with this?"

Murph replied, "Sure I will Malcolm but do you think I am the best man for the job? My skill is overseeing large construction projects, not security."

Malcolm said, "I understand that but I need someone that I can trust to run with this. You can do a lot of research on the internet. You can ask for assistance from the security team regarding existing security. I can arrange access for your computer to the outside world."

No one at the town site had direct access from their computers to the outside world. People could send messages to other people outside but they had to send them to a special address on the site first along with the address where they wanted the message to go. After the message was carefully screened it would be sent to the appropriate address. Any incoming messages to the special address the sender outside the site was replying to or sending were carefully screened as well and then sent to the recipient if the content was found okay. No casual internet browsing was allowed. Special internet firewalls had been installed to block any outside access and to block any attempted access from outside. A local internet site was set up with information from CNN and other sources copied and pasted into the site on a daily basis to keep people informed on what was happening in the outside world.

People could email each other within the site using special email accounts. Even these messages were carefully screened before being allowed to be transmitted. The people doing the screening were told that confidentiality was paramount and that he only needed to be contacted if the messages were a possible threat to site security. They were also told not to discuss the contents of any message with each other or anyone else. He knew there were possible extra-marital affairs going on but that was no concern of his or any of the security screeners.

One day Malcolm got a call on his two way radio from the guards on the road to the site.

"We have a vehicle here with three men who claim to be from the U.S. government. They won't answer any questions except to say they are to report to you. What do you want us to do with them?"

Malcolm replied, "Hold them there and I will be there in a few minutes."

Malcolm asked for four of his personal guards to accompany him and had one of them drive to the site gate. There was a unmarked truck there with three men standing near it.

Malcolm spoke to the guard supervisor who told him they just showed up unannounced and said they would only speak to him. Malcolm thought these were the Special Ops people who would be coming. He started walking toward the three men accompanied by his personal guards with their hands on their weapons.

"I'm Malcolm Beacham." Malcolm said to one of the three men, "What can I do for you?"

The man answered, "Do you have any identification on you to prove you are Mr. Beacham?", said the man.

Malcolm showed him his identifications. The man slowly reached into his jacket pocket and slowly took his hand out while carefully watching Malcolm's personal guards who all had their hands on their weapons. He did not want to startle any of them. He handed Malcolm a letter sealed in an envelope. Malcolm opened it and read it. It was on White House stationary from the Office of the President of the United States. The letter was brief. It read:

Dear Malcolm,

The three men before you are the Special Ops people we discussed. Please give them your full cooperation.

Many thanks,

Charlotte Henderson

(signature)

President of the United States

Malcolm kept the letter and walked back to the guard supervisor.

"Let the truck in.", he said. Malcolm climbed back into his car along with his personal guards.

They drove back to the launch site followed by the truck. Once there the three men got out of the truck and stood in line as if on parade.

Malcolm went to them and introduced himself and welcomed them to the launch site. "I'm sorry for the delay at the site entrance but we keep security tight for obvious reasons."

"Yes sir.", replied one of the men.

Malcolm asked, "Who is your team leader?"

The man that had spoken first replied, "I am. Colonel Black at your service sir. This is Lieutenant Colonel Jacobs and this is Lieutenant Barker, pointing to the other two men.

"We are pretty informal here", said Malcolm "we are all on first name basis. Colonel Black did not reply. "Please call me Malcolm.", he said to Colonel Black. "May I see what is in your truck?"

Without a word Colonel Black turned and went to the rear of the truck followed by Malcolm. Colonel Black, Malcolm doubted it was the mans real name, opened the back of the truck and inside were three space suits of United States designation along with some weaponry that Malcolm could not identify.

"When are you planning to go up to the spacecraft?", asked Malcolm.

He felt funny referring to the ship as a 'spacecraft' rather than a 'space station' to outsiders now the secret was out in the open.

"As soon as conveniently possible.", answered Colonel Black.

Malcolm said, "You are aware I hope these spacecraft you see are robot cargo carriers. They were never designed to carry passengers?"

Colonel Black said, "Yes sir" then quickly changed it to "Yes Malcolm, we are aware of that. Do you have a gymnasium on the facility?" Malcolm confirmed they did.

Colonel Black said, "We will need six padded exercise mats."

Malcolm said, "I'll take care of that. We can launch you tomorrow if that is okay?"

Colonel Black assured Malcolm that would be fine. All these men were very serious looking. They all looked trim and in top notch shape. He noticed they never smiled. It was all business with the mission as their only objective.

Malcolm said, "I'll arrange for the exercise mats and for some accommodations for you and your men."

Colonel Black thanked Malcolm and Malcolm turned to one of his guards and asked him to make the necessary arrangements.

"Yes Malcolm." he said and left to do his task.

Malcolm nodded to the three men and said, "Please stay here until someone comes and escorts you to your accommodations."

Colonel Black asked, "Will we be guarded all the time we are here?"

Malcolm replied, "Not unless you think its necessary."

Colonel Black replied, "No, we don't require any guards."

Malcolm was 100% sure these three could handle their own protection if necessary.

Launch Facility – The Next Day

The next morning Malcolm met with the three Special Ops men.

"We have your mats that you requested. Do you need any assistance loading the cargo carrier? Some of those items look fairly heavy."

Colonel Black replied, "No assistance is necessary except maybe for some help getting into our space suits.

Malcolm asked, "How much space experience have you had?"

Colonel Black replied, "None. We were given about a two

hour orientation before coming up here."

Malcolm was stunned. They were going up into space with no space training? Did Charlotte know what she was doing? If something went wrong he was not taking the blame for any of it. Colonel Black asked to see the cargo container. The three men discussed it amongst themselves for a few minutes. Colonel Black walked back to where Malcolm was standing and asked if any other cargo was going up with them and their equipment. Malcolm checked with the team of loaders and showed them the equipment and told them there would be three passengers. The loaders said there was enough room for some extra equipment but not much. Malcolm told them to help the Special Ops people to load the cargo module and to take orders from them. Malcolm watched as the team loaded the cargo module. The first thing to go in was two laser cannons. Some cargo was placed in between wherever there was space and then the Special Ops men placed the mats where they thought best. Colonel Black asked for assistance in getting the three of them into their space suits and asked when the rocket would be ready to leave. Malcolm told them the rocket would be ready to leave in about two hours time as soon as the cargo module was hoisted onto the top of the rocket.

Colonel Black said the three of them must be in the cargo module before it was lifted and secured to the top of the rocket. Malcolm told them to be ready one hour before liftoff suited and ready to go. Malcolm assigned three men to go with the Special Ops people to assist them getting into their space suits. An hour before lift off they were back at the launch tower suited up and ready to go. He noticed the three of them carried some nylon straps with them. These were probably to be used to strap in the three men. He was correct.

The three men entered the cargo module and laid down on the mats and asked for help in strapping in. Some of the cargo loaders assisted with this. They knew what to do as much of the cargo sent up was strapped in to prevent damage. These straps had special release mechanisms to allow the three men to get out of the straps easily once in space. The three of them looked like real astronauts with their suits and helmets on. Malcolm sincerely hoped all would go well for the three men.

The cargo module was lifted into place and secured to the top of the rocket. It was 30 minutes to lift off. Launch Control went through their usual per-launch testing and everything looked fine. The final countdown had begun. Everyone backed well away from the rocket and went into the bunkers. The final fifteen second countdown had begun as usual. Malcolm wondered if the three passengers inside the cargo module could hear the countdown. At 3 seconds before liftoff the first stage engine ignited followed by the solid rocket boosters and the rocket began its slow ascent and passed the top of the tower. It kept going quickly gaining speed as it went. Malcolm had been told the G forces at the beginning of lift off once the rocket had picked up some speed was high. He hoped the three passengers would be okay.

Inside The Cargo Carrier

The three Special Ops men grimaced as the G forces built up but the gym mats were helping a lot to pad them from the cargo. After a bit they heard the sound of the solid rocket boosters being ejected and later on the first stage detaching and the second stage igniting. They had a momentary break from the G force between the time of the first stage release and the second stage ignition. But the G force was back. Hopefully it would not be too much longer thought Colonel Black. In a few minutes they heard the sound of the second stage being detached and the third stage igniting. It was a lot less powerful than the other two stages so was much easier to bear. The worst of the liftoff was over.

They felt the rocket reverse its position and the third stage fired briefly to slow the rocket down and then tiny retrorockets guided it to the side of the International Space Station. They waited several minutes and they heard a crew outside unlock the cargo carrier. The crew had been told in advance of their human cargo and to tell Launch Control when they arrived. All three Special Ops men popped their safety straps and made their way slowly out of the cargo module and into the International Space Station's air lock. One by one they entered. One of the people in the station helped them off with their helmets and looked carefully into each face and asked if they were okay. All three men answered to the affirmative. Launch Control was advised the three passengers had arrived safe and sound.

Malcolm breathed a sigh of relief. "Those are three very brave men.", he thought.

The ISS made contact with Houston to let them know their "cargo" had arrived safely.

Washington

The Chinese ambassador had been summoned to the office of the Secretary of Defense, Charles Debin. At the appointed time the Chinese ambassador was escorted in and shown directly into Charles' office. Charles got out of his chair and walked over to greet the ambassador.

"How have you been Lung?", asked Charles.

"Fine, fine.", said Lung.

"Please sit.", said Charles and indicated a chair at a small round table in the corner of the room.

"Would you like anything to drink?", asked Charles.

"No, nothing at all thank you.", said the ambassador.

"I guess you are wondering why I asked you here?", asked Charles.

"I have a pretty good idea.", said Lung.

"Its about the spacecraft that's currently under construction as we speak.", said Charles.

"Yes", said Lung, "I thought it would be about that."

Charles asked, "What does the Chinese government think about this project? You must know it is not an American project. There is no way we could finance such a large project of this nature with the state that our economy is in."

Lung said, "Yes, we assumed that. But why was so much care taken to hide it from us?"

Charles responded, "It was just as much a surprise to us as it was to you. We thought it was a privately funded space station just as the cover story said it was. We only found out through our informants that you had found out it was a spaceship. We were as surprised as you were. We have already talked to the project director and he has told us the whole story."

Lung asked, "Which is?"

Charles continued, "The project is to build a extrasolar spacecraft to travel to Alpha Centauri to find the possible habitable planet that was discovered there and try and start a colony. The trip is going to take over 200 years to complete. Its the descendants of the original crew who would arrive there. Hopefully they will find the planet and be able to start a colony on it. When and if your country decides to make such a trip the colonists there will be more than happy to help you set up your colony and hopefully our two cultures could develop the planet together."

Lung's eyes narrowed a bit and then opened, "We don't see it that way, we see it as an American ploy to get a head start to one day take over the galaxy in several thousand years or so."

Charles laughed and said, "No, no. Nothing of the the kind was being thought. That is all fantasy. Do you recall the Outer Space Treaty way back in 1967?"

Lung replied, "Yes I am. But you Americans are well known for breaking treaties even with your own indigenous people."

Charles paused and then said, "That was then but this is now. We are not too proud of the way things were handled way back then but we have matured a lot as a nation along with the rest of the world. We want to see space as being open and free for all the people of earth, just as Antarctica is now."

Lung replied, "That is Antarctica but this is something much, much bigger we are talking about."

Charles replied, "That is so true Lung, which makes it that much more important to keep our word, both of us, both our countries."

Lung said, "Yes it is but what guarantee is there you will keep your word? Why were we not invited to participate?"

Charles responded, "Well we feel the same way. We were not asked either. Again, this was a privately funded project."

Lung replied, "You keep saying that but we still think America knew about the project and was doing what ever you could to help."

Charles replied, "Now that we know what the project is and what it is for, we are trying to help any way we can. The project was created to save humankind, not just Americans but the human race."

Lung asked, "What do you mean?"

Charles replied, "The project was created because Malcolm Beacham and several others like him believe we are not going to survive as a species much longer if things keep on deteriorating the way they are. They believe someone is going to push the button which will result in a nuclear holocaust."

Lung was quiet for a moment thinking about what Charles

had just said. It would not be China who starts a nuclear war, it would be the trigger happy Americans, Lung thought to himself.

Lung said, "My people are upset we were not asked to participate. If what you say proves to be true then the Chinese race will not continue. If we had been allowed to participate and some Chinese were part of the crew, then it might be a different matter altogether."

Charles sat back in his chair and wondered if this was the time to play his ace card the President said he could play if it was really necessary.

Charles said, "I have been authorized by my government to ask you if you wish to put four of your people on the ship for the trip. Four of our people would have to be removed from the crew to make room for them. They would have to have the same skills as the people we are taking off."

Lung thought about that offer for a moment, "That is very gracious of you Mr. Debin, but only four out of thirty?"

Charles said, "That is what I have been authorized to offer you."

Lung sat and thought for a moment, "I will have to confer with my government about your gracious offer. I will get back to you."

Charles said, "Okay, that's fine. Please do that and get back to me."

Charles stood up signaling the end of the meeting. Lung and

Charles shook hands and Lung bowed his head slightly in the Chinese way of respect and Charles did the same.

"I hope to hear from you soon, Lung.", said Charles.

Lung said, "You will, I am sure of it."

After Lung had left Charles picked up the phone and called the Presidents secretary.

"This is Charles Debin. Put me through to the President right away.", said Charles.

He waited a moment then heard President Henderson ask, "How did it go Charles?"

Charles said, "It went as well as expected. They still think we knew of the project the whole time and were hiding it from them. I played my ace card and Lung said he would get back to me."

Charlotte said, "Okay, all we can do is wait for a response. Nice work Charles."

She hung up the phone. Charles was not offended. That was the way Charlotte was. She said what needed to be said and ended the conversation. All business and to the point.

In Space

The three Special Ops men were resting in the ISS after their launch ordeal. They had a chance to look out some of the port hole windows to look at the construction of the spacecraft and the space wheel.

"That's gonna be a big bastard.", thought Colonel Black.

That wasn't his real name of course, that was his mission name. The two space laser cannons were floating freely in space near the ISS. They were going to have to start shifts pretty soon to stand guard with the space cannons in case the Chinese tried a sneak attack on the spacecraft.

"If they tried that we would nuke those Commies back to the Stone Age.", thought Colonel Black.

But of course he knew the Chinese would return fire and do major damage to the United States. And then other countries may get involved and there goes the whole shooting match. WWIII. It would be a mess. That was what this spacecraft was all about, saving some of civilization in case that happened. At least that is what he had been told. He was just waiting for a message from earth to get ready and man the laser cannon if it was thought the Chinese might try and shoot the spacecraft out of the sky. The only problem was would they try a sneak attack or would they try a preemptive strike against the U.S. first and then fire a missile at the spacecraft?

If it was him he would be out there now with the space cannon waiting for a sneak attack, not cooped up here in this tin can archaic International Space Station. He was still trying to get used to weightlessness along with the other two of his team. Every direction he looked seemed to be "up". It was a difficult feeling to get used to. He watched the astronaut construction crew assemble the space wheel. Each piece was carefully put in place and then welded. You could see the bright arc welders from here. He wished he was out there working with them rather than languishing here. Maybe he might suggest that he and his men help in shifts, even if its just moving pieces around, so if something did happen then at least one of them would be out there with a laser cannon to take action. Perhaps he would try and contact Houston and suggest the idea but he had his orders and he was used to doing whatever was asked of him. That's why he was in Special Ops. They were the people the military called on to do the difficult or the impossible jobs they felt no one else was equipped to handle.

Special Ops also had a high mortality rate. They were sent on missions and disappeared, never to be seen again. The government would absolve themselves of any involvement if a Special Ops member was ever captured. They were just a soldier or a common spy if anyone of them were captured. That was what they were told to tell, nothing more. Usually they tried to bluff their way out of a situation by claiming they were a tourist who had lost their way. Sometimes that actually worked but not most of the time. But if they thought they would be tortured to get the truth out of them they all had a method of committing suicide to forever hide the truth. No Special Ops member had ever blown his cover. It was a matter of pride and duty.

China

Lung contacted his superior, Lu, in Beijing to recount his meeting with Charles Debin, the U.S. Secretary of Defense. His superior said he would relay the information to the Premier but he bet that if the offer was accepted the Chinese crew members would be killed enroute to the distant star system. China would be unable to do much of anything about it short of starting WWIII. They could stop manufacturing for American companies but America would simply look elsewhere for cheap labor. That would hurt China more than it would America. After the phone call Lu called the office of the Premier to request a meeting. He was told it would be a couple of days before a meeting spot would be available. Lu said it was a matter most urgent. The phone was silent for a moment then the operator came back and said for him to come right away and the Premier would see him for a couple of minutes.

Lu called for his driver and had him go to the Premiers heavily fortified office location. After passing through several checkpoints the driver stopped in front of the building. Lu got out of the car and asked the driver to park and wait. Lu hurried to the Premiers office passing through another two check points staffed by armed guards. When he got there the Premiers secretary asked Lu to wait. Lu sat down and several minutes later a phone on her desk rang. She picked it up and said something that Lu did not catch and then motioned Lu to enter the Premiers office. When Lu entered the office the Premier was not looking too happy.

The Premier said, "What is all this about? Hurry up, I have another appointment."

Lu quickly recounted the conversation between Lung and the U.S. Secretary of Defense.

"Who does he think we are?", bellowed the Premier, "Fools!! Tell Lung the answer is no! The Americans have kept this secret until our spies found the truth. We would not know and the spacecraft would be long gone had we not found out the 'space station' was actually a 'spacecraft'!"

The Premier made a spitting sound and walked back and

forth a couple of seconds and then told Lu that he would think about the offer. Maybe he could sneak four of his spies on board posing as scientists or whatever they were supposed to be and take over the ship. Four against twenty-six, not very good odds. But maybe some "accidents" could occur and some of the crew could be lost and then takeover would be easier.

A spacecraft load of Chinese arriving at the new planet would be perfect. It would save the Chinese billions building their own generation ship. The cowardly Americans would be outraged but would do nothing to start a nuclear war over it. They didn't have the stomach for it. He already had rockets, the Americans he was sure, did not know anything about, in silos aimed at special locations in America. America was so trusting. They might as well have flashing lights indicating where their military bases were as well as their missile silos. And everyone in the world knew about Cheyenne Mountain. He knew if he launched first the Americans would retaliate but he had troops well hidden and ready at a moments notice to go to America quickly by air to attack with surprise and establish a base to take over the country. He had arrangements, if necessary, to have ships at sea posing as freighters that would be full of Chinese troops that would be rotated on a regular basis. They could be on American shores in just a few short days. He knew America had a substantial submarine fleet but a lot of them were in the Pacific, not the Atlantic. They used to be in the Atlantic but since the Russians and the Americans were chummy with each other, America had substantially reduced their submarine presence in the Atlantic.

China too had their own submarine fleet. America knew that too and America kept close eye on them. He knew they were watching and they knew that he knew they were watching. It was an underwater standoff. The Premier told Lu he would give it considerable thought and dismissed him. Lu left quickly because he knew the Premier was in a bad mood and you didn't stick around too long if that was the case. You got out of his way.

Houston

For years the Houston Control Center had been run with minimum staff members to monitor satellites still in orbit and to watch over the ISS to be sure its orbit didn't decay and made a tweak in its guidance if it strayed a bit, but now it was fully manned again. All eyes were on the ISS and the new spacecraft and satellites watched intently at the view displayed over China for any activity. There was a launch to their space station, probably a resupply rocket. The missiles track was observed closely. If it deviated one bit the control center would be on high alert. The space wheel was coming along slowly but surely and was taking shape. The body of the spacecraft was virtually complete and was being packed with supplies. Some equipment to be placed in the space wheel that would not be affected by null gravity and no air pressure was already being shipped up. The U.S. had considered getting involved by reviving the Houston launch pads but had turned down the idea. For one the U.S. couldn't afford it, they were near bankrupt and by the time the launch pads were readied the spacecraft would be almost complete if the present construction rate continued and it didn't look like it was slowing down.

This Malcolm Beacham had done his homework. His people had chosen a rocket design that was simple to assemble from mainly 'off the shelf' parts and cheap when you considered that it was a rocket capable of reaching low earth orbit. It cost many times less for Malcolm to launch one of his rockets than it took America to launch one of the old space shuttles and did the same sort of job, getting stuff into orbit. The space shuttle could hold a bit more, not that much, but it cost much more too.

Malcolm had asked if one of the old Space Shuttles could be used for one more launch. Asked why, Malcolm had told them that he had no cheaper way to transport the 30 spacecraft crew from the earth to the spacecraft. He had figured out the number of Russian launches it would take and it was a staggering cost. He was sure the Space Shuttle could do the job cheaper by packing everyone into seats mounted in the cargo hold. Houston told him they would get to work right away and let him know. The Atlantis, the last Space Shuttle to be used had been mothballed and put on display at the Kennedy Space Center and they would have to figure out if it could be restored to flight readiness in a short time. The old assembly building was still there. They told Malcolm they would work on the problem and get back to him. Malcolm called the U.S. President and talked to her about his plan and he knew it would be costly but to persuade Houston it had to be done and as cheaply as possible. She promised to make the call and talk to the head of the engineering team and tell them that.

A scrambled coded message came in from the ISS. It was Colonel Black with a suggestion to allow at least one of his group to be outside the ISS helping the spacecraft assembly crew with any help they could so they could be ready at a moments notice to man one of the laser cannons in the event of a surprise missile attack on the spacecraft. A reply was sent that his request would be passed on and an answer sent shortly.

"Great.", thought Colonel Black, "Maybe I'll get an answer in a few days."

About two hours later an astronaut on the ISS handed Colonel Black a message. The message was addressed to him with a one word reply...."Approved." He alerted his men and they worked out a duty schedule. Colonel Black said he would take the first shift. The other two men helped him into his space suit and did the usual checks that everything was sealed and escorted him to one of the ISS's several air locks. He heard the air lock cycle the air and then the outer door opened. He was looking down at the earth far below. He had a moment of vertigo as he had that momentary falling sensation that he was told to expect. He steadied himself until he got his "space legs" and then used the suits maneuvering jets to get over to the space wheel. He had been told to go slowly with everything which he did. As he got closer he marveled at the size of the wheel.

He pressed the communicate button on his suit and spoke into his helmet microphone.

"Do you guys need an extra hand?", he asked.

One of the space suited construction engineers answered, he did not know which one. "Sure, jump in. We can use all the help we can get."

He could almost hear the grin in the other voice. He saw a worker slowly go over to a large piece of the space wheel and followed. He made a sign if the worker needed any help. The worker waved him over.

Colonel Black went over to the other side of the large piece but the other worker spoke into his microphone. "Get the other one behind it. Go very slowly with it. The engineers at the space wheel will either tell you or direct you with hand signals where they want it."

Colonel Black said, "Thanks, its great to be out here doing something than sitting inside that tin can."

The other laughed and replied, "I know what you mean."

The engineer must have recognized him as one of the Special Ops guys. "I hope he doesn't think I am a trained astronaut.", thought Colonel Black, "I'm just flying by the seat of my pants here. I sure hope I don't crash anything." Colonel Black took hold of the piece and watched how the worker moved his piece and did the same thing. "Easy does it.", thought Colonel Black. He grinned. This was almost fun. It was the first time he had cracked a smile since the first of the mission. He would have to teach the other two how it was done. Easy does it. Go slow.

Somewhere Under The South China Sea

The Ohio class nuclear submarine, the USS Georgia was on patrol under the South China Sea. She was accompanied by the Virginia Class attack submarine, the John Warner. Both submarines were ordered to their present position and to get there by stealth which literally meant "get there without being seen or heard". Both subs slowly made their way to their present position and were standing on station. They were ordered just to wait and listen and await for further orders. No explanation was given. The crews knew where they were, near the coast of China south of the Pratas reef in deep water, about 300 feet below the surface, well out of range of view by any prying satellites. Sonar stations were manned all the time by two crew members just listening. They were to report anything unusual to the COB (Chief of the Boat) who would alert the appropriate sub crew and the Captain.

They had been on station for a month now and had heard little. There was a few distant contacts now and then but nothing unusual, nothing of immediate danger. No contact was allowed between the two subs. Silence was the order of the day. Everyone was careful to wear noise dampening footwear and be very,very careful not to make any sharp sound like dropping a tool. Such a sound could travel underwater a long way and another sub from China, maybe nearby, standing on station as they were might hear. Seaman Trent was manning communications when a flash message came in on the ELF (Extremely Low Frequency) receiver. Due to the long wave lengths used the message came in very slowly, a few characters a minute. It was the only way to get a message to a deeply submerged boat. A sub was always referred to as a "boat", never a "ship". It had been that way since as far back as anyone knew. It took several minutes for the entire message to be received. It was encoded of course so Trent took the message directly to the COB and handed it to him.

"This just came in on the ELF Sir", Trent said.

COB immediately took the message to the Captains cabin. It was "night" on the boat so the Captain would be sleeping. The sub kept regular surface hours for shift rotations and to allow the crew to keep regular time. The COB went to the Captain's cabin and knocked gently. He listened carefully. He didn't hear the Captain stirring so he knocked a little louder. He heard the Captain up and about and then a sleepy "come in". COB went in and the Captain was sitting on the edge of his bunk rubbing his eyes, trying to wake up.

"This just came in on the ELF.", said the COB.

The Captain took the message and took out the code book. The first few characters in the message was the days code word. He checked the message and the book and handed both to the COB.

"The message is authentic.", verified the COB.

The captain turned on his computer, logged in and went to the message decode area where he typed in the days date and the days code word. The screen was silent for a moment then a screen showed that said "Please enter coded message." The Captain was not a great typist and two fingered the coded message in one character at a time. He pushed the key to signify the end of the message. The decoded message showed on the screen: To USS Georgia. Return to base.

ELF messages were always short. "I'll be out in a minute.", said the Captain.

COB left the Captain's quarters and waited a discrete distance away. A couple of minutes later he came out dressed in "at sea" work clothes but his rank was conspicuously displayed. Both men went to the navigation nerve center of the boat.

The Captain told the Navigator to "Return to base. Very quietly." The Navigator verified, "Aye Sir, altering course."

The Captain said, "Sonar men! Please keep your ears wide open. Listen for both surface and submerged contacts.", ordered the Captain. "Aye Sir!", both sonar men replied in unison.

The Captain assumed the John Warner had received a similar message and would be returning with them. Another boat would be on its way to replace them on station. They were there in case China tried an attack on the spacecraft or America itself or both. Their orders would be, he was sure, to launch nuclear warheads at specific targets on mainland China. He hoped that would never happen. The Chinese weren't stupid. They knew that America had subs like his just waiting to launch nukes at them so they would have to think twice about it. That's the way the game was played. Hold a loaded gun pointed at each other. Neither side would fire because both knew that if one did the other would also. It was just like the Cold War between Russia and America that his grandfather used to talk about.

Somewhere in the Atlantic

Unknown to Malcolm or very few others, each freighter was carefully escorted by a small fleet of Virginia Class Attack Submarines. This had been done as soon as the United States became aware of the true nature of the spacecraft. They wanted to protect all the supplies and parts going to the launch facility. Groups of subs would wait off the shores of Baltimore for a freighter heading to Canada and then escort them all the way to the launch facility. Some subs were sent to Hudson Bay to stay on station there waiting for any unauthorized or unknown submerged boats to be heard on sonar.

The sound signature of another United States sub was known but so were the sound signature of a Chinese or any other nations sub known. The subs encircled the freighters by up to a couple of miles away to be able to hear any other submerged contacts. The propellers of the freighters made a deafening noise to the sonar men aboard the submarines so they had to get away a fair distance away to hear anything else. The lead sub didn't have too much of a problem and the sub bringing up the rear was using a towed sonar array to listen mostly to the rear. The subs at the side of the freighter had the most difficult job because even though they were a couple of miles away the noise from the freighters props sounded like a chain being spun in the water at high speed.

Freighter propellers were not designed to be quiet, they were designed to push the ship through the water with the greatest efficiency. Sub propellers were designed for both efficiency and quietness. It had taken years to get to the present sub propeller design which had been improved radically over the years since WWII. An American sub could be going 20 knots and not generate hardly any sound signature at all. Not only were the subs propeller designed for quietness but the whole shape of the sub was designed for the quietest operation when gliding through the deep.

Early 2026
At The Launch Facility

The main construction of the spacecraft was almost complete. The body of the spacecraft had been completed, all engine components had been installed. The space wheel was nearing completion. Much of the launches were now carrying equipment and supplies for the space wheel interior and for storage in the spacecraft body. Malcolm had contacted NASA and asked discretely for the best launch date and route to take getting out of the solar system and being able to use some of the planets as slingshots to speed up the spacecraft. NASA said they would work on the problem and get back to him. He wanted to use the spacecraft liquid fueled engines just to break orbit and get the spacecraft up to a reasonable speed and then use the planets themselves to accelerate the craft before leaving the solar system and trying the Bussard engine. It was the biggest gamble anyone had ever taken. No one knew for sure if the Bussard engine would work. All the calculations said it would but the real test would be with its actual use.

Several days later NASA got back to Malcolm with the best launch date, 21St of November 2026. That was only months away. He checked his computer and the project time line. Everything was on track as best as it could be. Money was running low but there should be enough to complete the spacecraft. If he had to he could approach the Bill & Melinda Gates Foundation for a few extra billion as they said they would be happy to donate more to the project if really required. Malcolm had already been laying off quite a few trades people in the town with bonuses as promised as they weren't needed anymore. The main jobs were now unloading the freighters and the odd aircraft that came in with supplies and parts, building rockets, loading the cargo modules, launching the rockets and assembling the last bit of the spacecraft. In a few days the space wheel would be very carefully moved over the body of the spacecraft and attached. That task alone was going to take several weeks to accomplish. They hadn't figured out a way of getting from the space wheel to the body of the spacecraft and back again without stopping the wheel. An air lock would have to be used to get from the wheel, into space and into the body of the spacecraft and back again.

Once the spacecraft had cleared the solar system it would be on autopilot until it reached Alpha Centauri where a crew would have to go down to the navigation section in the nose of the spacecraft to pivot the craft 180 degrees and then fire the liquid fueled engines to slow the craft down and search for the planet. Hopefully everything would still work after over 200 years of flight. And hopefully the training of the crew to perform this task would have been passed on to succeeding generations. The spacecraft had an extensive computer library on board that contained the sum of all human knowledge considered necessary for establishing a colony, creating primary industries and developing higher levels of technology, including what to do at the end of the trip.

The Chinese

The Chinese Premier was getting more worried as the days went on. He had to stop the spacecraft from leaving. The Chinese wouldn't have their own generation ship built for at least 50 years. He couldn't allow the Americans as the only nationality to populate the new planet and maybe others beyond in the centuries ahead. It was up to him to stop that from happening but he knew if he launched a missile at the spacecraft the American response would be swift and brutal. His spies had told him that three Special Ops personnel had been sent up to the ISS a few months ago with some armaments, probably radar guided laser cannons was their best guess. So the Americans had provided for some protection in space for the spacecraft. He had sent subs into the Canadian arctic in stealth mode to try and get close to the launch facility but they were detected by American subs and told to return or be fired upon. The Captains of the subs told him they were grossly outnumbered so fighting their way in would have been suicide.

He called his aide, gave her a list of people and told her to arrange a meeting at his office as soon as it could be done. He had to talk it over with his most senior staff as to what would be the best course of action with the least amount of danger. He knew the Americans would do everything to prevent a nuclear war so destroying the spacecraft would be the easy part but would the Americans retaliate by launching nukes at China or would they simply shoot down the Chinese Space Station? If that was all they would do it would not be a huge loss but an acceptable one to prevent the spacecraft from leaving. Another space station could be rebuilt fairly easily but a country.....? That was another thing altogether.

But if America tried nuking China they must know that China would retaliate. He could not rely on the Russians anymore. Russia and America were quite close especially as this project of theirs had given the Russians quite a bit of business at their launch center sending men up into space and back again as construction crew rotations were necessary. He had to act soon. The spacecraft, now called Hope, his spies had informed him would be leaving soon, probably sometime in late November his astronomers and space exploration people had told him, when the planets would be in the correct position to accomplish a slingshot course to get out of the solar system with a good amount of speed. He had learned some time ago the spacecraft had an experimental Bussard engine that no one knew for certain that would work. The spacecraft would have to be traveling very fast for the engine to ignite. He didn't have a clue how it was supposed to work so he had one of his engineers spend a couple of hours explaining it to him. It was supposed to accelerate the spacecraft up to 2% of light speed which would make it the fastest man made craft ever built.

Washington

President Charlotte Henderson was pacing her office thinking. If the Chinese were going to try something to destroy or delay the launch of the spacecraft they would have to do something fairly soon. The ship would be leaving orbit in November. The CIA had already told her the Chinese knew that as well. If the Chinese tried to destroy or disable the spacecraft what should America's response be? She did not want to start a nuclear war over it but it may come down to exactly that. They could of course destroy the Chinese Space Station but that would be a small response in retaliation for destroying the most important spacecraft ever built. The final decision was hers and she honestly did not know what course of action to take. She knew if she attacked China with nuclear weapons they would respond in kind. America, years ago, had developed an anti-missile which, it was hoped, would intercept and destroy any incoming missiles. Tests had proved it worked but that was a test. Would they work when it came to the real thing? She knew that NORAD was on high alert status watching for any activity such as a launch from China in an attempt to destroy the spacecraft and she had three Special Ops personnel in space that would be alerted in the event of an attack.

They had two of the latest design radar controlled laser cannons to be used in the hope of destroying any incoming missiles threatening to destroy the spacecraft. One Special Ops member was outside the ISS at all times ready to go at a moments notice to use the laser cannon. If China tried to destroy the spacecraft and failed or if they tried a preemptive attack on the Untied States and failed there too, what should America's response be? If China succeeded in either attack what should America response be? If the Chinese attempted a nuclear strike against the United States and even only partially succeeded that would almost certainly call for a retaliation strike against China which would be very swift indeed as American subs were on station near China to launch nuclear missiles at a moments notice. She had to talk to someone. She buzzed her secretary with an order to get Charles, her Secretary of Defense, to come to her office right away.

In Beijing

All the Premiers top staff were in his office as he had requested. A request from the Premier was never ignored or argued with. It was an order, be there or else. The agenda was of course what to do against the U.S. or the spacecraft or both? What would Americas likeliest response be in either scenario? The spacecraft had to be destroyed or at least badly damaged to prevent it from leaving orbit. He listened as each of his ministers gave the Premier their thoughts on the matter. It seemed all suggestions had some danger of some sort of retaliation but it was almost universally agreed the Americans would avoid a nuclear war if at all possible. The most likely retaliation would be the destruction of the Chinese Space Station which everyone agreed was expendable as long as the spacecraft was destroyed. The Premier agreed that a missile launch against the spacecraft would be the best course of action.

Nuclear attack against the United States would almost certainly guarantee major damage to both countries as the

United States would certainly retaliate in kind and the spacecraft would still be there. If an attack against the United States was to be done then a simultaneous attack against the spacecraft would have to be attempted at the same time. The Premier made his decision. An attempt would be made to destroy the spacecraft. The United States, it was universally agreed by everyone in the room, likely would not start a nuclear war over it. The worst that China could expect would be the destruction of the Chinese Space Station and a recall of all ambassadors from Beijing and a declaration from the United States that a state of war existed between the two nations. The Premier made his decision and gave the Second Artillery Corps a command to fire a missile at the spacecraft (now called Hope his spies told him) with the intent of destroying it or at least heavily damaging it. Then he would wait and see what the United States response would be.

NORAD – Cheyenne Mountain

Cheyenne Mountain is the hub of the North American Aerospace Defense Command or NORAD as it was known. Whenever NORAD was on high alert as it had been for quite a while as the spacecraft Hope was being finished, it was fully staffed. The base was deep under Cheyenne Mountain which was composed of mostly solid granite. Excavation for the facility began in May 1961, and was completed in May 1964. The NORAD Combat Operations Center became operational on February 6, 1966. The Operations Center itself lies along one side of a main tunnel bored almost a mile through the solid granite heart of the mountain. The tunnel is designed to route the worst of a blast's shock wave out the other end, past the two 25-ton blast doors that mark one wall. The center was designed to withstand up to a 30 megaton blast within 1-nautical-mile (1.9 km).

The main observation room was full of monitors being closely watched by alert operators. There was a huge screen showing the entire planet along one wall. Any detection of a rocket launch from any nation whether it was detected from ground-based facilities or by spy satellites would instantly appear on the big screen. The operators at the monitors would attempt to calculate the rockets destination and keep the General, who on this shift was General Adams, advised of any incidents.

A launch from China was being closely observed. Most rocket launches from China were to its Space Station high in orbit. The tracks for these launches were well known but this one was a little different. The operators attending to that launch notified General Adams who came over quickly to see for himself and make a decision what the next course of action would be. He notified Houston right away to notify the Special Ops personnel who were up near the ISS with the radar controlled laser cannons to be ready to destroy an incoming missile attack to the Hope. His next act was to pick up the red phone that was a direct link to the President. The phone was picked up on the first ring.

"This is General Adams from NORAD. Put me through to the President right away!", he demanded. The next voice he heard was that of President Henderson.

"This is General Adams from NORAD. There has been a missile launch from China that looks like it is going straight to the Hope spacecraft.", he said without any preamble. "I have already notified Houston to tell our Special Ops guys up there to be on the watch for an incoming missile."

President Henderson said, "Thanks for the heads up. Do

what you can and I will try and get the Chinese to abort the missile!"

General Adams said, "Good luck." and put down the phone. "He turned to one of his operators and said, "Take us to DEFCON 1! All military branches.", he said brusquely.

DEFCON 1 had not ever been used even during the Cuban Missile Crisis in 1962. DEFCON 1 was the maximum defense readiness position short of all out war. The operator quickly notified the appropriate operators of the order who sent the orders out to all U.S. military installations. He could not even imagine the chaos this would cause. Never in the history of the U.S. had DEFCON gone to a 1 immediately, not even during the Cuban missile crisis when it was at DEFCON 2 at its height. Submarines all over the world no matter where they were or how deep they were would be rising to missile launch depth and opening all missile silos in readiness. All missile installations in the U.S. and Europe and elsewhere in the world would be initiating launch codes in preparation for launch.

In Space

"We just got a call from NORAD. It looks like our Chinese friends have launched a missile at Hope. Call those Special Ops guys up there and warn them and tell them to destroy that missile if they can!!", said the Launch Director.

One of the Controllers punched a button on his console which gave him instant access to the ISS. It took only five seconds but it seemed like an eternity for someone to come on line.

"Tell those Special Ops guys there is an incoming Chinese missile headed your way!", he said.

The astronaut on the other end said, "Right away!" He pushed the Com button and said, "Colonel Black. Please respond ASAP!!"

Colonel Black replied, "Colonel Black here, what's up?"

The astronaut said, "Houston says there is a Chinese missile headed right for us!"

Colonel Black replied, "Okay thanks!" and headed right for one of the laser cannons floating in space near the ISS.

It was about two minutes away if he headed over slowly but this was an emergency. He hit the jet pack assist hard and he started to hurtle forward rapidly. As he approached the laser cannon he quickly rotated himself 180 degrees and hit the jet pack controls again. He had had a chance to practice quite a bit over the last couple of months using the jet packs on the space suits to move around in space and now it was second nature to him. It was a good idea of his to suggest to Houston to allow him and his guys outside on rotating shifts to help with construction. That way one of them would be outside ready to act at a moments notice and give them lots of practice using the suits propulsion system.

He reached the radar guided laser cannon and flipped a switch to turn it on. It was powered by a large battery pack which could be recharged by the sun. It was fully charged and ready to go. He flipped the switch to turn on the radar aiming device which showed the incoming missile.

"Damn! That thing is moving fast.", thought Colonel Black.

He centered the sites on the incoming missile and pushed the red firing button. The unit was made for the easiest possible operation because the designers knew that whoever was using it would not have a lot of time trying to figure out something complicated. He felt the hum through his gloves from the laser cannon as it automatically aimed at the incoming missile. He could not see it by naked eye but the radar could. As soon as a lock was established the laser cannon started to fire. It sent short bursts of highly charged laser bursts at the incoming missile. The radar was recording direct hits but it appeared that no damage was being done.

"Come on you Son of a Bitch!!", said Colonel Black to himself. He didn't realize that his helmet mic had been left on.

"What was that?", said one of the astronauts. Colonel Black did not reply. He just switched off the mic.

Washington

President Henderson ran out to her secretary and yelled, "Get me Charles on the phone right away!!"

He quickly dialed the President's Minister of Defense right away. The phone rang about three times and finally Charles answered, "Bentin here."

Charlotte's personal secretary handed the phone to the President. "Charles?" She shouted into the phone. "The Chinese have launched a missile at Hope! Get a hold of those bastards and tell them to abort or we'll be prepared to take drastic retaliation."

She slammed the phone down and raced into her office. Charles quickly called his counterpart in Beijing. The phone was answered after a couple of rings.

"Po? You've launched a missile at the spacecraft, the Hope! You better abort it or be prepared to suffer the consequences!", yelled Charles.

"What are you talking about?", said Po. "You know damn well what I mean!!", yelled Charles.

Po was obviously stalling for time until the missile reached its target. "Damn you, Po!!", yelled Charles. "Abort the damned missile!!"

Po was silent for a second and then said quietly, "Or what?"

Charles yelled back, "Abort the missile NOW or be prepared for a full retaliation!!" Po smiled to himself. He could of course give the command to abort the missile but he was not about to do that.

In Space

The Colonel Black's laser cannon was firing shot after shot at the incoming missile but it was having no affect. He noticed a movement out of the corner of his eye and turned to look. It was one of the other Special Ops people with the other laser cannon. He had already turned it on and was preparing the unit to fire at the incoming missile. The other laser cannon started shooting blasts of laser energy at the incoming missile but it still appeared to be having no affect.

"That damned missile is getting real close!", thought Colonel Black.

Suddenly there was a great flash in the distance as the incoming rocket was destroyed.

"Wow! That was too close!", thought Colonel Black. "Thanks for getting out here. I don't think one laser cannon was enough to finish that thing off.", said Colonel Black to Jacobs who he finally recognized.

"Glad I could help.", said Jacobs matter-of-factly.

Houston

One of the Controllers called out, "Flight! The missile has been destroyed in space before it reached the ship."

The Flight Controller replied," Thanks Paul, I am sure everyone will be pleased to hear that."

He wondered if it was the Special Ops guys that had destroyed it or was it Cheyenne Mountain? Those military boys had all kinds of nice toys that few people knew about. Or maybe someone in the upper levels of the government, maybe even the President herself that told the Chinese to destroy the missile or suffer the consequences. She was known as a tough old broad who never bluffed. The ISS called down and told Houston it was the Special Ops guys that had shot the missile down with the laser cannons but that it had taken two of them to do it.

President Henderson got on the phone to Charles and after it was picked up said, "Nice work Charles, how did you do it?"

Charles replied, "It wasn't any of my doing. I got Po, the Minister of Defense for the Chinese military on the phone and threatened him with dire consequences but he wasn't about to destroy the missile. He at first denied knowing what I was talking about and then you could almost feel the little weasel on the other end of the phone grinning."

The news from Houston was quickly relayed to Cheyenne Mountain and the White House. According to Houston it was our boys in Special Ops that finally took it out. Cheyenne Mountain was told by the President to go to DEFCON 3, be vigilant and hold. She was sure they had not seen the last of what the Chinese may do to destroy or delay the launch of Hope.

Washington

The President saw her other line blinking on her phone.

"One second Charles." It was General Adams from NORAD who told her that it was the Special Ops guys that had managed to take the missile out but that it had taken two of the laser cannons to do it.

"Tell those guys they earned their pay for the week and tell them thanks from me.", said the President.

"I'll pass that along to them Madam President.", said General Adams.

President Henderson switched back to Charles. "It seems it was our Special Ops guys that destroyed the missile."

Charles said, "So it was a good decision to send those guys

up with the laser cannons."

The President told Charles that it was then she said, "I have to let you go. I have a call to make."

Charles knew the President was going to contact the Chinese Premier himself and read the riot act to him. He was sure the next time the Chinese tried anything like this again it would be their last time. Charlotte buzzed her private secretary and told him to try and get the Chinese Premier on the line.

After a few minutes he buzzed her and said, "The Premier is on line 1 Ma'am."

Charlotte took a deep breath and picked up the phone. "Hello.", she said.

"Hello. How nice of you to call.", said the Chinese Premier.

"Damn that low life, trying to butter me up. Well have I got news for you!", thought Charlotte. She told the Chinese Premier in no uncertain terms what would happen if they tried anything like that again.

"You got lucky this time.", she said. "We were able to destroy the missile in time. And recall your ambassador or we'll throw him out of the country ourselves. He's got 48 hours to make arrangements. Our ambassador is being ordered home." She slammed down the phone, not even waiting for a reply from the stuttering Premier.

At The Launch Facility

Malcolm got the word the Chinese had just tried to shoot

down Hope but that it was the Special Ops guys that his launch facilities had sent up that had saved the day. It was now June and the space wheel was being moved into position. Launches were still taking place sending up equipment and supplies. He checked with Launch Control to see how things were going with getting the wheel in position.

"Its a slow process. It can't be rushed. That thing has an awful amount of mass. It has to be moved very slowly into position. Getting it moving is the easy part, getting it slowed down or stopped without it damaging something is very hard to do unless its moved slowly.", said the Flight Director.

Malcolm understood. He had been talking enough with the ground controllers to know that things in space cannot be done fast because even though things don't have any weight in space they do have mass whenever they are moved. It was fairly easy to get something moving but then an equal amount of force had to be applied to stop it. And something the size of the space wheel was the biggest item ever assembled in space. Even the International Space Station was dwarfed by the sheer size and mass of the wheel. It took another week until Malcolm heard the space wheel had finally been attached to the body of the spacecraft.

"Now the space wheel is attached we can really call the ship by its name. Hope. Hope for all humankind on the planet.", thought Malcolm.

In Space

The space wheel had been attached to the spacecraft body. Everyone cheered as the last bolt was tightened into place on the track that went all around the spacecraft body. It fit like a glove as it was designed to do. The air locks lined up fine. A suit would usually have to be worn to pass from the air lock on the wheel to the air lock on the body of the spacecraft. An L-shaped tunnel affair could be mounted to the air locks to lock the two together for transfer of items that could be damaged by the vacuum and cold of space such as the plants that would soon be transferred up to the hydroponic "farm". Special containers had been designed to ensure there was air inside and to keep out the cold of space during transfer from the ground to the spacecraft body where the hydroponics were located. There would be other edible items shipped up to give the crew an occasional break from eating hydroponically grown food. They would be shipped up using the same type of containers. A tin can of anything in open space would explode like a bomb if it were not shipped up in a protective container.

The only thing left to do engineering-wise was to start the space wheel turning to see if that worked the way it was designed. It had to work. That is where the crew would live, work and sleep all their lives. There had to be gravity or they would not survive very long. They could make do with a couple of hours of exercise every day like they did on the International Space Station but no one had stayed on the Station longer than a year. No one knew how long that exercise alone would keep a human healthy in space. These people would be in space for all their lives. He asked for a test of the space wheel to be done as soon as possible. The engineers had assured him it would work but he didn't want to find out at the last moment that it didn't and then have to scramble to fix something that may have been overlooked. Equipment such as computers, monitors and other necessary equipment were still being transferred from the ground to the wheel. Malcolm asked for all launches to continue but no more equipment to be moved into the wheel until it was tested for rotation. All equipment and supplies were to be "stockpiled" floating in space near the ISS until the space wheel had been tested for rotation.

Malcolm was told a few days later that testing was ready to start. He went into Launch Control and asked for a camera view to be transmitted to the ground from the ISS so he and others could watch. The little reactor attached to the outside of the spacecraft body had been sent up using one of the huge new Russian rockets that could handle a load like that. It had been put into operation after the electrical generators had been installed and all primary power had been connected to the space wheel. The space wheel would be rotated around the body of the spacecraft using the same technology used on earth that was used on high speed trains. Electromagnets would hold the space wheel away from the body of the spacecraft a fraction of an inch all the way around and on the sides. The space wheel sat in a kind of grooved track that went around the body of the spacecraft. If everything worked the way it should, the space wheel would never touch the body of the spacecraft. The electromagnets would also provide the motive power to spin the wheel similar as what was done on earth to move the high speed trains, except not nearly as fast. No moving parts would be in contact with each other, nothing to wear out.

The electric generators that had been selected were touchless as well, so no wear and tear at all. Anything at all that rotated had been designed to be touchless wherever possible especially in systems necessary to maintain life and equipment. Power transfer between the spacecraft body and the wheel was accomplished by transferring the electricity between the two sections by many transformer-like assemblies around the base of the wheel and then fed into power converters in the wheel to switch the power to 120 volt 60hz used by nearly everything in the wheel. It didn't matter what power was transferred to the converters. It could be anything from low to higher frequency AC power.

Launch Control was told the wheel rotation test was about to begin. At first Malcolm could see nothing moving and then slowly, slowly the wheel started to turn. It was calculated that 3 revolutions a minute would be all that would be required to provide half gravity for the inhabitants. The wheel was spinning a little faster. He held his breath. He had asked that a couple of astronauts be watching where the wheel and the body of the spacecraft met to be sure there was no touching between the two. After about ten minutes he was told the wheel was at full design speed. It could be sped up more or slowed down but as long as it would spin at design speed that was all that Malcolm cared about at this point. He had astronauts inside the wheel to experience the gravity and they said it felt funny after being in null gravity for months but that it felt great to feel "heavy" again. The astronauts also tested the AC power aboard the space wheel and found that it was perfect. The test was successful so far. Malcolm asked for the wheel to be spun for about an hour and then could be slowed down and stopped for the rest of the equipment to be moved into the space wheel.

Kennedy Space Center

Activity at the Kennedy Space Center (KSC) had been moving at a frantic pace for months. The Space Shuttle Atlantis which had been mothballed and out on display at the Kennedy Space Center Visitor Complex had been moved to the assembly building and restoration work had been on the go ever since. All of the old mothballed Space Shuttle parts had been checked over and Atlantis had been refurbished. Never in the history of the Space Shuttle had one been readied for space so quickly, never mind being assembled from a mothballed Shuttle and spare parts. Work was done with full crews around the clock. A couple of solid rocket boosters were found and quickly attached. There were so many men and engineers checking things out, assembling and repairing things that it looked like a bunch of ants pouring over a carrion. The Shuttle crawler was checked out and found to still be serviceable. It was the huge vehicle that moved the Shuttle stack from the assembly building to Launch Pad 39. The crawler has a long history. It was first designed and used during the Apollo missions of the 1960's and early 1970's to transfer the huge Saturn V rockets and Apollo spacecraft from the assembly building to the pad. It had still been used for the all the Shuttle missions.

After two months of work the newly resurrected Shuttle was finally declared ready and the crawler started to move the Shuttle "stack" as the Shuttle assembly with its external fuel tank and solid rocket boosters was called from the VAB to Launch Pad 39. Once there it would be checked over again by Kennedy Mission Control and fueled for its journey and unusual cargo. It would be the first and the last time a Shuttle would be used for transporting such a large human cargo. The crew was going to be at the minimum of two required for a launch and reentry, a Commander and a Shuttle pilot would be flying the Shuttle. The other 5 seats would be occupied by passengers. The rest of the 25 people would be in the payload bay. Everybody including the two crew members would be in space suits needed to move from the Shuttle to the space wheel and the crew needed in the navigation section in the nose of Hope's body. Launch seats had been installed in the payload bay for each passenger. It was going to be tight but they would all fit and they would only be there for less than 10 minutes for the trip into space. Each passenger was given a "crash" (hopefully not) course on launch procedure and what to expect in the weightless environment of space. Since many of them did not have any space experience at all they would all be given injections prior to launch time to avoid space sickness. Some people get really ill in a null gravity environment where everything is "up" and there is that fear of falling when floating in earth orbit looking down at the earth. But they would be fine. The Shuttle, the ISS, Hope and them would be rotating around the earth at over 17,000 miles per hour. There would be no sensation of speed because everything else around them was going the same speed. And there is no atmosphere up there so no air would be blowing in their faces.

The Shuttle arrived at the launch pad on the crawler after its slow journey from the VAB. The external tank was fueled with liquid hydrogen and oxygen. Many checks were done by Launch Control and it was discovered that one of the four computers that acted in tandem to run the Shuttle was faulty and was disconnected. It was decided the three remaining computers would be fine. Four computers were usually used in tandem to run critical systems in case one or more of them failed. In the Shuttle's hay day a launch would have been scrubbed if one of the four computers was down. Even if one of the other three computers failed they would still be okay. The passengers arrived and were hoisted into the payload area of the Shuttle and strapped into their seats and their helmets were put on and their oxygen supply was enabled. Many passengers were quite nervous and a few were down right terrified. They had all been injected with anti-vomiting medication to combat the effects of weightlessness. The really nervous passengers were given shots in the neck to calm them down. Some of them actually fell asleep after their shots. Injection in the arm or elsewhere was impossible because of the space suits. A final check of the Shuttle stack was done by Launch Control and no serious faults were found. A countdown was started for rendezvous with the International Space Station and the Hope spacecraft. The passengers had no choice but sit and wait. A speaker system had been installed at the last minute along with a video camera to keep an eye on the passengers from the cockpit of the Shuttle.

The countdown was coming to the final few seconds, some passengers started crying and the Mission Commander tried his best to calm everyone down and assured them that everything was going to be okay. The Commander was expecting this would happen but it was the only way to get everyone up into orbit. No one was given suit rockets. They were told they would be put into groups and would be tethered together to be towed to the spacecraft by an experienced astronaut. Once they had arrived and were aboard the space wheel or the navigation area at the front of spacecraft they were told the worst would be over and space wheel would be run up to give them gravity and a break from weightlessness until more equipment was needed to be put aboard the wheel where the wheel would have to be stopped so the air locks could be used.

The countdown was progressing normally, no stops so far. It had been decided the launch was going to happen even if minor faults were found which would not seriously jeopardize the mission. The last 30 seconds were being counted down. The passengers were told there would be a lot of noise and shaking at takeoff but this was normal. They were also told about the G forces to be experienced during liftoff and all of them had spent some time in the G force simulator so they knew what to expect. The final 15 seconds were being counted down. All still looked good so far. No major problems were discovered.

The last 10 seconds of the countdown was broadcast into the Shuttle cargo bay and at 3 seconds to liftoff the Shuttles main engines fired and 3 seconds later the SRB's were fired. The Shuttle started to slowly rise off the pad. The passengers and the crew aboard were subjected to quite a bit of vibration from the firing of the solid rocket boosters and the Shuttles main engine. Everyone in Launch Control was holding their breath. The Shuttle stack cleared the tower and started gaining speed rapidly. Soon the Space Shuttle was getting hard to see. The solid rocket boosters were detached and allowed to fall back to earth by parachute where they were meant to be retrieved and reused. Since this would be the last Shuttle flight ever, the solid boosters would not be retrieved. The Shuttle main engines were still firing. At the proper time the engines were shut down and the external tank was ejected. The International Space Station and the Hope spacecraft came into view. The OMS rockets were fired to place the orbiter near the Hope spacecraft.

The payload doors were opened. A crew of astronauts were waiting for them with lengths of rope for the passengers to hold onto as they were towed to the space wheel. Everyone had made the trip successfully. Everyone was unbuckled and and a rope was tossed into the cargo bay for several of them to hang onto. Several people at a time were gently lifted out of the Shuttles cargo bay. The astronauts towed them slowly to the space wheel and put them in the air lock 4 at a time. After about 20 minutes all the passengers had been transferred. The ISS notified Houston the passengers had arrived safely and Houston relayed the good news to Malcolm.

Since the main part of the construction had been completed most of the construction workers boarded the Shuttle for the return trip back to earth. The Shuttle itself did not have enough room for them all so most had to be placed in the cargo bay in the temporary seats used by the previous passengers. They were given the go ahead for reentry and used the OMS rockets to re-enter the earths atmosphere. This had to be done at the precise time to enable a landing back at the Kennedy Space Center. The Shuttle glided back safely, landed and rolled to a stop. The mission was a resounding success. The rest of the astronauts left in space would return to earth using the International Space Station Soyuz escape crafts that had been left there in case there was a situation on the ISS that necessitated leaving in an emergency situation.

China

The Premier was fuming. Those damn Americans! They were so lucky. They had a defense team up in space that had destroyed the rocket sent up to pulverize the spacecraft. He was pacing his office wondering what else he could do. If he sent another rocket up the Americans would likely destroy that one too and the American President had warned him that if anything like that was attempted again there would be "dire consequences". What that would be she never did say but he assumed the Americans would at least destroy the Chinese Space Station in retaliation. It was doubtful the Americans would go to nuclear war unless the spacecraft was destroyed and not even then he thought. He still had a couple of months left. He and his cabinet would think of something to do to destroy the spacecraft with the least amount of risk to China.

At The Launch Center

Malcolm was more than pleased, he was overjoyed. Spacecraft Hope was nearly complete, the crew was on board and the last of the supplies and equipment were being ferried up into space. It had been a long hard project. He was exhausted but happy. Everyone on the ground and in space had done a super job. He felt like dancing a jig. The people on the space wheel would be making sure that all the equipment was working as it should. He mentally went over in his mind all the amenities in the space wheel. There were living quarters for all of course. They were small but entirely functional. Each living unit had its own screen to play movies and games and display other information from the main computer. There was a main kitchen and dining area where all food was prepared. The dining room also doubled as a common area where people had somewhere to go to talk, play card games and just to generally socialize. There was a running track that went around the entire inside wall of the space wheel for those that were into jogging or just wanted to keep their cardiovascular systems healthy.

Most of the food would come from hydroponics with the odd break on special occasions to eat more regular food. The hydroponic food would be flavored to simulate a wide variety of normal food. All waste products would be recycled and automatically re-manufactured into edible food product. There was even a surgeon on board with a small well equipped operating room to take care of nearly all expected problems such as gall bladder removal or appendicitis. The operating room would also be used for child birthing and for euthanasia when the time for that came. The surgeon would also double as the ships General Practitioner. There was a small quarantine area in the wheel so if a disease outbreak happened the infected ones could be isolated and treated so as not to infect the rest of the crew. The quarantine area could be expanded if necessary. The medical facility had a wide range of drugs and pills to treat minor problems.

All the crew had been carefully screened on the ground and all were 100% healthy with no one having to take any medications so no problems were expected to arise for quite a while. There was no alcohol of any kind on board. There just wasn't room for any of it and since Malcolm himself did not drink he didn't see it as a necessity. All crew members were aware of that fact and it didn't bother them as all of them were professionals in their own area of expertise and were very light drinkers if they drank at all. They would all be busy with tasks of running the ship, teaching the children and passing on to them their area of expertise for the next generation of the voyage.

There would be many generation that would be born, live and die on board ship never knowing what living on a planet was like. Some members of the crew were there with the needed expertise of starting a new colony. Their main task would be to train their off spring with their knowledge of how to establish a colony once the planet was located. They would also be responsible for teaching the other members of the crew the basics of living on a planet again and establishing a colony. There were many documentary style programs in the computers storage showing what life is like on a planet so future generations could see what living on a planet would be like.

Aside from the propulsion engines of the spacecraft the computer was the most important piece of equipment on board. Triple redundancy was built into its design. All memory storage was done with solid state chip electronics. He remembered the days when computers had spinning hard drives that would crash on occasion necessitating their replacement and reloading of all software from scratch. Hopefully nothing like that would ever be necessary with the Hope computer system. All data was triple stored so that if the memory failed in one part of the computer the other two parts would compensate until the failed parts were replaced. The Central Processor Units were also triple redundant. If one CPU failed the other two would pick up the slack.

It was similar to the computers on the old Space Shuttle. Only one computer was needed but the designers put in four of them. If a computer failed while on a mission the other three would be able to easily pick up the slack and be used to complete the mission. Even if two computers went down the Space Shuttle would still be able to re-enter the atmosphere under computer control and be landed. All the Shuttles were "fly by wire" which meant there were no hard connections from the controls on the flight deck to the engines and the control surfaces on the wings of the Shuttle. All functions were fed through the computers and then the appropriate response would be sent to the engine or the flight control surfaces on the wings. It was the same on Hope. Most of the flight would be under computer control through the solar system.

Manual control may have to be taken over to navigate through the Oort cloud of debris surrounding the solar system after its creation billions of years ago. Little is known about the area because of its extreme distance from earth but there are a lot of theories. The inner edge closest to the sun was theorized to contain a lot of larger debris. This area is where most of the comets originate. It is hoped the outer edges of the Oort Cloud farthest from the sun is very sparse in larger debris but high in stray hydrogen atoms, enough to collect and ignite the Bussard engine and accelerate Hope to its expected speed of 2% of light speed.

All data in the Hope spacecraft computer was also available on optical disks kept in a library as well. Backup of new data stored in the computer memory would be incrementally backed up to external solid state memory devices and eventually to optical disk and transferred to the library. There were many technical, fiction, non-fiction, children's books and teaching aids for the kids to use. There would be no classroom. It would be up to the parents to "home school" the children. If something disastrous were to happen such as the sudden unexpected death of a crew member with knowledge of a certain kind, another crew member or one of the children could be brought up to replace them. They would use the technical library in the computer to teach themselves the skill they had to learn. All people on Hope were expected to have a primary and secondary knowledge of chosen disciplines. That way if someone was really ill or had died unexpectedly, another crew member that had secondary knowledge of that discipline could take over in a pinch.

There was a lot of data in the computer concerning establishing a colony on the newly discovered planet. A landing party would go down to start establishing a colony. The rest of the crew would stay aboard Hope until a colony was firmly established and then portions of the crew would use the landing craft to go down to the planets surface to join them. The landing craft were of Russian design. They were quite large and would be able to hold quite a few passengers and/or a lot of cargo for transport to the surface. They were simple in design and would operate like most of the other early design Russian spacecraft. They would go through the planets atmosphere protected by a heat shield and then land by parachute on dry land. They would have limited engines. Just enough to maneuver away from Hope and begin the long fall to the planets surface. They too would be computer controlled to maintain a steady descent and direction to land close to the colony site.

Yes, everything that could happen on the voyage had been thought of and a plan to handle it. That's what he thought about the project when he went to see the President of the United States who brought up a few scenarios that he had never even thought of. Sometimes it took another person looking at things from a different angle to realize problems that no one else had considered. He hoped that nothing such as that would have happened when planning the trip, that something that no one had thought of happening may happen and there was no protocol for dealing with the situation. The people on board the ship had been made aware of living life on board and dealing with all known problems but they had also been warned that something could happen that no one expected and it would be up to them to come up with a solution. There was no one else to provide any help. If they were close enough to earth they could send a message with the problem details and the experts on earth could advise them what to do. But when the ship was out of realistic range when it would take months or years for messages to be received then they would have to handle the problem on their own.

Inside Hope

Things were organized chaos on the space wheel as everyone checked and double checked that everything was working as it should. Once in a while someone would come across a problem and a solution would be found and it would be fixed. There were extra launches planned into the schedule in case something really bad was found and the parts necessary to fix the problem could be sent up. So far that hadn't happened. There was spare parts for almost everything. There was even a small machine shop to make a part if there wasn't a spare part for it as long as it was something mechanical. There were spare parts for most of the electronics aboard, especially the computer, although everything that was chosen was picked for its reliability and endurance. Anything that had a moving part in it, a search had been done to see if there was something else to replace it that didn't have a moving part. The electronic parts that were selected had to go through a "burn in" cycle at the manufacturer to be sure the part would not fail in a short time, something sometimes called "infant mortality" where a part would fail shortly after being used. But if the part worked for a certain length of time it would be expected to work for years afterwards. That's what warranties were for. Unfortunately that doesn't help when you are in deep space and a long way from home. You could not just run down to your neighborhood store and exchange it for another one.

The engine to break out of earths orbit had been checked thoroughly by the crew assembling it. Malcolm had told them to use the checklists provided by the engine manufacturer and to check and double check everything. If they found everything to be okay they were supposed to let the other engineer recheck it to see if the other had missed something. Malcolm did not know if either of them had caught something the other one missed. They weren't saying if they did. The engineers on board Hope rechecked everything again and had done everything possible to the engine short of a test firing and had found nothing wrong.

The moment of truth would happen when the engine was fired up for the first time. There were lots of spare parts for it too. The engine had been assembled at the manufacturer and test fired to check that everything worked as it should and then it was carefully taken apart, packed and sent to the Launch Site in pieces. It was simply too big to be shipped up to Hope assembled as one unit. The Bussard engine was another story. It had no moving parts. That was why Malcolm and his team had selected it. All that could be done with it was to check that all the electromagnets for collecting and compressing the hydrogen molecules were working and the engineers on board had confirmed that. The engine could not be used until the space craft reached the Oort Cloud and hoped the theory was correct there was a large concentration of hydrogen molecules on the outer edge of the Cloud, enough for the engine to ignite and accelerate Hope to its expected top speed of 2% of light speed.

China

The Chinese Premier had conferred with all his top ministers, officials and scientists and no one had a sure fire way to destroy the spacecraft without the United States taking drastic retaliatory steps against China. Sure, they could shoot down the Chinese Space Station. That has already been decided as an acceptable loss. But the Premier was sure the United States would do something far worse. He was sure after speaking with or actually getting yelled at by the U.S. President, he had little chance to get in a word, the U.S. would take more drastic action than that. His MSS spy network had recently discovered the U.S. had developed an anti-missile and had them deployed all around the perimeter of the U.S., some in Canada, Europe and some of the subs also had them which he knew were not far off shore of mainland China. If he sent another missile aimed at the spacecraft the U.S. would attempt to destroy it the same way they destroyed the first one and then they would possibly send nuclear missiles at China knowing they would retaliate in kind. But if the U.S. had these anti-missiles and they worked as well as was claimed then a strike at the U.S. would be unsuccessful. China would be in ruins and America would be unscathed, assuming all the missiles from China were stopped. If only one or two were able to get through it would only be a small part of the U.S. that would be destroyed.

China had few allies to help in the attack and none of them were nuclear armed to the extent the U.S. was. North Korea had nuclear capability but they had a very limited arsenal and nothing long range in the missile category to reach the U.S. The same situation was in Iran. Iran had a real hate for the U.S. and Israel but had limited launch capabilities. If a nuclear war started the first thing Iran would do would be to nuke Israel off the map. Russia could not be counted on either. They had a considerable arsenal but it was unlikely they would side with China. The U.S. and Russia had got real friendly with each other over the last few years, even more so as the Russian launch facilities had been used a fair bit to ferry workers up to the International Space Station to build the spacecraft Hope. And it would be leaving soon. His spy network had informed him that an American Space Shuttle had been taken out of mothballs and resurrected to use to ferry the crew up to Hope and to transport most of the workers back to earth. They also were able to find out the exact date of the launch, 21st of November. That was only weeks away. The only hope of destroying the spacecraft Hope would be to fire two missiles at it. The last time they had barely been able to stop one, two would surely destroy the spacecraft. But then the U.S. would probably nuke China in retaliation and even if China tried to retaliate by launching their missiles at the U.S. there was a good chance most of them would be destroyed if his spy network were correct, and they were rarely wrong, that the U.S. had a working anti-missile. But he HAD to destroy Hope if the Chinese race was to survive and continue.

The United States was sitting at DEFCON 3 which meant their entire military was on alert and could act at a moments notice. They may even raise that the closer the launch date became. Damn! Why hadn't he done something sooner. He had found out too late that the "privately funded space station" was a cover story for the whole thing. Now as the launch date was getting close the U.S. would do everything in its power to protect the spacecraft.

Washington

President Charlotte Henderson had her Defense Minister in her office and was talking about what other measures they could take to protect Hope until it was launched. The U.S. had a working anti-missile but it was designed to stop incoming missiles coming into the United States from somewhere else on the planet. They weren't designed to be used to fire on a missile in space. That scenario was not considered when the anti-missile was being designed. The missile was too big to transport into space all in one piece but maybe....

Charlotte started thinking. "Could those missiles be broken down into smaller components and reassembled in space?", she asked Charles.

Charles admitted he didn't know but a quick phone call would confirm it.

"Do it, now!", said Charlotte.

Charles went to his bosses desk and picked up the phone. He consulted his contacts in his personal pocket computer and dialed a number.

"Put me through to Dr. Hamilton right away. This is Charles Debin, the Minister of Defense.", he listened to the response. "I don't care where he is or what he is doing I have to talk to him immediately. Please get him on the phone!", Charles said rather irritated.

It took about three minutes but Dr. Hamilton came on the phone. Charlotte indicated to Charles to enable the speaker on the phone which he did.

"Hello Charles, what can I do for you?", Dr. Hamilton said. Charles responded, "I'm in the Presidents office and we have some questions to ask about the anti-missile."

Dr. Hamilton all of a sudden sounded a little nervous, after all, the President of the United States, Charlotte Henderson, was listening.

"What...what do you want to know?", asked Dr. Hamilton.

Charlotte replied, "We want to know Doctor, if the missiles can be disassembled easily and shot up into space in cargo containers and be fairly easy to reassemble once up there."

Dr. Hamilton replied, still a bit nervous, "Well they weren't designed for that but I can look into it."

Charlotte replied, "We need to know as soon as possible. They would have to be fully fueled and ready to go once assembled."

Dr. Hamilton replied, "We could dispense with the outer skin, that would not be necessary in space as there is no atmosphere to contend with. That would save a lot of space. We could disassemble one after removing the outer skin and break it down into stages for later reassembly in space. Its possible. How big are the rockets going to be to send the components up into space?"

Charlotte looked at Charles who said, "The cargo capacity is almost what the old Space Shuttle was capable of."

Dr. Hamilton said, "We would have to break it down even more then. The missiles are fairly large."

Charles replied, "Okay, here is what I want you to do. Break a couple of them down into as small a pieces as you can and still be fairly easy to be assembled back again in space. We'll take it from there. Be sure to provide detailed instructions on how to reassemble them. Is there any way you or someone from your team that knows them really well would be willing to go into space to assist with the reassembly?"

Dr. Hamilton said, "We have a couple of engineers on staff

that used to be astronauts. I could ask them if one of them would be willing to go."

Charles said, "These are cargo carriers we are talking about. They aren't designed for human space transport but we have sent up three Special Ops guys who made the trip okay. They used some gym mats and fashioned launch cushions out of them.

This would be quite the adventure." Dr. Hamilton said, "Can you give me a few minutes and I will ask them?"

Charles said, "We are really pressed for time on this one, can you get the two of them on the phone right away? We would like these things in space as soon as possible, like yesterday. Its for protection of the Hope spacecraft. We are expecting the Chinese to make one last desperate attempt to destroy it and we really need those anti-missiles up there as soon as possible. I would need your team working on this around the clock. I'll have an air transport on your runway with engines running waiting for your solution."

Dr. Hamilton said, "Give me one sec....." And he was gone. He was back on the phone in about three minutes. He sounded out of breath. He said, "I have the two of them here. I told them of your idea while running back here and Dave said it sounds like the adventure of a lifetime and he would love another chance to go back into space even if he had to be strapped to the outside of the rocket."

Charles chuckled. "That's great! Put him on the phone will you?"

Dave spoke, "Dave here! I hear you are looking for a

volunteer to go up and assemble one of our anti-missiles in orbit?"

Charles said, "It would be two of them. That's right Dave. It won't be your usual mission. We would have to send you up in a cargo carrier along with the missile parts. The rockets we are using are only for sending cargo up into orbit but we did send three Special Ops guys up a few months ago and they survived the trip fine. They used some gym mats as a makeshift launch couch."

Dave said, "Hey! This sounds like an adventure of a lifetime. Count me in!"

Charlotte came on the line, "The President here. You would be doing your country a great service. I really appreciate your enthusiasm."

Dave said, "The President? The President of what?" Charles and Charlotte grinned at each other.

Charles spoke, "THE President, the President of the United States."

There was a moment of silence and then Dave spoke, "Wow!! Yes, Ma'am. I would be more than willing to do this for you Ma'am!"

Charlotte replied, " We owe you a big one. There will be a medal or something in it for you I am sure. I really do appreciate your doing this for us and for your enthusiasm for this project."

Dave replied, "I owe you a big one. I never thought I would

get to go into space again. I can't pass this opportunity up."

Charlotte said, "Can you put Dr. Hamilton on the phone again for me, and thanks once again Dave."

Dr. Hamilton said, "Dr Hamilton here."

Charlotte said, "Get busy Doctor. I want everything ready to go in 48 hours or less. Drop everything you have going and concentrate on this project. Have the missiles disassembled into as small a pieces as you can for easiest assembly in space. There will be an Air Force cargo jet waiting at your airport to transport the missiles and Dave to our launch site in Canada."

Dr. Hamilton said, "Yes Ma'am, we'll get right on it right away. You want two missiles is that right?"

Charlotte said, "Yes that's right. Two of them."

Dr. Hamilton said, "We'll get on it right away and work around the clock as you wanted."

Charlotte said, "Thanks Dr. Hamilton." and hung up the phone.

"Here's hoping.", said Charles.

Charlotte said, "Get a transport plane to that airport. Have them there in 36 hours from now. Tell them to wait for Dr. Hamilton and his crew with the missiles and Dave."

Charles said, "Right away Ma'am!" And he left the office.

At The launch Site

Malcolm was taking a breather in his office when the phone rang. "Malcolm here.", he said.

It was the Flight Controller. "Malcolm, can you come over to Launch Control right away? The President wants to talk to you."

Malcolm said, "I'm on my way." And put the phone down. "Now what?", he thought as he hurried over to Launch Control.

When he got there the secure safe with the only phone to the outside world was open. The Flight Controller handed Malcolm the phone.

"Malcolm here.", he said.

"Hi Malcolm. This is Charlotte. We have every belief the Chinese may try one more shot at bringing down Hope before the launch. But we have a plan." Charlotte quickly briefed Malcolm on it.

"Okay.", said Malcolm, "We'll be ready for when they get here. We will have two birds on the launch pad ready to go."

Charlotte said, "Make it three just in case with two more ready to go."

Malcolm said, "Okay, will do." Malcolm hung up the phone and swore under his breath. "Damn those Chinese."

Nellis Air Force Base

In the middle of the night a large cargo jet landed and taxied close to some hangers. The pilot shut everything down and the plane just sat there. The crew had their mission. They were told to wait until the next morning and they would be contacted. There was some cots in the back that the crew slept on. This long range cargo plane was made for in flight refueling which made it unnecessary for it to land until it reached its destination so two crews were often aboard. While one crew flew the other would sleep. Nellis Air Force Base was near the famous "Skunk Works" and "Area 51" where a lot of aircraft development took place in relative secret. The crew was told very little, only that they were to transport two trucks and a man up to some place called Moosonee in northern Ontario Canada. The pilot had expressed some concern whether his large transport plane a C5 Galaxy, would be able to land there. He was assured it would., the runway had been extended a few years back and large cargo jets landed there all the time.

Early the next morning the crew awoke and grabbed a bite from their flight grub boxes and waited. About two hours later two trucks arrived and a man got out and came over to the plane. "Can you open your rear cargo doors?", he yelled.

"Who are you?", the pilot said.

"I'm your contact, Dr. Hamilton.", answered the man.

The two crew members looked at each other then the pilot flipped a switch which lower the rear ramp for vehicles to drive up into the belly of the plane. He heard the trucks drive to the back of the plane which then shook a little as the two trucks drove single file into the planes cargo bay.

The copilot went to the cargo area and chained down the vehicles so they wouldn't shift or roll during flight in case of bad weather or a rough landing.

A couple of minutes later the two drivers appeared and stood beside Dr. Hamilton. "Okay, you can close it now!", he yelled back.

Dr. Hamilton looked at his watch. "Dave should be here by now.", he thought.

A car came barreling across the runway and screeched to a halt near Dr. Hamilton. A well built man in his early 50's jumped out of the car and ran over to Dr. Hamilton.

"I hope I wasn't holding everyone up.", Dave said. He was assured he hadn't.

"Here is your passenger to take with you.", yelled Dr. Hamilton to the pilot who was two stories above him in the cockpit of the huge jet cargo plane.

The pilot told Dave to come around the side of the plane where he opened a door and a set of stairs flipped down allowing Dave easy access into the plane.

Once Dave was on board the pilot flipped the same switch and the stairs magically folded up and disappeared into the side of the plane.

"Okay, get going. They are waiting for those parts up north.", Dr. Hamilton yelled up.

The pilot waved and he and his co-pilot did their preflight checks and started up the massive engines. Once all instruments were checked and all looked well the pilot waved again and started to taxi toward the runway. He put on his headset and contacted the tower for takeoff instructions. He taxied the jet to the runway the tower had indicated and sat their for a moment and then the engines revved up and the huge jet started down the runway quickly gaining speed. It did not take long and the nose wheel assembly started to lift followed by the main landing gear wheels. The jet was airborne and on its way to the northern launch facility. The wheel assemblies disappeared into their pods under the belly of the plane.

The pilot had been given the co-ordinates for the location and had already programmed them into the autopilot. He steered the big jet in the general direction and when they had reached their altitude they had been told to fly at he flipped on the autopilot and went to the washroom. Dave was sitting in one of the flight deck jump seats and was talking to the co-pilot when the pilot came out of the planes washroom.

"What's in the trucks?", asked the pilot. "Don't ask.", grinned Dave.

At The Launch Facility

Malcolm looked at his watch and looked up at the sky. The anti-missile assemblies should be on their way by now. He figured they would be here by mid-afternoon. He went to check things at the launch pad. Three rockets stood ready with the cranes at their sides ready for their cargo. He hoped the cargo holds were big enough to hold the assemblies. He had given Dr. Hamilton the dimensions of the cargo carriers and the maximum takeoff weight the rockets could handle. It would be up to Dr. Hamilton to make sure the rocket assemblies were the right size to fit in the cargo carriers. He went into Launch Control to chat with the Flight Director for something to do to pass the time.

Washington

"Charles Debin for you on line one Ma'am", said Charlotte's secretary. She said thanks and picked up the phone and punched line one.

"Charles?", she said.

"Good news Ma'am. The cargo jet has just left Nellis Air Base a little while ago right on time.", said Charles.

"That's good to hear. Keep me posted.", said the President. Charles assured her he would.

At The Launch Facility

About 2:30PM Malcolm heard the sound of a jet coming towards the launch facility, circle around and headed for the Moosonee Airport.

A short time later he got a radio call from the main gate. "I got two trucks and a man here that says you are expecting him. He says his name is Dave. He wouldn't give his last name."

Malcolm told them to let him in and have two drivers drive the two trucks to the launch facility. Shortly the two trucks pulled up and a well built guy in his early 50's bounced out of the truck. Malcolm went to meet him.

"You must be Dave?", asked Malcolm.

"That's me!", said Dave and grinned back.

"I'm Malcolm, the project manager for the spacecraft Hope.", said Malcolm.

"Its a pleasure to meet you.", Dave said. "I hope you have some spacesuits here. I was going to bring mine but I was told you have lots here."

Malcolm assured him that he did and waved over one of the men near the launch pad. "Take Dave here and get him a suit. He's going up.", said Malcolm.

"Sure thing boss.", said the man. The two of them went toward a building on the site.

"Lets get these trucks over to the launch pad and get these parts into the cargo bays.", yelled Malcolm to a small group of men waiting. The men trotted towards the trucks and all climbed in the two vehicles and drove them over to the launch pad where another group appeared and they all worked together to load the rocket parts into the cargo bays. They had done this so many times over the last three years they could do it in their sleep.

The cargo bays were able to hold most of the parts for the rockets. One more rocket would be required to send the rest up. A few more supplies were loaded in for Hope.

"I hope someone told you how you were you were going to

be sent up?", Malcolm asked.

"Yeah they did. You sent up three Special Ops guys and they made it okay?", asked Dave. Malcolm nodded.

"Okay, I'll do it the same way then.", Dave said.

Malcolm waved over one of the men walking by. "Are you doing anything important right now?" , asked Malcolm. The man said no.

Malcolm asked him to go over to the gym and bring two gymnastic mats back in a hurry. "Yes Sir!", he said and took off at a run.

Malcolm told Dave how the Special Ops guys had rode into space on gym mats for cushions inside the cargo carrier. Dave assured him that would not be a problem. He told Malcolm he was "tickled pink" to have another chance to go into space again. Malcolm asked him if he had much astronaut experience. Dave told him he had been into space 7 times in 15 years including a six month stay at the ISS.

Malcolm said, "Well get used to being at the ISS again for a while until we can figure a way to get you back."

The ISS still has those old Russian Soyuz spacecraft attached for emergency use. He told Dave he hoped there would be enough room in them for everyone to come back all at once. Dave asked if there were space tools in the ISS. Malcolm told him there was lots as they had built the Hope spacecraft using the ISS as temporary quarters.

The rocket cargo bays were loaded and ready to go. The

crane lifted Dave up so he could inspect the cargo. The guys had done a good job. The crane lowered him back down and Malcolm told him to go get suited up. Dave trotted away to a nearby building with another guy to help him. Several minutes later Dave appeared with his spacesuit on. Malcolm told him which rocket he would be going up in. The mats were already there along with straps to hold him in place. Dave was lifted in a special cage made for human cargo and stepped off into the cargo bay. Two men were there to help him get in and strapped in. Launch Control had already started the countdown. It would be another 20 minutes until liftoff. Dave removed his helmet to wait out the time and with three minutes to go slipped his helmet on and locked it in place and started his air supply.

The cargo bay had already been closed and latched. It was pitch black inside. He could just make out the countdown proceeding outside. He was told his rocket would be the first of the three to go. With two minutes to go everyone including Malcolm headed for the block houses. A rocket had never blown up on the pad before but there was always a first time. The only failure they had was one rocket that had lost its guidance and had gone off course and had to be destroyed. Luckily the cargo carrier had detached by remote from the ground and had been parachuted down saving the precious cargo for another launch.

The final few seconds of the countdown had started and the rockets solid boosters and its first stage ignited. The rocket slowly lifted off the pad and as soon as it passed the top of the tower it started to pick up speed. Malcolm figured Dave would be starting to feel the full affects of the G force. Inside the cargo carrier Dave was pushed against the mats. "Its not as comfy as a launch couch but it will have to do.", Dave thought to himself. He heard the solid rocket boosters fall away while the first stage continued to burn. After a few more minutes he felt weightless for a second as the first stage stopped firing and fell away and then the G force was back as the second stage took over. Soon it dropped away and the third stage took the rocket into low earth orbit. He felt the rocket pivot around and the third stage ignited briefly and the small OMS rockets maneuvered the rocket next to the ISS. He heard someone outside opening up the cargo carrier and he floated out.

"Hi guys!", he grinned and waved.

Down at the Launch Site the second rocket was lifting off. As soon as it was on its way the third rocket would be right behind it. Crews were already readying a new rocket to move to the launch pad.

"Its gonna be a busy day.", said Malcolm to himself.

In Space

Workers were gently moving the anti-missile parts out of the cargo module. As soon as it was unloaded the rocket was pushed out of the way. The OMS and the third stage ignited briefly to send the rocket into the earths atmosphere to be burnt up. The second rocket was already on its way. Dave carefully unwrapped the pieces and started to tell the other astronauts how everything was to be put together. The other astronauts started on their tasks, Dave had supervised taking the rockets apart so they would be fairly easy to put back together again. They were all fully fueled and ready to go once pieced back together. They would not look like rockets because they would have no outer skin. It was not needed in the vacuum of space. Dave took out the last piece. It was the control console which he would use to guide the rocket toward an incoming Chinese rocket if in fact they launched one. The console could configure the rocket to automatically go after anything incoming. It, like the laser cannons used radar for aiming. As soon as it was a close as could be to the other rocket it was designed to explode destroying both rockets.

The second rocket was on its way and he saw it approaching the ISS and watched as it automatically docked with the ISS. A crew opened the cargo carrier and carefully unloaded it. It contained the rest of the parts for the first rocket and some of the parts for the second one. He took a look at Hope floating in space with its space wheel turning. "It looks beautiful.", he thought. He could see people inside the space wheel through the port windows working checking out equipment in preparation for the flight. The second rocket was unloaded and he directed the correct parts over to complete the assembly of the first anti-missile. Soon he could fire up the console to do some tests. The tests were pretty much automatic. A light would flash if something was found wrong. He would also be able to hear an audio sound but not here in the vacuum of space. This crew was good. They had been working in space for quite a while and had everything down pat. After about two hours the first anti-missile was complete and Dave turned on the console. The anti-missile started to respond and he started his first series of tests. The crew was already assembling the second anti-missile and went over to offer help. He had to make some changes in the way it was being put together. He used his helmet communicator to advise them what needed to be done.

Washington

Charles was spending almost all his time in the Presidents office. He was using the phone and was keeping the President updated on the assembly of the anti-missiles.

"Our Chinese friends may be planning another attack on Hope soon.", said the President. She had found out through channels. "I hope those anti-missiles will be ready to go into action if needed soon.", she said.

Charles assured her the first anti-missile was completed and being tested as they spoke and the second one was being assembled. The third rocket was on its way up with the parts for the second missile and a fourth missile was being readied for launch as they spoke which would send the rest of the parts for the second anti-missile. The Special Ops guys were outside in shifts taking turns manning the laser cannon. Another agent was inside the ISS suited up and ready to go out at a moments notice if needed to man the second cannon. That would probably take care of one missile but if China decided to launch two missiles they would likely not be able to stop it. A launch was detected from China and its track was carefully watched. It appeared to be a supply run to the Chinese Space Station. Houston had relayed that information to the ISS who relayed it to Dave.

"They probably did that just to keep us guessing.", thought Dave. Dave went over to the console. All the preliminary tests had passed. He started the second and final series of tests. By experience he knew that if the first tests passed the second tests would likely pass as well. The astronauts in the ISS were giving Houston a blow by blow account of how the process was coming along. Charlotte was ready to nuke

China if they tried anything. She had already made up her mind on that. China would of course retaliate but Americas new anti-missiles should mostly protect them. She was told the theoretical success rate should be at least 90%. That was way better than the alternative. The second missile was almost complete. They just had to wait for the fourth rocket to arrive with the rest of the parts. They got a message from Launch Control the rocket was on its way.

China

The Chinese Premier, Chang was getting more and more frustrated and worried. Hope was days away from leaving earths orbit and he had to decide what to do about and do it very soon. If he destroyed Hope the Americans could destroy the Chinese Space Station but that would be a very small retaliation indeed for destroying Hope. He knew that. Would the Americans risk a nuclear war over it? That was the big question. Both countries would be badly hurt or destroyed completely if that happened and what would the Russian's do? He had to disregard them. They would likely not choose sides and decide to wait and watch as both China and the U.S. destroyed or badly damaged each other. If Russia did choose a side and launch their own missiles at either one of them they would risk being retaliated against as they would be drawn into the war. No, they would just sit and wait, thought Chang. He could not risk a nuclear war but that ship had to be destroyed. The big question was, would the Americans risk a nuclear war over it? The American President was known as a bit of a hothead in global political circles. She was also know not to bluff. If she said if China launched another missile at Hope that America would retaliate. If the missile was destroyed America would yell and scream again and possibly, maybe destroy the Chinese

Space Station in retaliation. They would not go to war over it. But if the spacecraft was destroyed.... that was another matter entirely. One missile was not enough to destroy Hope. The Americans had somehow managed to destroy the missile with some sort of laser canon or something. No one in China knew for certain. All they knew was the missile had been under attack for several minutes and then had blown up.

He picked up his phone and called his Defense Minister. "Po?", "said the Premier when Po picked up the phone.

"Yes Premier." said Po.

"What do you think? Should we attack the spacecraft again with one or two missiles?", asked the Premier.

Po was silent for a moment. "What about American retaliation?", said Po.

"I know, I was thinking the same thing. What do you think the risk would be?", asked the Premier.

"That's what we don't know, isn't it?", sighed Po.

"We have to decide on what to do and do it quickly. The spacecraft is due to leave in two weeks time.", said the Premier. "We could send two missiles up and see if the Americans are willing to risk a nuclear war over it. Other than that I am at a loss at whatever else we can do.", said Po.

The Premier was silent for a moment. He felt like exploding in exasperation. "I'll call back!", said the Premier and hung up.

In Space

The fourth missile arrived at the ISS and the astronaut engineers unloaded it and finished off assembly of the second anti-missile. Dave went ahead and started to test it after it was assembled. One of the astronaut engineers asked how the missiles were going to be launched here in space when they were designed to be a land to air intercept missile. Dave replied that he would be able to do it from his test machine or they could be activated from the ground and that NASA in Houston had been given the equipment necessary to activate the missiles. The equipment had been delivered the same way the anti-missiles had been delivered to the launch site. NASA still had operational sites scattered around the planet with a clear view of any part of space above the planet that could be transmitted to Houston via satellite. The likeliest site that would be keeping an eye on everything was Australia. The Australians also had some of the anti-missiles as well in case of a surprise launch from China to the U.S. or even to them.

"I'd sure like to have a look inside that thing.", said Dave to no one in particular.

"Why don't you ask Houston to look after the fort while we go over to have a look and get out of these suits for a while.", said one of the astronaut engineers.

"Really!! Okay lets go! I'll ask the guys in the ISS to relay a message to Houston and then we can go.", said Dave.

"Its already taken care of.",came a voice in his helmet. "Go have a good time.", said someone from the ISS.

At The Launch Site

Everything should be aboard Hope thought Malcolm but he had asked for two more rockets to be set up and waiting just in case that someone remembered something that had been forgotten or some equipment that had failed a test and they needed a replacement sent up right away. The workers were just finishing off setting those rockets up. It was less than two weeks to the launch of Hope. Malcolm prayed that everything would work as planned. All equipment on board Hope had been triple checked to be sure it was working. The fly by wire control systems had been checked for any problems with communicating with the engines and the attitude and control of the OMS system. The OMS (acronym for Orbital Maneuvering System) system on board Hope were not going to be used for orbital maneuvering primarily but for slight direction changes in space when required.

The acronym had been used for decades on nearly all spacecraft whether orbital or not. As with nearly all spacecraft the OMS system on board Hope was computer controlled to keep the spacecraft attitude level at all times. It would not really matter all that much because the personnel in Navigation in the nose of the ship would not notice if the ship was level or not because they were in a null gravity area of the ship and the people in the space wheel would not notice either because of the artificial gravity produced by the rotating wheel but the OMS was keeping the ship level with respect to the earth. In deep space there would not be any reference to go by. They could be upside down but in relation to what? It didn't matter.

Malcolm's radio went off. "Could you come to Launch Control right away? There is an important phone call for you.", said the Flight Controller.

"On my way.", said Malcolm.

When he got there he went straight to the secure lockup for the only phone at the launch facility that could make or receive calls to the outside world for security reasons. He picked up the phone.

"Malcolm here.", he said.

"Malcolm? Can you come down to Washington right away? We have something important to discuss.", it was President Henderson.

"Can't we discuss it now?", Malcolm said sort of irritated.

"I don't want to discuss this on an open line. Its very important. I can have a jet there to pick you up in about three hours.", said the President.

"Okay.", said Malcolm. "I'll be waiting at the airstrip."

He went and told Murph to hold the fort until he got back that he had to leave 'on business' again. Murph said he would look after things. Murph knew how the site ran as good as Malcolm and had 100% confidence in the man.

About two and half hours later he hitched a ride on one of the trucks going to the airport and saw there was no jet there yet. He waited and looked at the sky for the jet that was coming to pick him up. It must be important if Charlotte wanted to speak to him personally and to send a jet just for him. Soon he started to hear the sound of a jet in the distance and started looking up in the sky. He finally spotted it, just a dot in the sky far away and coming fast. As it got closer he noticed it was a jet fighter, not a jet passenger plane as he expected. The little jet landed and taxied over to the hanger. The canopy opened and the pilot yelled out that he was looking for Malcolm Beacham. Malcolm indicated that was him. The pilot started to shutdown the engines then climbed down from the cockpit.

"Can you have someone fuel me up for our trip back?", he asked.

Malcolm asked, "Our trip? We are going back to Washington in that?", said Malcolm.

"Sure are!", said the pilot grinning. "Have you got any flight suits here?"

Malcolm said he didn't think so. "Its lucky I brought one for you then.", said the pilot. He went back into the cockpit, reached in and grabbed a flight bag, climbed down and handed it to Malcolm. "Here you go.", he said.

"I've never worn one. I've never had to fly in a fighter jet before.", said Malcolm.

"You'll love it!", said the pilot smiling. "Lets go get you suited up."

A fuel truck was coming to top up the fighters tanks. Malcolm and the pilot went to the hanger into a change room and he helped Malcolm get partly undressed and into the flight suit.

"You'll need this as we will be flying quite high and fast. It would be pretty cold without it.", the pilot said.

Malcolm was not too sure about all this. He had never flown in a fighter jet before. Also he did not have his security people with him. He figured he wouldn't need them, he was, after all, going to the White House.

Malcolm and the pilot went out to the fighter jet and the pilot helped Malcolm into the rear seat. "It sure is cramped back here.", thought Malcolm.

The pilot strapped Malcolm in and handed him an oxygen mask and told him how to use it and that he would tell him when he needed it. The pilot gave Malcolm a headset with a microphone that Malcolm put on. The pilot jumped into the front seat and waited for the fuel truck to finish fueling the jet and drive away and the started flicking switches. The powerful engines engines started up and whined loudly and higher pitched as they spun up.

"All set?", said the pilot.

"As set as I'll ever be.", said Malcolm into the microphone.

The pilot gave him the thumbs up sign and started taxing the jet toward the runway. He could hear the pilot and the tower talking through his headset.

"The takeoff is pretty fast but once we are up in the air its smooth as a babies bottom!", said the pilot.

The pilot waited a few seconds for the tower to give him the okay for takeoff and then throttled the engines up. Malcolm was pushed back into his seat as the jet accelerated quickly down the runway. He could feel and hear the wheels rumbling on the asphalt and then all he heard was the engines as the jet leapt off the runway and into its element. They climbed steadily and leveled off.

"We are going up to 30,000 feet so put your oxygen mask on now.", said the pilot.

Malcolm did as he was instructed and turned the air valve on as he has been shown.

"Okay?', asked the pilot.

"Okay", replied Malcolm.

"I'm Major Pat Michaels.", said the pilot.

"Nice to meet you.", said Malcolm in return.

Pat was right. There was no real sensation of speed now they were up at their chosen altitude but he guessed they were going damn fast.

Washington

About two and half hours later Pat informed Malcolm they were about to land. Malcolm had dozed off and woke up at the sound of the pilots voice. He heard the pilot conversing with the tower at Ronald Reagan Washington National Airport. The tower was telling the pilot what altitude to take as they approached the airport and then told him what degree turn to make to land on the appropriate runway and finally to follow the glide path in for a landing. The fighter jet bumped a little on the runway and then slowly rolled to a stop. A staff car was racing across the runway towards the jet. The pilot had climbed out of the cockpit and was helping Malcolm out of the cramped rear seat as the car pulled up along side. There was a driver and two security men in suits in the car. Malcolm climbed down from the fighter using the indicated foot holes and jumped to the ground.

"Did you enjoy the flight?", asked Pat.

"Yes, it was very cozy back there. I must have fallen asleep, I remember the takeoff and us getting up to altitude and you asking me to put on the oxygen mask and then I was looking at the clouds beneath us and then we were here.", said Malcolm.

The pilot chuckled. "Not bad for your first flight.", Pat said.

"I'll be here to take you back. I was told your meeting would be fairly short.", said Pat.

Malcolm nodded and then climbed into the back of the staff car. Soon they pulled up in front of the White House and he was quickly escorted into the President's outer office.

The President's secretary told Malcolm, "Just go ahead in, they are expecting you."

Malcolm thought, "They?", and walked in. The only people there were the President and her Secretary of Defense. Malcolm still had on his flight suit. It was getting warm so he unzipped it a little.

"Sorry for the rush to get you here but you don't have any

secure phones up there so I had to get you down here.", said the President.

Malcolm looked worried. "What's happening?", he asked.

"We have reason to believe our Chinese friends might try something desperate soon to prevent the launch of Hope. Our agents are reporting a lot of activity around the Premier's office and at some of the Chinese missile launch centers.", she said.

"What do you want to tell me that you couldn't tell me on the phone?", asked Malcolm.

"We want to launch Hope earlier than originally planned.", she said.

"But Houston has already given us the best launch date to use the planets slingshot effect.", said Malcolm.

"Yes, I am aware of that. But I have already contacted Houston and asked them to calculate an earlier launch date. Does that present a problem for you?", asked the President.

"How soon?", asked Malcolm. "In one weeks time.", said the President.

Malcolm scratched his cheek. He was unaware he did this when he was stuck for an answer. "I'll have to get back to you on that but it should be okay.

The crew are checking and rechecking everything as we speak and so far few problems have been found. What problems were found were easily fixed. If something goes wrong on the way after launch there is no way to turn back to get it fixed.", said Malcolm.

"Don't they have spare parts?", asked the President.

"Well of course but we want those used in emergency situations only. We don't want them to start using spare parts when they are still in the solar system. That's why everything is being triple checked. We have three teams checking everything. If all three teams say its good to go then I am confident that nothing will go wrong for a long, long time, if ever, for the duration of the voyage.", said Malcolm.

"And how is the check schedule coming along?", asked the President.

"I wish you had asked me that before I left. I could have found out.", said Malcolm.

The President picked up her phone and punched the pad for her secretaries line.

"Get me launch control at Houston and have the call transferred in here please.", she said without waiting for a reply.

Malcolm and the President talked over a few other minor issues when her phone rang.

"Hello.", said the President. "One second please." She handed the phone to Malcolm. He asked the name of the other person and identified himself.

"Can you contact Hope and check to see if anyone knows

how the ship checks are coming along? Where they are at, how much longer they plan to be?", asked Malcolm. He listened for the reply and then told the person to call him back at the President's office as soon as they knew.

Malcolm was getting quite warm now but he couldn't unzip his flight suit much more without embarrassing himself. The President seemed to sense this.

"Can I get you a cool drink, Malcolm?", she asked.

Malcolm replied that would be nice and she buzzed her secretaries line again and asked for a pitcher of ice water and two glasses. In a few minutes an aide knocked and the President told them to come in. The aide placed the tray on the side table and walked out shutting the door behind her. Malcolm went over to the table and filled a glass with ice water and nodded toward the President. She nodded back so Malcolm poured ice water in the other glass and took both glasses back and handed one to the President. She thanked him.

The phone rang and the President picked it up. She listened and then said "One moment.", and handed the phone to Malcolm.

He talked with the person in Houston Launch Control for a minute and then hung up. "Hope says the checks are almost done. They should be all done in two or three days at the latest."

The President said, "That's great! That fits our plans perfectly. We are sure the Chinese know the launch date and may try something in the last week but if we launch early when China is on the other side of the planet, Hope should have built up to breakaway speed and be on her way while China will be on the opposite side of the planet of Hope's breakaway location. I have already discussed this with Houston."

Malcolm said, "The breakaway rockets were built to have enough power for breakaway without putting a lot of stress on the space wheel, the people and equipment inside it. We figure one and a half revolutions may be required to reach breakaway speed, so my engineers have told me."

"Damn!", said the President. "Our spacecraft designs assume breakaway speed in three quarters of a revolution. I was told that by Houston on their secure phone link to my office."

Malcolm replied, "Our design did not take any of this into account. We were hoping to keep the cover story of a space station alive and well until launch time and then just take off leaving everyone with surprise, including the Chinese and even the United States."

The President replied, "Well you didn't take into account the Chinese spy network. They are very good. We know who some of their agents are and keep them under surveillance all the time but there are quite a few we just don't know about. One of them spotted a crate in a warehouse in Baltimore that was from somewhere different and they apparently opened it and probably took pictures of the engine parts inside. Your launch control contacted Electro HydroDynamics to tell them the crate looked tampered with. We took it from there. The spies then made their way to Electro HydroDynamics in Texas where they found the blueprints for the Bussard engine with your name scribbled in the corner of one blueprint. That gave them the link they needed that proved the space station was indeed a ship. Its fortunate for you that we did find out what they had discovered otherwise Hope would be a pile of space rubble right about now and WWIII could be happening. If we hadn't been able to stop that first missile......"

Malcolm looked worried, "We had hoped something like that wouldn't happen. We had hoped the Chinese would buy the story of the space station but someone thought to investigate further."

He thought it might have been Murphy who had called the company as he was one of the few people that had access to the outside phone line.

The President said, "The Chinese were probably wondering why a new space station was being built especially when there was the ISS is still up there and could be restored to operational status in a couple of weeks."

Malcolm said, "Part of the cover story was the new space station had a space wheel incorporated into its design to provide artificial gravity for extended stays."

The President said, "We also surmise the Chinese were also wondering why a bunch of Capitalists were investing in such a huge and expensive project as this when the return on investment was almost zero."

Malcolm had to agree. There were serious flaws with his original cover story. The Chinese would of course wonder about that.

"Okay, I agree with your decision to launch a week early. How are we going to tell about the change of plans to Hope?", asked Malcolm.

The President said, "We don't until the very last minute. Hope will be notified about a launch date change and to expect an upload of the new automatic flight plan to their computers and be prepared to launch at a moments notice. That is why I brought you here to talk to you privately rather than risk a wire tap in the phone network that would tip off the Chinese to the change of plans. I want to catch them with their pants down.", she said.

Malcolm smiled. This woman was no dummy. She thought through every contingency and had a plan for it.

"Okay", said Malcolm. "Lets go ahead with that plan. I won't of course tell anyone at the launch site of our discussion."

The President said, "No! Don't tell a soul up there, no one. That was the next thing I was going to tell you. We suspect there might even be a Chinese spy or two at the launch facility."

That would be a surprise to Malcolm because everyone had been screened very carefully. But it was a spies job to get past screening of that sort with falsified papers so it could have happened. Damn! The President and Malcolm said their goodbyes and Malcolm left to be driven back to the airport. The flight back was uneventful but now Malcolm was worried. He had to be careful with any communication with Hope. He had to have Hope ready to launch in a weeks time but he had to be sure it was ready. He would tell the people on Hope to be sure the checks were done in plenty of time so they could play around with the new systems and equipment to get ready for the new launch date on the 14th. He would not mention to a soul about the launch date change. No one.

At The Launch Center

Malcolm got a drive back to the launch site with a truck going in with supplies for the town.

"A town that will not be needed in a week.", thought Malcolm. He went straight to the Launch Center and walked in and asked the Flight Director how things were with Hope. The Flight Director assured Malcolm that everything was fine. The triple checks were almost finished and except for a few minor problems that were easy to fix, nothing serious was found. Malcolm told the Flight Director to let him know when all checks were complete and if Hope needed anything else shipped up. The Flight Director told Malcolm that some requested items were in a cargo bay already.

Malcolm thought," I must think of an excuse to send the cargo up before the week is up."

He asked the Flight Director to call Hope and ask them if anything else would be required other than what had already been requested. Hope replied that likely nothing else would be required and Malcolm ordered the missile to be launched.

Hope - A Space Novel - Chapter Three

Launch Day – Nov. 14th 2026

Malcolm woke early in the morning. Actually he had hardly slept at all the night before. He went to the Launch Center and spoke to the Flight Director. He was assured everything was okay.

"Wait until 10AM", thought Malcolm. That was the time that Houston was supposed to start uploading the new flight information to Hope's Navigation computers.

He was sure that the Nav crew aboard Hope were going to be calling down to Launch Control to confirm the new launch time for Hope. He was going to have to tell the Flight Director at that time the change was indeed legitimate and quickly tell the Flight Director the reason for the change in plans and to let it happen and to assure Hope the reason for the change in plans and to get everyone on board ready for takeoff. Malcolm glanced at his watch, it was 9:15AM. The last shipment of requested parts had been sent up the day before. The cargo carrier had been no where near full. I am sure someone would be wondering why it was sent up when they still had a week to go. Malcolm was hoping that nothing else was required.

A light on the Flight Director's board lit up signaling that a call was coming in on the only phone to the outside world. He went over and unlocked the safe and answered. "Its for you Malcolm", he said.

Malcolm took the phone. The voice at the other end said, "Is the bird ready to fly?" Malcolm knew what that meant. He replied, "Yes, as ready as it can be." The voice said, "Okay" and hung up.

Malcolm decided to tell the Flight Director ahead of time about the change of plans. He quickly recounted the meeting in the Presidents office and the plans to launch Hope a week early and to try and catch the Chinese off-guard so the chances of them doing anything would be minimized.

He knew the Chinese would have missiles aimed at Hope just waiting for the Premier's word to launch. He was hoping that the ship would be well on its way before the communications got to the Premier and back to Chinese Missile Control to be of any effective use. Malcolm checked his watch. It was 9:35AM. Time to contact Hope and tell them of the change in plans and to expect new launch data from Houston. He spoke directly to the duty Captain on Hope. There was someone in Nav Control in the nose of Hope all the time. Not that they would be needed as Hope would be launched by command from Houston. Malcolm just hoped the break orbit rocket would work. He had been assured it would as it had passed all tests short of an actual firing.

The artificial gravity in the wheel was going to be affected. He hoped the Captain had got the applicable information to the space wheel so the people there could secure any lose material for the change in gravity. It was expected the artificial gravity would change from the outer ring of the wheel to its back side as it became the "floor" as soon as the escape rocket fired. The time was now 9:45AM. Houston should have almost finished uploading the new commands to Hope's computers. The two anti-missiles were in orbit and ready to be fired on any incoming missiles from China. It was assumed that China would use two missiles this time as one missile was destroyed in an earlier attempt. The Special Forces guys were outside as well with the laser cannons at the ready just in case. The Russians had assured the U.S. that it would send up a craft to rescue the men from the International Space Station if necessary if they could not all fit into the Soyuz emergency craft. The time was now 9:55AM. Almost time. Malcolm was starting to sweat as his mind raced to think of anything that had been overlooked but he could think of nothing. The countdown was starting to proceed. Hopefully the Chinese were still unaware of the change in launch date. The computers on Hope were on automatic and had taken control of the launch.

The final countdown was almost complete. 10-9-8-7-6-5-4-3 main engine start. The engine was working the Flight Director assured Malcolm. The Flight Controllers were not informed and started to panic as they realized that the Hope's engines had started. The Flight Director quickly assured everyone of the change in plans and just to monitor the spacecraft. The breakaway engine thrust had been carefully controlled so as not to put too much stress on the space wheel. Hope was moving and accelerating slowly as planned. So far everything was okay. American spy satellites were carefully monitoring missile launches from China. None had been detected so far but he could only imagine the panic that was happening as frantic calls were made to the Premier.

China

The Premier's phone rang, he picked it up. His secretary said in a stressed voice the Missile Command Center was on line one and that Hope was leaving orbit.

The Premier was stunned. The launch was not scheduled for another week! "Are you sure?", he asked. "I'll put them on line now.", she said.

A frantic voice on the other end was almost unintelligible with confusion and shock and was trying to tell the Premier that Hope was leaving orbit. The Premier knew it was now or never. He had to make the decision now that he had been contemplating for over two weeks. He knew if he destroyed Hope the Americans would at the very least destroy the Chinese Space Station but he feared much worse. He ordered the immediate highest defense posture and told the frantic man on the other end to launch the missiles at Hope. He felt he had no choice. The phone was hung up with a quick, 'Yes Premier!", from the other end.

The Premier slumped into his seat. He picked up the phone again and called the Missile Command Center. When the phone was answered he said, "Premier Chang here. Launch a preemptive attack against the United States. Everything we have."

There was a stunned silence on the other end of the line and then a, "Yes, Premier!" and the phone was hung up. Well he had done it now thought the Premier. He had to take a chance that more damage would be done by a preemptive strike rather than waiting for the U.S. to strike first.

Washington

DEFCON had been at 3 for quite a while but now was raised

to 1. All subs were at launch depth and had been for some time. All land based nuclear missiles had their launch codes input and were simply waiting for the button to be pushed. Cheyenne Mountain was on full alert as were all anti-missile sites in and around the U.S. The U.S. President and her staff had already been moved out of the White House and were situated in a secure bunker miles away from Washington at a closely guarded location. It was assured that Washington was one of the cities that would be targeted by anyone including the Chinese with a nuclear strike. They would also try and take out Cheyenne Mountain but there were back up sites in case of that eventuality. Cheyenne Mountain saw by satellite reconnaissance that missile launches had been detected from China headed to the Hope spacecraft. It was hoped the spacecraft would be out of range of these missiles given that Hope had a good head start. But was it enough?

Washington had been in contact with Iran and North Korea. They were told in no uncertain terms not to get involved. If any missiles were detected being launched from either country the United States would consider that as an act of war and would act accordingly. President Henderson was especially worried about Iran as they had threatened previously to "wipe Israel off the map" and may take this situation as an ideal chance to do exactly that and assume the U.S. would have their hands full with their own defense and attack. But she was not bluffing. She was prepared to authorize a nuclear strike against Iran in case of that eventuality. The North Koreans would of course try a strike against South Korea and maybe even Japan but they too had been promised swift retaliation in either event.

The space based anti-missiles were under control of Houston and the incoming Chinese missiles were being closely tracked. President Henderson wondered whether to wait to see if the space based anti-missiles were going to succeed in their task or should she launch a preemptive attack against China? She pondered that decision. What was her response to be?

China

The Chinese Missile Command Center was alive with activity as controllers carried out their tasks in launching preemptive strikes against the U.S. as ordered by the Premier. The Chinese missiles were launched and were headed on their way. WWIII was effectively over. Once the missiles were launched the fate of each side was already decided.

The duty General from Cheyenne Mountain called again and told the President there were inbound missiles coming from China toward the U.S. Did she want to just defend with anti-missiles only or did she want a retaliatory strike as well against China?

She thought about it for a moment. She told the General to order the retaliatory strike. "Well now its done.", she thought. "WWIII is started."

She hoped that only the U.S. and China would get involved. Russia had given assurances they would not choose sides and not get involved unless directly attacked. That would be all she would need if the Russians decided at the last minute to back China but she doubted that would happen as the Russians had more love for the U.S. than for China and they knew that if attacked, the U.S. would retaliate guaranteeing major damage to both countries. Russia and the U.S. had been slowly lowering their missile stockpiles but the U.S. still had a formidable nuclear missile system arsenal.

Somewhere Under The South China Sea

The Ohio class sub the USS Georgia had returned and was on station at missile launch depth when the message to launch was received. The order was verified by the Captain and the COB. The well trained crew had been expecting something like this and were preparing the Georgia's missiles for launch. Everyone knew the seriousness of what they were about to do. They were about to join WWIII. The Captain was advised all missiles were ready to launch. The missiles had already been programmed days before.

The Captain hesitated for only a moment and then said quietly, "Launch!" The sub shook a little as each missile was thrust from its silo by compressed air and burst into the open air above the water where they were designed to ignite and fly swiftly to their targets. It was thought the Chinese had no anti-missile defenses. He almost felt sorry for them. All missiles were programmed to destroy all military installations and known missile launch locations to minimize the civilian casualties but he knew those would be high none the less.

Cheyenne Mountain

Nuclear missile launches had been ordered by the President. The duty operators were well trained and went ahead with their tasks relaying commands to the missile sites to launch. Each missile had been programmed with the destination to destroy key points in China. In a moment the missiles were on their way. Farmers in the Midwest looked up and saw the missile silos open and the missiles being launched from their silos. Never in all their time since they were installed had they thought they would ever be used but there they were, on their way. The newspapers had been full of news about the new spacecraft orbiting earth, the aborted attempt by the Chinese to destroy it and the President's warning to the Chinese that if it was tried again the consequences would be dire.

On Hope

Houston had already informed Hope of the incoming missiles from China headed their way. Houston was ready to send the two anti-missiles in space to hopefully destroy them before reaching Hope. Operators in Houston were carefully watching the two Chinese missiles waiting for the opportune time to launch. It was hoped they were both operational. Both had been tested and passed but it was not 100% certain they would work. The people in the space wheel had been told what to expect as their center of gravity would likely change and it did. There was a combination of the spacecraft acceleration and the spinning wheel giving the center of gravity somewhere between the outer edge of the wheel and the "side" of their usual world. The two space based anti-missiles worked and had been launched by Houston and were targeted at the incoming Chinese missiles. The two sets of missiles were closing fast. At about 100 miles from Hope the anti-missiles exploded. One Chinese missile was destroyed but the other was damaged but still functional and was closing fast. The Special Ops guys in space were on station with their laser cannons just in case. They were notified by Houston the anti-missiles had only destroyed one Chinese missile, the other was still coming their way. Two of the Special Ops guys used the radar guided laser cannons to begin firing on the incoming missile. Direct hits were being registered but it seemed as though they were having little affect. The missile was only 50 miles away and coming fast!! At 25 miles distance the Chinese missile blew up in a fiery fireball. A stream of debris was still headed their way.

The crew in the space wheel could see the explosions in the distance well behind the craft. Hope was picking up speed and soon reached breakaway velocity at about the time predicted by the Houston computers. Malcolm was unable to give Houston the mass of the spacecraft accurately but he was able to give them the type of engine being used to propel Hope out of orbit. Houston was able to guess the mass of Hope and came close to figuring out the breakaway point. Hope was on its way to Mars to perform the first slingshot maneuver to speed the spacecraft up on its way out of the solar system. The escape engine kept firing to propel Hope to 36,000 miles per hour in relation to earth. This would bring them to Mars in about 235 days where they would be pulled toward the planet faster and faster by its gravity and then slingshot around the planet at a fairly low altitude but high enough to stay out of Mar's upper atmosphere. They did not of course aim directly at Mars but aimed at a point in space where it would be in about 235 days. As the spacecraft was leaving earth orbit they could clearly see nuclear missiles detonating in China and the Chinese nuclear missiles being destroyed over the oceans before reaching the continental United States.

The stream of debris from the destroyed Chinese missile was all around them. One piece hit one of the Special Ops guys and he was disintegrated immediately. One of the pieces hit the ISS and damaged one of the modules causing the death of three construction astronauts in that area. Doors between all sections had been closed as a precaution otherwise everyone could have been killed. The remaining crew had no way home except for the Soyuz spacecraft docked at the ISS in case of an emergency but there may not room for them all. Now that one Special Ops guy and three construction astronauts had been killed that increased their chances of being able to use the escape craft to get back to earth. They had to hope the Russians would fulfill their promise of sending a rescue craft to get the rest if necessary.

Cheyenne Mountain

The controllers at Cheyenne Mountain were closely watching the incoming Chinese missiles. The anti-missiles were poised and ready to strike. They could be individually programmed to go after a particular missile or could be launched and the internal radar aboard each missile could seek out and destroy any incoming missile. The controllers decided to target most individual incoming missiles with a particular anti-missile rather than risking the chance of two anti-missiles going after the same incoming missile and missing a second one in close proximity. Missiles were headed for Washington, Chicago, Philadelphia, Houston, Boston, Omaha, Manhattan Island, Colorado Springs, Minot (North Dakota), Pittsburgh, Los Angeles, just to name a few. All these locations were known areas of financial, industrial and military targets by the Chinese, some of the areas were known from the Cold War era with the then Soviet Union decades before. The controllers were timing the anti-missile defenses to intercept incoming Chinese missiles over the oceans to minimize the effect of debris and nuclear hazards from broken nuclear warheads hitting the ground. Popular opinion thinks that blowing up a nuclear bomb will detonate it but it will not. It takes a detonation triggered around the nuclear material of just the right timing to cause a nuclear reaction. Blowing it up would not cause a nuclear detonation.

Nuclear missile strikes against China were aimed at primarily military targets such as Luoning where a large concentration of hardened missile silos were known to exist. These sites would be hit with deep penetrating nuclear strikes to ensure maximum damage to the hardened silos to prevent a possible second wave attack. One incoming missile was missed by the anti-missile defense system and was heading straight for Kansas. Another anti-missile was quickly launched in hopes of intercepting it before it reached the state but it was too late. The Chinese nuclear bomb detonated on ground impact for maximum damage to the missile silos located there. The news was relayed to President Henderson by the General at Cheyenne Mountain. It could have been far worse. The Chinese had been contacted and threatened with a second wave of missiles if they did not immediately and unconditionally surrender. An answer was quickly received, they would surrender. Most of China's military strike capability had been destroyed. Great damage had been done to industrial areas. There were heavy civilian casualties but as much care as could be was taken to minimize that impact. There would be a lot more casualties over the next few days and weeks from nuclear exposure and fallout.

On Hope

Hope was continually updated on the nuclear strikes by Houston. Some people on board Hope had family and friends in Kansas and openly wept on hearing the news. The engine on Hope was shutdown as it had reached the calculated speed for the mission. All they had to do was wait until they neared Mars and hoped that Houston was still around to assist with the navigation around the planet or the navigators aboard Hope would have to make course changes manually if any were required. The entire flight path through the solar system was programmed into Hope's guidance computers so if everything was done properly there should be no intervention required by the crew. But the option was if Houston was destroyed or otherwise unable to transmit the possible necessary minor course corrections they could be done aboard Hope if necessary.

The crew aboard Hope checked all systems and the mechanical integrity of the ship, especially the space wheel. Everything checked out. Hope had survived the breakaway from earths orbit and the acceleration needed to get to Mars. The fuel for the rocket was checked and found to be enough for the braking needed when reaching the Alpha Centauri star system. There were three navigation crew on rotation in the navigation area in the nose of the ship. There were sleeping areas for those crew not on duty. There was no gravity in the nose like there was on the space wheel.

Whenever the crew was in their seats they had to strap in to avoid floating about freely. They were kept busy with constant communication with the space wheel and Houston. It was also part of their job to check cargo in the hold of the ship and the hydroponic garden. The garden had been designed to be self-maintaining in a closed environment. Very little intervention was required. Houston informed them the war was essentially over on earth. The United States had survived the Chinese attack except for some destruction in Kansas, mostly just west of Ness City, a largely unpopulated area but where there was a large concentration of missile silos.

Washington

The President was continually updated on the situation. She was proud of the performance of the military. Everyone had performed their jobs as they were supposed to with no hesitation. It was the opinion of the military that the President stay in the bunker for at least the next 48 hours until it was considered safe to return to the White House. She considered going back right away but she decided to do as suggested and stay put just in case and asked to be continually updated. After a couple of days in the bunker and no retaliation from the Chinese or anyone else was expected she was informed it was safe to go back to the White House.

She ordered China to disarm totally and to expect the arrival of U.S. troops and aid starting within the next few days. She received word through channels this would be done. China had no other choice. America would help China rebuild but not at the expense of the American economy. Since the decision to proclaim martial law, this gave the U.S. President unparalleled powers such as canceling all elections and jumping hoops over many civil liberties until order was restored. This including those enjoyed by corporate big wigs who had made billions at the expense of closing down manufacturing plants and laying off millions of workers over the last 60 years. It was going to be a whole new world.

An immediate tariff tax was placed on all products enroute to the United States from the off shore manufacturers. Corporations were ordered to start tooling up to produce products in U.S. plants. Those Chinese plants that had survived the American nuclear attack would have their production supply chains moved to the U.S. This was going to take time and the average American was just going to have to wait until production was phased out overseas and moved back to America. It would be turmoil in the short term but eventually it would work out in the end. It was not going to be painless.

Now that she had the troops at her disposal her first task was to take over the commune farms that had been selling food at ridiculously high prices and start moving food into the cities to feed the population. City gangs would be broken up. It would be almost civil war taking the cities back by force if necessary but it would be done. Many gangsters would die and some of them would be ordinary citizens recruited by the gangs. They would of course be given the opportunity to disarm and give up but if they didn't the troops were ordered to move in and take back the cities by whatever forceful means were necessary.

At the Launch Facilities

Malcolm's job was done. He had been in Launch Control the whole time until Hope was on its way and out of danger. Now his job was to dismantle the whole operation. He asked Murphy to get everyone in the town site together in front of the launch pads in two hours time. During that time he managed to get a temporary stage set up and a small amplifier, speakers and a microphone for himself. After two hours he went up on the stage. Everyone from the town was assembled to hear what he had to say. There were rumors flying especially in the last few days. Now he was going to tell everyone the truth as to what the project was all about. As he stepped up on the stage, which was a temporary stack of shipping crates, there was a smattering of applause.

Malcolm waved to acknowledge this unexpected response. He didn't have a speech prepared on paper but he knew what he wanted to say:

"Thanks everyone for coming. You have all done a great job and the project is now complete. You are to be congratulated. Give yourselves a hand."

Malcolm waited until the applause quietened down and then continued. "As I said the project is complete but for many others it is just beginning. You have been told that we were building a privately funded space station. That is not entirely the whole story."

The crowd started buzzing and Malcolm waited until everyone was quiet again. "What was being built was not a space station but a spacecraft."

Again the crowd started stirring and Malcolm called for quiet. "The spacecraft is called Hope and was built to travel to our nearest star which is commonly known as Alpha Centauri or precisely Alpha Centauri-A around which has been detected a planet that it is hoped will support human life. The spacecraft is a generation ship because it will take more than 200 years to get there. It will not be the original crew that will arrive at the destination of course but their distant descendants."

The crowd really started to buzz now as people started to make comments to one another. Malcolm had to call for quiet again before continuing. "It was thought things were getting so bad here on earth that myself and people like me thought the human race was in serious trouble and may not survive so a plan was hatched to build the ship and send it to

Alpha Centauri-A in the hopes of finding the planet and starting human civilization again. That hope still remains.

Our job here is done and theirs is just beginning. As we speak the spacecraft is on its way to Mars and the outer planets to use their gravity as a slingshot to speed up the spacecraft to enable it to leave the solar system. This step alone will take several years. Once the ship has made it out of our solar system an experimental engine called a Bussard Ramjet will be used to hopefully accelerate the craft to 2% of light speed. Without doing that the trip would take many centuries more so it is hoped the engine will operate as predicted.

As you may have heard or not there has been a nuclear war here on earth." Again the crowd was really talking now and getting louder. Malcolm had to call for quiet a few times before continuing. "The nuclear exchange was between the United States and China. Fortunately the United States had anti-missiles which did an excellent job of protecting us but unfortunately Kansas was hit near Ness City but it was in a remote area and casualties are assumed to be light."

Some people broke down in tears as they probably had friends or family there. There was a lot more talk in the crowd.

Malcolm let this sink in for a couple of minutes and called for quiet again. "Kansas was the only place in the United States or in all of North America to be hit. We were lucky.

China was not so lucky. They have been hit hard and most of their known military camps and missile capability as well as their manufacturing capability has been mostly destroyed.

Because of China's dense population civilian and military losses are expected to be extremely high. The United States is the main reason the spacecraft survived at all to be launched from earth orbit. The Chinese spy agency found out the truth about it and promised to shoot it down. They thought the United States knew about the truth of the project all the time but was hiding it.

The Chinese were upset because they thought the United States was going to get the jump on them in colonizing the galaxy. Even after many assurances they refused to believe otherwise. One attempt was made to destroy the spacecraft as it was being built in orbit but with help from the United States that attempt was thwarted. They were threatened with dire reaction if another attempt was made. A launch date was determined and it was also thought the Chinese had found out about that too so the craft was launched a week earlier than planned under utmost secrecy. The Chinese fired on the spacecraft again and again their attempt was thwarted but they also tried a preemptive nuclear attack on the United States at the same time. American military defense launched a retaliation attack which hit China hard as I explained and they were told to surrender immediately and unconditionally or risk a follow up attack. They have surrendered so WWIII is already over."

The crowd was really talking now. No one knew of the events of the nuclear exchange. Malcolm waited again for the crowd to settle down before continuing. "This project owes the United States a lot for the protection they have given us. The truth about the project was not given to them, they found it out from the Chinese spy network who found the truth first. Once the United States found out I was called down to Washington to meet with the President and tell her what the real project was all about. Once the truth came out the President said the United States would do whatever they could to protect the ship and they did."

"Now this camp is no longer needed. Everyone will get the bonus as promised in your contracts and transportation back to wherever you want to go. Some of you may have had homes or friends and family in Ness City. For that I am truly sorry. Please let the exit people you will be seeing know if there is somewhere else you want to go. Everyone will receive further instructions as to where to go and who to see in the coming days. As of now all security is taken down. The internet is freely available and open and the camp gates are now open so if anyone wishes to go into Moosonee for a change of scenery they can. You can now make phone calls to the outside world but please don't all go running off and try to make calls all at once. If you do that you will likely crash the phone system here at the camp. Use email if you can and make your calls brief when you do make them at least for the next day or so. There will be no charge for phone calls. There will be shuttle buses running between the camp and Moosonee. The buses will start immediately and will be available between 10 AM and 2 AM everyday with runs every hour on the hour. That's all I have to tell you. There is little else I can tell you because everything you have just heard is the complete truth. If anyone wants any other information they can talk to me at the side of the stage. I'll be there for a few minutes." A few people did want to talk to Malcolm and he did his best to answer any and all questions.

Someone from Launch Control came over and told gave Malcolm a note. It was from Charlotte. She wanted him to call her "as soon as it was convenient". Malcolm smiled. When the U.S. President said that it really meant to call her now. Malcolm headed off for Launch Control. A few controllers were still at their consoles communicating with Houston. Why he did not know. Houston had complete control of the spacecraft project now. Malcolm picked up a phone and dialed the number he had been given. It was the White House switch board. He identified himself and gave the code word in the message to prove it was really him. He was put on hold for a moment.

The next voice he heard was that of the U.S. President Charlotte Henderson. "How are you doing Malcolm?", she asked.

He replied, "I am just winding down activities here at the launch site. I just told everyone about the project and about the events of the last few days."

The President asked, "And how was the news received by everyone?"

Malcolm replied, "Very well all in all. A few people were upset that Kansas had got hit because they probably had friends and or family there but everyone realized that it could have been much, much worse."

The President said, "You got that right. We got lucky. Fortunately we still have a good military and everyone did their job perfectly. Without them you and I would not be having this pleasant conversation."

Malcolm said, "Yes, that's very true. What is the reason for your call?"

The President said, "I need YOUR help this time Malcolm."

Malcolm was thinking "She needs my help? For what?" Malcolm replied, "What kind of help do you need?"

The President said, "I'll need you here in Washington. I have a huge task ahead of me to rebuild America's manufacturing and I need you to talk to the heads of many corporations and get them on side with our plans. It won't be an easy job. I want to start bringing back manufacturing to America. I know I am going to get a lot of resistance from a lot of companies currently manufacturing off shore especially in China. I don't want them running off to another country. I want them back here in America."

Malcolm said, "I don't think I am the right person for the job, I....."

Charlotte cut him off. She said, "You're the perfect one for the job. If you could talk those people into giving you billions for your project you can convince them that bringing manufacturing back to America is the right thing to do in the long run."

Malcolm started to try and object again and again Charlotte cut him off. She said, "You owe me Malcolm. I want you, I need you for this job."

Malcolm was silent for a moment. She was right. Hope would be a pile of scrap metal floating in space right now if it wasn't for her help. "Okay, you got me. What do you want me to do?", he asked.

The President asked Malcolm to get down to Washington as soon as he could so she could give him an overview of what she needed done. She promised him his own office with all the staff he needed to get the job done.

Malcolm said, "I'll be down as soon as I wrap things up here."

The President said, "No! Leave that to someone else. I am sure you have everything in place. All you need is for someone to take care of it for you. I need you here, Malcolm."

Malcolm said, "Okay, let me assign someone to act in my stead to take care of things and I will be down there as soon as I can."

Charlotte said, "Do you need transport to get here?"

Malcolm said, "No, I can arrange something from here."

The President said, "Okay, I'll see you soon." And hung up.

"Typical Charlotte.", thought Malcolm.

She was right of course, if it wasn't for her and the U.S. the project would never have succeeded. Spacecraft Hope would be scrap metal in orbit right now. He did owe her something in return. What she was asking seemed huge. But as with any large project you broke it up into sections and stages and tasks and then assigned people to them. The more he thought about it the more he thought he could do it. The man he had in mind to take over closing down the town site was Murph. The big man had built this town and the launch pads and got it done on time. He had also taken care of the security at the camp later on. He was sure Murph could handle the job. He got back to his office and called Murph to come see him.

When Murph arrived he asked the big man to have a seat. He needed a shave and his hair was a little long but Malcolm had realized a long time ago that under that rough exterior was a smart man who could get things done.

Malcolm opened his computer and showed Murph what needed to be done to shut down the camp and send everyone on their way. Malcolm had planned for this in detail some time ago as the end part of the project. It was quite detailed and needed a little time to fill in some holes with Murph.

Murph said, "You don't worry about a thing Malcolm. I'll get 'er done."

Malcolm smiled. He knew the big man would. He had every confidence in him. "I'll be sure you get an extra bonus for taking this on for me.", said Malcolm. Murph just grinned back

In Washington

Malcolm arranged transport to Washington. There were flights leaving the Moosonee airport all the time. He caught the first available flight down to southern Ontario and made connection flights that eventually ended up at the Ronald Reagan Washington National Airport. He called the White House switchboard and identified himself and was soon put through to the President. She told him to stay where he was and she would send a car for him. When the car arrived he got in the back seat and was driven to the White House. When he arrived he identified himself again and was ushered to the Presidents outer office where he waited a short time until her secretary indicated that he could go into the Oval Office.

The President met him as he came in the door and extended her hand. "Thanks for coming Malcolm. I am glad you decided to accept this project." Malcolm felt he had little choice. "I have a small building that is currently sitting idle and I would like you take it over. It is mostly still furnished and technicians are over there as we speak to make sure the communications infrastructure is working. Go over there and make sure that everything you think you will need is there. You don't have a staff yet, that will be your first priority. I have arranged for a stack of resumes to be sent over for you to choose the employees that are best suited for the job. You will have to build the organization from the ground up." Malcolm liked that idea. He liked to choose his own staff.

Charlotte continued, "Get over there and the techs will show you your office. Make sure that is has all the furnishings and equipment you will need, then you can start going through the resumes to pick the starting people for your staff. I have given you carte blanche for this project. If there are any roadblocks you need cleared just call me and I will try my best to help. I have also reserved a suite in a good hotel nearby until you can get some accommodations for yourself. I think you will be here for quite a while.", said the President.

Malcolm had to agree, this project was going to take quite a while, maybe several years to fully implement.

"I have a car and a driver at your disposal. It should be waiting out front for you. The driver should have a cell phone for you so you can call him whenever you need to get somewhere quickly.", said Charlotte.

Malcolm asked if it was okay to check into his suite first to freshen up and rest a bit before going over to his new office location. The President said that was fine but she hoped he would be able to start going over resumes today to start choosing his staff. Malcolm assured her he should have some time in the afternoon to start that process. The President wished him the best of luck and to keep her updated. Malcolm said he would and that ended the meeting. He went out to the waiting car and asked the driver to take him to his suite.

Later on that afternoon after he had a chance to freshen up and get a little rest he called for the driver again and was met at the front of the hotel and asked to be taken to his building. Once he arrived he took the elevator to the top floor as he was instructed and was shown by the techs where his office was. It was quite large and well appointed with the latest in communications and computer equipment. On the desk was a note that directed him on log on procedures to access the resumes he needed. He went through them all quickly and picked an "A" list of possible candidates. His first priority was to get a good office manager who could take charge and run the office.

He read the resume of Samantha Jackson and liked what he saw. She had the education and experience he needed. He called the contact numbers listed in the resume but was told that she had been laid off from her last job two years ago due to downsizing. He called the contact number of her residence and was told the phone was out of service. He tried the cell phone and got the same result. He made a quick call to Charlotte and asked if he could call someone to find a person who he had in mind that he could not reach. She gave him a name and number of a person to call. It was someone in the FBI. He gave the person all the details that he had and then hung up the phone and went through the rest of the resumes picking a few that he thought would make good office staff and a administrator for his Office Manager. The phone rang after a couple of hours. It was the man from the FBI. He told Malcolm he had located Samantha. She was currently living in a downtown shelter. Malcolm asked that he arrange a drive for her over to his building. He wanted to personally interview this woman.

After about 40 minutes the FBI man came into his office accompanied by a tall, slim, attractive black woman he assumed was Samantha. She looked to be in her mid 30's. She had short curly black hair that he could see she had teased quickly for the interview.

"Please have a seat.", he said to Samantha and offered her a coffee which she gratefully accepted.

She had the look of someone who was downtrodden and in despair and who had given up hope. He could understand that with the economic state of America. He told Samantha the type of person he was looking for and would she be willing to work on his staff? Her whole attitude changed in an instant. She was bright and vibrant and suggested some ideas of how she would like to run the office.

After a while he told Samantha, "We have some business to take care of first. I want to get you out of the shelter and into some housing. Give it some thought where you want to live and what furniture you will need and a car to get back and forth." He asked her if she had any other family. She told Malcolm that she had two boys, 12 and 14, living in the shelter with her but did not mention a husband. When asked she told Malcolm her husband took off three years ago and she had not seen or heard from him since. Malcolm told her to hire a live-in helper to look after the house and the kids, to prepare meals and so forth as this job was going to consume a lot of her time and he did not want to have her worry or take time to do domestic chores at the house. She wondered where all this money was going to come from as she had none.

Malcolm assured her that everything would be taken care of. He asked her to contact a real estate company in Washington to help her choose a house and a domestic agency for the live-in help. She told Malcolm that she had a friend in the shelter that she trusted 100% with her kids and had known for the past two years and would it be okay if she filled the job. Malcolm told her as long as she passed a background check that it should be okay.

Malcolm handed her a credit card. It was a gold American Express card that she could use to pay for everything she needed and not to worry about what she ran up on the card. He asked her how much time she would need to get everything in place. She told Malcolm she would need at least a couple of days maybe three. He told her to get going and that there was a car and driver waiting downstairs for her to use at her disposal. He handed her a cell phone with a wall and vehicle charger and gave her his cell number that he wrote down on a piece of paper and told her to call if she needed any help.

She almost bounced as she left the office. Malcolm smiled to himself. It was amazing what a little hope could do to change someones attitude in an instant. He called Charlotte and told her of the developments and that he too would need to look for a place to live and would be unavailable for a few days while he got all that settled.

In Washington – The White House

The first order of the day was to put an immediate freeze on all home repossessions. Food banks would have to be set up and quickly. People had to eat. Emergency supplies were to be moved from warehouses to the food banks and from the farms. The President spent most of her time delegating these tasks. She expected and got some resistance but she told any detractors to "just get it done" and that was that. The lights in the Oval Office burned long into the night almost every day as the flurry of orders went out. Her staff was getting worried about Charlotte's health and the possibility of burn out but Charlotte had a known history of being able to take on huge amounts of work over long hours without it phasing her. Everyone in her office staff co-operated with her and worked hard to be sure that what she wanted to get done was done.

The biggest resistance was of course the multi-billion dollar corporations. She threatened to have the government take over their operations unless the changes she wanted were made. A few resisted and called her bluff until a line up of military trucks pulled up with staff cars full of "suits" ready to take over operations.

Ships were diverted to China to assist with treating the population exposed to radiation and repairing the infrastructure. The same had been done when America had defeated Japan and assisted in defeating Germany almost a century ago. Corporations were directed to have teams go to China and organize the movement of industries producing their goods from China back to the United States. This was no simple task as many companies were involved in the making of parts that made up the finished product. All the parts necessary were shipped in from suppliers all over China to a central plant where the final product would be assembled and shipped back to America and the rest of the world.

Creating new factories in America to make all these parts needed was going to take time but let it take time. It had taken decades to dismantle the manufacturing base of the American economy and it would take time to reverse it. Hopefully not decades but only a few years in most cases. Plants that were still in operation off shore were allowed to continue in operation until the phase over was complete but they were told in no uncertain terms that expansion was not an option and that reduced capacity was to be expected. Some parts would continue to be made "off shore" but certainly not the entire product as was being done now. Wages would have to be established for American manufacturing plants and the unions would have to be told not to interfere and would be strictly regulated and not allowed to hold companies at ransom over pay increases for workers to justify their own existence. Charlotte knew that unions had made many important changes in the salaries and working conditions for the workers many years ago but most of that was now tightly controlled by government regulations but it had been too little too late as most manufacturing in America had already been moved off shore by the time they were introduced.

Now that Hope was safely on its way President Henderson could concentrate on reviving the U.S. economy. She had been mulling over a plan the last few weeks and now with the destruction of China's industrial might it made her plan that much easier to implement. She intended to bring back manufacturing to America. It could not be done overnight of course but within 5 years a lot of it should be "on shore" again. Corporate America was going to be in for a shock. No more or very little off shore manufacturing. That should never have been allowed to happen. The average American worker was going to be on side with the plan she was sure. There should be lots of jobs for anyone that wanted to work. The biggest criers were of course going to be the upper echelons of the multi-billion dollar corporations whose job it was to make sure their products were made the cheapest way possible. Well guess what guys? Those days are over. Get ready to make your products here in the good ol' U.S. of A.

Charlotte had been informed that Chicago was almost liberated from the gangs that had controlled most areas of the city. There were still a few hold outs but they were being mopped up quickly. There had been significant loss of life, mostly on the gang side but that had been expected. Order was slowly being restored and people were once again walking the streets without fear as police patrols were again keeping order. Martial law was still in affect and would be for some time to help protect the citizenry and keep order. Other cities were reporting similar success as gangs were defeated, dismantled and protection handed back to the local police assisted by local garrisons of military forces in case of gangs attempting a come back. Gang members of former law-abiding citizens recruited by criminal elements were allowed to go home without penalty on strict conditions they were to sever all relations with their former gang bosses.

Jobs were created repairing the infrastructure in the cities from all the damage caused by taking back control. Wages were low but most people understood the situation and were just glad to be working and doing something useful again.

Houses that had been repossessed earlier were being offered back to their former owners at manageable payments. It was almost like the restructuring of America after the stock market crash of 1929.

Base industries had to be restarted and the manufacturing plants above them in the supply chain of manufacturing had to be slowly started again. Back then it took over a decade to accomplish but Charlotte did not want to wait that long and neither did anyone else. This had to be done quickly to keep up the moral of the people. Charlotte's martial law proclamation was protecting her position and allowing her to get done what she knew had to be done. There was of course opposition to her course of action but mostly from self-serving politicians used to getting their own way and lining their pockets at the expense of tax payers. Those days would be gone as well if she had her way. She just hoped that she could hold herself together long enough to make it all happen but she had many on her side who were working as hard as she was to make the changes.

Europe and the rest of the world was following America's lead and were slowly taking back control, sometimes with states of civil war existing in these countries but progress was being made. The death toll was high as both sides in the conflicts fought to maintain control. The Russian Premier contacted Charlotte directly and asked if Russia could be of any help. Charlotte held an emergency session with her cabinet to consider the offer and if accepted where the Russians could be of the most use. It was feared that Russia may take advantage of the present situation to expand their empire as had been done in the Cold War. After a full day of conferences it was decided to take up the Russians offer on several conditions including not taking over countries as had been done in the past but just to help restore order and once that had been done, to withdraw and allow the governments in those countries to self-govern themselves once again. This proposal was presented to the Russian ambassador in conference with the Russian Premier and he agreed to the conditions that were presented. The Russians had never forgotten the fall of the Soviet empire in the last century when America could have swept in and taken over the country but instead had assisted creating the new Russia and becoming allies instead of enemies.

Leaders of a number of European countries were told to expect the arrival of Russian troops but to give them every cooperation as they were there to help not to invade and to make them aware of the deal that had been made with the Russians. It took a bit of arm twisting and convincing with some of the countries such as Czechoslovakia, Poland, Hungary and others that once were under Soviet control. Civil war was averted in all countries that needed help to restore order with the help of the Russian forces.

The strain of the last several months were starting to show in Charlotte. Charles offered to step in with the help of the Vice President to continue her work while she took some time off to regain some sort of sanity in her life. It took a bit of convincing but she finally agreed to take a short leave of absence. It was either that or she knew herself that she was going to implode emotionally and physically. The 14 and 16 hour days had taken their toll on the U.S. President. She decided to take her rest at Camp David in Maryland. Once or twice she had tried to get on line and continue some of her work but the medical staff at camp David had intervened and almost forced her to rest and be assured that if anything happened that needed her response she would be notified immediately.

Malcolm Beacham

Malcolm and Samantha both had found houses that would suit their individual needs and Samantha's friend from the shelter had passed her background check and was living in Samantha's house to look after it and Samantha's kids. Now Malcolm and "Sam" as Samantha had asked Malcolm to call her were pouring over resumes looking for good office staff. They had to be good negotiators, familiar with corporate law and be free to travel and be away from home for extended periods if need be. Sam had suggested a couple of people from the shelter where she had been as they had been corporate executives at one time but had lost everything. He asked Sam to call them in for interviews. They both had extensive experience in corporate upper echelons and seemed to be good negotiators. He gave them the same deal as he had given Sam, a few days to get a place to live, buy some decent clothes and report to work when all that was done.

He needed a name for his new department. He asked Sam for some suggestions and wrote them on a white board along with a few of his own. They discussed the pro's and con's of each most of the morning and thought up a few new ones along the way that Malcolm added to the list. Lunch time was coming so Malcolm suggested a break and then come back to it after. Malcolm asked Sam if she knew of any decent places nearby and she suggested one called "Mario's" so they went there. It was a small Italian place that was not high class but appeared clean homey looking. They both took a seat and chatted over lunch. Malcolm was amazed at the change in Sam from the hopeless looking woman that first walked in the door a few days ago. She looked full of energy and was enthusiastic with the task at hand.

After an hour or so they had finished lunch and walked back to the office. On the way Sam's hand touched his and he almost jumped as if hit by an electric spark and quickly drew his hand away. What was the matter with him? Sam was attractive but was he scared of her? Was he scared of getting into a relationship with any woman? It had been a long time. Malcolm's work was his world. He had no social life. It had been that way for a long, long time, maybe too long?

Once they got back to the office they went back to picking a department name. It had to be something that indicated hope for the people and a better way of doing things in the long run for the corporations. Malcolm was head of Microsoft but he didn't have to worry. All of Microsoft's development was done in America in Redmond, Washington. It had been headquartered there for decades and that's where most of its development took place. Microsoft did not make all software products, they did have some hardware such as the Microsoft Phone and other products.

These were of course currently being manufactured off shore, most of it in China. Malcolm made a few conference phone calls and laid out what he wanted done. He met some resistance as was expected but reminded these detractors that it was the President who was telling all corporations including Microsoft to bring back manufacturing to the United States. Microsoft could act as a good role model for other corporations as it had always been a "Made in America" company when it came to its famous Windows operating systems that were used on most of the worlds computers. Malcolm checked from time to time but things were running fine and decision making had been turned over before the Hope project to someone else. He was still CEO of Microsoft but really in name only.

A few people now staffed the newly created office so they could get a start on what needed to be done. Everyone seemed to know what was expected of them but Malcolm decided to have a staff meeting anyway just to make sure that everyone was on the same path. The building had a large board room that would be sufficient for his needs. He asked everyone to meet there tomorrow morning for a short presentation and question and answer session. The next morning at the appointed time he and Sam went to the board room and nearly everyone was there. They waited a few minutes for others to arrive and then Malcolm took the lectern in preparation for his presentation and speech.

Malcolm started, "I think everyone here has a good understanding of what we are going to be doing but I thought it would be a good idea to get everyone together and make sure everyone knows what is going to be expected of them and why it will be the best thing for America. As you know in the last several decades companies have been sending manufacturing off shore and closing plants here in America and laying people off. Manufacturing and even new product design is being done off shore. Even those industries were not affected. Help lines and even telemarketing companies started moving off shore for cheaper labor. This has left fewer and fewer jobs in America and got us where we are today with unemployment at over 40%."

"The President of the United States has tasked us with convincing companies to bring manufacturing and support back to America. Our job is to make that a reality. Its not going to be easy and we will meet a lot of resistance but we don't want to have to force companies to comply but to try and work with them to make it all happen. The President is ready to start placing ever increasing tariffs on goods entering the United States that were manufactured in other countries that could have been made here in America. The recent war with China has destroyed a lot of industry over there so the manufacturing capability in China has been severely crippled. This is the best time to convince companies to come back home rather than trying to rebuild in China or go to other countries to continue their off shore manufacturing processes. With the President's idea of imposing tariffs on import of off shore manufactured products and our help with convincing companies to move their manufacturing facilities back to the United States it will be a win, win for everybody especially the American economy and the average American worker."

"The President and her staff have been in contact with other governments like Canada and the European Union and they are all on board with this idea because they are facing the same challenges as we are. We are not going to cut off all off shore manufacturing as these countries depend a lot on off shore manufacturing at present to maintain jobs in their own countries. Some piece part manufacturing will be allowed but the large percentage of the product must be manufactured here in the United States. Canada has said it will support our initiative as long as they get a share of the manufacturing pie. We have promised them they would. Okay, any questions?"

There were quite a few questions and Malcolm wrote them down on his personal computer and on the white board in the room and did his best to answer them. Most of the questions dealt with what to do with companies who resisted and tried to find other ways and means of getting their product manufactured off shore with cheap labor and import them into the U.S. Malcolm replied their job would be mainly proactive and to think up ways that companies could use and to plug the leaks and watch for anything unanticipated and stop those in their tracks as well.

He stressed that their job was to work with these companies to comply with the new regulations rather then fight against them. Help them to get organized and set up and not to worry about the unions as they had been held at bay for the time being. They were one of the reasons that companies started going off shore as unions in prior days had struck and demanded higher and higher wages until the companies said enough and closed the plants and moved off shore. He vowed that was not going to happen again.

Workers would get fair pay for their work but it was not going to be skyrocket wages. He was sure that people would be happy just being able to work again and bringing in a salary. There would be an advertising campaign to educate people to live within their means but that would not be their job, someone else would be looking after that. Everyone seemed happy when they left the meeting as to what their job was and how to approach it. Sam and Malcolm along with other staff would be putting together a list of companies they had to work with then to assign companies to each staff member to work with to make it all happen.

Sam and Malcolm went back to his office to continue with a name search for their newly created department. It had to be something catchy that would give hope to the average American that better days were coming and also a name that would relay his departments direction in helping corporations to bring back manufacturing and R&D to the United States. They had a long list on the white board and they started by removing names that didn't convey the right message.

At the end of the day there were only three names left: Rebuilding America, American Pride and Working for a Better America. Malcolm had an idea. He went out to the general office and called everyone into his office for a few minutes. He showed everyone the three names that had been selected as possible candidates for the new department name and what the name would stand for. He asked for a by hand vote. He read the fist name and some hands went up. He did a quick count and then did the same for the other two names. The clear winner was Rebuilding America. That was it. That would be the new department name. Malcolm thanked everyone and dismissed them. Now he would have to get letterhead paper and business cards made up reflecting the new departments name.

Washington

Martial law was still in place which gave the President unprecedented powers to keep law and order but that had mostly been achieved. Now the Republican political party and the population wanted martial law lifted and new elections held to let people decide on the best course of action to take. President Charlotte Henderson was still resting in Camp David when the news came in. She had been there for two months and seemed fit and ready to tackle her duties and campaign her doctors had decided. She was allowed to return to the White House. The first things she checked was the status of everything and found that in her absence her staff had done a wonderful job with making the changes she had wanted. She found out soon that most people wanted martial law lifted as it was felt it was no longer necessary. She could not justify it any longer and was forced to admit that she had run out of ideas to keep it imposed. The cities were in control once more, food supply was stable with the agriculture industry returning to normal. Shelters had been improved and people were being fed. People were being allowed to move back to their homes that had been repossessed and had not yet been sold off. Jobs were created to repair the infrastructure in the cities that had been damaged or destroyed by violence in taking back control.

She wondered if an election was called, and it would be once martial law was lifted, if she would be re-elected so she could continue her work and whether she would be strong enough to go on a long grueling campaign trail. She firmly believed that what she was doing was the right thing and hoped that the majority of Americans would see it that way too. She knew that she could not justify martial law any longer and would have to lift it. She was getting pressured from all sides to do so. She resolved to go on television in a few days and announce the lifting of martial law and then she would have to deal with the consequences. She told her secretary to make all the arrangements and let her know when the television networks could give her an hour to make the announcement leaving time for questions from the press.

Her secretary got back to her in about three days and gave her a date when the networks could give her an hour. The date was a week away. She better get her speech ready and hope for the best. It was going to be a job selling her economic recovery plan to America and was hoping the press would be on side with her.

Presidential Address to the Nation

The night of The Address to the Nation had arrived and Charlotte was as ready as she was going to be. She had her speech all ready. The room was filled with reporters. Rumors were already flying that she was going to lift martial law. There are few secrets in Washington. Her personal staff was with her trying their best to keep her calm. She knew that once she was out there and giving her speech she would settle down. This could be one of the most important speeches in all of American history. The time was counting down so she waited for her Chief of Staff to finish his warm up speech and announce her arrival. Finally she heard him say, "And now please stand for the President of the United States."

Charlotte walked out and stepped up to the podium to a round of applause. She waited for the applause to stop and everyone to take their seats. She began her speech:

"My fellow Americans. It is my pleasure to address you tonight. This country has been through one of its most trying times since the Civil War but we survived. {applause} Everyone knows the problems our country has had to deal with from economic meltdown, the highest level of unemployment in the history of the United States and a period of out of control gangster control of our cities and our farms. With the support and courage of our Armed Forces we have taken back the cities and made them safe once again. {applause} But we have a lot of work to do to revive this country. The groundwork is already in place and hopefully with your understanding and courage we can make it happen.

All home repossessions have been stopped. Homes that have been repossessed but not yet sold will be given back to the families that were foreclosed. Those living in shelters will be given first priority on jobs to give these people hope once again."

"Affective immediately martial law will be lifted. {loud applause} Our cities are once again safe and people can walk the streets again without fear as local police can now maintain order."

"I will be introducing a new country wide law similar to that now used in California. It will be the three strike law. Any person arrested and found guilty of any crime and given a prison sentence will be given three chances. On the third violation they will be put in jail for life and considered a danger to society. This should go a long way to bringing peace, safety and order to the country as a whole." {loud applause}

"I am hoping that I will have full support of all levels of government to bring manufacturing back to America. For far too long we have outsourced America to the point there are very few jobs anymore but all that is going to change if I get the backing I need from you, the people of this great nation and the rest of the government. We need products to be made here in America by American workers, not made off shore in other nations. That is what has killed and continues to kill our economy. {heavy applause} With your help and backing I am proposing the following changes. Corporate America will be encouraged to manufacture here in America and not in some far off country. Tariffs will be put on goods manufactured in other nations and brought into the United States by American corporations when those products can be made right here in the United States." {more applause}

"These tariffs will start off low as off shore manufacturing will need a transition period to move manufacturing to the United States and open plants here to provide jobs for American workers. These tariffs will be steadily increased making it less attractive to keep on manufacturing off shore. Some off shore manufacturing will be allowed but carefully screened to ensure that at least 75% of all products are made here in America by American workers. {more applause} We know we will get a lot of backlash from corporate America but they will just have to understand they can't keep on out sourcing American jobs any longer. We have hit rock bottom. This trend has to stop and stop now! {loud applause} I have already created a new government department whose job it will be to help corporate America make this transition. We don't want to be seen in the position as ordering them to make this transition but to give them all the help and cooperation they need to make this happen. We want them to be on side with us with this transition. I look forward to the day in the not too distant future when we export more than we import and we will be proud to see 'Made in America' on most products once again." {loud applause}

"On another note, everyone knows about WWIII. It was very short as predicted it would be, if it happened at all. With the help and the courage of our Armed Forces, America was mostly spared the brunt of the attack. The only damage we suffered was some destruction in Ness City and some of the surrounding areas. It could have been a lot worse. {applause} Our retaliation to attack from China was swift and final. China attempted a preemptive attack on the United States and we mostly defended ourselves and retaliated destroying most of China's attack capability with a lot of damage to manufacturing areas. Civilian losses were high due to China's dense population. Unfortunately more losses are forecast from radiation and fallout. China was ordered to immediately and unconditionally surrender or be attacked again. They wisely chose to surrender." {applause}

"Our ships and planes are either there or on their way with aid for the population along with assistance from our Allies. That's the type of people we are. We assisted Japan and Germany when they were defeated in WWII to get back on their feet. Now both these countries are strong allies of the United States. {applause} Some European governments were having a hard time taking back control when gangster elements and civil war took over a lot of these countries. We were contacted by our Russian allies and they offered their help. We took them up on their offer under the condition they would not try and occupy these nations but to leave once order was restored. They agreed. They did not have to do this but they are considered allies now and they put their money where their mouth is and loaned a hand when it was needed. We are indebted to them for their assistance." {applause}

"What some of you may not know is that a generation spacecraft was built in space with private money is now on its way to Alpha Centauri in the hope that it will find the possibly habitable planet that has been found there. It is a generation ship because Alpha Centauri is more than 4 light years away. We cannot travel any where near the speed of light and it has been calculated that it will take over 200 years to make the voyage. It will be the distant descendants of the original crew who will start a new colony on the planet. All launches to the spacecraft with parts and supplies were done from a remote launch site built in northern Canada. The space vehicles used were of civilian design in

America and made by plants in the United States providing jobs for Americans. {applause} Space facilities were not used in the United States because even though it was a privately funded project the average American would not see it that way and would have been angry the government appeared to be pouring money into the space program when we had serious problems here on earth and they were correct. This project was mostly kept secret from the general populace."

"The spacecraft project could have left some of the astronaut construction workers stranded in space in the International Space Station after the spacecraft left orbit but the Russians promised to rescue them if necessary. The Soyuz spacecraft at the International Space Station were considered adequate for the job. Unfortunately four people were killed in space when the Chinese tried a second attempt to destroy the spacecraft. This was unfortunate but it left the rest of the people in space a way home using the Soyuz emergency craft at the International Space Station. We hope to revive the American space program in cooperation with the Russians and many other nations to design and build spacecraft and to hopefully reuse the International Space Station which was restarted as a base for the astronaut construction crew that built the spacecraft to live in."

"It is hoped the space program will be revived again providing still more jobs for Americans and give something for Americans to be proud of once again. {applause} The spacecraft project was possibly the catalyst for China's attack on the United States. Even we did not know of the spacecrafts true mission. The cover story was the spacecraft was actually a space station. The Chinese found out the truth and thought we knew all about it and were trying to get the jump on them in galaxy colonization. Our spy network discovered the findings of the Chinese spy network and we tried to convince the Chinese government that we did not know of its intended purpose either and were caught off guard as they were. We talked to the builders of the spacecraft and found out its true purpose and agreed to protect it until its launch."

"But the Chinese still believed that we were in on the plan and tried once to destroy the spacecraft. With the help of three Special Ops people in orbit with state of the art radar controlled laser cannons they managed to destroy a missile attack on the spacecraft. The Chinese were warned not to attempt it again. We sent up into orbit two anti-missiles in pieces to be assembled in space to protect the spacecraft. The Chinese fired off two missiles at the spacecraft when its launch date was moved up by one week in utmost secrecy in the hope to catch the Chinese off guard and they also attempted a preemptive nuclear attack on the United States at the same time. This resulted in the beginning and the end of WWIII. Iran attempted to take advantage of the situation and launched a nuclear attack against Israel despite being warned not to attempt it or be destroyed. We had given Israel some anti-missiles for defense so destruction of Israel was avoided but our Ballistic Missile submarines in the area were ordered to launch an attack against Iran as soon as missile launches were detected. Most of Iran is now in ruins."

"There was a love hate relationship with China. China is known to have banks of computers whose job it was is to crack into United States and other countries government and military computers. Corporate America loved using China's huge population as a cheap place to setup manufacturing plants to produce products while all the time closing down plants here in the United States and other countries laying off millions of workers in the process. Even help and telemarketing lines were being outsourced to India and other countries putting still more people out of work. To wrap up my speech here is what I propose:"

"Bring back manufacturing to the United States and stop most off shore manufacturing to provide more jobs for Americans." {loud applause}

"As more and more Americans get back to work and start being tax payers again I hope to realize a very large drop in taxes as the years go by. The more money circulating in the economy keeps it running well. The more money you take out of the economy in the form of taxation does nothing but hurt it further." {applause}

"Reduce redundancy of government services and streamline government services to make it easier for the average person to receive the help they need when they need it and to reduce government red tape and spending. {applause} This would not be done until the economy is running well and then only in stages."

"To bring more transparency of government. Everyone from the President on down will be accountable to the average U.S. citizen how their tax money is being spent. Government will be run as a corporation with all Americans as shareholders and will expect a yearly breakdown of expenses." {applause}

"Revive the American space industry to provide still more work for Americans and give people the pride they used to have in the United States space program. This will be done in cooperation with our Russian allies and other countries contributing to a planetary space program that I envision. There is no reason why we should waste money to try and outdo each other when much more can be accomplished when we work together. The International Space Station is an example of that."{applause}

"I will now take questions from the press. Please be brief to give everyone a chance."

She felt the speech had gone over well and felt confident that she would have the backing of the press and the American people as a whole. She could not wait until she saw tomorrows papers and internet news web site reviews and comments about her speech. She hoped that it would be favorable. She felt that she had brought America back from the brink of destruction and total anarchy and that the American people would recognize this and support her in her future efforts.

The Next Day

Charlotte woke early in the morning as usual. Actually she had not slept well in anticipation of seeing the press reviews of her speech. Several Washington and national newspapers were in her office as usual. She turned on the television and selected one of her favorite early morning news programs. She listened to that while checking the headlines of the papers. All of the headlines had to do with her speech from last evening. She quickly scanned the reviews in the papers while listening to the discussion on the television. It was mostly favorable. One paper tried to blame her for starting WWIII. She had considered that would happen but there is one in every crowd. All in all the reviews were favorable.

The hosts of the early morning news were discussing her speech from last evening and had as guests some political analysts. They were discussing her plan of reviving the American economy and the chances of the corporations bringing back manufacturing to the United States. It was universally agreed that prices for products would end up rising because of the lack of cheap labor in the United States. They had a point but the auto industry which had mostly built all their cars here in the United States and Canada had managed to survive. If they could do it so could everyone else. Work smarter, not harder was her motto. Malcolm was of the same thought. She had not heard from Malcolm in a few days. She would have to touch base with him to see how he was doing.

Malcolm

"Malcolm? A call for you on line one.", his personal secretary said.

Malcolm said, "Take a message and I will call them back in a little while."

He was talking to Sam and did not want to be disturbed. "Its from the White House.", his secretary said. Malcolm knew it was probably Charlotte and immediately took the call.

"Malcolm here.", he said.

Charlotte asked, "Did you catch my speech last evening?"

Malcolm replied, "Of course I did. I thought it was great. I think you will have the backing of the American people."

Charlotte said, "Thanks Malcolm. How are things on your end?"

Malcolm replied, "We are just starting to make initial contacts with the corporations. I was waiting for your speech before going into high gear."

Charlotte said, "I would like you to come to the Oval Office to discuss some strategy. Are you free this afternoon?"

Malcolm smiled, "I'm always free for you Charlotte." He could almost hear her smile on the other end of the phone.

"Could you be here for 1:30 PM in my office?", Charlotte asked.

"Of course. Can I bring one of my people with me?", asked Malcolm.

Charlotte said, "Of course. See you at 1:30.", and she hung up.

Malcolm checked his watch. It was now 10:30. He turned to Sam and said, "We will have to have an early lunch. We will be going to meet with the President at 1:30.", said Malcolm.

"What!", exclaimed Sam.

Malcolm laughed, "Don't worry. The President is very nice. She won't bite your head off. Go and clean up anything you have on the go and clear your calendar for the afternoon. We'll go for lunch at 11:30 and then come back here and go over to the White House."

Sam said, "But I'm not dressed to meet the President!", she said.

Malcolm said, "You look fine. Don't worry about it."

At around 1 PM they left the office to go to the White House. Sam looked nervous but he was sure she would be okay once they were there and Malcolm would be doing most of the talking anyway. He wanted Sam to be there as an example to the President of the type of people he had working with him. He was proud of Sam. She was doing a great job running the office and keeping work flowing. They arrived at the White House and the guards recognized Malcolm but checked his ID anyway as a matter of protocol and checked Sam's identity as well. He drove up to the White House and parked the car. The two of them entered the White House and were checked again for ID and checked with security wands to be sure they were safe to be allowed to go further. They recognized Malcolm of course but they were doing their job and checking anyway by the book.

They were escorted to the Oval Office waiting area where Malcolm told Charlotte's private secretary that he and Samantha (he used her full name) were here at the President's request. He asked Malcolm and Sam to take a seat and the President would see them shortly. After a couple of minutes he motioned to Malcolm and said they could go ahead into the Oval Office. Malcolm and Sam walked in and Malcolm shook hands with Charlotte and introduced Samantha to the President. Sam was nervous and did not know what was expected of her. Was she to curtsy or anything like that? The President extended her hand and welcomed Sam to the White House and they shook hands. This made Sam feel much better. Charlotte asked Malcolm and Sam if they would like any refreshments.

Malcolm looked at Sam. She was stuck for words so Malcolm said, "Just water Charlotte."

Sam was surprised that Malcolm and the President were on first name basis. She did not know of most of the prior history of his dealings with the American President. Malcolm and the President discussed strategy to be used when dealing with the corporations. Sometimes he would ask Sam for her opinion and asked her the occasional question and said at the time that Samantha would be the best one to give that answer to give her the chance to talk. The President asked how he had recruited Samantha so Malcolm gave the President a quick run down of how he had located Samantha and that she was doing an amazing job. Charlotte seemed very pleased that Malcolm could recognize talent and personality even though Samantha had been living in a shelter.

The meeting lasted about 45 minutes and then the President checked her watch and said she would have to let them go because she had another appointment coming up and told Sam she was pleased to meet her and hoped that she would like her new role. Sam thanked the President and she and Malcolm left the Oval Office. Once they were back in the car and on their way back to the office Sam took a deep breath and let it out.

"Nervous were you?", he asked Sam.

Sam replied, "Well its not every day you get to meet the President of the United States."

Malcolm replied, "Well get used to it. I am sure we will be

meeting her more in the future and I may even have to send you over on your own once in a while. You will have to get used to meeting and dealing with powerful people. But always remember they are just people like you and I."

"I will have to tell you a bit about my history in dealing with the President. We know each other quite well. She helped me a lot in the past so when she need my help for bringing manufacturing back to America, how could I refuse? I was project manager for the spacecraft on its way to Alpha Centauri."

This took Sam by complete surprise. "Oh my God! I never knew that!", she exclaimed.

Malcolm replied, "Few people do. The project was shrouded in secrecy as it was thought if the true nature of the spacecraft got out there might be problems. I was right. It was one of the reasons for WWIII. But I firmly believe that it was not the only reason. I am sure that WWIII would have happened anyway. It was only a matter of time. That was the reason for building the spacecraft, to save humanity and to continue on another planet in case the worse case scenario happened and the planet was destroyed or world wide loss of civilization happened."

Sam was silent for a moment then said, "Where did all the money for the project come from?"

Malcolm said, "I am not at liberty to say. Lets just say I was able to convince other people with good finances to invest in the project as a way to save humanity in case of the worst case scenario."

Sam said, "It looks now that the worst is over. Why not recall the spacecraft?"

Malcolm said, "I considered that but I am not convinced the worst is over. You know the old saying. The light at the end of the tunnel is sometimes the headlight of an oncoming train."

Sam did not say anything. "What else could happen? China is no longer a threat. The Russians are no longer a threat and are now considered allies. No one other country has a nuclear arsenal as big as the United States and Russia.", she thought.

What she was not considering was that there were other threats. That's what Malcolm was worried about. Nuclear war was only one threat but there were others.

Malcolm and Sam

Work at the office continued as usual. Companies were contacted and staff were assigned the responsibility of dealing them to convince and assist them to bring manufacturing and research and development back to the United States. Malcolm and Sam continued to go to lunch together usually. There were days when it wasn't possible due to work load. Samantha was becoming more attracted to Malcolm and wondered sometimes if there could ever be anything more between them other than work. One week she had a plan. She did not know what Malcolm did on the weekends. She had asked him one or two times and it seemed he lived a solitary life. She knew there was no Mrs. Beacham and she knew that Malcolm did not have a girlfriend. If there was she would never consider getting closer to Malcolm other than as workmates. Friday was coming up and she had some planning to do. She got on the phone and made some arrangements.

Friday came and Malcolm and Sam were preparing to leave and go home. She knew where he lived and discretely followed him and parked a short distance away. She walked to his front door and rang the bell. She was nervous. She hoped that things would go the way she hoped they would. Malcolm answered the door looked surprised to see Sam standing there.

She said, 'Well? Are you going to invite me in?", she asked smiling.

Malcolm opened the door to let her in and asked, "Is there anything wrong? Is everything okay at the office?"

Sam assured him that everything was fine at the office and not to worry.

"Have you had supper yet?", Sam asked.

Malcolm said, "No, I just got home. I usual eat supper later whenever the mood hits me."

They walked into his home and she looked around. It was rather spartan but very neat and tidy. There were few pictures on the wall or anywhere else. She sat down on the couch and motioned Sam over to sit beside her. He looked uncomfortable. They chatted about work and various things and then the door bell rang.

Malcolm started to get up but Sam said, "Don't worry. I'll get it." Malcolm looked surprised.

Two men came in with packages and Sam directed them into the kitchen. Sam gave them a tip and let them out the door. "Okay, lets eat. Where do you keep your dishes.

Malcolm indicated the cupboards where the dishes were kept.

"Do you have any table cloths and place mats.", she asked Malcolm.

Malcolm said he did so Sam asked if he could put a table cloth on the dining room table and a couple of place mats. Sam put out the dishes and the cutlery.

"Do you have any candles?", asked Sam. Malcolm said no but she found a dimmer switch on the wall and turned the lights down a little.

Sam went into the kitchen and opened the packages which contained a wonderful dinner of chicken breasts stuffed with spinach, along with mixed vegetables and baked potatoes and a bottle of chilled Sauvignon Blanc white wine. She knew that Malcolm didn't normally drink so just in case he didn't have one, Sam had also asked for a cork screw to be added to the order. She put the strawberry deserts in the fridge to keep them cold. Sam put the food on the plates and asked Malcolm to take a seat. She put a plate in front of him and a plate for herself. She opened the bottle of wine and poured a little for Malcolm and some for herself.
"Wow, this is a surprise.", said Malcolm. Sam smiled and thought to herself, "You haven't seen anything yet."

They ate and Malcolm asked about her kids and how they were doing. She asked Malcolm if he had any children. He never talked about any so assumed he did not have any. She learned that Malcolm had never been married. He said he had a few brief affairs but nothing serious. "His love was his work.", thought Sam. "Hopefully I can change that." They finished dinner and Sam got up and took the dishes away and poured a little more wine into Malcolm's glass. She brought in the dessert which was a strawberry shortcake with lots of whipped cream. They continued their conversation and sipped the wine. When that was finished Sam got up and cleared the table and put all the dirty dishes in the dishwasher. Malcolm was still sitting at the dining room table. She took the bottle of wine off the table and asked Malcolm to come sit in the living room. Malcolm sat down on the couch and Sam sat down close beside him. She put the bottle of wine on the table.

"Tell me about the spacecraft project." she asked Malcolm.

He started to explain how it all had come together, the launch site in northern Canada and the general design of the ship and a description of the crew. As he talked she moved closer to Malcolm and put her hand on his knee. He looked uncomfortable with this.

Malcolm asked her, "What time do you have to go to put the kids to bed?"

Sam replied, "I don't have to tonight. Maria is looking after everything for me." Maria was Sam's live in house keeper.

Malcolm said, "I don't think this is a good idea, I...."

Sam cut him off with a quick kiss. "I think its the perfect idea.", she said as she snuggled up close to him.

Malcolm was looking very uncomfortable now. Sam took Malcolm's chin and turned his face toward hers and gave him a long deep kiss.

"Do you still think its a bad idea?", she asked? Malcolm did not say a thing but responded to her kiss and they were soon in each others arms.

She rubbed his chest and lowered her hand down to his belly and rubbed seductively.

"You haven't shown me your bedroom yet.", Sam said. In a few minutes they were in the bedroom and Sam started undressing.

Malcolm stood there fully clothed. "Well?", she asked. She went over to Malcolm and started to unbutton his shirt and helped him off with it then his pants.

She continued undressing slowly until she was completely naked. She stood before him and asked if he liked what he saw. Malcolm didn't say a thing. He just looked and nodded. He already had an erection Sam noticed. She went over to him and took off his underwear allowing his manhood to spring free. She gently caressed it and took one of his hands and placed it on one of her breasts. He started to softly rub and knead her breast. She backed away and led Malcolm by the hand to the bed. She turned it down and climbed in.

"Well? Are you coming in?", Sam said seductively.

Malcolm climbed into the bed and they snuggled together. She reached for him again and took one of his hands and drew it down under the sheets. He started feeling around and put a finger in her vagina and started gently massaging her clitoris.

She moaned into his mouth and then rolled over on her back and drew him on top of her. Malcolm entered her and they made love slowly while kissing the whole time. She moved against his thrusts feeling him deep inside her. It had been a long time for her and she was enjoying this. After several minutes Malcolm could not control himself any longer and thrust deep and hard in her and came for a long time in a shuddering orgasm. He started to apologize to her for cumming so quickly but it had been a long time for him.

She kissed him tenderly and told him, "Don't worry, we have all night."

They snuggled down in the bed spoon style with Malcolm behind her. She woke a few hours later feeling Malcolm in her again. She thrust back to him and made love spoon style for a while and then she got up on the bed on her hands and knees and asked Malcolm to enter her from behind. He slipped himself into her again, gripped her hips and began thrusting into her slowly.

"Oh! That feels so good.", she whispered. He was hitting the right spots. He hoped she would be able to come before he did. She could feel her orgasm building deep inside her and then started cumming herself. Her vagina was spasming which pushed Malcolm over the edge and he had his second orgasm of the night. She waited until he was done and slipped out of her and then turned around while kneeling on the bed, gently kissed and rubbed each others bodies and then crawled back under the covers.

"Did you get off that time?", Malcolm asked.

"Oh, did I! It was wonderful!", she said giving him a big hug. They kissed for a little while and then dozed off in each others arms.

Morning came and Sam opened her eyes to see Malcolm gazing at her. She smiled. "Good morning.", she said.

"Good morning.", Malcolm replied.

"How long have you been awake?", she asked.

"Not long.", he replied. They kissed again and were getting into the mood again when Sam said, "Don't move. I have to go to the bathroom."

She went and cleaned herself up the best she could from the night before. She found a face cloth in a drawer to accomplish this. She opened the door and found Malcolm standing there. "Me too.", he said.

She smiled and squeezed his semi-erect penis and went back to the bedroom. Shortly he came back and she reached for him and found that he too had cleaned himself up. They kissed for a while and then she slid down the bed and took him in her mouth and gently sucked and massaged his penis with her tongue. She knew it was having an affect from the moans coming from him. When he was fully erect and she knew he was going to cum if she continued so she stopped.

"Make love to me again.", she said.

Instead Malcolm started kissing her face, her neck, her breasts, down her belly. She felt his tongue. "Oh my God!! He might not have been with a woman for quite a while but he sure knows where to go!", she thought.

She could feel another orgasm building and let Malcolm continue until she came in shuddering waves. "No more, no more. I'm too sensitive."

She laid there for a moment enjoying the afterglow and then went to Malcolm and gently pushed him down on the bed. She climbed on top of him and reached for his penis and inserted it into her. She began slowly rocking back and forth and Malcolm had his eyes closed and was moaning. After several minutes of this he rolled them over so he was on top and started thrusting deep and hard and came in a shuddering orgasm. Sam kissed his lips and his face and then he rolled off and took her in his arms. She smiled, snuggled up next to him, drew the covers over the two of them and she drifted off to sleep.

China

The American missiles had done a good job at destroying any hope of a retaliation against the United States. Most defense and known missile defense areas had been targeted and destroyed. The death toll was high but that was unavoidable due to China's densely packed population. Emergency services were trying to keep up with the flow of injured and dying. There would be a lot more deaths in the coming days and weeks from radiation exposure. The United States and other countries said they were sending aid. It would likely not be enough for China's huge population. Some Chinese soldiers did not want to surrender and talked about firing on anyone approaching Chinese waters. This was anticipated so the first landings would be military. They were told to fight back if fired upon and shoot to kill. It could be several days before any medical help arrived. Planes could be sent in but it was thought they may be fired upon by resistance forces vowing to fight on. Some military recon flights had been flown and all that was seen were craters and scarring from the nuclear attacks. None were fired on from the ground.

One fighter even dared a touch and go landing at an airport without being fired on. China did accept an unconditional and complete surrender. Maybe assistance flights could be sent in without harm. This was discussed in Washington and a couple of flights were sent in. Fighter planes flew escort and were flying overhead as these mercy flights landed. The planes were met by Chinese airport workers that seemed happy to see them. The ones that could speak English were rounded up and told what to tell the others and ask where a first aid station and temporary field hospitals could be set up. They were directed to some nearby hangers where the aid workers set up triage centers, field hospitals and so on. Some of the Chinese airport workers were recruited to work as translators for the medical teams.

It was not long before trucks and bus loads of injured began arriving. The treatment center went into high gear treating the wounded. Most were happy that help had arrived. Some were shouting and yelling at the aid workers for the United States destroying their country but a quick exchange of words with the Chinese translators settled them down. Temporary waiting areas were set up in other hangers and on the tarmac as more and more people arrived. Triage teams went to these areas and took the more critically wounded first. Some had to be left to die as it was considered futile to attempt to save the most serious cases as they probably would not make it any way. If three could be saved at the expense of one it was considered a good trade off. The critically wounded with the best chance of surviving were the ones that got treated first. Washington was quickly advised of the situation and more flights were sent in from the United States and other countries.

Kansas

Kansas had taken a hit just west of Ness City and some of the city was destroyed or badly damaged. Emergency teams were quickly on site attempting to save whoever was left. There were some dead and dying on the streets as frantic people had attempted to flee the city before the bomb went off. Some people who were not hurt or not hurt badly were asking emergency teams how they could help. Some were recruited to carry litters, the rest were sent to waiting areas to be transported out of the area after the wounded had been taken care of. The lightly wounded were transported on buses to other hospitals in the areas around Kansas. Helicopters filled the skies as badly wounded survivors were flown out. More buses were sent in for the wounded that could survive transport. All hospitals within 200 miles of Ness City were placed on full alert to expect heavy loads of casualties. After 48 hours the wounded had been removed and troops had restored order.

A New Economic Hope

Major American corporations who were doing most if not all

their manufacturing off shore were being told to start bringing it back. Old factories that could be re-opened would be or new ones built. Any manufacturing equipment that could be salvaged in China or moved from other countries was to be dismantled and started to be sent back to the U.S. Any plans of moving manufacturing to another country was discouraged by the threat of tariffs, steadily increasing, on goods entering the U.S. that had been manufactured by American companies off shore. Of course there was a lot of rebellion by the corporations but they were told in no uncertain terms there was to be no other choice. This would increase the price of consumer goods, mostly paid for with disposable income, such as big screen TV's and other electronics and the like but the American auto industry had adapted and survived. If they could compete with a "work smarter, not harder" attitude then the rest of America's corporations could do the same.

Canada was co-operating with this plan as well because their economy was tightly bound to the U.S. economy. The European Union was on board with the plan as well as their economies were suffering for the same reason. The Canadian government did the same with their corporations as well, telling them to start manufacturing on Canadian soil or face huge tariffs on off shore produced goods. Most companies in Canada were simply satellite offices of U.S. corporations anyway. There were many import companies in both countries that were going to be out of business as time went on because of the new rules. They would have to change functions and act as wholesalers for the manufacturers once they were set up and operating.

A 5 year schedule was drawn up dictating a time line that was to be followed in bringing manufacturing back. During this time less and less off shore produced goods would be allowed into the U.S. with corporations starting up manufacturing in the U.S. At the end of 5 years most corporate manufacturing would be done in the U.S. as it had been done almost sixty years ago. Some off shore manufacturing was going to be allowed, mostly for small component parts but not the whole of the product. 75% of the product would have to be manufactured in the United States or the corporation would face stiff penalties. President Henderson was hoping to make it into law that could be backed up with fines and jail time for repeat offenders. It was going to be a rough few years but it would be worth it. North America was going to prosper once again. People would have jobs again and the unemployment rate would return to less than 3% as it used to be once upon a time after WWII.

Washington

Martial law had been canceled and for the most part, peace was in the cities except for the usual crimes. The Republican party was calling for an election and Charlotte knew there was nothing she could do about that according to the Constitution. She was lucky so far that martial law had been thought of as necessary and had kept her as President long after her term should have been up. A date was set for the Senate, State and Federal elections. The parties would have to select new leaders. She was hoping she would be selected again and then voted in as President once more so she could finish the work she had started. She was going to campaign vigorously on that platform also pointing out how peace and order in the country had been restored on her watch.

The next election date for the Presidency was the 6th of November 2034. She will have been in power for 8 years due to the declaration of martial law. Now that martial law was lifted the elections could be held on schedule. The House of Representatives and the Senate had both voted to allow her to run again for President even though she had served two terms. But that was because of martial law. If that had not been declared she would have to step aside for a new candidate to take her place as president-elect for the Democratic Party.

On Hope - 2027

Hope had reached Mars many months ago and had performed the first of the planetary slingshot maneuvers to gain speed. Earth looked very distant as a tiny bright light in the vastness of space. The navigators were now down to two shifts. One shift had gone back to the space wheel. The wheel had to be stopped temporarily to allow the crew to airlock themselves from the body of the spacecraft into space and once again into the wheel. Once this was done the wheel revolution was started again. It took a couple of hours to prepare the wheel to be stopped as personal things in quarters and equipment had to be secured for weightlessness. Even ordinary things like coffee cups had to be covered with their specially designed covers or drank, washed, dried and secured before weightlessness. It was of course uncomfortable to the crew as most were not used to the weightlessness of space. The airlock operation was done quickly so as to minimize the effect. Hydroponic harvests were moved at the same time and stored for use. This process alone would have to be done at regular intervals on the trip. The Captain thought one of the things that would have to be done was to minimize the time it took to get everything ready to stop the wheel in case an emergency came up and the wheel had to be stopped in a short time.

Several crew members were starting to pair up and share quarters or were known as a "couple" even if they lived in separate quarters. This had been expected and even encouraged but it had also been implanted that a couple may not necessarily be able to have a child together. The offspring of people aboard had already been determined to keep the gene pool as varied as possible. A woman may end up with two children, both from different fathers, neither of which was her current partner. Fertilization could be done naturally or by artificial insemination, whichever method was the most comfortable to all concerned. No children would be required for the next little while but soon they would be as it would take about 25 years to educate the children in basic education and then in their required profession to take over that position when it was time.

The spacecraft had three Captains, one for each shift. Captain Jacoby was currently Captain of the day shift and was considered "First Captain." Every section was to report to him giving the status of their particular section. Nothing unusual was reported. News programs were still being received from earth along with other programming from Houston to keep the crew informed of things on earth and for entertainment. As Hope got further away in the years to come these programs would become less and less frequent and eventually stopped altogether except for essential communications. Regular time and date was kept on board Hope to give the same familiarity of the passage of time as it had been on earth. The navigation section gave regular updates to the Captain. He was especially concerned with space objects that Hope would have to avoid. Getting through the asteroid belt could be difficult but deep space probes in years past had encountered no problems. Objects in the asteroid belt were many miles apart and in the past the odd minor course change had taken care of any near misses. No space probe had ever collided with an object in the asteroid belt. The Oort Cloud was a different thing altogether. It was thought to exist but had never been proven. Hope would be the first spacecraft to travel out that far and it would be just the beginning of their long voyage.

Doctor Fred Randolph on Hope was going through his exam room and surgery for the umpteenth time making sure that everything was in its place to be there when he needed it. Extra supplies were stored in the body of the spacecraft if he ran low on anything. He hoped his services would not be required for quite a while. Everyone chosen for the voyage was in perfect health with clear medical records and no significant family medical history problems. Hope was stocked with most common antibiotics. It was thought unnecessary to stock any vaccines as everyone was given vaccines against all common diseases long before launch. In a closed environment like Hope there should be no need to carry vaccines as there should be no germs. As far as surgery went Doctor Randolph could perform most common surgical procedures like gall bladder and gall stone removal, appendix removal, intestinal problems, C-sections, child births and so forth. Anything else he could look up in Hope's extensive medical database.

He was also told he would be the one performing euthanasia when necessary. His replacement may be the one performing one on him when it was his time. Everyone was informed of this eventuality and had signed off on it. Everyone was also asked to draw up a Will where it was documented what type of ceremony, if any, the person wanted before and after the procedure. He had checked everything three times before launch and had just finished another extensive check and everything he needed seemed to be here. He sighed, turned and walked out of the medical room, locking the door behind him.

Democratic Party Convention

It was pandemonium in the Chicago Stadium arena. The arena had gone by several names over the years as major U.S. companies paid millions for the rights to name the arena after their company. But in recent years with the economic downturn no company could afford such extravagance and so the arena was now simply called The Chicago Stadium arena named after the original arena that had been torn down decades ago. And to think all this chaos is the basis for our democracy thought Charlotte. So far several votes had been cast with no decisive winner. She had a lot of support but would it be enough? She certainly hoped so.

It had been decided by a House of Representatives vote that she could run again for the Presidency even though she had served two terms but that was because of extenuating circumstances of martial law. She and her supporters were debating in the arena with representatives from other states to gather support for Charlotte. Another vote was about to take place. The various states were starting to put their backing to the few remaining candidates. Charlotte was among them. One by one each state representative announced who they were backing. Quite a few were switching their votes and backing Charlotte. If this kept up she would be the Democratic candidate for President. She had her fingers crossed!! Another vote was taken and more supporters joined her ranks. It was soon obvious she would be the President-elect for the Democratic party. But she still had to get the backing of the votes from the Electoral

College in each state during the elections. The vote would determine whether it would be a Democratic or a Republican President. The American people had to vote as well to pick the representatives for the House of Representatives. She needed a majority in the House to be able to push through the new regulations to force corporations to bring back manufacturing and Research and Development to America.

On the 15th ballot Charlotte was declared a clear winner to be the next Democratic Party President-elect. Now the nation would have to choose between her and the Republicans who would be leading the country for the next four years but for now it was celebration time! Malcolm and Sam had been invited to the convention and made their way onto the arena floor to congratulate Charlotte. That would have to wait for a while as Charlotte was surrounded by her party delegates and supporters. Signs and posters from other election hopefuls littered the floor. After about 20 minutes Malcolm and Sam got near Charlotte, at least close enough to wave and congratulate her. Charlotte waved back with a huge smile.

6th of November 2034

The country wide vote was taking place. The Electoral College vote was clearly Democratic but what would the average American voter say when voting for their choice for the House of Representatives and the Senate? She hoped for a clear majority all around if she was to accomplish what she felt would be her life's work in the next four years. She stayed glued to the television set in her office accompanied by her closest friends and advisers. The voting booths were closed and the votes from each state started to trickle in. The early results were looking good. It looked like the average American believed in her restructuring plan. She had campaigned hard on it and pulled no punches. She had told the American people changes were not going to happen overnight but that changes were going to come and be enacted as soon as possible, in fact some corporations had set up some new manufacturing facilities due in a large part to Malcolm and his team. She had made sure to mention that fact on her campaign. She was asking the American people to vote Democrat across the board to give her party a clear majority to get things done as quickly as possible.

Concessions were being made to major corporations in the form of loans and tax breaks to assist them with the transition of bringing manufacturing and R&D back to America. The end result would be lots more jobs for the average American worker and their families as many goods would be made here in America and not in some far off land using cheap labor. This would increase the cost initially of many goods but it was hoped that corporations would find cost cutting measures to make up for this. One big saving was the expense of shipping goods half way around the world to North American and European Union markets. The European Union was mostly on side with her. This had to be a global effort or it would not work.

Already prices on some consumer goods were starting to rise as companies had to increase prices to cover the cost of higher wages in the United States and because of the tariffs that were starting to be charged on off shore manufactured goods. Charlotte was hoping the average American would realize this as the price to pay to get jobs back in America again and not be short sighted and vote against her and her plan and allow off shore manufacturing to continue. Prices would rise, yes, but taxes would come down as more working Americans started paying taxes again and America was able to pay down its huge deficit which was in the multi-trillion dollar range and had been for some time. It was all the government could do to pay just the interest on the money owed never mind paying down the debt. Most corporations were seeing the light and were trying to play ball with the new plan but there were some hard liners who were trying to do the end run around the system or play the waiting game and see what happened if the Republicans got voted in.

It was nearly midnight when it was clear the Democratic Party was announced as having a clear majority in the Senate, the House of Representatives and the Presidency. The American public had not let her down. They trusted what she was doing was the right thing and had voted the Democrats and her back in as President of the United States. A huge cheer went up in the Oval Office as her staff rose and gave her a standing ovation. Champagne corks were going off left and right and cheers were echoing off the walls. Malcolm and Sam were over at Malcolm's house and were watching the results on TV and hugged each other as the announcement came in that the Democrats led by Charlotte Henderson were again leading the country.

"Time for bed.", said Samantha as she gave Malcolm a big hug and snuggled up to him. They had yet to spend a night at Samantha's house because they wanted to wait until the time was right for him to stay the night with her two boys in the house.

They had already met Malcolm of course and they seemed to approve of him. Samantha's kids knew she was spending nights at Malcolm's when she wasn't home but Samantha didn't want to push things too quickly just yet in front of the kids. Malcolm went along with it. Samantha was a good mother and knew her kids and would know when the timing would be right for Malcolm to start spending some nights over at her place. She hoped that her and Malcolm and her two kids could all live in the same house someday soon and hopefully marry and have kids of their own

On Hope

Hope was well on the way toward Jupiter. Earth looked very tiny in the distance as did Mars. Hope was still receiving news broadcasts from earth and things on earth seemed to be on the mend and it was being discussed whether the trip to Alpha Centauri was necessary at all. Some wanted to turn around and return to earth. This was radioed to Houston but Hope was told to continue as things were not as rosy as they seemed. The United States was waiting for a response from the Middle East after destroying Iran.

The Middle East

Iran had taken a few good hits during the war and was still in devastation. The United States offered help but it was flatly refused. Other Arabic countries in the Middle East had come to Iran's aid even though Iran was looked on as the "bad boy" by most other Arabic countries. Al-Qaeda was of course really upset and was planning a retaliation strike at the United States. The Department of Home Land Security in the United States was expecting some retaliation attempt by Al-Qaeda and was on high alert for everything and anything. For years all cargo whether shipped, flown in or driven in to the United States was carefully screened looking for anything that could contain parts to make a weapon, particularly a nuclear weapon. All known nuclear weapons world wide were carefully monitored to ensure none went missing and could find their way into America. All nuclear material in America was carefully guarded in case some terrorist group already had a bomb but were just waiting for the chance to get their hands on some enriched uranium for it. It didn't even have to be weapons grade nuclear material. As long as it was radioactive then a "dirty bomb" could be made and set off somewhere in America, probably in Washington or New York to irradiate a large part of one or both of those cities.

Somewhere in the West bank a meeting was taking place by Al-Qaeda operatives to discuss just what was the best course of action to take to strike back at the United States. Al-Qaeda already controlled most of Iraq once again and the Taliban controlled most of Afghanistan. It was as though the two Middle East wars had never happened. All that money spent and lives lost for nothing as is the case in most wars. A terrorist war is the hardest war to wage because you never had a clear idea who the enemy was. It could be the man walking across the street from you. You just never knew. In a conventional war it was far easier. There were battle lines and countries that were fought over and won or lost but in an internal terrorist war all the rules were different. Actually there weren't any rules, that was the problem. There were no boarders, no land to take control of, just people and since everyone appeared to be the same you just never knew who the enemy was. America learned that lesson in Vietnam but had hoped it would be different in Afghanistan and Iraq. It wasn't.

In Iraq there was great celebration when the American forces first went in and it was assumed the war would be over in a few months but it dragged on and on with heavy losses on both sides and billions of dollars spent, all for nothing. Other neighboring Arabic countries were accused of harboring hostile forces and even allowing training camps but little could be done about it without expanding the war further which could not be done because it would be far too expensive and also upset relations between some Arabic countries friendly to America. Mohammad El-Erian (no relation to Mohamed Abdulla El-Erian) was the leader of Al-Qaeda for the last three years and had the final say in all matters. He had been listening and debating all possible retaliations against the United States. He had finally come to the decision that suicide bombers would be used as the first strike against the United States. They had more than enough operatives in America who had vowed to give their lives in the holy war against America and be assured of their place in Heaven seated next to Allah. Once the suicide bombers had rattled America and demoralized them then other attacks could be considered but suicide bombers had always been used as the first wave of any Jihad attack.

Yusuf Mohammad Hussain

Yusuf Mohammad Hussain was an engineering student at Frostburg State University in Maryland. His cell phone went off between classes. There was a short message waiting for him. He listened to the message and then slowly closed the phone and put it back into his pocket. He knew he would get a call someday but was secretly hoping never. He was beginning to hope it would never come as he was starting to like life at the university. He had made a few friends and tried his best to blend in. He even had a girlfriend which was against Al-Qaeda rules but you know what they say, one thing leads to another. They had started as friends and ended up becoming lovers. He never told her about his past or

Al-Qaeda. He had been given a cover story which he always used even with her. He told everyone he was from Saudi Arabia which was one of the Middle Eastern countries that had friendly relations with America although it was a bit strained these days since America had nuked Iran.

He was supposed to meet his girlfriend tonight but the phone call that he had just received told him to call a number and for further instructions. He was sure he would be asked to go to an Al-Qaeda "safe house" in the country to get instructions as to what his mission would be. He knew what it would likely be and he didn't look forward to it but if he didn't follow through he would be killed anyway so he might as well do what was expected of him. Allah was waiting for him.

He caught up with his girlfriend Martha between classes and told her that he had to meet someone later that evening so he would not be able to see her. She was of course disappointed but she knew that he had a life other than just the two of them as she also had a life apart from being with Yusuf. She was Christian but did not practice it and he was Muslim and practiced Islam and prayed to Allah the required five times a day. But she could not resist him. She found him extremely handsome in a adventurous sort of way and he was a very good and passionate lover. He made sure she was satisfied any time they made love which was often. They had been together almost a year. She had yet to break the news to her parents that she was seeing someone of the Muslim faith as they would not be happy about that as she was sure that his parents back in Saudi Arabia would not be happy that he was seeing a Christian girl. She didn't know what the future held for the two of them but she was enjoying it for the moment as she was sure was he.

After Yusuf spoke to Martha he went to see one of his friends and asked to borrow the car. He rarely did this and always returned the car with a full tank of gas so his friend did not mind. His friend would not be needing the car that evening so he said sure that Yusuf could borrow it. Yusuf called the number that was in the message and identified himself along with the password he had been given. He was given directions to drive to a point in the country and to call again from there for the rest of the directions. That evening after class he drove out of the university and into the country to the location specified and called again. He was given the rest of the directions and was at his destination in about 10 minutes.

He parked the car and went to the door and knocked. A man in a thobe, a Muslim robe, answered the door and beckoned him in. Once inside he saw there were several men, some young as he and some older. He was shown to a chair and a discussion followed. A holy Jihad had been called against America and it was the sworn duty of all faithful Muslims to obey the order. It was considered an honor to be chosen and die fighting ones enemy. He was told what his duty would be. It was as he thought, he was to be a suicide bomber. He was to use a vehicle that would be packed with explosives and driven to a yet to be determined location and blow it up. The location was kept secret right up to the last few minutes so as not to tip off the American infidels.

Washington

American spies in the Middle East had picked up information that a terrorist Jihad was planned against the United States and could come in a very short time. Details were sparse but the likelihood was high. The Department of

Homeland Security was on high alert and every known person with possibly links to Al-Qaeda was being carefully watched. This was even announced on the news and everyone was asked to keep their eyes and ears open and to report anything suspicious no matter how trivial it may be to their local authorities who would check it out and if warranted would inform Homeland Security. It was suspected that suicide bombers would start targeting sites in Washington or New York and possibly other cities. These strikes may come all at once or be staggered. Not enough information was known but every person available in the FBI, the CIA, NSA and Homeland Security was chasing down every lead.

Yusuf had thought a great deal about his mission. It was his duty and an honor to be selected for this mission and he was honor bound as a devout Muslim to carry out his mission. He had been given directions to pick up a vehicle at a location just outside of Washington. He had asked Martha to come with him. He loved her very much and wanted her to be in heaven with him. He told her the vehicle he was picking up had a friends stuff in it and he was to drive it to an address his friend had given him and to unload the vehicle once they got there. Once they arrived at the location the vehicle was a SUV with all of the back portion packed with "items" and covered with several sheets. He told Martha they were to keep the dust off.

He had opened an envelope earlier that he had been given that was his target. It was the Department of Justice at 950 Pennsylvania Avenue in Washington. This surprised him. He thought his target would have been the White House but security was very tight there. He drove down Pennsylvania Ave. towards the Justice building. Martha asked Yusuf when they would arrive at their destination. Yusuf assured her they would be there very soon. He could see the Justice Building coming up. He pulled up on the curb as close the the building as he could get and reached for the switch under the dash to trigger the explosive.

Martha was about to ask what he was doing on the curb when he turned to her and said, "I love you." and threw the switch.

In an instant the bomb, which was very simple in design, mostly fertilizer, blew the SUV into tiny pieces along with the occupants inside. A large gaping hole in the side of the building and a crater where the SUV once stood was all that was left as evidence of the suicide vehicle. The Justice Building was severely damaged with most of the front of the building blown away. The Jihad had begun.

President Charlotte Henderson heard the explosion just down the street from the White House. She was hearing sirens as emergency vehicles raced past the White House to the scene. She was informed shortly that a suicide bomb had targeted the Justice Building. There was severe damage and casualties were expected to be high. Soon other reports were coming in that three other terrorist bombs had gone off, one more in Washington and two in New York. Road blocks were hastily thrown up to protect the areas that were bombed but also to check other vehicles in the area for more suicide bombers. None were found. Homeland Security was at the head of the investigation with the FBI and the NSA assisting. There was not much left as evidence at the bomb sites, just scattered wreckage of vehicles and bits of DNA evidence and small body parts of the participants. In the days that followed some universities and businesses reported that people of Middle

Eastern descent were missing. The investigation immediate concentrated in these areas. The countries of origin of the missing individuals were identified, some were misrepresented. Some had supposedly come from Saudi Arabia but were traced to Iran, Yemen, Pakistan and Afghanistan. A hurried meeting with the President and her Secretary of Defense and other chief advisers was held.

The President did not want a repeat of the Iraq and Afghanistan conflicts which were both abysmal failures. No, this time it would be different. There were already two Battle Forces in the Mediterranean Sea that were on high alert. Suspected terrorist training camps were targeted and fired on with Cruise Missiles. Heavy damage was done and protests from the countries where they resided were lodged with the U.N. and the American State Department but were told these countries were repeatedly warned not to provide safe harbor for terrorists groups or the Al-Qaeda training camps. Further attacks were promised unless these countries cleaned up these issues. Cries of displeasure were coming in from all over the world including Russia. The United States did not want to have Russia as an enemy but wanted to continue with friendly relations as had been shown for the last several decades. Russia had had its own problems in Chechnya and had taken drastic action against that rogue state so they should understand the American response better than anyone.

On Hope

Hope received the news broadcast about the terrorist suicide bombings in Washington and New York and Hope was told that more attacks were anticipated. A Middle East and American war seemed more likely as time went on. Hope was also told of the cruise missile attacks against suspected terrorist training camps in various Middle East countries and the world wide condemnation of these attacks. Even Russia was upset at the U.S. Even the most militant people on Hope that wanted to return to earth realized that Hope's mission was more important now than ever in view of the recent events. The political scene on earth could deteriorate rapidly bringing about more military action, perhaps even more nuclear reprisals, a WWIV was not out of the question.

Washington

President Henderson realized that she had a major crisis on her hands. She asked Homeland Security to enlist the help of the FBI, NSA, DEA, any and all agencies that could lend a hand in following leads of suspected terrorist groups. They were granted special rights to investigate any dwelling that was suspected of being a terrorist safe house or bomb making facility. Homeland Security already had a list of suspects and locations. All agencies that were involved were given a list to investigate immediately and a date and time was picked for a coordinated effort so groups would have the least chance of warning others of impending investigations. A date and time was picked for the following week. Most would be night time raids depending which time zone they were in. At the appointed time the raids were conducted. People suspected of having terrorist ties were rounded up. Suspected terrorist locations were raided. Several locations were found to have bomb making supplies or evidence of bomb making activity. All suspects were immediately jailed without trial or charges until a full investigation was done under the umbrella of Homeland Security powers. This was not gone unnoticed by the news agencies. Newspapers and news web sites were full of information about the terrorist raids. People were calling their local police with information on Middle East neighbors or even other Americans suspected of having terrorist sympathies.

Police check points were set up going into the cities and any suspected vehicles were pulled over and inspected. Most were found to be okay but the roadside checks did manage to catch a few terrorists transferring bomb making supplies and in a couple of cases managed to catch some vehicles packed with explosives to be detonated at a predetermined location. With all this surveillance and activity it caught quite a few terrorists and a large cache of bomb making supplies but all were sure there were still some well hidden places that just had not been found yet. The investigations and the check points were maintained to keep up the pressure. Major sites were guarded around the clock with police units overlooking all roadways into the areas.

President Henderson was worried about the public paranoia of Muslims. She knew that many innocent Muslims were being persecuted unfairly. Most Muslims were good American citizens working hard to raise their families and to help the country back on its feet. She started to get reports of Muslims losing their jobs and some reports of murders. It was time to get on the television for another speech. She asked her secretary to make the arrangements "with all haste" she said. She also asked for a prominent Muslim leader to appear with her for her speech and to ask him to contact her ASAP as to what she expected him to say to the American people and the American Muslim community.

Her secretary did his best and managed to get the President one half hour on most of the major networks the following evening. He also managed to get Hassan Mohammed Ibrahim, a high level Imam or Muslim cleric who would be contacting her later in the day. When Hassan called she asked him if it was possible for him to come to the White House for a quick meeting. He said he would be most pleased to do so. He arrived at the appointed time of 3PM for the meeting. The two shook hands and President Henderson expressed her sorrow for the problems the terrorist attacks were having on good American Muslims and that she was going on the air tomorrow night to try and convince Americans that most Muslims are good Americans and not to let the acts of a few terrorist extremists taint all Muslims in America.

The Imam said he would be pleased and asked what was expected of him. She said she was going to give her speech and then the Imam would get his chance to speak to America both in English and in Arabic to inform America that all Muslims were not terrorists, only a very few radicals and to tell all Muslims the current situation should improve shortly and to keep up the faith. She also promised that each and every incident of Muslims losing their jobs since the terrorists attacks would be looked into to either get their jobs back or to get another job. Hassan seemed to like this idea very much and for about 15 minutes they discussed what each would say on the air.

After the meeting Charlotte shook hands with the Imam and said she would see him at the White House news room tomorrow evening. She rang her secretary and asked that an Arabic translator be on hand as well to interpret what the Imam was saying.

Washington News Room - The Following Evening

The President and the Imam, Hassan, a Catholic Priest,

Father Hannigan and an Arabic interpreter were waiting off stage listening to Charlotte's White House Chief of Staff speaking and soon they heard, "Please stand for the President of The United States."

The two men and Charlotte walked out and Charlotte stood behind the podium. Everyone in the room sat back down again.

"My fellow American's", Charlotte began. "The last few days have seen some startling terrorist activity. I want to thank each and everyone for being so vigilant but I also want to remind everyone that not everyone wearing a Hajib is a terrorist. There are many good Muslim American's that have moved here to make America their new home. They want the same things that we all do. A peaceful country to work, raise their families and practice their chosen faith. Over the last several days have seen random attacks and open criticism of anyone of Arabic descent. I should not have to remind you that almost 100% of these people are American's, NOT terrorists. We have even been given good information by many Muslims who do not support the terrorist attacks because they too see terrorism as an attack on their homeland as do we. I am asking each and everyone one to cease and desist any and all segregation and attacks against the Muslim community. Remember. They are American's too. Thank you."

Charlotte left the podium and was replaced by Hassan, the Iman of the Muslim faith. He spoke in English first and begged the American people to spare his people, fellow Muslims, from further attack and that he too deplored the terrorist attacks. He spoke at length in Arabic. The interpreter back stage was listening carefully as she was instructed to do. The Imam was speaking to all Muslims to work with their fellow American's against the terrorists. He followed up his speech with a short prayer in English and Arabic.

Father Hannigan spoke last paralleling the Presidents wish that all American's please respect their Muslim and Arabic neighbors and reminded them that most bomb making facilities were not in open neighborhoods but were in isolated areas. He urged all American's to exercise restraint when dealing with their Arabic neighbors. He closed his short speech with a prayer for peace.

Charlotte took the podium again and thanked the Imam and Father Hannigan for their supporting words and thanked all American's for their patience in these trying times.

Charlotte said, "We are working around the clock with many government agencies and local police forces to flush out the terrorists. We will get them all. Please don't persecute innocent citizens. Thank you for your time."

She turned to leave and a few reporters tried to ask questions but she ignored them as the security officials escorted them from the stage to the back. Charlotte spoke to the translator who had been listening to the Imam's speech.

"Did you detect any hidden meaning in the speech?", asked Charlotte. The translator admitted she hadn't but the speech had been recorded and would be analyzed for possible code words or phrases. Charlotte felt she could trust the Imam but just in case....

Al-Qaeda Headquarters in the West Bank

The leaders of Al-Qaeda were discussing the effect of the suicide bombers had on America. Everything had gone pretty much as expected. America was now a bee hive of activity looking for more terrorists. The American's had been quite thorough and had found many bomb making facilities but Al-Qaeda still had other methods of attack. Recently a new type of terrorist bomber had been thought of. Instead of the bomb being carried on the person or in a vehicle, the bomb material could now be surgically implanted into an individual making it almost impossible to detect. Several feet of intestine could be removed and replaced by bomb material.

A suicide bomber need only walk into an area and self-detonate creating maximum damage. If enough of these human bombs could be deployed it would be very demoralizing to the American people. What was worse Al-Qaeda had managed to recruit several American's who were sympathetic to their cause or Arabic people who could pass for American with perhaps a little plastic face surgery. Several safe houses had not yet been discovered. Al-Qaeda operatives were only given just enough information to do their job. They did not know the whereabouts of other safe houses other than the ones they operated out of. This was to safeguard the locations in case the American's got desperate and decided to use torture or hypnosis to try and get more information from their captives but it was well known the American's did not have the stomach for torture. And if it were found out that torture was being used the average American would be appalled.

The headquarters location would have to be changed soon as

it was moved about on a regular basis just in case that somehow the American's found out where they were operating from. This was discussed at length and it was decided to move into Iran. The best hiding place was often in plain site. It would be the last place they would look.

The decision about their next target was to be the New York Stock Exchange at 11 Wall Street in Manhattan. It was heavily guarded but entry was not impossible. Bombers could shoot their way in and then self-destruct once inside. It was felt that a sufficient number of bombers coupled with a bomb laden vehicle outside the building would do the maximum damage. Many months of planning were necessary but at last a plan was hatched. Directives were sent out and the people involved were notified.

Several bomb vehicles were readied in case one or more were stopped before reaching their target. Ten bombers in all were selected and provided with concealed weapons. All had been surgically implanted with explosives and were directed to get as far into the Stock Exchange as possible before self-destructing. Destroying or heavily damaging the Stock Exchange would put the American economy in a tailspin for weeks to come.

A Monday was selected as the best day to strike because trading would have just begun based on results from last weeks trading. The ten terrorists walked to the Stock Exchange and attempted to gain entrance. As was anticipated they met resistance and immediately killed the guards at the entrance. They then ran as far into the Stock Exchange as they could. Some even managed to get onto the trading floor. One by one they self-detonated creating massive casualties and damage. Meanwhile two of the five vehicles had managed to get to the outside of the building and exploded. One vehicle was chased by police units and was heavily damaged but still managed to reach its destination and exploded. The New York Stock Exchange was heavily damaged both inside and out. The stock exchanges in the rest of the world immediately ceased operation and went into lock down mode in case attacks were attempted against them.

Charlotte Henderson was immediate notified of the event. Police and military units cordoned off the area for blocks around and all other possible targets were heavily guarded. Investigators poured through the carnage looking for clues as to who and where the bombs had originated. It was obvious that America was under attack and a whole new defense was going to have to be thought up to defend vital operations. Homeland Security had done a good job but obviously not good enough. New investigative procedures would have to be drawn up and instigated immediately. It was very obvious that Al-Qaeda was serious in its intent to cripple America through terrorism and destruction to demoralize the nation.

On Hope

Hope had been notified about the attacks against America. Everyone knew that events on earth where again spiraling quickly out of control. Hope's mission looked more important than ever. Hope was approaching Jupiter. Day by day the massive gas giant was getting bigger. Jupiter's gravity was pulling Hope toward it preparation to slingshot around the planet and put it on course for Saturn, the next planet to slingshot around and gain still more speed. Hope's speed was 36,000 mile per hour as it slingshot past Jupiter on the way to Saturn.

The navigation section of the ship was manned at all times and the radar was aimed forward to give lots of advance notice of Hope heading into an asteroids path. After checking the doppler shift in light from Jupiter and stars whose doppler shift was known from earth, it was found that Hope's speed was about 58,000km/hr. The Captain wondered about trying out Hope's Bussard engines but he wanted to be in the Oort Cloud first. The Bussard engine was theorized to propel Hope to 2% of light speed, that is if it worked. That didn't sound high but was actually about 360,000km/hr. He wanted to be sure that he wasn't going to collide with anything in the Oort Cloud. No one knew how dense it was. It was assumed it was less dense than the asteroid field between Mars and Jupiter but he didn't want to take the chance.

In the space wheel everyone was busy training and cross-training others in their field of study. Many people had joined up as couples which had been expected and encouraged. Some of these couplings had taken place even before Hope had left earths orbit. Margret Blake (everyone called her Maggie) had paired with Tom Simms, a Geoscientist. His skills would be passed down through the generations to his distant relative whose job would be to establish the first habitation on the newly discovered planet. Maggie was an Astrophysicist whose job was to research the solar system as they passed through it, the Oort cloud and beyond. They had met during training on earth and had established an instant bond. Once aboard ship they immediately chose to live together in one of the ships living quarters. It was pretty cramped but they were together and didn't mind the closeness at all, in fact the closer the better. They enjoyed a healthy sex life together and had made friends with other couples on the ship.

Margaret was at her station as they were going through the asteroid belt heading to Jupiter. They had passed Mars some time ago and she was able to do a lot of study as they came toward Mars and used its gravity to sling shot around that planet and gain more speed for their journey. There was not much more learned about Mars or its moons as many earth probes had landed on the moons and on Mars itself. A manned mission to Mars had been planned but the economic crisis on earth had put a stop to that as the United States and other nations stopped all their spending on space and other projects and concentrated on just surviving. Her mother and father had been lucky. Their house was paid for and at first they lived comfortably enough but then their investments they had worked so hard for all their lives took a beating on the stock market. The bank where most of their savings were held had gone bankrupt and most of the money was lost. They were surviving on the government Social Security payments each month but there were rumors they might stop as the government went deeper into debt and could no longer afford the program. They did not know what they would do if that happened.

Her parents had taken in another couple, friends of theirs, who had lost their house when they both lost their jobs and their savings. It was around that time that Maggie had been contacted about this mission. She had gone through the initial testing fine and then found out it was for a deep space mission to the outer planets, a project being privately funded by a group of investors. A new space station being built in orbit to serve as an assembly and launch base as the ship that was scheduled to be built would be far too large to be launched from earth. It was during this time that she had met Tom and they had fallen in love. Then the truth had been revealed to them. The real voyage was to a distant planet around Alpha Centauri. Their entire life would be spent aboard the space ship they had been told was a space station. They had both been given 48 hours to decide if they wanted to go on the voyage. Both of them knew they would live and die aboard ship and it would be their distant relatives who would reach the distant planet with the hopes of colonizing it.

Tom had no relatives on earth. His parents had been killed during one of the uprisings and wanted to go on the voyage. He had finally persuaded Maggie to go with him. She agreed because she was so in love with him that the thought of not being with him was too much to bear. She was not allowed any contact with the outside world at this stage of the training. She would never see her parents again. They would be told of her decision to go on the voyage after the ship had left orbit. That is assuming it would leave orbit. There were rumors of steady unrest in the outside world and the threat of WWIII as China was threatening to blow the "space station" out of orbit. As it turned out they nearly succeeded. The last view she had of earth as the ship left orbit was the explosions in China as nuclear warheads found their mark. One Chinese nuclear missile had managed to make it through the North American anti-missile defense shield and had detonated in a lightly populated area of Kansas. China was heavily damaged with huge losses of life and infrastructure. China's manufacturing capability was mostly destroyed in the process.

She did not know what her parents would think of decision. She had been in contact with them a few times since the launch and at first they had been quite upset they had not had a chance to say good bye in person but once they knew the truth of the mission and the need for ultimate secrecy they understood but were still quite disappointed with the fact that a physical goodbye was impossible.

She and Tom had been notified they could not have a child together. He could not be the father. The father was someone she barely knew. She knew the reasoning behind this decision. It was all to do with genetics and the need to keep the gene pool as diverse as possible. They were both upset they would never be able to have their own child but knew this would probably happen. Maggie had immediately opted for artificial insemination as taking another man's sperm in the traditional way, especially someone she hardly knew, was out of the question. Her and Tom had been told the procedure would not happen for a couple of years yet. Some other couples had already been inseminated. One couple had got lucky. They had been chosen as the only couple on board that was allowed to have a child together. Maggie was envious.

Hope was equipped with a forward-looking radar that had been designed to watch out for asteroids and other debris that Hope was heading for and sound an alarm if anything was detected. This would give the ship plenty of time to avoid collision. So far the alarm had not sounded. The ship was also equipped with an automatic avoidance system that was designed to avoid any objects if there was no human intervention. This was considered a backup system just in case. The ship would automatically change course slightly to avoid the object and then come back on course. The ships auto-pilot would be using the Alpha Centauri star system itself as guidance once they cleared the Oort cloud and were in deep space between the stars. It was during this time there would be no one in the pilots cabin in the nose of the ship. There would only be periodic checks to make sure everything was still functional. It was not expected there would be any debris in deep space but the automatic collision system had been installed as an added safety measure. By the time anything was detected, the wheel was stopped and anyone air locked into the body of the ship to make the course correction manually, it would be too late.

Maggie (as she preferred to be called) was trying her best to analyze the composition of any asteroids that were close by. So far nothing remarkable had been found. They were all essentially just rocks in space. It was theorized the asteroid belt was debris left over from the formation of the solar system that never cohesed into a planet or they could have been a planet once that had exploded or been destroyed by a large meteor strike. It was generally accepted that is was debris that never formed it into a planet. The distance between Mars and Jupiter seemed to prove out this theory. Mars was some distance behind but was still a tell-tale small reddish marble in the blackness of space. Jupiter was somewhere ahead but unless you knew exactly where to look it was hard to spot. Hope had performed the sling shot maneuver perfectly around Mars and was now headed off at an angle toward Jupiter. The planets were rarely perfectly aligned, in fact it only happened once every several hundreds of years, so slingshotting around the planets made a zigzag course necessary.

Tom had been hard at work training one of the other crew in Geoscience as a secondary skill. In the unlikely eventuality that something happened to him the crew member he was training could train another member of the crew. There were lots of training materials stored in Hope's computer banks so even if there was no one on board with his skill someone could, given enough time, train themselves in the skill. It was boring work so training sessions were kept fairly short as there would be lots of time to pass on the knowledge, a whole life time. That thought bothered Tom a little, a whole lifetime aboard Hope. At first he was excited to begin the voyage but as the months went on he was having second thoughts about the whole thing. The news from earth told them of the increasing attacks by Al-Qaeda in the United States and some European countries. The United States was taking action and attacking known training camps and weapons stockpiles in mid-east countries.

This action was of course making the entire Arab world very upset but the American government was not about to risk another Iraq or Afghanistan fiasco. Oil shipments from a lot of the mid-east countries was being slowed or stopped altogether which made oil prices skyrocket to ridiculous heights. Increased resources were being thrown at alternative energy such as solar, wind and fusion power. Actually fusion power had been under research for several decades and had been accomplished but the riddle of how to get more energy out of a fusion reactor than was being put into it to sustain a reaction still had to be solved. From what he had heard some advancements had been made but not near enough to make it a feasible power source anytime in the near future. A whole new set of theories had to be found, he thought, to solve the problem. But once the problem was solved then America and all the rest of the western world could do with a lot less oil. In fact importing oil would be a thing of the past. The Middle East would return to its previous state of medieval life before the automobile was invented which required huge imports of foreign oil for gasoline and oil fired electric plants which made some people in the Middle East extremely rich. That was the problem. Some Kings and Princes in the Middle East were worth billions upon billions but this wealth was not shared very well so the common man in the Middle

East still had a meager existence.

Tom decided to break off the training for today and go visit the love of his life, Maggie. At least she was busy doing something relatively useful to keep busy. She was always so cheerful that when Tom was feeling down he would go visit Maggie and listen to her chatter on about planet and asteroid composition. He could hardly wait until the day was done and they could spend time together and then make love as they did almost every night. Some couples on board were rumored to be starting to swap mates for fun but the thought of sharing Maggie with another man was unthinkable. They had never discussed it and he hoped she thought the same way. Maggie saw Tom coming and gave him a big smile. His mood had not gone unnoticed. As much as he tried to hide it she knew his enthusiasm for the voyage was starting to decrease. This worried her. They had been on the voyage for only a year and several months and already this was happening to him? How would he be in 10 years, 20?

She was hoping they would be able to have a baby to take care of soon. It wouldn't be his baby but it would be theirs born from her womb. Hopefully this would give his spirits a lift. If his mood kept going down she was going to have to talk to him about it and see if there was anything for him to get interested in to peek his mood.

"How's it going babe?", he asked. Always the same question.

"Fine.", she answered as always."Nothing really new to report out there. Just rocks, rocks and more rocks, but I keep hoping to spot something really good. Maybe I can find a giant diamond.", she laughed.

Tom thought, "That's my Maggie. Always so upbeat. Maybe I should go see Doc and see if he could get some meds to improve my mood." But he knew the chances of that were almost nil to zero as medication on board Hope was strictly limited as it had to last for several generations. Actually this eventuality was considered for the first generation. They knew what it was like to live on a planet under open skies and earth beneath your feet but future generations would know nothing but the ship. It would be home to them. "To them....", thought Tom.

Washington – The White House

Charlotte knew that something had to be done and done quickly. It was obvious that Al-Qaeda had declared war on America. When the World Trade Center towers were brought down in 2001 America went to Afghanistan to root out Al-Qaeda but that resulted in several years of war without eradicating them. America had managed to kill Osama bin Laden but all that did was infuriate Al-Qaeda even more. It also strained relations between the United States and Pakistan as bin Laden had been hiding in Pakistan "in plain sight" in a heavily guarded compound right near a Pakistani military base. How could Pakistan not know that bin Laden was there, the world was asking? How indeed!

Now it appeared that Al-Qaeda had brought the war to America. How do you fight a foe who are willing to die as suicide bombers and can masquerade as normal American's? All it takes is a handful of people to get past heavily patrolled defenses and do massive damage. She had to call a meeting with Homeland Security, Defense, the FBI and anyone else she could thing of and do a brainstorming session on the best course of action. They may have to lock down the nation for self-protection. Charlotte called her secretary and gave him a list of people who she wanted in her office in two hours. No excuses. She didn't care what they were doing. Just tell them to "be there."

On Board Hope

Tom was really depressed and he did not know what to do about it. The more he thought about it the more he came to realization that he could not live out his life aboard Hope. He wandered the corridors thinking about what to do when he came to the airlock doors. He stood there a while looking at them. If he went out into space without a spacesuit death would be quick. Tom looked up and down the corridor. Because they were on a wheel the corridor disappeared quickly as the corridor turned out of sight. Tom pressed the button the for the airlock door and it opened. It was quite large inside as during the building of Hope large items had to be locked aboard and during flight items from the hull section and hydroponics had to be locked into the wheel as well. Tom stepped into the airlock and looked at the control board. It seemed pretty easy to operate. There was a large sign on the wall, "SPACE SUITS REQUIRED BEYOND THIS POINT"

Meanwhile Lisa Menard who was at the control console in the wheel noticed a flashing light on her console. It was the airlock door signal. No airlock maneuvers had been announced.

She immediately called her supervisor and showed him the console signal. "What the.....". He started to say.

He flicked a switch on the console and pushed a button.

"Why are you in the airlock! Identify yourself!", the supervisor said.

In the airlock Tom heard the supervisor's voice and hesitated then chose to ignore it. He pushed the button to close the inner airlock door. He looked at the panel and pushed the button to open the outer airlock door.

"The inner airlock door is closed.", said Lisa as the lights indicated the inner airlock door was closed.

"Was any maintenance scheduled for the airlock?", asked Lisa.

"No.", the supervisor replied, "If there was we would have been notified." Lisa almost shouted, "The outer door sequence has started!"

Inside the airlock Tom heard a hissing sound as the air in the lock chamber was pumped out. "What was happening?", he thought.

Tom had failed to consider the airlock had to be evacuated of all air before the outer door would open. It was getting hard to breathe and he started to panic. He looked at the control board frantically to look for a way to abort the outer door sequence. What he did not know was once the sequence was started there was no way to stop it. The console had been designed to be as simple to operate as possible for future generations in case they started to lose the technical ability to operate complex systems. He punched the inner door button frantically without success. The inner door would only open once the lock was pressurized to equal the air pressure in the wheel.

Tom was gasping for air that was quickly being evacuated. Soon he was unable to breathe at all. He was trying to inhale but there was nothing to inhale, no air. He felt himself beginning to black out when he saw the outer door opening and the blackness of space beyond. The heat was quickly expelled into space and replaced by the cold silent vacuum of space. Tom's last conscious thought was how dark, cold and silent space was. His lifeless body floated out into space and was quickly spun away from the wheel from the centrifugal gravity produced by the wheel's turning.

Lisa said, "Whoever it was is gone.", she said. Her and supervisor exchanged glances and he quickly called for someone in engineering to check the airlock.

In a few minutes he got a call back. "Barry here.", they said. "The inner door is closed but the outer door is still open. I'm not seeing anyone."

The supervisor replied, "No you wouldn't because if it was a person they would have been spun away from the wheel."

The supervisor quickly made an announcement that had never been made on Hope before. "All personnel, all personnel. Please go to assembly areas. Please go to assembly areas. Code red, code red."

This command was to be used in emergency situations where all occupants of Hope were to go for a head count and if necessary to be assigned tasks in case of a catastrophic event.

Washington – The White House

It was 1 PM and everyone that she had requested to be in her office was there. Refreshments had been set up for everyone.

Charlotte began. "I am pretty sure you know why you are all here. Al-Qaeda has obviously declared war on us and we have to decide what the best course of action will be to protect ourselves. Homeland Security, the FBI and other agencies are doing a good job so far but as you know Al-Qaeda still has the ability to attack. The problem as you know is these radicals are prepared to give their very lives to accomplish their missions. We may have to take some drastic actions to combat them and protect ourselves. That is what this meeting is about, to decide what we can do. Martial Law is an option but the law under Homeland Security gives them arrest and detention rights far and above most law agencies. Does anyone have any ideas to start us off?"

Everyone looked at others in the room. Finally Paul Harrison the head of FBI spoke. "We have to restrict their movements and use better detection methods when they are moving bombs or bomb making materials around. We could have sensors installed at key points to detect those. We could also do random checks of all vehicles such as trucks and SUV's which seem to be their favorite delivery mechanisms to get a bomb where they want it to be."

George Patricks, head of Homeland Security gave Harrison a disgusted look and said, "We are already doing lots of spot checks of vehicles even during rush hours which is frustrating a lot of people but that would be the opportune time to transport something so everyone better get used to it. We are trying our best to get vehicles to be inspected off the road as far as possible but all the rubberneckers slow down the traffic. As far as sensors go, we thought of that but most of these bombs are just crude fertilizer bombs. They are easy to construct. You can go on the internet to find out how to make one. Al-Qaeda has been using them for years. We have been monitoring the purchase of large amounts of fertilizer and that's how we tracked down many bomb makers and Al-Qaeda cells in the beginning but now they are getting smart. We think they are buying smaller amounts, some here and some there and in some cases stealing it. It makes things quite difficult. One pattern we have found is that most Al-Qaeda cell headquarters are in rural areas so we have been advising residences to be especially vigilant and to call us about any suspicious activity. That netted us some arrests as well. We have used some interrogation methods that are a little extreme but quite within the law such as sleep deprivation to get information which sometimes has led to good results."

Charles Debin, Charlotte's Secretary of Defense was the next to speak. "I know it would be considered profiling but we have to keep a close watch on all people of Middle Eastern descent. Anyone from that particular group should be considered a suspect and closely watched. We will probably get a lot of backlash from the Muslim community but we also have the right to protect ourselves. At the beginning of the Second World War after Japan bombed Pearl Harbor everyone of Japanese descent was rounded up and placed in concentration camps and their property seized. In a lot of cases the Japanese roundups were 2nd and 3rd generation American's but that didn't matter. To the political leaders of the time they were still Japanese and might still support Japan instead of America. It was feared that Japan may have had a whole network of spies and terrorists in America already."

Everyone in the room contemplated Charles's words and the

implications behind them. They may have to take the drastic action of rounding up anyone of Middle Eastern heritage and hold them, interrogate and investigate until the crisis was over.

George Patricks said, "We could institute the death penalty for any bomb makers suppliers and suicide bombers but that may only raise them to the level of martyrs. What I would suggest is an immediate stop to all people from any Middle Eastern country or anyone of Middle Eastern descent no matter where they are coming from."

Charlotte said, "So there really is not a lot more we can do that we aren't doing already. We just have to keep the pressure up and ask American's, real American's, to be especially vigilant and to keep reporting suspicious activity. Okay, we'll wrap this up unless anyone else has anything to add?" Charlotte looked around the room.

Everyone looked at Charlotte and then at each other. No one had anything to add. There were ideas put forward if things got worse but no one wanted to commit to anything drastic such as a roundup and holding of people of Middle Eastern descent.

Charlotte said, "George, I want you to initiate your plan of stopping all people of Mid East descent from entering the country. At least that will be a start but I fear that all the terrorists Al-Qaeda need are already here." Everyone looked grim for they all knew what Charlotte had just said was true.

On Hope

Everyone had stopped what they were doing and had gone to

their assembly areas. A headcount had been taken of all groups and everyone was present except for Geoscientist Tom Simms. Several pages were announced on the ship including the navigation section but there was no response. Maggie started to weep and then broke down crying. Everyone gathered around her to comfort her but it was of little use.

"That bastard!", she thought, "He was the one that was all excited about this trip and convinced me to go and now he decides to do this...."

The doctor was soon at her side. "Come with me Margaret.", he said gently as he placed his hand on the small of her back.

Maggie numbly walked along beside the doctor until the got to the ships small infirmary. Doctor Fred Randolph talked to Maggie at length about Tom's state of mind over the last little while.

"I knew there was something wrong but I never expected this.", she said. "I knew he was depressed but I figured it would pass. Whenever I asked him if anything was wrong he would always answer 'nothing' with a little smile but I knew there was something wrong but I never in my wildest dreams expected anything like this."

She broke down sobbing again. "We always had a good sex life but lately he was so robotic. There didn't seem to be any emotion in it. I was starting to wonder if he was tiring of me and was attracted to someone else. That was my worse fear. I tried to be upbeat and happy for him and told him many times I loved him because I did. He was the one who convinced ME to come on this voyage and I did because I loved him so much. I left everything behind, my life on earth, my parents, everything, to be with him."

The doctor could see the rage beginning to build in Maggie. She felt betrayed. "What am I going to do now? Everyone is paired up on the ship. I won't have anyone."

The doctor knew that some crew members were swapping mates and it was rumored some were even involved with group sex. He didn't dare mention this to Maggie. She probably already had heard the rumors. She wanted someone to be her one and only like Tom but there wasn't anyone. Maggie was a normal healthy attractive young woman with needs and desires. What was she to do now? The doctor had no answer. They talked for a while longer until Maggie said halfheartedly she better get back to work. The doctor thought to himself that work would help take her mind off things for the short term but what was going to happen to Maggie in the long term? Other women on the ship were going to be wary of her now because they may think that Maggie would be out to steal some other woman's mate but the doctor knew Maggie well enough that would never happen. But then no one expected Tom to commit suicide, did they?

Al-Qaeda – The West Bank

The Al-Qaeda leaders had changed headquarter locations many times to make it harder for the American's to track them. They had got the news from America that Al-Qaeda's latest terrorist bombings had been successful but the missions were getting harder to implement. The American's were finding safe houses and bomb making facilities and security was extremely tight. Vehicles were being randomly searched all the time and a few had been caught transporting bomb making materials. Anyone of Middle Eastern descent was suspect and America had stopped all travel by Middle Eastern people into the country.

One of them spoke, "We must change our tactics. I think we should lay low for a while to make the American's think they have defeated us but meanwhile we should gather all our assets and plan a massive attack in the future when America seems to have let down their guard."

All seemed to agree. After the Stock Market had been bombed America had stepped up their surveillance and it was getting difficult to acquire bomb making materials and plan terrorist missions.

NIF & PS

NIF & PS is the National Ignition Facility and Photon Science center in California where research was being carried out to design a workable fusion reactor. Fusion reactors have been under research around the world for decades, since the 1970's. A fusion reactor actually works in reverse to a nuclear or 'fission' reactor which splits atoms to release energy. A fusion reactor fuses atoms together at the atomic level thus the name 'fusion reactor'. Our sun and all the stars are fusion reactors. They work because of the immense gravity created at the star's core raising the temperature of mostly hydrogen creating a plasma that breaks away the electrons at the atomic level allowing the atoms to fuse together releasing massive amounts of energy and creating new elements. Hydrogen was the most often used element and when fused it would create helium. Other elements are fused together as well thus producing all the different elements we see on earth. At the end of a stars life it will explode spreading all these elements through space which will eventually over a period of billions of years will create another solar system with its own sun and planets like ours.

Actually the amount of energy released by the fusing of two atoms is quite small but when you are dealing with trillions and trillions of atoms the result is a huge amount of energy indeed. Our star, the sun, is 93 million miles away but on a sunny day you can feel the heat from it on your face proving this power. The earth receives only a tiny fraction of the suns energy output. Scientists have been trying for decades to create the same conditions here on earth. We can't use massive amounts of gravity so lasers are used to heat the hydrogen fuel into a plasma until a fusion reaction takes place. This process has been done in labs all over the world but more energy has to be used to start the reaction and sustain it than the energy output achieved.

The scientists at NIF had just made a significant breakthrough using a new type of low power, high output laser which looked promising on paper. This may be just the break they have been looking for. Plans were made to replace the existing lasers in a working prototype reactor rather than building a new one. The project took about six months to complete and the newly designed reactor was ready for its first trial run. It would take several hours for the lasers to heat up the hydrogen pellet fuel. The lasers had all been carefully aligned so their total output was concentrated in the middle of the crucible, surrounded by magnets to suspend the plasma. The reactor was beginning to heat up. The energy output from the lasers was almost bang on to what had been predicted. The crucible had been redesigned as well to hold the pressure created by the plasma. Between the lasers and the pressure in the crucible it was hoped between the two that a higher amount of power could be achieved than what was needed to fire the lasers and power the magnets.

The hydrogen pellet ignited with a brilliant flash brighter than a dozen suns. The light could be seen even through the thick walls of the crucible. Anyone in close proximity had to wear protective glasses for the glare. The engineers monitored the power input to the lasers and the power output enough to power a small steam turbine to generate electricity. The power output was six times the power input to the lasers and the electromagnets surrounding the crucible holding the plasma. They had done it! The secret to fusion power had been cracked! They decided to let it run for several hours all the while monitoring its performance but all looked good. They powered down the lasers in steps to allow the plasma to cool gradually until fusion stopped and then continued in graduated steps until all laser power was zero. A report was immediately sent to Washington of their success.

Washington

The report of the fusion reactor success was received and went through channels until it crossed Charlotte's desk. She knew hardly anything of the mechanics of a fusion reactor but she did know that it was a source of virtually free power and far safer than nuclear power. No special fuel was needed as in a nuclear reactor which made it so attractive. That and the added value of being far safer. There was no chance of a runaway as there was in nuclear reactor. If you wanted to stop it all one had to do was turn the lasers off. She picked up the phone and called the U.S. Secretary of Energy, Mr. Samuel Zambrowski. He was not in his office so Charlotte left a message with his Administrator to have him call her ASAP. Within 10 minutes Mr. Zambrowski was calling back.

He and Charlotte discussed the success of the fusion test reactor and told him to go ahead and build a full scale reactor "with all possible haste." With price of oil going through the roof America desperately needed a cheap source of power and this looked like it would be it! America had cut its need for foreign oil to the bare bones but a fair amount still came in from off shore sources. Europe was in far worse shape as virtually all their oil was imported. This discovery would of course be shared with them and soon the rest of the world. It could be the start of the dream of true world peace. Cheap power for everyone.

Charlotte thought, "The only ones who were going to be pissed were the OPEC countries but they had held the rest of the world hostage with high oil prices for far too long, now it was pay back time."

Aboard Hope

Hope was nearing Jupiter and the slingshot manoeuvre around the massive gas giant had been calculated and in Hope's computers. The slingshot had to be precise so as to head them off in the exact direction to Uranus, the next planet to slingshot around and increase Hope's speed even more. Jupiter filled almost the whole of the view from the cockpit in the nose of the ship. A crew was on stand-by in the cockpit in the event something went wrong which was considered a near impossibility as slingshot manoeuvres had been done for decades with planetary probes and always with great success. Once in a while a small mid-course correction was needed but that rarely happened. Houston was "driving" the ship and monitoring its progress through the solar system. If any course correction were needed they would be radioed up to the ships computers and it would be taken care of with a slight tweak in direction with a short firing of Hope's engines. The fuel calculations for this eventuality had been taken into consideration during the ships design.

As Hope began its slingshot manoeuvre around Jupiter it affected the center of gravity aboard Hope. Not a lot but the people in the space wheel could feel the tug of the giant planet. Hope's speed had increased as it headed toward Jupiter and it was now slingshotting around the planet. There would be a slight reduction in speed as Jupiter's gravity tugged at Hope as it sped away from Jupiter but the end result would be a significant speed increase from when they were far away from Jupiter and not being affected by the giant planets gravity well. The slingshot manoeuvre had been performed perfectly according to Houston and no course correction was needed at this point. As they neared the half way point to Uranus, Hope's direction would be checked again but for now it looked right on target.

Al-Qaeda Headquarters – Iran

Al-Qaeda Headquarters had been moved to Iran as it was assumed the American's would believe that is the last place they would look which would be the likeliest place, right under their noses. It appeared that it had worked. American spies were searching everywhere except Iran because it was believed that would be the last place for them to setup a headquarters. It was carefully concealed with many direction changes needed to find exactly where it was. Several top Al-Qaeda operatives were in attendance.

One of the operatives said, "America has stepped up its defenses. It is almost impossible to get a bomb to its target. Many of our facilities and personnel have been discovered. The American's have caught on to our little trick of buying or stealing small amounts of fertilizer and stockpiling it. We do have some stockpiled but we have to use it wisely. We can use it all in one big attack or small co-ordinated attacks. What do you all say?"

Everyone was thinking and looking at each other. Use it all in one big attack and then have nothing left for another attack or use it in small attacks?

Finally one of the operatives spoke. "I vote we use it in small attacks but spread out over time so the American's think we have lots of bomb making materials left. That will keep them guessing for a while. It will mean they will probably tighten up their security even more after each attack or we could go for several co-ordinated attacks at the same time to give the same impression."

Everyone pondered this idea and after more discussion it was decided to do small co-ordinated attacks. The orders would be sent out over the internet tomorrow in carefully coded messages.

Several days later America was rocked by five separate explosions as Al-Qaeda terrorists detonated bombs in five separate cities at carefully chosen targets. There was soon a meeting in Washington with Homeland Security, the FBI, CIA and a few other agencies to discuss the matter and how much more they could do. They had tightened up security as much as possible and yet the terrorists had managed to squeeze by security and set the bombs off. Each bombing was carefully analyzed to see what could have been done. The terrorists had used smaller vehicles in all cases. None were done by big vans, trucks or SUV's but by smaller vehicles packed with explosives. The explosives were probably carefully hidden inside the doors, under the wheel wells, inside the frame, anywhere that a quick search would not reveal. Will more attacks come? Was this the start of a new round of terrorist attacks? The general population in the cities were getting real nervous especially ones that worked in high profile targets and you couldn't blame them. There were patrols around these targets but the targets just attacked were "below the radar" lower profile targets. Was Al-Qaeda getting too scared to go after high profile targets and now concentrating on lower profile ones just to heighten everyone's anxiety? It was general agreed this was the case. The conclusions of the meeting were sent direct to the President.

The Oval Office

"Those damn bastards!", Charlotte swore after reading the report. She was referring to the terrorists.

What should her next step be? She was getting REAL close to ordering the round up of all people of Middle Eastern descent.

"That would be my absolute last option.", she thought.

What else could she do before getting to that stage? Al-Qaeda had picked lower profile targets this time which meant they considered the high profile ones were too high a risk of success but manpower was stretched to the limit. They couldn't guard EVERYTHING. According to her advisers Al-Qaeda was squeezed very tight and it was assumed they had very little in the way of personnel or bomb making materials and any further terrorists attack was unlikely but they had managed to detonate five car bombs. Obviously intelligence was wrong. What to do? Let's say believe what my advisers are telling me and this was a last ditch attack with everything they had left and there would be no more or they had lots more and this was just the beginning of a new round of attacks. She decided reluctantly to sit and wait for further developments. She called the head of Homeland Security, George Patricks, of her decision and to get his opinion. They discussed it for a few minutes and agreed. Let's wait and see what happens but keep up the same security on the high profile targets and attempt to keep lower profile targets under security as well. Right now security was being handled by patrols, both in vehicles and on foot and there were carefully placed camera's at many locations that were monitored 24 hours a day. She didn't know what else to do. It was decided to wait and see. She hoped they were doing the right thing.

Several Months Later

Several months had passed and all was quiet as far as terrorist attacks were concerned. A few Al-Qaeda cells had been discovered and raided. Few bomb making supplies had been found.

Manufacturing in the U.S. Was slowly picking up and the jobless rate was starting to come down. As more people started working again taxes, both state and federal started to come in again. Charlotte had reduced government spending to the bare bones as had state spending. Prices for consumer goods bought with "disposable income" rose as was expected but everyone was forewarned this would happen. The auto industry needed a break. Salaries at the auto plants were way too high and had been for years by pressure and frequent strikes over the years by the unions. High level talks were held with the unions and the heads of the auto plants. It was explained that salaries must come down to a more believable level. The salaries in the plants that had returned to the U.S. were a lot lower but at least people were working. When compared to the auto workers salaries there was a huge difference. The majority of vehicles being produced were electric with some gasoline vehicles still being produced, especially long haul buses and trucks.

The price of vehicles would of course be reduced to reflect the lower wages being paid to assemble them. Charlotte expected a big backlash from the auto unions and she was right. Threats were made of an industry wide strike if a move was made to lower salaries. It was explained that salaries would not be lowered all at once but in small steps to allow the workers to adjust to the new levels. The theory was that the reduced prices in autos would stimulate sales and would help the economy overall. In the end the hammer came down. Charlotte directed that her advisers were to tell the unions they had no choice in the matter. If strikes were held the strikers would be laid off and new people hired to take their place and the military would be brought in to maintain order. It was either go with the flow and accept the changes or there would be dire consequences.

The unions would still be there to monitor working conditions and so on but salaries for the time being were off the table. Union meetings were held and as expected there was a lot of commotion and threats but they were told in no uncertain terms this was the way of the future. Salaries must be balanced across the whole of the U.S. industrial base so as not to undermine the process. There were a few wildcat strikes. The workers were ordered back to work or risk being fired. Some went back while others dug in their heels and refused. These workers were promptly fired with a lot of yelling and screaming from the workers and the unions because the word had been given and was being reinforced. Of course there were accusations of Charlotte trying to turn the U.S. into a communist country. Most people outside the auto industry applauded the move and supported her decision. Why should a worker in an auto plant get almost three times the salary for putting vehicles together versus someone working in another industry doing a similar job? It was just leveling the playing field for everyone.

Hope

Hope was nearing Uranus preparing to do a slingshot around the gas giant. No mid-course correction had been required. The Houston computers had done an excellent job in astrogation getting them to where they were. Once out of the solar system Hope would be on her own. She would be light years away and any chance of getting a signal to Hope for a course correction would be almost futile. It would take years for a signal to come back to earth to be analyzed and then several more years for a signal to be sent back to Hope for a course correction which would lengthen the closer they got to their destination. Once Hope reached Alpha Centauri it would take four years for a message to reach earth and four more years for a reply to be sent.

Hope had been designed with this scenario in mind. Hope would be concentrating on Alpha Centauri and any course correction, if needed, would be performed by Hope's on board computers. Even now it was taking many hours for signals between Hope and earth to be completed and they weren't even out of the solar system yet. Hope was coming up on Uranus quickly. The planet filled most of the port windows in the navigation section at the nose of the ship. Everyone hoped the slingshot manoeuvre was calculated correctly as this would be the last one before Hope left the solar system. Pluto was currently on the other side of the sun but had not been considered for a slingshot manoeuvre because of Pluto's small size. Besides, Pluto's status had been downgraded from a planet to a simple asteroid many years before.

As predicted the slingshot around Uranus was a success. There was some discussion about using Uranus's slingshot to return to earth as things appeared to be picking up but the general consensus was to continue with the mission as things appeared to be getting better but Al-Qaeda was still considered a threat and it was largely unknown what they would do. There were still rogue nations like North Korea to worry about. The Russians were being trusted for now but if some idealist got into power that could change quickly.

Washington

Charlotte received word the fusion reactor in California was complete and was undergoing testing. So far everything appeared great and lined up perfectly with all the expectations and predictions. In a few days the fusion reactor would become fully operation and put onto the California electricity grid. It should replace at least four coal, oil or gas fired electric generating stations. That would be a big saving in fuel not to mention less pollution in the environment. Plans were already on the drawing board to start building more fusion generating stations across the U.S. In the most needed areas.

A new day was dawning. A day when dependence on foreign oil would cease. That would be a day to celebrate for sure. OPEC had heard the news and threatened to boost oil prices through the roof or even stop exports unless the U.S. stopped its fusion generating program. A quick meeting with her Energy Secretary confirmed the U.S. had a stockpile to ride out such a scenario. It would be tight. There would have to be gas rationing and maybe even rolling blackouts for a short period of time but if the fusion reactors were built all at once with all possible haste the U.S. would survive without foreign oil even if OPEC decided to make good with their threat right at this moment.

The European Union and Russia had both been advised of the fusion reactor breakthrough and the plans for building them had been sent. It was up to them as to when construction would start. She hoped soon because most of Europe depended heavily on imported oil. The Russians were an oil exporter and had agreed to supply oil to Europe at the fixed price as of today. If OPEC raised their prices Russia would not to take advantage of the situation. Bless those Russians. They have been a big help. She just prayed that would continue to be the case. A lot of the world's conflicts were all about energy. She hoped the fusion reactors would solve that problem and give every nation the source of cheap and always available electric power.

Three Years Later.......

A lot had transpired in the last three years. Most of the fusion generating plants that were planned for the most needed areas had been built. There had been another federal election but Charlotte Henderson was no longer President. She had served two consecutive terms, three if you count the time the U.S. had been under marshal law prior to WWIII with China. The person in charge was now Peter Williams, a Democrat, as was Charlotte. The Democrats had won easily since the U.S. economic situation was improving in leaps and bounds. Peter was following Charlotte's direction in getting the U.S. manufacturing base restarted. OPEC had tried to control the flow of oil by restricting supply to the world's nations plus hiking the price considerably. Their plan backfired as the U.S. had sufficient reserves until the fusion reactors were built. The plan to gradually lower the salaries of the autoworkers had worked. Cars were being produced at a much lower price and most of them were electric due to the consistent lowering of electricity rates due to the fusion reactors and the ever higher gasoline prices and gas shortages. Gasoline had to be rationed as expected which steered people to public transportation or to electric vehicles.

Aboard Hope

Hope had long since passed Uranus and even Pluto's furthest orbit point since Pluto's orbit was elliptical and was sometimes closer to earth than Uranus. The sun was just a tiny glowing point in space. It was hoped the Oort cloud existed as theorized and the Bussard engine would work or it would be a VERY long trip to Alpha Centauri indeed! The ships sensors had not picked up any increase in free floating hydrogen that was expected in the Oort cloud.

Mana Halikona was watching over the sensor board when there was a sudden rise in the amount of hydrogen atoms being detected outside the ship. It stayed level for a few seconds and she was about to call the captain when it dipped back down again. "Just a stray cloud of atoms.", she thought.

After a few minutes it jumped up again. She watched the reading and it was staying at fairly constant level for several minutes.

She decided to call the Captain. "Captain. This is Mana at sensors. The hydrogen levels have jumped considerably. They went up once and then came back down. Now they have jumped up again and are staying high."

The Captain replied he would be there right away and within minutes he was at her side. "Its been holding steady since you called me?", he asked.

"Yes sir.", Mana replied.

He punched the ships intercom button and said, "All hands, this is the Captain. High hydrogen levels have been detected outside the ship and are holding. Please refer to your guides for preliminary procedures for Bussard engine start. Each section report in to Central Control when you have finished. This is a first class protocol."

First Class Protocol meant drop whatever you are doing and complete the task at hand. Each section was shutting down all non-essential systems and equipment. Most power from the reactor must be made available to the Bussard engine systems. There were huge electromagnets to collect and eventually hold the plasma and lasers that would be used to heat the hydrogen collected into plasma for the engine to ignite. The Captain went to Central Control and brought up the Operations Guide and on the screen and turned to the section "Bussard Engine Start-up." The section for turning off all non-essential systems was being completed as he read over the sequence for the engine startup.

"Send a message to Houston that we appear to be in the Oort cloud and are starting the Bussard engine. We will let them know if it is successful or not." He knew the message would take over a day to reach earth.

All sections had reported in and acknowledged that all non-essential systems were shutdown. Even the lights were turned off completely or only a minimum left on as necessary. He activated the huge electromagnets to collect and hold the hydrogen. There was a scoop at the nose of the ship just under navigation that would aid in collecting the hydrogen atoms and guiding them to the engine where they would be held until enough had been collected for engine start. The guide was quite vague on how long this would be as it was not known how much stray hydrogen was in the Oort Cloud. A camera was mounted some distance from the engine that could be zoomed in to view the area in the middle of the magnets where the hydrogen would be collected and compressed as much as possible. Not a lot was needed, just slightly larger than a marble. He checked the camera and zoomed in for a look.

He could not see any activity yet. "This could take a while.", he thought.

Hours passed and he checked again and there was a noticeable small round object being held in place by the magnets but it wasn't nearly marble size.

Houston Mission Control

One of the controllers that was monitoring transmissions from Hope called the senior controller who everyone called "Flight." This was a title that had been used since the early days of rocketry and was still used. "Flight, we just received a message from Hope. They appear to be in the Oort Cloud and are collecting hydrogen to hopefully be able to start the Bussard engine. They said they would send another message later on to let us know if the engine worked or not."

Flight said to the controller, "That's great news! Keep me informed." The controller acknowledged.

As Flight had been ordered he called the White House and left a message for the President of the situation on Hope. The President, Peter Williams, immediately called Malcolm Beacham as Charlotte Henderson, the last President had told him that Malcolm had been the head of the Hope construction project and was to be made aware of any important developments on Hope. President Williams asked his secretary (the same one who was Charlotte's secretary) to call Malcolm and give him the news.

When Malcolm heard the news he was elated but also worried. The Bussard engine was experimental and it was theorized to work but had never been tested in space. At least it was collecting hydrogen. That was a very important first step for without hydrogen the engine would not work at all. Samantha or "Sam" as she like to be called came into the office. She and Malcolm had recently married. They had both sold their separate houses and had bought a larger house because they had discussed having a baby. Samantha was already pregnant. She was in her first Trimester and just beginning to "show."

Sam said, "Time for lunch?"

Malcolm replied, "Yes! And I just got some great news! Hope has apparently reached the Oort Cloud and has started to collect hydrogen. We'll soon know if the Bussard engine will work or not."

Sam replied, "What happens if it doesn't work?"

Malcolm looked worried. "I don't know. Without that engine working it will take a very long time for Hope to reach its destination. There was even some talk of bringing Hope home if the engines did not work."

That scenario had already been discussed whether the engines worked or not. Things on earth had improved dramatically since Hope's departure and it was being bandied around if the mission was still needed. Hope was supposed to be humankind's last ditch effort to save itself since things had been looking so bad on earth. After much talk it was decided to allow Hope to continue. If a colony could be started on the planet orbiting Alpha Centauri it would be a foot hold in space for further colonization of the galaxy. Hopefully at sometime in the future the light speed barrier could be broken and faster ships could be built. As it was it was going to take about 200 years for Hope to reach its destination.

Several generations of humans would be born, live, work and die on board ship never having set foot on a planet. What would those of the generation that reached its destination think about living on a planet? The ship would have been their home and many of their descendants home. He hoped that training for the mission would be passed down from generation to generation as was planned for.

On Board Hope

Hope had been collecting hydrogen for two days and the little round ball of hydrogen was nearing the size needed for engine start. Captain Jacoby wondered if they should collect more hydrogen than was needed "just in case." No one knew for sure how much propulsion the engine would produce or for how long. Everything was theoretical. It was hoped that it would be enough to propel Hope up to the expected speed of 360,000 kph need for the rest of the trip. Maybe he would collect just a bit more than was needed.

China

China had been severely crippled by the war but was slowly getting to its feet again. There had been many casualties. Over a third of China's population had been killed outright or had died from their injuries or radiation exposure after the war. There was still a feeling of hatred toward America by the general population. An American campaign had been running for quite a while explaining to the Chinese people that it was China who had hit the button first and that America was simply defending itself. Some people believed it but a lot didn't. They had been given contrary information by the Chinese government. On the face of it the new Chinese government had supported America's campaign but through the backdoor information was going out to the contrary. America and Europe had tried their best to help China get back on their feet but they too had their own problems. The Chinese economy was not very good as most manufacturing had been moved out of China. Only some manufacturing was allowed with exports to the U.S. and America. Russia had helped China much more than the rest of the world and the two countries were now very good comrades. Russia had even helped China get its space projects started again. It was Russia that had sent two ships up to the Chinese Space Station to rescue the crew after the war.

America was closely watching the events unfold between the two countries. Russia was still friendly with the U.S. but was much more so with China. For a start they were both communist countries. Russia was supposed to be democratic and on the surface this was so but most of the infrastructure was still owned and run by the State. It was the same in China. People were allowed and even encouraged to start and run their own businesses but all the major infrastructure and most manufacturing that was left was State owned and run. Russia knew that it was China that had started the war but was appalled by the lack of assistance given to China after the war. Immediately after medical teams had been sent in to help the injured but after that little help was given. It was Russia that had stepped in and helped get China back to where it was today. The two countries were very friendly indeed which worried America.

On Board Hope

Hope had been collecting hydrogen for about 5 days and the little ball of hydrogen was a little bigger than needed. That pleased the Captain. He would much rather have a little extra just in case. He gave the order to start the firing sequence of the lasers to heat the hydrogen to a plasma state so the engine would ignite. As soon as the lasers were switched on it was realized they were drawing more power than expected. The reactor was being taxed to the limit. He immediately gave the order to reduce power consumption even more.

More systems were turned off. Even one of the computers was shut down. Hope had three computer all running in tandem. In a worse case scenario Hope would run fine with one computer but three had been installed. Triple redundancy. The power draw from the reactor dropped a little but was still a bit high. He considered stopping the wheel. That would save a fair bit of power but most of the people, including himself, were not used to zero gravity. He had been to Navigation in the ships nose a few times but hated going there through the airlocks into space and then locking into the body of the spacecraft. Once in the body of the craft there was zero gravity because unlike the wheel there was no artificial gravity.

He was in Central Control and was monitoring the power draw from the reactor. It was at around 97% which he considered a bit too high. There was little room for error. He ordered more systems and lights to be switched off and watched the power draw drop to 95%. A little better but he would like to see less. He brought up the specs on the wheel to see how much power it consumed to maintain revolutions. Maybe by stopping the wheel he could get the power levels down even more. He checked the specs for the amount of power needed to start the wheel rotating again and quickly realized that if the wheel was stopped it would not be able to be restarted until after the Bussard engine was shutdown and no one knew for certain how long the engine would have to run for Hope to reach its trip speed. It could be a few days, it could be a week or more. No one knew for certain. He asked the controller to carefully monitor the little reactor and to let him know ASAP if there were any problems.

The controller contacted him about 30 minutes later to let him know the temperature was rising in the reactor and approaching its operational limit. He checked the Bussard engine and saw the ball of hydrogen was now white hot but had not ignited and turned to plasma yet. He made the announcement to the crew of Hope that the wheel would have to be stopped to conserve yet more power. Moans and groans could be heard throughout the ship. Hardly anyone liked weightlessness. After the all clear from all sections that everything had been secured for weightlessness he gave the order to Central Control to stop the wheel. Stopping the wheel was easily done. Just turn off the command to the rotating magnets that drove the wheel around and wait for it to stop. The space wheel rode in a track that went around the belly of the ship. It was held away from the ship by a series of magnets similar to those used by high speed trains on earth. Once the magnets were powered the wheel was moved away from the track and then the magnets would start rotating in sequence around the wheel causing it to rotate, again similar to moving the high speed trains on earth. The wheel never touched the track when turning. When the wheel had stopped then power to the magnets would be turned off. If the wheel touched the track at this point there was no fear of damage as it was not rotating.

As the wheel slowed one could feel the lessening artificial gravity until the wheel stopped turning. The Captain ordered power to the magnets to be cut. He watched the power draw from the reactor and it dropped to 84%. That was MUCH better. He looked at the reactor heat and noticed it was coming down. Now all they had to do was wait.

Iran

Iran had been almost blown off the map after it had tried to send nuclear missiles at Israel during WWIII. They thought they could get away with it and America would be too busy with China to do anything about it but America and Israel had anticipated this contingency and America had armed Israel with some of its anti-missile missiles which had destroyed Iran's attempt to obliterate Israel. Iran had paid the price by being attacked from ballistic missile submarines in the Arabian Sea. America had warned Iran this would happen if any move was made to attack Israel and they had paid the price. After the attack America had offered Iran emergency assistance to its people but Iran flatly refused. Help was given by other Arab nations in the Gulf. Now Iran wanted to get even. Al-Qaeda had asked Iran to provide them safe haven and Iran welcomed them with open arms. Iran was slowly re-arming itself with weapons from the black market and from Russia which was short of cash as were most other nations. These arms shipments were very secretive and America did not know about most of them. For one thing America did not believe that Russia would help them re-arm so this scenario was basically overlooked.

Some of Iran's nuclear facilities still existed as did some of their launch platforms. America knew about some of them but not all. A plan was secretly in the works to destroy an American battle fleet in the Arabian Sea. At the center of the battle fleet there was always an aircraft carrier. Nearby were destroyer escorts and supply ships. Under the water subs patrolled the depths listening for intruders. Iran doubted that America would nuke Iran again for destroying most of a battle fleet. They may choose to invade Iran but the leader of Iran, a hard-liner named Hassan Sharifi did not care. He just wanted to show America that Iran still had some teeth and exact some measure of revenge. The aircraft carrier Abraham Lincoln was patrolling the area with her escorts of support ships. Iran would send one nuclear missile at night. It really did not matter whether it was day or night because the American radar would pick up the incoming missile anyway. A night attack would just add to the confusion and more loss of life. Few people knew this was going to happen and it would be Hassan himself who would give the order whenever it suited him.

Aboard the Abraham Lincoln

It was night time and things were quiet aboard ship. A minimal crew was on duty, one of them Tom Watson, a radar operator. The radar gear was set up to give an alarm if there was an incoming threat but it had never gone off so he disregarded the screen. He busied himself playing computer games to keep himself awake during his shift. Things were really quiet so he decided to go down one level to the drink machine and grab a Coke and return. He would only be gone a minute or two.

Just as he was taking the Coke can out of the machine he heard the incoming alarm go off. He sprinted up the gangway to the radar screen and saw the blip of the incoming missile. He immediately hit the ships alarm which shrieked throughout the aircraft carrier.

Men scrambled to their combat positions, most assuming this was another drill but an announcement of, "Incoming bogey! This not a drill! Repeat. Incoming bogey! This not a drill!" put those feelings to rest real quick.

The speed of the object coming toward the ship was very fast, faster than a normal fighter plane. A missile was very likely. But who had shot it? A quick check of its direction confirmed that it probably came from Iran.

"Those crazy bastards!", swore the Captain.

A surface to air missile should take care of it. Two were set off toward the bogey and the radar showed the path of both missiles and the incoming bogey. They were closing impossibly fast. About 25 miles from the ship the radar showed them as one blip. There should be an explosion as the two missiles and the bogey exploded but the radar showed that somehow the bogey had managed to avoid the two missiles and was still coming. The two missiles had turned and were chasing the incoming but the radar operator and the Captain knew it would be too late. Another two missiles were quickly fired and the first two were destroyed by remote control. This time at least one of the missiles hit the bogey and there was an atomic explosion. The incoming missile must have been equipped with a proximity or G-force fuse so that if it detected an explosion near the missile the warhead was programmed to go off. Several ships sustained heavy damage and human casualties were high. A lot died instantly while others were either blinded and/or had their skin fried and were not expected to live more than a few hours. Even the Abraham Lincoln had sustained some damage and loss of life.

Pandemonium reigned as the injured writhed in agony and those trying to help were working in the darkness. The Captain immediately contacted Washington for immediate instructions. The President, Peter Williams, was awoken and told of the news. Within an hour most of the military Joint

Chief of Staff were at the White House to discuss the necessary response.

"Nuke the bastards!", said one older General.

Others nodded in agreement. The President called for other options. "We don't want a ground war. We don't want a repeat of Iraq and Afghanistan.", said another.

This action could not go without a response. America thought they knew where all Iran's remaining nuclear ability was and had gone in and dismantled it. Even though, they were watching closely but they never expected this. The Iranians must had some missiles, or at least one, that missed inspection.

"I say we carpet bomb the whole damn country!", barked another General.

Again heads nodded in agreement. The President pondered what to do and it had to be done fast. What if Iran had more nukes to fire and finish the job. Then what?

A large part of the surface battle fleet had been either destroyed or heavily damaged. A response from them was out of the question for the moment. But the subs should still be operational, at least most of them. This battle fleet had four subs. A message was quickly sent to the Abraham Lincoln asking about the subs. The Captain confirmed that all four subs had survived.

"Tell them to fire cruise missiles at all known missile launch and nuclear facilities in Iran. Come daylight I'll get fighters to recon from the battle group in the Med to try and detect from the air any other possible targets and destroy them as well. We'll try and contact Hassan and find out what they hell is going on."

The Captain acknowledged and sent the appropriate commands to the subs that rose to near surface and started firing cruise missiles at known and suspected targets in Iran.

He hoped that Russia would not side with Iran. It was suspected the Russians had been supplying armaments to Iran. At all costs relations with Russia must be kept at its present level. After the war with China, America had few nuclear options left, not enough to defend against a surprise attack from Russia.

Aboard Hope

A message was sent to Hope telling them of the latest developments. It reassured many aboard the voyage was still necessary as some people were starting to talk of reversing and going back to earth. Malcolm Beacham himself had predicted that things could go from bad to worse very quickly. It looks like he was right. America had survived a nuclear exchange with China and now the Iranians, who everyone thought had no more nuclear capability, had made a first strike response at an American battle fleet in the Arabian Sea and almost succeeded in destroying it. The report said several ships had been destroyed or heavily damaged and a retaliatory strike against military targets in Iran was underway. What would be the outcome? Did Iran have any more nuclear weapons that had been missed and were they prepared to use them? America had already used one nuke against Iran during the America-China war when Iran made a surprise attack against Israel. Iran had been warned not to try an attack against Israel during the conflict but they had gone ahead and attempted it and had paid the price. The news report also said the America was weighing further response against Iran but had to be careful not to anger Russia that was an allie of Iran. It was suspected that Russia was re-arming Iran. If it turned out the missile that was used against the Abraham Lincoln battle group was of Russian manufacture then all hell could break loose.

The Captain received an urgent message from radar control. Several large asteroids had been detected and Hope was heading right for one. It was still quite a ways off and Hope had ample time to turn to miss it but everyone thought the hydrogen cloud they had just passed through was the Oort Cloud and the theory of an asteroid belt outside the solar system were wrong but it looked like it wasn't. The Bussard engine was near to begin firing and as Hope sped up that would mean less time to maneuver around any asteroids in Hope's path. The astrogators were busy plotting a path around the large asteroid. A change of direction was obviously needed and the decision was made to pitch the nose of Hope down in order to slip under the asteroid. But a propelling forward force was needed. In space just changing a spacecrafts attitude will not change its direction. It will just keep going in the same direction. A push was needed to send it in its new direction. This meant firing Hopes engines for a short burst to change direction. This had been calculated in to Hopes fuel requirements as the occasional course change was anticipated. The main engines were fired for about 15 seconds, just enough to change Hopes direction to pass under the asteroid. Another burn was going to be needed to bring Hopes direction back on course.

Suddenly a call came in from Central Control. The Bussard

engine had ignited!

"If it doesn't rain it pours.", thought the Captain.

Now they had not only the main engines burning but the Bussard engine was firing too! The Captain immediately ordered the main engines to be shutdown. Hope looked like it was going to easily pass under the asteroid as predicted. Once they passed under it more asteroids were spotted on radar...a lot of them....but they were spaced fairly far apart and most were quite a distance away forward so they posed no immediate threat. He gave orders to radar control to keep a sharp lookout.

He made his way to Central Control. He wanted to see the speed increase the Bussard engines were giving Hope. He and everyone else could feel a small amount of gravity as the rear wall of the wheel became the "floor" because of the forward push of the engine. It wasn't much of a gravity but it proved that Hope was speeding up. He wanted to see the speed increase as would be proved with doppler readings of the stars. Their speed could be determined by how fast they were moving in relation to the stars. The doppler reading had already been done back on earth so once that was reached the Bussard engine could be shutdown. It was theorized that 2% of light speed could be achieved but what if the engine was capable of more? The fuel for the main engines had been calculated to slow the ships speed from 2% of light speed. Any faster and they would run the risk of running out of fuel. No, he better stick to the plan. He wouldn't be alive when they reached their destination anyway. It would be his great, great, great, great grandson that would have that privilege.

White House - In The Oval Office

President Peter Williams had called most of his Chiefs of Staff for a high level meeting about what to do about the Iran situation. All known and even some suspected missile sites had been blown up with Cruise Missiles but there still might be some that were hidden. Would Hassan risk another attack betting on the fact that America would not risk a nuclear attack again on Iran? The Russians had been uncharacteristically quiet. If they were going to make a protest they would have done it by now. Maybe it was time to contact the Russians to get some idea of a limited nuclear response against Iran. The damage to the Abraham Lincoln battle fleet could not go unpunished.

Peter Williams said he would contact the Russian Premier and lay his cards on the table to see what the Russian response would be. So far, relations between America and the Russians had been good. They had stayed out of the America-China nuclear exchange and also said little if anything about the nuclear attack on Iran after they attempted to destroy Israel while the America-China exchange was going on. But America could not risk a nuclear exchange with the Russians if it came to that. America had used most of its stock pile attacking China. Both America and Russia had been slowly bringing down their nuclear stockpiles for a number of years but America had called a halt due to the rise of China and other world countries like Iran, Pakistan and North Korea. Peter Williams had even suggested that America quickly rearm itself with nuclear weapons to bring them up to the level of the pre-America-China exchange but that could take several years and quite a bit of money the U.S. just didn't have.

Peter decided to risk a call to the Russian Premier to get his reaction. He asked his secretary to set up the call and let him know the date and time to expect the call. His secretary was back in touch in a couple of hours to let Peter know the call would take place in about three hours time. He was going to be the only one in the Oval Office on the phone but he bet the Russian Premier's office would be filled with members of the Politburo. When the appointed time came his phone rang. It was his secretary who told him the Russian Premier was on the line. Peter told her to put the call through. Peter recognized Vladimir's thick accent at once.

"Good evening!", said Vladimir.

"Good afternoon.", said Peter

"Ah, this time difference. Its 10 PM in Moscow.", said Vladimir.

"I'm really sorry to bother you at such a late hour. I did not know you would get back to me so soon. I thought we would be talking tomorrow or the day after.", said Peter.

The Russian Premier laughed and then said, "No matter, I was working late anyway so decided to call you back as soon as I was finished. What is on your mind, Peter."

Peter did not mind at all the Russian Premier had used his first name. That was a good sign the Premier was in a good mood. He smiled as he imagined the Premier with a glass of vodka or cognac after a long days work. "I have a delicate subject to talk about.", said Peter.

You probably want to talk about Iran. I'm so sorry to hear

about the attack on your battle fleet in the Arabian Sea. Such a senseless loss of life. The Iranians should know better after the thrashing you gave them after trying to attack Israel during your little spat with China."

'Little spat.', though Peter. He assumed the Premier was being facetious with that remark. '*Little spat* indeed!'

Peter said, "Yes, we certainly did not expect it. We had no choice but to respond to Iran's unprovoked attack on our ally Israel during our 'little spat' with China. We had our hands quite full so any other action was not possible at the time and we had warned them.....but now they have seen fit to try and destroy one of our battle fleets. They almost succeeded. The nuke went off about ten miles away from the center of the fleet. Their intended target was the aircraft carrier, the Abraham Lincoln. Some ships were completely destroyed and many others severely damaged with a very heavy loss of life. Our response so far has been to destroy any known and some suspected missile sites but we are still worried. I am concerned if we turned up the heat what your feeling and response would be. We are allies but we know you have been helping Iran get back on its feet. They refused our help completely."

Peter did not want to use the word 'rearm' in reference to the help the Russians were giving Iran.

Vladimir said, "Yes, we have been helping Iran in humanitarian ways. We knew you were assisting China and I commend you for that. We learned through channels that you had also offered help to the Iranian people but they had refused your assistance."

Peter said, "Yes we did but as you also know America went through a tough time with several terrorist attacks against us and we have traced the planning for those attacks to Al-Qaeda which we have learned now have their headquarters somewhere in Iran. We would very much like to root them out and put them out of commission once and for all."

Vladimir was silent for a moment and then said, "So the reason for your call is what would be our response to your going into invading Iran and destroying what is left of Al-Qaeda?"

Peter said, "Yes Vladimir, that is exactly the reason for my call."

Vladimir was silent again for a moment then he said, "Who is in the room with you?"

Peter responded, "No one. I am calling from the Oval Office and there is no one else here and no one else is monitoring this call. We did discuss what we should do and I said I thought I should contact you first to get your reaction to our proposed action. It may not come to that but if it does....." Peter left the sentence dangling as the rest was meaningless to say. It was not necessary.

Vladimir was silent for a moment again and then said, "I would have to talk with my aides and get back to you. This could be very serious indeed."

Peter said, "I understand Vladimir. When do you think you would be able to get back in touch with me."

Vladimir said, "I am not sure. The wheels of bureaucracy turn very slowly sometime in Mother Russia but I will try and get back to you in a few days with a response or at least an update. How would that do?"

Peter said, "That is fine Vladimir. I understand you would want to discuss it with your advisers. Get back to me in a few days and let me know or at least an update."

"Yes, I will do that my friend. Thank you for letting me know your intentions. It is appreciated.", said Vladimir.

The line went dead. The Russian Premier had hung up. The call had gone pretty well as Peter had suspected. He couldn't condemn the Russians for wanting to talk it over before giving him a response. He would do the same thing. He would advice his staff of the conversation and wait for the Premier's response.

Aboard Hope

Houston Control was still monitoring all radio transmissions between earth and Hope. Hope had just advised them they were encountering an asteroid field in the Oort Cloud. So the theory was correct. There was a ring of debris around the the outer reaches of the solar system well past the orbits of the outer planets and Hope had already had to dodge an asteroid. The good news was the Bussard engine appeared to be working. Its thrust was low as predicted but that was good because a high thrust could have been dangerous to the wheel mechanism and the ship in general. A gentle thrust over a longer period of time was preferable. What would be a concern was how long would Hope be under thrust from the Bussard engine? The wheel had to be stopped because the lasers being used to keep the hydrogen plasma ignited were drawing too much power. Everything in the ship that was non-essential was turned off but even so the reactor had been running at 97%. The Captain had made the decision to stop the wheel which had brought the power draw from the reactor down to 84% which was much better. They didn't want to tax the reactor too much because if it failed the mission was doomed.

Hope was doing doppler readings to figure out their rate of acceleration and how long it would be to reach the expected speed of 2% of light speed and would they be going too fast before exiting the Oort Cloud to avoid another possible collision? Hopefully they would clear the Oort Cloud before that happened. The engineers and physicists on Hope had calculated that Hope was accelerating to give the equivalent of 0.165887 Gees which was slightly more than 16% of the G-force of someone standing on earth. It did not seem like a lot but the acceleration would be enough to propel Hope to 2% of light speed in a week. This was within the range anticipated. Dry rations had been provided for emergencies so mostly everyone was eating those. Everything aboard Hope had been designed to operate with the "floor" of the wheel at its outer edges. Now that Hope was accelerating and the wheel was not turning the "floor" was now at the back of the wheel. It was nice to have *some* gravity but when that gravity was off angled to where it was supposed to be made life somewhat difficult. The radar console was manned 24/7 in the event Hope had to be maneuvered out of the way of another asteroid. Other stations were also being maintained around the clock in case the maneuvering jets had to be fired to change Hope's direction.

Washington

A few days later Peter's secretary buzzed him in the Oval Office to tell him the Russian Premier, Vladimir, was calling and wished to speak with him. Peter told him to put the call through. His office phone rang and he picked it up.

"Vladimir? How nice of you to call.", said Peter.

Vladimir said without any preamble, "I am afraid I have some bad news for you. The Politburo voted down any further aggression towards Iran."

Peter was silent for a moment. "But they attacked and almost destroyed one of our main battle fleets. We can't just let this action go unpunished."

Vladimir replied, "I understand but it was you who chose to use nuclear weapons against Iran. They felt they were just getting even."

Peter said, "They attempted an unprovoked attack at one of our allies, Israel, after we told them not to attempt it during our 'little spat' with China. They chose to ignore our warning and launched a nuclear warhead at Israel."

Vladimir said, "Yes they launched something at Israel. Was it a nuclear device? You don't know. Israel was able to destroy it. That should have been notice enough not to try again."

Peter was silent for a moment. Vladimir was correct in one thing. The United States was not certain it was a nuclear device launched at Israel but he would bet his bottom dollar it was. "And when were we supposed to retaliate? When

Israel was a smoking ruin? May I remind you of your little skirmish with Chechnya? It was under similar circumstances."

Vladimir said, "That was a little different. We were invited in by the ruling government to put down an uprising and then the rebels decided to turn their attack on us. We were just defending ourselves."

Peter said, "It is the same with us. Al-Qaeda attacked us in America with suicide bombers. We have the right to protect ourselves also. We just want to go in and make sure that Al-Qaeda is finished and make sure there are no more nuclear weapons we have to worry about and then we leave to let them sort themselves out."

Vladimir said, "I am sorry but my government will not allow that. Enough damage has been done. If they had another missile I am sure they would have used it by now."

Peter said, "I don't feel like staying awake nights thinking about that and I am sure our men and women in the battle fleets don't want to either. The bottom line is what are you prepared to do if we do decide to go in on a ground assault to be sure they are no longer a threat to us?"

Vladimir was quiet for a moment and then said, "I would not advise such action. I don't know that the Politburo would vote to do in that case."

Peter said, "I will have to let my cabinet and advisers know of our discussion and we can decide what we are going to do. I can tell you this. If Iran attempts another attack it will be their last."

Vladimir said, "Good night my friend." And hung up.

Peter sat there with the phone to his ear for a moment and then placed it gently back in its cradle. He buzzed his secretary and said, "I need to talk with the Secretary of Defense and the Chief's of Staff as soon as possible in my office. Set it up as early as possible and let me know when everyone can be here."

His secretary acknowledged the request and Peter stood up and started pacing back and forth in the Oval Office deep in thought.

Aboard Hope

Hope was still navigating her way through the Oort Cloud and had not had to make any other course directions. The Nav section of the ship, Central Control and the radar console were manned at all times. Hope did have a collision avoidance system but it was primarily in case of a collision with a single asteroid. No one knew what would happen if Hope's computer system navigated them around one asteroid only to be heading toward another one, then another course correction to avoid it. The collision avoidance system was designed to navigate around a single asteroid and then return to course using Alpha Centauri as a target.

Rena Williams was at Central Control in the early morning hours when she smelled smoke. She checked the board quickly and saw nothing wrong. No alarms were going off and everything seemed to be working fine. All of a sudden a red light appeared on the console warning of a problem with communications and then an alarm went off. She could visibly see smoke coming out of the cabinet. She immediately hit the alarm button to summon help right away. They had all been trained to keep all cabinets and doors shut in the event of a fire. Keep the fire contained and also keep out any air from reaching the fire and fueling it. Within minutes which seemed like hours two of the people who were designated as emergency personnel appeared on the scene. She quickly advised them of the problem. One of them grabbed a fire extinguisher and stood ready. His partner grabbed the cabinet door and opened it. A burst of flame shot out and the other went to work quickly with the extinguisher while his partner went to kill the power to the console. In moments the fire was out.

The Captain and several of the crew had arrived by this time. The Captain asked to wake up the maintenance people and get them over here on the double. Three maintenance people were there in a few minutes. The Captain asked them to analyze the damage and let him know how long repairs would take. Navigation in the ship's nose was advised of the situation and told to take over watching for asteroids and take whatever action was necessary until repairs were complete. It took about an hour but the source of the problem was found. The communications section of Central Control had short circuited causing the fire. There was extensive damage but mostly contained to communications. Spare parts were pulled but only the receiver could be repaired. The transmitter part of the communications circuitry was burnt to a crisp. The main circuit board was completely destroyed. They had spare parts for the board but not the board itself. It was considered the entire circuit board would never be destroyed.

The Captain asked if a new board could be made but was told it was a multi-layer board and there was no hope of making another one. Hope could receive messages from earth but could not respond. The daily check in time was approaching and when the time came they could hear Houston calling but had no way to transmit back to them. All telemetry and speech back to earth was impossible. Houston would think that Hope had been destroyed in the Oort Cloud.

On Earth

The President, Peter Williams, was told immediately of what had happened, that they had lost contact with Hope. Peter called Malcolm Beacham who had been the project leader for Hope of the news and that they were trying to raise Hope. He was told of Hope's near miss with an asteroid in the Oort Cloud. The Bussard engine was firing and Hope was traveling very fast, maybe too fast to avoid another asteroid or perhaps several of them where there was no room to navigate around them. Maybe the Oort Cloud was populated far more heavily with asteroids than anyone previously thought. Malcolm was told they would keep trying and he would be notified if Hope was contacted again.

Malcolm put the phone down. "All that work and all this time and now this happened.", he thought.

Hope was earths last chance at survival. He was sure that earth had not seen the last of its troubles. He had heard on the news about Iran attempting to nuke a battle fleet in the Arabian Sea and America's response. He knew that America would want to go into Iran and make sure that no more missiles existed but what would the Russians do? It was well known that Russia was helping Iran and what if it was a Russian weapon that had been fired at the battle fleet? There was no way of knowing right now. But if America went into

Iran and found that out the fat would be on the fire for sure. America could not fight another World War, not with Russia. The United States had depleted most of its missiles against China. America still had some submarine missiles and some land based missiles but the Russians had a lot more. The United States could still do considerable damage to Russia but Russia could wipe America right off the map.

Hope's engineers worked for several days trying to jury rig something that would work but all attempts proved futile. The transmissions from Houston went from daily to continuous trying to get Hope to respond.

Houston Mission Control

Robert "Bob" Myers was the head of the project of communicating with Hope. He didn't hear any word of successful contact but called for the umpteenth time anyway to ask if there had been any contact.

"Nothing yet sir.", said the controller. "We will let you know as soon as we make contact."

It had been several days since a successful contact was made. The last contact said there was no unusual problems. Hope had to dodge around one asteroid, maybe they came up to a situation the ship could not avoid and been destroyed. That thought was in the back of everyone's mind even though no one voiced it. They could send a probe out to the Oort Cloud to investigate. They knew of Hope's exact course but to build a probe, launch it and get it out there would take several years. The probe may end up with the same fate. But at least the probe could be fitted with a camera and when it was close to Hope's final last known position it could be turned on to continuous mode in the hope of seeing what happened to Hope. The whole scenario would be like looking for a needle in a haystack when the haystack is moving at several 10's of thousands of miles per hour.

Aboard Hope

They could hear Houston calling repeatedly but could do nothing about it. It was frustrating to everyone. Finally after several days the Captain ordered the receiver to be turned off. There was no new transmissions being received, just the same message over and over to respond. He asked the engineers not to give up rigging a new transmitter until every possible avenue had been researched. The engineers had already done that, even taking spare circuits meant for other systems and trying to modify them from the ship's schematics but nothing worked. Earth was now deaf to Hope. Hope would continue on its journey and earth would think that Hope had been destroyed. If Hope arrived safely at their destination in two hundred years they would have no way to tell earth they made it. Maybe if earth survived and made another attempt in the years to come sometime in the distant future and reached Alpha Centauri they would see a thriving colony. Then it could be told what happened. He or anyone else on board would not be alive to tell the tale.

Houston

After two weeks a meeting was held as to what to do. Keep trying or give up? It was decided to leave all the equipment on automatic and set it to auto-record if anything was heard from Hope. The recording would be checked from time to time to see if anything had been received. Weeks stretched to months and nothing was heard from Hope. The auto-recording equipment was left on in any case and checked once a month but Hope was never to be heard from again.

The Oval Office

The Presidents Secretary of Defense and the Chief's of Staff were all in attendance. The topic was what to do about Iran. President Peter Williams recounted his talk with Russian Premier and the fact the Politburo voted against allowing the United States to invade Iran. Everyone was of the same mind, that Iran's attempt at destroying a battle fleet could not go unpunished. And what if Iran had more nuclear missiles the U.S. did not know about? They would all be wondering when or if a similar incident would happen.

Would Russia risk a nuclear war over it or just get upset? The United States could not afford to get into another nuclear exchange with anyone, especially the Russians as their nuclear capability had been badly depleted in the exchange with China. That wasn't the only problem. There was a severe shortage of anti-missiles which had largely saved the United States from being badly damaged. They would have to pick and choose which targets to save and allow the others to be annihilated. Russia was a huge country. They could still inflict a lot of damage but the United States would take the worst of it.

After hours of talking it was decided to take the risk and if it looked like Russia was going to follow through with their threat they could always pull out. The Russians could be invited as observers or even as allies in a joint mission but no one thought that was going to go over well as Russia was helping Iran get back on their feet again. They may well be helping them to re-arm. What if it was discovered the Iranian missiles were of Russian manufacture? That would really mess things up. Rather than a full out advertised invasion of Iran it was decided to run several covert missions into suspected areas of Iran. There were areas that spy flights and satellite images just could not see. It had to be done from the ground. If these missions were done carefully enough they would suspect who it was but have no proof. Without proof the Russians could or would likely do nothing. They could suspect but that was all. The same with the Iranians. A top secret plan was devised and a name picked for it. Operation Clean Sweep.

Two Months Later

At a secret SEAL training base Colonel James Christensen was giving a last minute briefing to his troops. There was a large map of Iran on the wall and he had a laser pointer that he was using to point to references on the map.

The American SEAL units were created in the Vietnam war as the elite of the Special Forces who completed top secret missions. It was a matter of pride that no member of a SEAL unit had ever been captured.....alive. If a member of a SEAL unit was ever captured and escape was considered impossible they were to neutralize themselves so they could not give any information to an enemy force. The enemy would not even know they were a SEAL.

"We will be taking off from the John F. Kennedy in the Mediterranean Sea in one of the new B-5 stealth bombers. We will fly to a height of 95,000 feet in a circular pattern and then do a glide into Iran airspace. We'll be doing a night jump using our standard night black parachutes. We'll free fall to minimum height of 1,400 feet before opening the chutes. Once landed we'll bury everything, chutes, helmets, the works and then join up here.", said Colonel Christensen as he moved the laser pointer to a new point on the map. He looked at all his men to be sure everyone was attentive.

"Once down and joined up we will proceed to this location where reconnaissance has been unable to penetrate, It is one of the locations where we believe the Iranians could be hiding more missiles, if they exist. If we find any our orders are to destroy and neutralize any ground personnel. Once the mission is complete we are to make our way to this location" (he moved the laser pointer to the new location) "where we are to meet our spy contacts who will transport us to this location" (again moving the pointer) where will be met by inflatables that will take us out to a sub and home.", he said.

Colonel Christensen looked at his troops. "Does anyone have any questions?" He looked at each one of the troops and made eye contact. No one had any questions.

Aboard Hope

Hope had reached her top speed of 360,000 kmh a week after the Bussard Engine had been shut down. Shutting it off was easy. The lasers that heated the ball of plasma were turned off and the power to the electromagnets that held the plasma in place were turned off as well. Captain Jacoby had given the command for the wheel rotation to be turned back on. Everyone was very glad to have gravity returned. Several people had made adjustments to their beds, work places etc. for the change in gravity direction when the Bussard Engine was firing. The acceleration was not all that much but it had to be compensated for. Slowly, life aboard the wheel returned to normal. Another slight course change had to be done to avoid another asteroid but they were back on course again. No asteroids had been seen for several days so it was assumed they had cleared the Oort Cloud. Even at Hopes great speed the stars hung in the darkness unmoving as ever so there was no reference point for speed anymore. The only way they could tell they were going as fast as they were was taking doppler readings from Alpha Centauri.

Maggie (Margret Blake) who had been partnered with Tom Simms who had committed suicide by opening the airlock and ejecting himself into space was now paired with the ships doctor. He had been counseling Maggie off and on since Tom's death and they had grown closer together. Now they were a couple and very much in love. Maggie's mood had shot way up and the doctor was quite happy with the arrangement. He was the only one on board who had decided not to pair with anyone as he thought it would interfere with his work but after years of loneliness that thinking had changed. At first he felt a bit guilty taking Tom's place but after a while and with some coxing from Maggie those thoughts disappeared.

Now that Hope had cleared the solar system and the Oort Cloud it was assumed there would be little to do except maintain ship operations and cross train others in their specialty. Some women were now pregnant. It would take a minimum of 25 years from birth to a fully trained member of the crew. In that time the original crew would be getting on in years and it was best to train others while they still had their minds working at peak capacity. For soon as they got older they new that many would develop some form of dementia and their usefulness would be at an end.

On the John F. Kennedy

Colonel Christensen and his troops had arrived along with the B-5 stealth bomber. All they had to do now was wait until the conditions were perfect. They needed a moonless night preferably with a overcast sky which rarely happened in Iran but they could always hope. The moonless night sky was a necessity. Two weeks went by and the moon was dark with a slight overcast over the landing area. It was the best that could be hoped for. Colonel Christensen and his men boarded the stealth bomber and took off from the deck of the carrier and circled up to their height of 95,000 feet. There was little air at that altitude. It was the ceiling for the bomber. They proceeded towards Iran and near the boarder all power to the engines were cut so the bomber could glide over the landing area and hopefully not be detected. It wasn't long before they got the signal they were nearing the drop zone. The SEAL unit lined up single file at the door getting ready. As soon as the signal was given they jumped out into the inky black darkness to begin the long fall to earth before opening their black parachutes. They all wore black jump suits and their faces and hands were all black. They should be invisible from the ground. Nothing could be seen below, they only had their altimeters to tell them how close to the ground they were. It took several minutes free fall to get down to the minimum height of 1,400 feet to pop their chutes. Colonel Christensen opened his suit and felt the hard tug as his chute opened and felt his speed decreasing. He could just barely make out the landscape below as he got closer and used the risers on his chute to guide himself to a good landing spot. He hit the ground and rolled. As soon as he was down he rolled up his chute and removed his helmet and small oxygen tank and mask and found a good hiding spot in the rocks and shoved everything in. He covered it all up with some sand and small rocks. He smoothed everything out so it would not look like anything was intentionally buried there. He checked his GPS unit and headed off at a trot toward the chosen meeting area.

In The Oval Office

President Peter Williams was in the Oval Office when his secure phone rang. He picked it up. The voice on the other end simply said, "The package is on the ground."

The President simply replied, "Keep me updated." The connection was dropped. He replaced the phone on its cradle.

"Now we will see what those Iranians have got for firepower.", thought Peter. "Whatever is left will be destroyed."

SEAL Team In Iran

Colonel Christensen and his men were jogging to their first contact point. They only had a few hours of darkness left. They had to reach their co-ordinates before daybreak. All the men were jogging along not even breaking a sweat. They had all trained for several years to become Navy SEAL's. All of them were in 110% physical shape. Stone hard bodies, well muscled and lots of stamina. They were the top 10% of the men who had volunteered to become SEAL's. SEAL training is the most rigorous in the world. To be even considered to being trained as a SEAL was an honor. To wash out was disappointing but there were other units that would take them, units not nearly so well trained but still very dangerous and feared by the enemy.

It was a couple of hours before dawn when they arrived at their chosen location. It was a mountain side with a lot of caves. Missile launchers could be hidden there and rolled out and fired and rolled back in with no eye in the sky detecting exactly where they had come from. This particular location was chosen because the flight path of the missile that had nearly destroyed the Abraham Lincoln battle fleet had been traced back to near this location. The SEAL troops spread out and surveyed the area. There did not seem to be anyone about. One of the SEAL's notified Colonel Christensen that he had discovered some tents near the mountain wall and a cave close by. All other units reported nothing found. Colonel Christensen ordered all troops to meet near the cave and the tents. The first order of business was to neutralize the troops in those tents and the cave and then investigate. Two SEAL's went into the cave keeping close to the cave walls and reported rocket launchers but no one nearby they could see. All enemy must be in the tents. They must all be neutralized as quick as possible before any radio signal could be sent they were in trouble.

Colonel Christensen gave his men instructions to lay explosives around the tents that hopefully would kill anyone inside. Any survivors would be shot. Timers were all set and they went a short distance away and waited. In a couple of minutes the explosives went off. Some yelling and shouted could be heard and the SEAL unit went in and quickly disposed of any survivors. They waited silently for any movement but heard none. They must have got them all. Colonel Christensen and his unit went into the cave to examine the rocket launcher and to see if there were more missiles. After a brief inspection one nuclear tipped missile was found along with the launcher. They were of recent Russian design.

"Those lying bastards!", thought Colonel Christensen. "The President is going to be real pissed when he hears this...."

He set up the secure satellite phone and called in and told Cheyenne Mountain using carefully chosen code words what had been found. News was immediately relayed to the President who called an emergency meeting of his Chief's of Staff and his Secretary of Defense and told them what the SEAL unit had found. There was much surprise and anger and suggestions of what to do but the States could not successfully win another nuclear exchange. They could do a fair amount of damage to Russia but the States would take the worst. How to handle this situation? That was the question. What should America's response be?

Colonel Christensen and his team disabled the missile and laid charges inside the cave to destroy everything. The explosion would likely destroy the shielding around the nuclear warhead making the cave and immediate area radioactive for quite some time. They would have to be far away when the detonations went off. Some trucks were found near by that would hold them all. It was decided to take two of them in case one died on them. They could all squeeze into one to complete the journey. They would drive near to the second co-ordinates and hide until night fall. The Iranians would of course find out what happened and have their guard up. The second target would not be as easy. They loaded the trucks with as much arms and explosives they could find to augment their own and drove away. About ten minutes later they heard the explosions in the distance as the cave and its contents were destroyed.

They reached the second co-ordinates just before dawn and found a hiding place for the trucks. They would have to be on their guard because the Iranians would probably figure it out where the next target would be and would be prepared. Colonel Christensen set up the satellite phone again and contacted the John F. Kennedy to ask if a air to ground strike could be co-ordinated on the co-ordinates to be provided. He also said he expected a formidable defense from the Iranians because they would be expecting his team.

On the John F. Kennedy

The message was received from the radio room and a transcript was sent to the Captain by a runner. The Captain read the message and called his staff for a quick meeting. He wanted to know if a night strike was possible. He was told it was but the President wanted this operation to be as clandestine as possible. A bombing run would certainly expose the mission. It was decided to call the President for his okay or denial of the request.

He went to the radio room and asked for a connection to the President and went into the secure booth where confidential conversations were held. He discussed the situation with President Peter Williams but was denied the use of an air strike saying the operation was to be top secret and a bombing run would expose it. He did okay a night drop of extra explosives, munitions and field rations.

The Captain relayed this information back to the SEAL team on the ground. Colonel Christensen wasn't pleased with the answer although he was expecting it. He relayed the info to his men. A plan must be devised to create as much collateral damage as possible to reduce the odds of them against the Iranians. He suspected the Iranians may start patrols around a wide area of the missile site so he ordered his men to pull back a couple of miles. They found a well hidden cave in which to hide. He radioed the John F. Kennedy with co-ordinates for the supply drop that night at 11PM.

At just before 11PM he was advised that supplies were incoming to the co-ordinates he had supplied. He was also given the frequency to the locator which would be attached to the pallet. At just before 11PM he could just barely hear a plane overhead. It was probably a stealth. Hopefully the Iranian radar would not pick it up. He tuned his GPS to the frequency of the dropped supplies. They were still on their way down. They should drop about a quarter mile from their position. He and some of his men went to the drop point. By the time they got there the pallet was on the ground. They hid the black chute and picked up the pallet and carried it back to the cave. There were field rations, water, ammunition, explosive charges and a few more "burp" guns, good for close quarter fighting. They would have to make do with what they had.

A plan was devised to sneak into the Iranian camp and plant explosives as close to the tents or other structures as possible and a few more around the area to cause as much confusion as possible. As soon as the explosives had gone off they would rush the camp and neutralize any and all Iranians they could find in the confusion and then inspect the cave and if missiles and launchers were found then see if they were Russian or not then destroy them. At this point their mission was complete. They would then go to the coast and wait for the sub to pick them up.

About 2AM in the morning they made their way in total darkness to the missile site. They all wore night vision goggles so they could see everything quite clearly. He hoped the Iranians had none. They found a small hill near the camp and Colonel Christensen used his night vision binoculars to survey the camp and the surrounding area. As suspected there were some guards around on patrol. It was discussed the best way to proceed was to neutralize the guards with stealth, plant the explosives and then hide a short distance away. As soon as the explosive charges detonated they would rush the camp and neutralize any remaining enemy. Each man was assigned a guard to take out. Colonel Christensen assigned one of the guards to himself. He would not ask his men to do anything he wasn't prepared to do himself. The SEAL team spread out and maintained close radio contact using lapel microphones and an ear plug. His assigned guard was the middle of a group of three.

They were spaced well apart but they would have to get as close as possible and when all three guards were turned with their backs to them they would attack and neutralize. They waited several minutes keeping in contact when all three SEALS indicated their targets had their backs to them they attacked. Colonel Christensen put his hand over the guards mouth and with one quick slash of his knife he cut the guards throat from ear to ear cutting both neck veins and the windpipe. He kept his hand pressed over the guards mouth until he hit the ground and all gurgling and struggling had stopped. All the SEAL's reported in that their targets had been eliminated. They proceeded to the next stage of the mission and stole into the camp. They placed their charges all set to go off at the same time except with a few seconds delay between the ones placed near the tents and the ones placed around the camp for confusion factor. This would give them a few extra seconds to rush the camp and take out the remaining soldiers.

Once the charges were placed they backed away until the explosive charges went off. Those were the ones near the tents. They heard a lot of screaming of dying and injured men along with shouts of others. Then the extra explosives went off. They quickly rushed the camp like ghosts and took out the remaining soldiers. There may be some in the cave. They crept up to the cave entrance and listened. He could hear excited chatter from inside. They stole quietly inside and killed three more soldiers. They quickly inspected the missiles and the launcher. The launcher was of indeterminate origin but the missiles were Russian. He quickly took several pictures as evidence while his men placed the charges then they left the cave. They inspected the tents and neutralized any remaining wounded. No witnesses. Unbeknownst to Colonel Christensen one of the Iranians had managed to get off a a quick radio message they were under attack. He had planned for such an event. He quickly grouped his men together and commandeered some trucks and headed out of the area quickly and made the coast.

Daylight was coming and they were still aways from the coast. The subs arrival was for that night. They would have to hide during the day and proceed again at nightfall. He found a cluster of rocks and trees to hide them and the vehicles and instructed his men to hide the vehicles from the air as much as possible in case the Iranians did an air search. While in hiding they did hear a few aircraft fly over their position and waited to see if any attack was coming. None came. As soon as Colonel Christensen thought it was dark enough him and his team continued their escape to the coast. They abandoned the vehicles a couple of miles away and carrying as much armament as they could easily carry they made their way by foot to the coast. The sub was due to arrive in two hours. As they got close to the coast they proceeded slowly and stealthily and then heard the voices of soldiers.

"Damn!", thought Colonel Christensen. The Iranians had anticipated their escape route and were likely waiting for them. There was a good chance there would be troops all up and down the coast as they would not know exactly where the pick up point would be. He and another SEAL went ahead to survey the area. There looked like there was four soldiers grouped together and talking. He looked up and down the coast but did not see any others. He heard a short radio conversation. They were likely being contacted at regular intervals. This was going to make things difficult. He and his partner went back to the rest of the group and reported. He set up the satellite radio and reported in to the John F. Kennedy and told them of the situation and advised them to get an ELF message to the sub to come in as close as possible to shore and to surface just enough to launch the inflatables but NOT to use any engine. They were to row to shore for the pickup. They also asked for someone to be manning the deck gun and possibly some sailors on deck with small arms fire for cover just in case. The John F. Kennedy replied back in a few moments the information had been forwarded to the sub.

The sub was supposed to arrive at 3AM. At a half hour to the appointed time the SEAL was in hiding near by. Colonel Christensen could hear more voices down the shore. There were four more soldiers coming. Damn! They met up with the four that were there and chatted for a few minutes. He hoped it just a relief and they would be gone in a few minutes. After about 10 minutes the four that were there left and wandered away down the shore. It was only 20 minutes until the sub arrived. He hoped the original four would be far enough down the shore where they couldn't run back soon enough to help their comrades. At precisely 3AM he saw the conning tower of the sub rise just off shore in the darkness. He saw through his night vision goggles several men getting the inflatables into the water.

There were three of them with two men in each ready to row to shore. It was no or never. Colonel Christensen and his men rushed the four soldiers from four different directions and tried to take them out silently but one of them was able to give out a scream before he was killed. Colonel Christensen and his men waded out as far as they could go to get to the inflatables. From down the shore in both directions he could hear groups of soldiers shouting and running. He and his men pulled themselves into the inflatables as he heard the deck gun on the sub start firing. Colonel Christensen and his men started firing back as well. Bullets were hitting the water all around them and some were hitting the inflatables as well but they were all built with Kevlar so the likelihood of damage was remote. One of his men gave a groan and fell toppled over into the bottom of the boat. They were nearing the sub. Most of the men on shore were dead or dying but a couple were still standing and firing but the subs deck gun took them out. As soon as all were aboard including the injured SEAL (Colonel Christensen hoped he wasn't a casualty) the inflatables were released and the sub glided away into the deep.

Colonel Christensen went immediately to the subs small infirmary and was told his man had taken a bullet just under the shoulder. It had passed through the top part of the lung and emergency surgery was about to be performed to try and save his life. Colonel Christensen asked to be notified as soon as possible as soon as surgery was complete and whether it was successful or not. About an hour later a sailor told Colonel Christensen the surgery was a success and his man would be okay.

"That;s what I call a successful mission.", he thought to himself. "No casualties and only one injury. Not bad, not bad at all."

He handed his spy camera with the evidence photos to the communications section who would offload the pictures and relay them to Washington. The President was going to be pissed with the Russians!!

In The Oval Office

President Peter Williams had seen the photos and swore under his breath. "Why did the Russians give nukes to the Iranians? They must have known they would use them.", he thought.

It was early morning in Washington but late afternoon in Moscow. He asked his secretary to connect him with Premier Vladimir as soon as possible. With in a half an hour he was speaking with the Russian Premier. After the obligatory exchange of pleasantries the serious talk began.

"We didn't invade Iran at your request but we did go in with a clandestine mission to see for ourselves what was there. There results were very upsetting. Our men got picture proof of Russian nuclear missiles at two sites we could not see from the air.", said Peter.

Vladimir tried denying how Russian nuclear weapons had fallen into Iranian hands.

"Don't you keep a watch on your arsenal and make sure they are all accounted for?", asked Peter.

"Well of course we do but....", started Vladimir.

"Explain to me then how the Iranians got hold of three, no make that four Russian nuclear missiles, counting the one that almost destroyed our battle fleet in the Arabian Sea?", asked Peter.

Vladimir replied that he did not know and Peter replied that if the Iranians received any more "aide" in the form of nuclear weapons that The United States would invade Iran and slammed the phone down.

Peter was fuming. He arranged a meeting with his Secretary of Defense and told him of the SEAL teams discovery and his conversation with Vladimir. They discussed what the Russian response would be and it was decided they could do nothing but wait and see.

Cheyenne Mountain

Operators were watching their screens as usual when one operator shouted out, "Launch of possible ICBM from Russia!"

The duty officer rushed over right away. The launch was indeed coming from one of Russia's known ICBM missile sites. He picked up the phone right away and spoke, "Get me the President right away!"

President Peter Williams was in a conference room with his Chief's of Staff and his Secretary of Defense when he was informed of a missile launch from a known Russian ICBM site.

"How many?", asked Peter.

The duty officer replied, "Just one sir."

"Expected arrival?", asked the President.

"About thirty minutes.", replied the duty officer.

"Let me know as soon as you know a projected target and if there are more launches. Go to Defcon 2.", said Peter.

"Immediately sir.", said the duty officer.

"So...the Russians have launched one missile so far against us. If they launch any more we will have no choice but to go to Defcon 1 and launch a retaliatory strike. I just hope our anti-missiles, the ones we have left, can protect most of the U.S. First targets will be military targets depending on where the Russian missiles are headed. We may have to nuke their high population cities as well.", said the President.

The high probability of WWIV was about to unfold. Meanwhile out on Anystreet U.S.A. The population was blissfully unaware of what was transpiring.

"The phone in the conference room rang again. It was the day shift officer from Cheyenne Mountain. Peter put it on speaker phone. "There is still only one missile inbound at this time sir. What do you want us to do?"

"Do you have a projected target yet.", asked Peter.

The day shift operator replied, "As near as we know, somewhere in the middle of the mid-west in a largely unpopulated area."

Peter thought, "Why would the Russians send one nuke to a largely unpopulated area and not a civilian or military target?"

"Do we have any silos in that area?", asked Peter.

"None sir.", replied the officer.

"Wait one.", replied the President.

A quick discussion ensued with about what to do. One Russian missile was inbound to a largely unpopulated area. What was their plan in doing that? It could be a test to see what the U.S. response would be. Maybe the best thing to do was let it come and see what happened.

He took the phone off mute asked the duty officer if there were any more inbound and got the reply their were none. He told the duty officer not to take any action but to remain on the phone and let him know what happened when the missile struck. The duty officer replied he would.

The room was silent as the duty officer counted off the minutes and then the seconds until the missile struck its target.

"10-9-8-7-6-5-4-3-2-1", counted down the duty officer and then a "Huh? There was no nuclear detonation sir."

"None?" asked the president.

"No sir, no detonation detected at all.", replied the officer.

"What the hell were those Ruskies playing at?", thought the President. "Maybe it was some sort of a test?"

He thanked the duty officer and told him and his crew to keep a sharp eye and let him know ASAP if there were further launches and to remain at Defcon 2 until further notice.

Much discussion followed. It was apparent the Russians were testing them. The response would be through diplomatic channels. Once all the hubbub was over he would have to talk with Vladimir again. The threat was far from over. WWIV still might happen. He would give the Russians notice they would be watching very carefully any ships or planes entering Iran and what was being transported. They would also be told that Russian ships could be boarded on the high seas headed for Iran for inspection and that any resistance would be dealt with accordingly. If America even thought the Russians were re-arming Iran the American's would invade Iran right away with no notice. America had the right to protect itself and its ships at sea. They would not start a fight but they sure as hell would finish it!

One Month Later

The American and Russian diplomatic channels had been buzzing with activity and President Peter Williams asked that he be kept updated on the proceedings. Defense Condition (Defcon) had since been lowered to Defcon 4. No more Russian missiles had been launched. It had been an obvious test to see what the "trigger happy" American's would do he thought. Well he had called their bluff and won. If he had launched even one retaliatory missile both Russia and America would have been into WWIV. Hell! It would be over by now with both sides picking up the pieces. News of the event had been leaked to the news world as usual and news channels were still talking about it a month later.

The end result was almost a "cold war" situation between Russia and America. America had told Russia in no uncertain terms they would be boarding any Russian vessels at random on the high seas heading for Iran for inspection. If any nuclear missiles were found aboard there would be hell to pay! Also that America would invade Iran to be sure no more nuclear missiles had snuck through. The attack on the battle fleet, The Abraham Lincoln, by Iran using a Russian nuclear missile was like an attack from Russia itself. America and Russia were in a stalemate position. Peter Williams gave the order for more anti-missiles to be built for America's protection. If Things heated up and WWIV happened then America had better be prepared to defend itself.

The European Community was 100% on side with America. If any fire fighting started America could certainly count on their European allies. Things were quiet for several months. The news channels had stopped talking about the Iranian incident and things were resuming some sort of normality. Peter figured it would be a good time to call Vladimir in Moscow and have a talk, that is if he would want to talk at all. He called first thing in the morning to hopefully catch the Russian Premier near the end of his day.

When he called he was intercepted by the Kremlin switchboard. He identified himself and asked to speak with Vladimir. He was told that Vladimir was unable to talk right and was there a message. He asked the switchboard to ask

Vladimir to give him a call at his earliest convenience.

About two hours later Peter's phone rang in the Oval Office. It was his secretary who said it was Vladimir and asked if he wished to speak to him. Peter asked for the call to be transferred through.

"Vladimir?", said Peter.

"Peter, how are you doing. What can I do for you.", said Vladimir.

Peter said, "Things have not been going well between our two countries for the last little while and I thought we could talk about that."

Vladimir was quiet for a moment and then said, "Yes, thing are not going well. Relations are a bit strained."

Peter thought, "A 'bit' strained?"

Peter said, "Yes, you could put it that way. I was hoping we could chat about that and work towards resolving those issues."

Vladimir said, "Its not really up to you and I. All the negotiations are being handled through diplomatic channels. I really wish it was up to just you and I. I am sure we could work something out you and I."

Peter said, "Can I ask you a question Vladimir?"

"Of course.", said Vladimir

"Why did you give the Iranians nuclear missiles?", asked Peter.

"To be very honest with you I did not know anything about it. The first I heard was when your SEAL units went into Iran and discovered them. They are destroyed, yes?", asked Vladimir.

"Peter said, "Yes they are destroyed. I only hope those were the only two sites that have them. If you did not know who in your government gave them to the Iranians maybe you could command a search for the people who did?"

Vladimir said, "That could take some time. Everyone involved will of course deny it and anyone who knows who did will not say but I can try. I certainly would not have authorized such a stupid thing."

Peter said, "I am sure you wouldn't Vladimir. You and I are of the same mind. We both want a peaceful world. Russia and the United States had such a good relationship. You helped us out greatly years ago when the world economy was flat lining and during the building of the generation ship, the Hope."

Vladimir said, "Yes those were very bad times. You have heard nothing from Hope?"

Peter said, "No, nothing. The last we heard they were in the Oort Cloud and had to dodge one asteroid. We are assuming they must have come up against some asteroids they could not avoid and were destroyed."

Vladimir said, "That is so sad. All that work and money

wasted. Maybe in the years to come another ship could be built, maybe a Russian and United States venture?"

Peter said, "I would like to expand that even further and include all earth's countries. It would be an earth ship not just a ship from our two countries. And hopefully some day we could build a new engine that can propel the ship faster once it is in intergalactic space to reduce the time to get to its destination. Maybe during the lifetime of the original crew."

Vladimir said, "Ah yes, we can dream can't we? Okay I will try and see if I can get an investigation started on those nuclear missile shipments to Iran. I am sure it was some motivated General with no love for the west who must have known what would happen if Iran was armed."

Peter said, "I agree. Good luck in your investigation. Nice talking to you Vladimir."

Vladimir said, "Nice talking to you too." And hung up.

Peter sat back in his chair. Was Vladimir being truthful? Was he unaware that nuclear missiles had been sent to Iran? He sounded genuine about the situation. He felt in his gut that he could trust the Russian. Hopefully his investigation, if one was done, would uncover the truth.

Two Months Later

It had taken a couple of months but Vladimir had been true to his word. It was all over the news. A renegade Russian General had been exposed and arrested for sending nuclear weapons to Iran in the hopes they would be used against the American's with no blame against Russia. It would be assumed that Iran had some missiles left that America had not found. He did not count on America sending in a SEAL team to uncover the truth and destroy the remaining missiles.

Peter asked his secretary to call the Russian Premier. In a few minutes his phone rang and the President answered.

"Hello?", he said.

"Hello Peter, its Vladimir. I assume you have seen the news?", he said.

"Yes I have.", said the President. "I am very happy you managed to uncover the truth. It will certainly improve relations between our two countries."

"Yes it will.", said Vladimir. "Why don't you come over and we can have a meeting you and I to discuss ways in which we can help one another and improve our relationship?"

Peter thought that was a great idea and he said he would check his schedule and see when he could come over as long as it fit with Vladimir's schedule. Peter had begun to have a lot of admiration for the Russian and genuinely wanted to meet him face to face. They agreed on this and after a couple of days a date was picked for Peter to go over to Moscow. The meeting was kept very hush hush from the news media. Of course once he was in Moscow the story would break but that was okay.

Moscow

It was raining when Air Force One touched down. The plane had immediately been escorted by two Russian MIG's as soon as they entered Russian air space. This was expected. Air Force One landed and taxied to the edge of the tarmac near the terminal. A red carpet was rolled out to the steps of Air Force One. A military band was playing the Stars and Stripes, the American national anthem. Peter saw the Russian Premier walking toward him. He had seen pictures of the large Russian so he knew what he looked like. Peter had brought his wife along at the insistence of the Premier. The Premier's wife met Peter's wife and embraced each other and talked. Peter and Vladimir shook hands and then Vladimir hugged Peter in the Russian manner. All four walked together as Peter reviewed the honor guard. He stopped now and then to talk to some of the guard. Some could speak a little English and seemed happy to talk.

Afterwards they boarded the Premier's ZIL 41052 that were still in use as official state automobiles. They were very roomy and comfortable inside. Crowds of people lined the sidewalks on their drive to the Kremlin. People waved American and Russian flagged and waved at the passing motorcade. Peter could not help but notice Russian troops with sub-machine guns lining the streets. He also glimpsed a few sharp shooters on the roof tops. The Russians were not taking a chance of having an American President assassinated on their soil. After a short visit at the Kemlin, Peter and his wife were escorted to a hotel not far from the Kremlin. One entire floor had been cleared for them with armed guards at each end of the floor and likely on the lower and upper floors thought Peter. He felt quite safe with the Russian protection.

The next day he was escorted back to the Kremlin for his official meeting with the Premier. Peter's wife was going to spend the time with the Premier's wife who spoke surprisingly good English. When Peter was escorted into the Premier's office he was surprised there were a few extra people there. He did not know if they were security or not until the Premier introduced them as top members of the Russian Politburo. Peter felt a little uncomfortable and outnumbered but he would have to put up with it. He soon learned why this was done. The Premier gave a short speech about the unfortunate circumstances surrounding the Iranians and their acquisition of Russian nuclear weapons. Then each member of the Politburo also said they were deeply saddened and offered their apologies and then left the room leaving just Peter and Vladimir.

On Hope - 2083

Scientist Edna Fowler was 68 years old. She was having trouble remembering things and had to resort to writing almost everything down. She had been diagnosed with moderate dementia. Years ago she had trained her replacement and now she was working with him. He was a bright young guy called Wayne. She could not think as fast as he could and had trouble understanding most of his work, things that she had taught him. Other people were noticing it too. No one had to be euthanized yet but even she was realizing she may be the first one. She had it in her Will that she wanted a party in her honor and then surrounded by friends and family she would be euthanized by lethal injection. Sodium Thiopental would be administered first to render her unconscious in seconds followed by Pancuronium a muscle relaxant which by itself would cause death by asphyxiation but this is quickly followed by a dose of Potassium Chloride which stops the heart. The whole procedure is completely painless to the person being euthanized. There was a meeting held by the Doctor, two of the ships Captains and one other member of the crew chosen at random. A unanimous vote had to be made to approve the procedure.

The Doctor was the one that had the sad duty of informing Edna of their decision. The Doctor also had the power to ask a family member or a good friend deliver the news. Edna must know it was only a matter of time and would not be surprised. Her performance had been noticeably decreasing for some time and this meeting should have been held over a year ago. The Doctor decided that he would give the news to Edna himself. He called her into his office closed the door and as gently as he could told Edna that it had been voted to have her euthanized. She didn't seem to be surprised and just nodded her head when she heard the news. The Doctor had a copy of her Will in front of him and asked her if she wanted to make any changes. She didn't. The party in her honor would be done that Friday night. She would have the choice of being euthanized right after the party or she could wait until the next day. Edna said she would like it done immediately following the party. The Doctor solemnly shook hands with the aging scientist and the meeting was over. Edna returned to her work and made sure her replacement knew all that he needed to know to take over. It was a silly question because he had essentially been taking over all her duties for over a year.

Friday evening arrived and everyone on board the wheel was there telling her what great work she had accomplished. Speeches were made and finally the time arrived. She was escorted into the Doctors surgery and strapped down to a gurney. The needles were inserted and she was asked if she had any last words or statement she wished to make. She shook her head no. The Doctor opened the valve for the

Sodium Thiopental to begin entering her veins and she lost consciousness almost immediately. The Pancuronium was next which paralyzed the body followed by the Potassium Chloride which stopped the heart. The monitors all went to a straight line showing that she was dead. Several people openly wept, others wiped away tears. No one said anything. The Doctor told everyone the procedure was complete and he and his assistant would take care of the final disposal. Some people went over brushed the hair out of her eyes or stroked her cheek. One or two kissed her forehead and then soon the room was empty.

Hope - A Space Novel - Chapter Four

George - 2097

"Happy Birthday George!!", exclaimed his mother as she carried in the birthday cake from the kitchen.

The family had just finished a birthday supper in celebration of George's 18th birthday. George grinned as he was expected to and accepted congratulations all around the table.

"You'll be done with High School this year. Have you thought about what you want to do after that?", asked Ben, his father.

His sister Trisha said, "Yes George. What are your plans? I'm going into Biology."

George knew what he wanted to do but was not prepared to go through with more schooling to achieve it. He had done okay in school, not great, but good. He had planned it that way. He could have aced every test but didn't want to do "too" good. He wanted to look "normal". He was interested in theoretical physics and had been secretly studying on the computer in his room. He had self-taught himself calculus and started studying basic physics usually taught to university students and had gone from there to studies taught to 4th year students...and beyond. No one knew this. He kept that knowledge to himself. School was boring. He did what was required to pass and that was all he was interested in.

His father was a physicist and a good one. He often saw the complex formulas on his computer screen and understood them. His father was working on a problem right now that George knew how to solve. He itched to sit down at the keyboard and do it but knew that his fathers computer was a forbidden zone.

After supper and the birthday cake was done he was heading back to his room and glanced in his fathers study and looked at the screen again. His father was getting close to solving his equation. He could not stand it any more. He glanced over his shoulder and listened. No one was in the area or coming up the stairs. He sat down at the keyboard and quickly finished the formula his father was working on and went back to his room.

George's parents were worried. George had few friends, no girlfriend, did not get involved with school activities and had to be almost forced to attend family functions and gatherings. He spent most of his time in his room. George was usually studying leading edge physics and keeping tabs on what was being investigated in the physic labs around the world. Whenever anyone knocked on his door he would quickly change the screen to something else and then ask them to come in. Ben went back to his study and sat down at the screen to resume his work when he realized the formula he was working on had been solved. His wife, Maria, was a physicist as well and thought maybe she had seen a solution and did him a favor by seeing the solution and solved it before it skipped her mind.

Ben called out, " Maria? Were you on my computer?"

Maria answered,"No dear. Why would I touch it. I know you don't like anyone fiddling with it."

Ben thought, "Then who?"

He considered George but he was just in High School and doing okay but not great. This work was way beyond his capabilities but there was no one else. Ben went to George's room and knocked.

There was a moments silence and then George said, "Come in!" Ben said, "George, did you touch my computer?"

George looked worried. He shouldn't have touched it and he knew it.

George answered, "Well I saw a solution and wanted to solve it before I forgot it. I'm sorry Dad."

Ben said, "How were you able to do it? That is way beyond your capabilities."

George looked uncomfortable. He didn't want anyone to know that he was bored with school and was self studying on his own. "I have been looking at some stuff and remembered something and saw the solution and just did it."

Ben said, "That's impossible! What I am working on has never been published anywhere."

George didn't know what to say. He just hung his head. Ben said, "Come here for a minute."

George thought he was going to be grounded for touching has fathers computer instead his father opened up a new page and asked his son to sit down. "Go ahead and do this test. I'll leave the room so you won't be nervous.", Ben said.

George looked at the screen. It seemed to be a series of questions, "Another IQ test.", thought George.

George went ahead and finished the test and then opened the door for his father to come in. His father looked at the screen and clicked the button at the end of the test that said it would reveal the IQ of the tester. It said 210.

"Impossible!!", said Ben.

He stared at the screen not believing his eyes. "Have you done this test before?", asked his father.

"Not this test.", George answered.

Ben called to his wife Maria and asked her to come into his study. When Maria came in Ben said nothing but pointed to the screen. She looked once and then looked again not believing her eyes. "Are you sure?", she asked.

"Pretty sure.", said Ben.

"So it was George that solved your formula?", Maria asked.

"Yes, it appears that way.", replied Ben.

He turned to George and said, "We are going to the University tomorrow and get you checked out and see what they think.", said Ben.

George did not know how to feel. His secret was out. He knew he was smart but was uncomfortable with it. He felt he didn't fit with any of his friends, the ones he had that is. His thinking was different than theirs. He grasped things far faster than they did and had to hold back on saying anything when they were stuck for an answer, especially in class.

The next morning Ben called the school and told them George would not be there that day. Ben and George went to the University and asked to speak to the Dean. He was told to make an appointment. Ben said it was urgent and to please fit him in. The receptionist asked if there was something wrong thinking Ben was an upset father angry with the University because of marks given to his son. Ben assured her nothing was wrong but had to speak to the Dean about something extremely important and would not to take up much time. The receptionist asked Ben to sit and wait for a few minutes and see if the Dean could see them for a couple of minutes. After about five minutes the receptionist told Ben the Dean would see them now. George hung back but Ben ushered him into the Dean's office and told the Dean what had transpired at home yesterday. The Dean listened and then asked Ben if he was here asking to enroll his son in the University.

George interrupted by saying, "I don't want to enroll, I want to do Theoretical Physics Research."

The Dean smiled and said, "But son, you have taken no courses, you have no PHD. You can't do research without years of study."

George assured the Dean he had been self- studying at home. The Dean asked if George had ever even taken an entrance exam. George said no that he hadn't. The Dean figured this young kid needed a lesson. He picked up the phone, called and talked to someone about an entrance exam. The Dean told them where to go and who to ask for, that George was going to be given an entrance exam. George thought to himself, "Another useless test.", and followed his dad out of the office.

They arrived at a classroom and were met by an older, distinguished looking man who asked if they were sent by the Dean. Ben said they were. He ushered George into the room and had him sit at a desk. He called up the entrance exam on the screen and told him he had 2 hours to finish it. Once the two hours were up the test was over whether he had answered all the questions or not. He walked out of the classroom and told Ben where to wait and told him there was a view screen to use to read or watch entertainment. Ben settled in for the long wait. In about 45 minutes George came out of the classroom and stood there looking around. Ben saw George and asked if there was anything wrong. George assured him nothing was wrong and that he had finished the test. Ben went to a desk where a young woman was sitting and asked her to call the entrance exam professor because George was finished the test.

The professor came by and checked the screen. "Too tough for you?", he asked George.

"No.", said George, "I'm just finished."

The professor checked the screen and was astonished that George had indeed finished the test. He glanced at his watch. "I'll be back in a moment.", he said.

He went to a special area in the test screen and entered a password. The computer quickly checked the test and presented the results. His face was ashen. "You got all the answers right! In under an hour!", said the professor unbelievably.

He asked George what courses he wanted to take. George told him the same thing that he told the Dean, that he wanted to do research. The professor could not believe his ears but decided to play along. He motioned to Ben and George and asked them to follow him. They walked for quite a while and arrived at a lab with a closed door. The professor knocked and waited. Eventually the door opened and a tall thin dignified man wearing thick bi-focals stood before them.

"When are you going to get rid of those glasses and get your eyes fixed like everyone else, Doctor?", asked the professor.

"Never!", no one is touching my eyes, they are okay the way they are and these work fine, thank you.", said the Doctor tapping his glasses.

The professor introduced everyone. "George. Ben. This is Doctor Spencer. He is the Universities head of Theoretical Physics." He motioned to George and said to Doctor Spencer, "Young George here has just finished our entrance exam in less than an hour. His father claims that George has an IQ of 210. Can you show George what you are currently working on?", he smiled at the other man with a look that said "teach this young whipper snapper he isn't as good as he thinks he is".

Doctor Spencer smiled and invited George into the lab and closed the door. About 30 minutes later the door opened and Doctor Spencer and George came out. Doctor Spencer wasn't smiling now.

He said to the professor and to Ben, "When can he start? I

want this young man to be one of my assistants." The professor stood there with his mouth open and did not know what to say. He glanced at Ben, then George, then back to Doctor Spencer. "You're joking, right?"

Doctor Spencer assured him he wasn't joking and that George had just helped him solve a puzzle in 20 minutes that he had been working on for the last two weeks.

"I want, I NEED this young man on my staff as soon as possible!!", Doctor Spencer said. "George here started me thinking in directions that I had never even considered and between the two of us solved the puzzle."

Two Months Later

George and "Bob" as he now called Doctor Spencer were talking. George wanted to research something on his own and was trying to convince Bob to let him do it.

"But many people have tried and failed to discover FTL (faster than light) travel.", said Doctor "Bob" Spencer.

"I know that.", said George, "But I want to look at the problem from a different perspective."

Bob took his glasses off. George knew that when Bob did that he was doing some real serious thinking and did not interrupt him.

Finally Bob said, "All right George. Go ahead. How much time will you need?"

George said, "I am not sure but I hope to have a good start

within two weeks where hopefully you will allow me to continue."

Bob said, "Okay, two weeks." and walked away.

"Can I use the big screen?", asked George. "I'll need it because I may be working on several equations at once that interlink."

Bob replied, "Whatever you think you'll need."

George went into one of the rooms where there were several keyboards and a huge display screen that took up most of one wall. George was thinking that it was too bad the screen wasn't bigger but it would have to do. George had been working on the problem at home and had made some head way but he needed the much more powerful computer here at the college and the immense screen to display everything he needed at one time. Doing the work at home was painfully slow. He took out his personal memory storage unit and plugged it into a special dock station where the main computer carefully analyzed it for viruses and then allowed George to transfer the data into his own memory area on the college computer.

He remembered some of the history lessons from High School where he had learned they used to use something called a "disk drive" which had spinning platters and data heads that wrote data onto the disk drive to store it and then read the data when needed but it was painfully slow and was susceptible to damage and had to be backed up to a tape drive or to another disk drive to preserve the data. Today this didn't need to be done. The memory on the newest computers was virtually indestructible and several generations of data could be stored so that you could easily go back to an earlier revision and start from that point.

If, in the event of a power failure and even if the back up power failed to come on, the data stayed in memory and would still be there when power was resumed. No backups were needed except if you wanted to transfer it to a personal data unit for transfer to a home or other computer. The main advantage of the college computer was its speed. It could process data at several hundred terahertz, many times faster than the old gigahertz computers made a few decades ago.

The computers made today used optical circuits instead of old fashioned metal circuits. All home computers used optical processors and circuit boards and were terahertz computers but not anywhere near the speed of the college computer which was several hundred times as fast. Instead of waiting hours for an answer he had only to wait a few minutes. He smiled as he thought of those old gigahertz computers that he saw in the museums. They would have to wait days, maybe weeks for an answer.

His equations started to appear on the screen. The huge screen was separated into several sections, each section contained its own set of equations. At the touch of a button he could expand any section to fill the whole screen. Even doing this was slow because his equations were so large and complex he had to scroll up and down at times to make changes. George sighed thinking of the limitations but he had to make do with what he had. It was the best available. George knew that trying to break the light speed barrier was impossible in our space dimension but many other dimensions had been theorized and he was sure that one of them could be used to go as fast as you wanted, not by using plain old speed but time warping. He theorized that time in at least one of these other dimensions could be warped or "folded" to go from one point in time to another very easily and so travel from one point to another in a very short time period. The only problem he had to solve was how to get into one of those other dimensions and then back to our dimension. His theory was that if you could get into one of those other dimensions, time warp incredible distances and then pop back into our dimension, you could travel huge distances after coming back into our dimension. He felt that a couple of weeks work, maximum, he would be ready to prove to Bob, if he could understand it that is, that he was onto something and would allow him to continue his work.

It had long been theorized there were other dimensions. This had been proven by Theoretical Physicists long ago but no one knew how to go from one dimension to another. This was what George was working on. After a week of constant work he felt he was close to a solution. It would take the building of a craft to be able to "disappear" into another dimension and return. It would be like a spacecraft with its own self-contained air supply and fully sealed. The first tests would be unmanned and if they were successful then a personed trip would be made. He knew it would not be him to make the trip. The University considered him to be too valuable an asset to lose so the trip would probably be made by someone in the military. The first tests would be done in the laboratory and then progress from there into space and actually attempt a trip to go to the moon at first and then a planet such as Mars and then to one of the outer planets. He hoped that a trip would be made to the stars if the dimensional ship actually worked. Now that would be exciting!

After the two week period was up Dr. Robert (Bob) Spencer went and checked on his young charge, George, to see what he was up to. Robert had his own work and had been fully involved with that and had not checked on George. He knocked on the lab door and George asked, "Who is it?".

Robert answered, "Its Bob."

George asked him in. The screen was full of complex equations. Robert looked at them and was able to make some sense of some of them but the others would take some time to understand.

"What progress have you made?", asked Robert.

George replied, "More than I thought. I think I am very close to a solution."

Robert said, "To break the FTL barrier?"

George answered, "No, that can't be done in our universe or dimension but what I have been doing is investigating other possible universes or dimensions where it might be possible via time warping."

Robert said, "Yes, that would take some doing. Others have tried but failed to find a possible way to do it."

George replied, "Yes I know but I think I am on the verge of something. I need to build a lab experimental cabinet of sorts that will be able to move under its own power into the other dimension or universe to prove my theory."

George tried to explain his work so far to Robert but George saw that Robert was barely comprehending what he was saying.

Robert just nodded his head and said, "How much more time do you need?"

George said, "At this time I don't know but hopefully not too much longer. Can I have that time?"

Robert thought for a moment and then said, "Why not? You have invested two weeks in it now and if you feel you are close to a resolution, why not keep working on it?

Do you need any help from me or anyone else?"

George said, "I will need help when it comes to building an experimental lab 'craft' to move into the other dimension and then the automatics to have it come back to our dimension otherwise when it disappears from our dimension we will not be sure where it went."

Robert agreed, "Okay keep working on it. I don't how much longer I can spare you for this project of yours but if you feel you haven't hit any roadblocks yet you might as well keep working on the problem for a while longer."

George thanked Robert and Robert walked out of the lab and closed the door. He barely was able to understand any of the equations that were up on the multiple display screens. He may as well allow George to keep working. He may be the greatest theoretical mind since Einstein or Hawking.

One Month Later

Robert was checking his young charge periodically and then one day George announced he was 'ready.' "Ready for what?", asked Robert.

"I need this built.", said George. He handed Robert a pile of paperwork.

Robert leafed through it and asked, "What is it?"

George replied, "Its the experimental dimensional shift ship that I was talking about. It will have to be assembled here on earth and then taken up into space to be tested. I will need help designing the hardware and the automation but when it is complete it should be able to pop into another dimension, time skip huge distances through folds in space/time and then pop back into our dimension once it gets to its destination."

Robert asked, "And where would that be?"

George replied, "We could plan a short hop to Mars and back and see how that goes. From the calculations from going there and back I should be able to easily calculate further distances. Right now I am not completely sure of how long it would take but if my initial calculations are correct a trip to Mars would take less than a minute."

Robert's jaw dropped, "Less than a minute!"

"Yes.", replied George.

Robert said, "Okay we have to figure out the cost and time to build and do a lot of checks and a trial run. The first trial will have to be unmanned. No one is going to authorize a manned flight on a machine that has never been tested."

George replied, "Yes I know. That is why we would have to put in the automation. We would have cameras on board so they would record the whole trip there and back. That was the hard part, the getting back. Getting there wherever you want to go was fairly easy, its the getting back part that was hard."

Robert looked puzzled so George explained. "When you travel to a distant location in space you have to know where to come back to. The planets have changed position. The universe is still expanding. All that has to be taken into consideration because you can't go the exact same distance and go back to the exact same place in space because everything will have changed. This would be especially true if we travel to other star systems."

Robert understood now. "So your automations would take all that into account?", asked Robert.

"Yes, an astrogation computer will have to be designed and built using my formulas to take it all into account.", said George.

"I'll have to bring this up with the university Board of Directors. This sounds like it could cost a lot of money. We may have to look at venture capital funding or even get the government and the military involved.", said Robert.

One Year Later

The 'ship' that was built from George's designs and calculations stood in a lab in the university. It was quite small for something that held so much promise. It had taken quite a bit of arm twisting and funding from various sources to complete it. Robert had wondered at times if it was all going to come together but after two months of furious negotiations all the funds needed had been raised. Then it his job was to get all the needed resources and expertise to build it. The university ended up hiring a project manager who took control and made sure the experimental ship was built on time and on budget.

The ship was going to be shot up into space and a course set for Mars and back again. The plan was the ship would leave our dimension, travel through space/time and arrive some distance from Mars. Automatic cameras would take pictures to prove it was actually there and then return, reappearing in our dimension. That was the plan anyway. George had wanted to have the ship leave from ground on earth but no one wanted the risk. If anything catastrophic was going to happen it would happen in space.

The ship was put on top of a small ferry rocket and sent into orbit. Camera's from the distant space wheel were trained on the ship to record the entire event. The ship was being controlled from earth at the university. At the agreed upon time George was given the okay to start the ships dimensional shift and hopeful voyage to Mars. George held his breath as did everyone else and clicked the mouse on the control screen to start the process. The ship simply disappeared. One second it was there and the next split second later it was gone. No bells and whistles, no bang, nothing. It just disappeared.

On Hope

The second generation of people on Hope were growing up. They had no idea what it was like to live on a planet. The ship was the only home they had or would ever know. The original crew were getting older and were training the new crew in their respective disciplines. When describing what to do when they arrived at their destination it seemed the new crew was wondering why? The ship was their home, not some far away planet. Go outside and land on a planet with no spacesuit? The thought was incomprehensible to them. It was explained that planets had their own gravity due to their size and also had an atmosphere like the ship had but even so it was hard to grasp by many. If this generation was having such a hard time visualizing a planet what would future generations be like? And there would be several more generations until the ship arrived at Alpha Centauri.

The Dimension Ship Experiment

Everyone was holding their breaths including George. The last thing anyone had seen was the ship just disappearing! If all worked out okay the ship should reappear right where it left from. George had calculated the trip to Mars would take only seconds, then a few more seconds for the ship to orient itself towards Mars, take a few pictures and then return.

Three minutes had gone by but the ship had not returned. George was getting quite worried. Had his calculations been wrong? Had the ship disappeared into the other dimension but had not been able to reappear back in our dimension or the the same thing coming back? Had his calculations been really off and the ship had returned but was somewhere else that it could not be seen? Earth was doing scans as was the personnel on the space wheel. Nothing was being detected.

All of a sudden the ship was there. It just popped back into existence! It would appear the experiment had worked! A ship was dispatched from the space wheel to investigate. All looked fine with the ship. The memory from the camera was removed and inserted into a portable camera and viewed. There in all its splendor was the Martian planet. The experiment was a success! Now, would a living passenger be able to survive the journey there and back? Another experiment was done with some mice as passengers. After inspecting the mice in a lab it was confirmed they were normal. Some of the mice were kept alive and they seemed completely normal. They were allowed to mate their offspring were completely normal as well. It would appear that living matter was not affected by dimensional travel. A call for a human volunteer was put out and of course George wanted to go but he was denied because he was considered too big an asset to risk. A Major Timmins from the Air Force was found who had volunteered to take the trip. He was shown all the data from the mice experiment and seemed confident he would be okay.

Major Timmins boarded the dimensional ship and strapped in. No one knew what kind of a ride was to be expected but the mice had been unaffected. A journey to Mars and back was planned. The plan was to go to Mars where Major Timmins would radio back that he had arrived, take a few pictures and then set the controls for the return trip. As expected the ship simply disappeared. A few minutes later the ship reappeared. Major Timmins was supposed to have radioed in that he had arrived at Mars safely. Several minutes later Major Timmins voice came across the millions of miles to say that he had arrived at Mars. He had beat his radio signal back to earth orbit!! This was really exciting. No one had thought about the ship traveling faster than light in the other dimension and that it would be faster than a radio message which travels at light speed.

Major Timmins was asked what it was like in dimensional space. He described it as just a gray area for a few brief seconds and then suddenly you were back into our space. There was nothing to see, just gray.

The next test was to be intense. An automated trip to near Alpha Centauri, take some pics and then return. The trip took a little longer but not by much and the pictures showed the Alpha Centauri suns in all their brilliance. This was followed up with a manned trip with Major Timmins in the ship. He came back with pictures and described the experience as "fantastic." It would have been no use to radio back because it would have taken over four years for the radio signal to be received back on earth!!

Establishing a Colony

It did not take long for a plan to be devised to establish a colony on the earth-like planet that was to have been Hope's destination. Many nations, including China and Russia were invited to be part of the project. Large transport ships would be constructed in space and filled with all the supplies needed by the first colonists to establish a base. Later transport missions sent machinery, equipment and supplies for building structures. After several years basic industries were in full operation with smaller industries and a scientific research center in full operation. Many discoveries were made once a new telescope had been set up. Habitats were built and volunteers were sent to inhabit them. Soon a large thriving colony was in full operation. What would the people on Hope have thought about all this?

In the Science Center on Planet Alpha - 2228

Brian Ellison was in a newly constructed wing of the Alpha Science Center doing some star charting when he noticed an object that looked like an asteroid coming toward the star system. It was quite a ways off. The only way he had detected it was from photographs taken several days apart and one photograph showed an object that had changed position slightly from a few days previously. He considered it rather odd because all asteroids were confined to within the star systems influence but this object was further out than it should be. He compared the two photographs and did a few calculations and saw to his amazement the object was traveling at about 2% of light speed. No natural phenomenon was known to travel that fast. He decided to alert his boss George McAdam. He picked up his personal phone and punched the number for George who answered right away.

"George?", Brian began, "I have something rather strange here. I am comparing two photographs taken several days apart and they show an object heading toward us from deep space traveling at high speed, approximately 2% of light speed."

George replied, "That sounds impossible. Have you checked your calculations?"

Brian replied that he had, using a couple of different methods, and that it always came out to the same answer. He was going to do a doppler shift reading once it got closer to be sure. George asked if the object would have any possibility of hitting the planet and Brian replied that it was too soon to know until more study on exact trajectory was done. George asked Brian to keep an eye on the object and keep him informed. Brian disconnected and set up the equipment to take another photograph of the incoming object. It was still too far away to be seen directly. The only way it could be observed was with a time lapse photograph of about an hour to gather enough light to show up. What disturbed Brian was the objects speed. Nothing natural could travel that speed. Meteors and asteroids have been known to travel as fast as 40 miles per second just before impact with a planetary body but this object was in deep space and not being influenced by any gravitational fields.

By rights its speed should be just a few miles per second at the very fastest but this thing was moving at over 60 miles per second!! He checked its possible origin and saw that it was in direct line with the Sol system. There was nothing between the Sol system and Alpha Centauri star system. The object had to come from somewhere but from the Sol system and at such speed? He pondered the problem for quite a while and then something that he had learned in school many years ago popped into his mind. Over two hundred years ago earth had launched a generation ship toward Alpha Centauri because at the time things were really bad on earth both economically and politically. He could not remember the name of the ship and contact had been lost after its launch several years later and it was presumed destroyed by unknown means. The theory was it was hit by an interstellar asteroid or some catastrophic event aboard ship had destroyed it. He decided to do some research on the ship. The first thing was to remember the name of the ship.....

He went onto his computer and did a search for earth ships launched in that era. There were quite a few in late 1950's up until the early 2000's until the economical conditions on earth deteriorated to the point where no nation except China and Russia could afford to launch any space vehicles. China was the only nation to have a working space station at the time. The International Space Station had been mothballed when America and Europe had run out of money and Russia lost interest in maintaining it and saw no further use for it. But a little more digging brought up the fact the International Space Station was restarted and used as a staging point for the building of a generation ship called Hope. THAT was the name of it! He remembered now. China thought it was an American project and thought America, although with a badly damaged economy, had built a generation ship to try and get the jump on everyone else to start interstellar colonization. This eventually led to WWIII between America and China. China was badly damaged in the exchange. America got lucky because of its stockpile of anti-missiles which destroyed most of China's incoming nuclear missiles. Only one had managed to get through doing some minor damage in the grand scheme of things.

He worked out the launch date of Hope and its planned arrival date at the Alpha Centauri star system and the projected date, if it was Hope, was only six months away. Could it be Hope? Could it be that Hope was NOT destroyed as had been theorized but had simply lost the capability to communicate? He picked up the phone and called George back and gave him an update on the object and his theory. George was silent for a bit and then said he too remembered in history lessons from his school days about the generation ship Hope. Now-a-days the inter-dimensional travel between earth and Alpha Centauri took a matter of hours. Humankind was already establishing colonies on other habitable planets in other star systems. The colony on Alpha as the planet they were on had been named, had been here for well over 100 years and boasted a population of several million. Because of fusion energy and other factors earth was now one large society. It had been tough convincing a lot of countries that was the way to go but after narrowly averting WWIV the United States and Russia had spearheaded a campaign for "boarderless" countries and after several years of negotiating most of the world's countries decided to join. There were a few long term hold outs, particularly in the Middle East, but eventually they too decided to join especially after fusion plants world wide cut the planets dependency on oil. A lot of these Middle Eastern countries had no exports other than oil and if no one was buying they had no income. There was even an "Earth money" monetary system but even that had become obsolete in favor of "credits" that were issued to everyone. Most work was now done by robots so hardly anyone had to "work" and this left a lot of time for research, development and education. Mankinds knowledge was escalating at a furious rate and all knowledge gained was shared world wide. Humankind had finally "grown up."

If it was Hope coming toward them he better find out how they were going to stop once they got here. At that speed they better start doing something soon or risk going straight into one of the Alpha Centauri's suns. He spent several days going over the trip details and the ships engineering. It was really archaic comparing it with what was available today. He found out it was up to the inhabitants of the ship to reverse the ships attitude 180 degrees and use the old style rocket engines they had used to break away from earth's orbit as breaking rockets to slow the ship down. It would be the 5th or 6th generation on board the ship that would be expected to do this. Had this training been passed down through the generations? All but the first generation would consider Hope their home. They would have no concept of what it was like to live on a planet.

He decided to give one of the psychologists a call and discuss it with them. He looked through the list and saw the name Debra Thatcher who he had talked to before. Maybe she would have some insight on this. Brian called Debra and left her a message. After about 15 minutes she called back and Brian brought her up to speed on what was happening and asked her if the present occupants of Hope would have any concept or reason to slow Hope down in the hopes of establishing a new colony as what the mission was created for or would they have evolved to believe that Hope was their home and had forgotten the knowledge that was supposed to have been passed down from generation to generation. Hope would have been their home, their parents and generations back, home. They would have no concept of a planet and the information as to what to do once they arrived lost in the mists of time. He and Debra seemed to conclude the same possibility. They did not know if the object was actually Hope but so far indications were that it was a high probability.

After his conversation with Debra he called George back and related his conversation with Debra to George who listened carefully.

"Maybe we ought to take a ship out there and see if it really is Hope or not?", George asked.

"I was thinking the same thing.", said Brian.

"Let me see if I can get anyone interested enough to send a ship out and see what is what. The inhabitants of Hope, if it really is Hope, may have no clue as to how to slow Hope down. We better get some engineers to work on the problem, how to gain access to Hope and what has to be done to slow it down. From the description we don't have anything here big enough to do the job from outside the ship. All our craft are large inter-dimensional freighters and passenger ships meant to travel through inter-dimensional space and then low power fusion engines to manoeuvre into Earth orbit. We have some light high speed craft to get around the system. We could use one of them to get a crew of engineers out there and hope they can board her and slow her down.", said George.

Brian fully agreed and said, "We better get on this quick because if it is Hope she will be here in a few short months." George said he would get right on it and gather the necessary resources and manpower for the project.

Two Months Later

A project crew of engineers had gone over every detail of Hope's systems and knew how to slow the ship down. The only way on board was through an airlock into the navigation part of the ship or through another airlock and into the space wheel part of the ship. The wheel was continuously turning to provide artificial gravity for the occupants of the wheel. Such an archaic method of producing gravity was no longer needed as artificial gravity had been developed decades ago. The only way to stop the wheel from turning was to use the airlock from outside the wheel itself. It could not be done from the navigation part of the ship. Would the present inhabitants of the wheel know enough or care enough to stop the wheel? They may consider the crew that was being sent out as invaders and not stop the wheel on that account. Contingencies had been thought about for just this scenario. The engineering crew knew the outer airlock for the wheel could be opened from outside but how to do it if the wheel was turning? It was decided to use portable magnetic clamps on the hull to hold a person in place until they were able to open the outer door. In case of a violent reception all engineers were issued light TASER-like weapons to subdue any attempt to stop them from boarding. These TASER units were not like the old style ones with wires attached but shot a bolt of charged electricity at the target person who would collapse and be incapacitated for several minutes paralyzed and unable to move. They were rarely ever needed as there was virtually no crime but security people carried them all the time just in case.

The little "system ship" as they were called left Alpha and headed out to what was believed to be Hope. There was no need to boost the ship into orbit with rockets as in the olden days. These ships could take off from a standard runway and attain orbital speed in just a few minutes. Once in orbit a fusion engine would boost the speed as high as 5% of light speed if necessary but was rarely done. This was one of those cases. Speed was of the essence. At top speed it was going to take several weeks to get out to Hope. It was decided to make an arc journey and come in from behind Hope and then slow to match its speed. It was hoped the people aboard Hope could be contacted by old style radio or even a sign held up that read "Stop wheel, we are here to help you." If that failed then they would have to make an aggressive entrance through the airlock to board Hope.

About five and half weeks later they reached Hope. It was

true. Hope had survived. Hopefully the mystery could be solved as to why contact was lost so many years ago. The system ship had matched Hope's speed. Hope was only two months away from arriving at the Alpha Centauri star system. Radio contact was tried on several known older frequency and amplitude modulation channels with no response. The crew of the system ship could see people in the windows of Hope and waved to them but got no response except they looked agitated and were wondering what to do. The system ship maneuvered close to one of the port windows and a sign was held up asking the occupants to stop the wheel. One of the occupants looked like an older man. He was thin and very gaunt looking. One could tell that he was very puzzled by the appearance of the system ship. There seemed to be a lot of chatter going on between the occupants but there was no indication the wheel was being stopped. One of the engineers held up a sign simply saying, "Can you read this?" but it too got no response.

Two of the engineering crew decided to attempt to gain entry to the navigation part of the ship. According to the technical manuals there were no codes, it was a simple matter of pushing a button to gain entry. The airlock was supposed to be evacuated of all air and then it could be entered. Once inside another button could be pressed which closed the outer door, the airlock would be pressurized and the inner door would open. Both engineers were armed in the eventuality that people were in the navigation section and resistance was met. The airlock sequence was completed and the inner door opened. No one was there. Both engineers stepped in cautiously but there did not appear to be anyone there. Lighting was on although some lights had failed over the centuries. They made their way to the navigation section at the nose of the ship and sat down, strapped in to the seats because there was no gravity and consulted their computer pads they brought with them that contained all of Hope's engineering information. They familiarized themselves with all the controls and figured out how to pivot Hope 180 degrees and fire up the old style rocket engine to slow the ship down. It was recommended to stop the wheel before performing this procedure. They communicated this information to the other engineers in the system ship.

Gaining access to the outer airlock of the wheel without it stopped was going to be a trick as the wheel was rotating about one and a half revolutions a minute. The specifications said the wheel should be turning at three revolutions a minute. They had no choice but to clamp onto the hull and hang on tight for the ride. Timing was going to be everything. Another possibility was considered and that was to attach to the center of the wheel and then "walk" magnetically to the outer edge of the wheel where the airlock was but this idea was abandoned because as they got closer to the outside of the wheel, inertia would increase and it would be harder and harder to hang on. The persons arms would likely give out before they got there. They just needed to get close to the airlock and then each of the magnetic clamps could be turned off one at a time allowing the person to "walk" as needed along the outside of the wheel to the airlock and operate it. The best way they figured was to manoeuvre the ship close to the wheel and open the hatch. As the airlock started to come around then jump up and try as to get as close as possible to match the speed of the wheel and lock on.

One of the engineers, James had volunteered to give it a shot. He went into the ships airlock and stood on the sill of the lock and watched as the wheel spun around in front of him.

He stood there for a couple of minutes gauging its speed then slowly crouched, jumped and was gone!! The other engineer was worried if he was able to clamp on or had spun off into space. Each suit had a locator beacon on it so in the worst case he could use the ship to track and rescue him. As the wheel came around again he saw his fellow engineer hanging on near the airlock and using the magnetic clamps to get to the airlock. It was slow going because he had to fight the inertia of the wheel every time he unlocked a clamp and reached out and secured the clamp into place. James finally reached the airlock and had managed to operate it and had stepped into it.

James did not know what to expect when he opened the inner door to the airlock. He held his hand TASER in front of him just in case and kept an open communications channel to his partner on the system ship. The airlock had pressurized and the inner door opened into Hope. He stepped cautiously through the doorway and looked around but did not see anyone. The gravity from the wheel turning provided some artificial gravity, enough to walk around but it wasn't planet normal. It was far below that. As he walked further into the ships interior he started to look for Central Control where the console was to stop the wheel. He saw a glimpse of someone or something moving quickly and hiding. He just got a glimpse but who or whatever it was was very skinny with spindly legs. It was probably from living in a environment with such low gravity thought James.

He kept up a continuous chatter with Kevin, his partner still aboard the system ship. As he approached Central Control he saw more people, if you could them that, gathered in a small group. Their clothes were in tatters and from their attitude he could tell they were very afraid and not sure of what to do.

He considered taking his helmet off but reconsidered it. It had been discussed that Hope may have become a plague ship with disease that the inhabitants were immune to but could be deadly to an outsider. He waved to the small group of people but got no response. He reached Central Control and looked at the console. It looked operational but most of it was covered in dust as though it hadn't been used in a long time except the section to stop the wheel. He assumed these people still retained the knowledge to be able to stop the wheel and harvest plants from the hydroponics section in the body of the ship. James looked around carefully. No one was behind him. He was wary of a sneak attack but these people seemed terrified of him. He was much bigger than they were and they were probably afraid to come near him. By the looks of them he did not think he would have much of a problem fighting them off. James took out his computer pad and consulted it to remind himself of the console operation. He made the selections to stop the wheel from turning. If they had read the instructions properly the wheel should stop with the wheel and navigation airlocks aligned.

He could feel gravity beginning to lessen as the wheel started to slow down. He looked at the main screen on the console and had to wipe the dust off to see it clearly. He made some selections to see the power output from the old style nuclear reactor that was supposed to supply power to the ship. It read about 45% and that with the wheel slowing down. He theorized the reactors fuel was running out and the wheel revolutions had to be slowed at some point, maybe generations ago, to save power. The inhabitants of the wheel had probably lost the knowledge needed to replace the fuel rods in the reactor but had retained enough knowledge to turn down the power to the wheel to conserve power and to stop the wheel in order to get to the hydroponics in the body of the ship. That was his theory anyway.

He signaled Kevin that the wheel was slowing down but Kevin would probably have noticed it anyway. Finally the wheel slowed and halted. There was now zero gravity in the wheel. The people were starting to panic now as they floated about terrified as to what was happening. He took a chance and stepped toward the nearest one and grabbed an arm and gently pulled them down and helped them to grasp something to hold them in place. He tried to smile through his helmet to show that he was trying to help and was not a threat. The person, a middle aged woman it looked like, slowly seemed to calm down. He tried to talk to her through the speaker in his suit but she seemed unable to understand what he was saying. Kevin had signaled Barry, one of the engineers in the navigation section of the ship that the wheel was stopped and they could begin turning Hope's attitude 180 degrees and begin the braking manoeuvre on his command.

He knew once the braking started that an artificial gravity would begin to assert itself against the rear wall of the wheel. He better get all the people gathered together against the back wall of the wheel in preparation. He took the hand of the woman he had helped and gently pulled her. At first she did not want to let go of what she had but with a little persuasion and she finally let go and allowed herself to be led to the back wall. He waved at the others with a 'come here' motion of his arm and hand. The others were still very afraid so he had to go and start collecting them one or two at a time and take them to the back wall. He used his suits air jets that were usually used when in space to move about. It took a while but he finally managed to get all of them to the back wall. He better have a look around the rest of the wheel to be sure he had got them all. He went in each room and looked but it seemed he had them all. There were 15 in all.

James notified the engineers in the navigation nose of the ship to begin the process of rotating Hope 180 degrees around then firing the braking engines to begin slowing Hope down. The engineers in the Nav section fired the OMS jets to slowly turn Hope around and stabilize it. Once this was done the main engine was fired. It was hoped the engine would still work after all these years and miraculously it did. As expected, this created artificial gravity at the rear of the wheel. The occupants were frightened as the "floor" was now the rear part of the wheel. He could hear them talking amongst themselves but could not make out what they were saying. He did not recognize the language they were talking. There was a word here and there he could recognize but the rest was gibberish. It was going to take some time, maybe several weeks to slow Hope down. He wondered what the people on Hope had been eating. He found some old packages laying around. The ship was a mess inside. It looked as if these people had been living as near savages for quite some time, most technical knowledge other that what was needed to survive seemed to have been lost. It was considered moving the inhabitants off Hope to some of the small system ships but that idea was quickly dismissed as there was still a threat of disease. Hope could be a plague ship.

James started exploring the wheel more thoroughly. He noticed where people had obviously been sleeping and living. In one room he found a body that was mummified and been left where it lay. He asked the engineers in the Nav section to check on the hydroponic section to see if anything was still growing. He was confirmed that it was still growing but was choked with plants that had obviously not been fully harvested in quite a while. He checked his tablet and searched for food preparation equipment the hydroponic plants would be placed to make eatable food. He talked to the engineers in the Nav section about harvesting some of the plants, placing them in transport containers and moving them into the wheel part of the ship. According to the old documents about Hope she had left earth orbit with a crew of 30. These people would be very difficult to re-educate to become useful human beings again.

There was little to do now except to wait while Hope decelerated. He and and the other engineer went and collected some plants from the hydroponics section, packed them in air tight cargo boxes and moved them into the wheel through the airlock. While he was in hydroponics he took a look at the ships stores. The extra food and so on for special occasions was all gone. It had been consumed during Hopes long voyage.

Three Weeks Later

Hope's speed had been reduced to several hundred kph and the rocket engine was turned off. As they approached Alpha 1 they would have to decelerate more to put Hope in a stable orbit.

Attempts had been made to communicate with the people on board Hope but they still had a hard time understanding them. Some of the people on Hope had been talking to some linguists on Alpha 1. The language being spoken was evolved from English with other languages mixed in. Some questions were asked about how they had lost all their technical knowledge but no one knew. It had always been this way. Hope was their home. There was no knowledge of reaching a planet and settling it. The thought of leaving the only home they knew, the spacecraft Hope, seemed unthinkable.

Several Weeks Later

Hope was maneuvered into a stable orbit around Alpha 1 and a team of medical specialists was dispatched to the ship in spacesuits. The biggest concern was to discover if Hope was a plague ship and if so, what to do about it. After several days of intense investigation and testing it was concluded that Hope was clean of any disease at all, especially any of unknown origin that may have mutated over the centuries. Now what to do with the inhabitants of Hope. All these people had been living in ¼ of earth gravity. They were all thin with underdeveloped legs. They could not survive on Alpha 1 whose gravity was slightly more than earth normal. They would have to remain on Hope which would be okay as Hope was the only home these people had ever known. They would be given special water that had birth control medicine mixed in just in case these people tried to procreate. The people on Hope would be the last of their kind.

It was decided to leave Hope in permanent orbit around Alpha 1. It would be a sort of museum to show the people of Alpha 1 what long distance space travel was like before inter-dimensional space travel was possible.

Hope – A Space Novel - Epilogue

Earth had evolved into a true earth society. There were no borders, no countries anymore. There had been no war for well over 100 years. Peace reigned the planet for the first time since the beginning of recorded history. Robots were used for most tasks which left the people time to concentrate on research and living a better life. Humanity had finally come of age. The population was under control, disease and famine were a thing of the past. New colonies were already being started on more distant planets orbiting other stars. None of this may have happened without the intervention of one man, Malcolm Beacham, centuries before. WWIII may not have happened in the manner it did. Earth may have been destroyed as he had feared and none of this would have happened. Humankind may well have died out as a species.

Humankind was settling the galaxy but all this activity and expansion had not gone unnoticed. There was another race in the Galaxy that had kept a discrete distance observing and they were worried about the expansion of the human race in the Galaxy.......and they were watching......and waiting......

(Authors Note: Stay tuned for a sequel to this Novel yet to be named that would chronicle the eventual meeting with this other galactic race. Would there be peace....or war? Watch for the sequel......)

THE END – or not?

Made in the USA
Columbia, SC
31 December 2017